Bloody Fairies

Nina Smith

Also by Nina Smith:

Hailstone

Dead Silent

First Printing, 2014

ISBN: 149928358X

ISBN-13: 978-1499283587

To my most dedicated readers, who have taken the journey into Shadow with me: Kate, Clare, Lizzie and Vivienne.

Also, a great big thank you to my lovely editor Fiona, and to the wonderfully patient and adventurous people who have participated in bringing my characters to life in The Shadow Project and in the cover artwork for this book: Eddie, Richelle, Rebecca, Jay, Tess, Belle, Damien, Joanne, Dwayne and Laura.

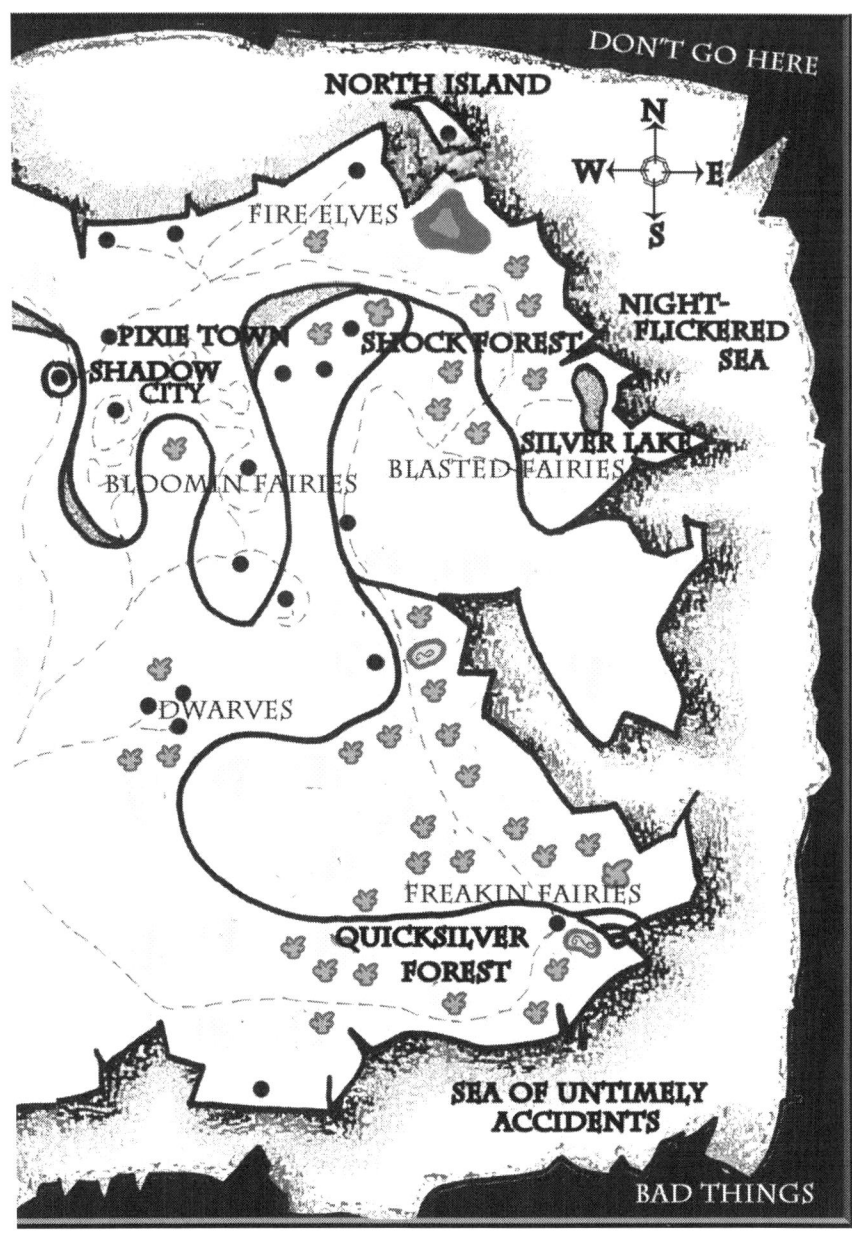

SHADOW is a penal colony created for a bunch of troublemakers as a result of some unpleasant goings on about three thousand years ago. It exists in a pocket of time and space you might think of as a bubble.

In those three thousand years, the descendants of the original exiles have established diverse tribes, cultures, religions and traditions.

This tiny world, once a simple prison, is now a thriving civilisation where many peoples live in uneasy accord.

While an official census has never been undertaken, it is believed the following is a comprehensive list of all the tribes living in Shadow. It's always possible others may be lurking about the place.

Muses: Work hard to inspire creativity in the world of humans, which they call Dream. They prize physical beauty, learning and art, and are sternly loyal to their king. They see themselves as Shadow's ruling class. Not everybody agrees–most people regard them as unnaturally tall and kind of irritating.

Bloody Fairies: Enjoy shiny things and war. While they have historically been known to abandon battles because they saw something shiny, for the most part they are a formidable fighting force.

Freakin Fairies: Obsessed with quicksilver, an abundant, toxic and very shiny element found in their territory. They mine the quicksilver and maintain a monopoly over it, creating a constant shortage of it elsewhere in Shadow. Rogue Freakin Fairies have been known to run a black market sideline in vibe, a drug deadly but almost irresistible to muses.

Bloomin Fairies: Live in giant pumpkin shells and like to grow things. These farming tribes are fiercely independent and very good at hiding whole villages amongst their crops.

Blasted Fairies: A reclusive clan famous for their penchant for blowing things up. Nobody's seen one for a while. Their origins are shrouded in as much mystery as their actual location.

Forest People: Serious types with hooves for feet. Very territorial, fond of big axes and likely to become political dissidents when they leave their forests. They are referred to colloquially as forest people not so much because they live deep in forests, as because nobody can ever remember their proper names. The two known tribes are the Fish-Tailed Green Dragon Dancer Tribe and the Three-Headed Red Elephant Tribe.

Vampires: They like blood. Mostly they prefer fairy blood, although pixies will do at a stretch. They're not so hot on muse blood, which makes them at best throw up and at worst go into anaphylactic shock. They live in the Darkness at the borders of Shadow, but have an irritating tendency to go invading due to the lack of fresh blood over there.

Pixies: Fond of darkness, depressing music and heavy makeup. Sometimes they write poems or draw their endless pits of despair in many shades of black. Most people try not to have anything to do with them.

Dwarves: Artisans, artists and architects, who have disdained hierarchy in favour of forming anarchist collectives for decision making. Easily the most intelligent citizens of Shadow.

Fire Elves: A tall, willowy people who have devoted three thousand years to their love affair with fire. They fight it, they dance with it, they juggle and create with it. While capable and skilled, fire elves have a reputation for being hot tempered and violent.

CHAPTER ONE

Fluffy Ducky was missing.

A tear pricked the corner of Hippy Ishtar's eye, but she blinked it back. She'd only wanted to let him out to stretch his legs. All eight of them. She didn't want him getting eight lots of leg cramps, but now he'd been gone for three whole hours, and that just wasn't like him.

She peered up into the thick, spiky leaves of the tree she'd been under when she let him out. Maybe he'd seen a lady spider. She bit her lip. Lady spiders had teeth. Big ones. She placed both hands on the ridged bark and stood on her toes to get a better look, but it was hard to see anything except shadows on shadows at this time of night.

"Fluffy Ducky!" she called. "Fluffy Ducky, are you up there?"

A long, thin, hairy leg extended lazily down from a branch above her head.

"Fluffy Ducky!" Hippy reached up toward the branch, hand open for the spider to crawl onto. "There you are, you naughty spider!"

The words bounced into the darkness. Too loud. Oops. Hippy tried to stay very still and pretend she wasn't there, but already the unmistakable stink of blood and metal pickled the air she breathed. Footsteps crunched on the loose white rocks. She reached for her fairy dust, but a fist closed around her collar and lifted her clear off the ground.

Hippy kicked out and pummelled the air with her fists, but that effort was pretty pointless, since she was facing in the wrong direction. She stopped fighting, folded her arms and scowled.

The hand turned her around. She gulped. A pair of feet encased in very large leather boots. Black pants, fastened with a leather belt. A crisp black shirt, all fitted and rigid. White-blonde curls nestled on thin shoulders. The moon peeked through the spiky leaves and gleamed on skin so white you could see the blue veins pumping through it. Sharp white fangs made soft dents in cracked lips when he smiled. It wasn't the nicest of smiles.

Hippy gave a high-pitched yelp.

A second pale creature joined the first in a rush of movement too quick to follow. Soft white ringlets cascaded over a delicate white face tracked with claw-like veins. She licked her lips. "What have you caught?"

"It's a Bloody Fairy."

The woman went instantly for the knife skewered through her belt. "Quick, let's kill it."

Her companion laughed. "Why? It's only a little one and it's not even armed. Fresh blood tastes so much better."

"Maybe you're right. I haven't had fresh fairy in a week." The woman took a step closer.

"Back off vamp!" Hippy yelled. "Or–or–or I'll-" A long, thin tendril of spider web glinted in the moonlight. "Or my Fluffy Ducky will get you!"

Both vamps stared at her. The man smirked. The woman snorted. Then they burst out laughing so hard the sound shook the leaves.

Hippy scowled. "Now my Fluffy Ducky's really upset."

"Your duck won't save you now." The man's fangs plunged toward her neck.

A shape sailed down from the branches of the tree, drifted for a moment in the breeze, then clamped onto the face of the woman.

She stumbled off balance, screaming. "Get it off!"

Distracted from Hippy's neck, the man knocked the spider flying through the air with one swipe.

"Hey!" Hippy yelled. "Don't be mean to my Fluffy Ducky!"

"Would you shut up about Fluffy Duckies?" The vamp grabbed her by the neck.

Hippy scrabbled for the numerous pouches at her belt. By the time she managed to rip one open and seize a crunchy handful of fairy dust, the vamp was breathing stinky vamp breath all over her throat. She squeezed her eyes shut, shrieked in disgust and shoved the dust into his face.

He dropped her.

Hippy landed on her rear end and scrambled closer to the tree. The vamp yelled something really nasty at her in Vampish and clutched his skin like it was going to melt off. Then he went grey and crumbled where he stood into a pile of ash and bits of bone.

The woman hissed in fury. "You're going to die for-" an

unmistakable thwack cut her off. Bone crunched. She swayed like a tree in the wind and fell over.

A Bloody Fairy blocked out the moon. She scowled and tapped a big, chunky spear against one hand. "What are you doing out here alone?"

"I lost my spider." Hippy scowled back. "Why d'you have to sneak up on my fights all the time? I was just starting to have fun."

"Dad said you're not to have fun unless I'm there. You're too flaky." Ishtar Ishtar pointed at the male vamp. "Hey look."

Hippy looked down at the pile of ashes. In the moonlight, the fairy dust glittered and shone. "A sparkly vamp." She giggled.

The one giggle was enough to set them off. The two fairies clutched their bellies, leaned on each other and bawled with laughter until their faces hurt. Only then did Hippy wipe the tears from her cheeks, kick the pile of vamp dust and admire the sparkling cloud that flew up into the moonlight.

The female vamp raised her head from the ground. Her pink-tinted eyes glinted with malevolent hatred. "You're going to die slowly, you nasty, short, horrible-"

"Hey Hippy, watch this." Ishtar's grin turned ferocious.

Hippy took a step back. "No, Ishtar, don't do it. Just use the dust."

Ishtar raised her spear high and drove it through the vampire's back before she could get to her feet. She slumped again. Blood spurted like a fountain from the wound and sprayed Ishtar's face and spear.

Hippy's stomach twisted. Her skin crawled. She froze to the spot.

"It's only a bit of vamp blood." Ishtar wiped the blood from her face and held the hand out to Hippy. "Here, why don't you wear some?"

Hippy dry-retched. The movement freed her from the spot. She bolted away from the dead vamps, the blood and her horrible, mean, nasty, awful sister.

Ishtar's shrieks of laughter followed her all the way back to camp.

Fluffy Ducky was still missing the next morning.

Hippy slipped away from camp while everyone else was busy competing to see who could throw their spears the hardest. Ishtar would win. She always cracked the melon into at least ten pieces. Hippy preferred not to bother. She knew how to throw a spear, why show off?

She slipped through the gates unseen and darted to the outer fortification, a twenty-foot-high wooden wall topped with pointy spikes that threw long, cold shadows over her walled village and the neighbouring muse encampment. The muses didn't feel the need for a second wall. Their tents and pavilions clustered together in the open like shiny white sails on a glassy sea.

They'd never needed walls to keep the vamps out before. The muses had turned up out of the blue just a few months ago, all dirty and bloody, and said they had to build a wall because the vamps had destroyed the Bitter Tower and were on their way. Hippy didn't really understand what they were on about. Ishtar said the wall was stupid because it meant there was less fighting.

Sunlight speared through the murder holes. The forest beyond smelled like mud and flowers. Hippy kept low until she found the little gate she'd left unlocked last night. She slipped through, closed it behind her, then hugged the base of a pile of big white rocks on the other side until she was far enough from the wall not to be seen running off.

It had been quiet lately. Too quiet, the elders said. There'd been no attacks for a week, barring the occasional vamp patrol like the one she'd encountered last night. That was fine by her. Hippy didn't mind being able to sleep now and again.

Stupid rules.

She resolutely turned her back on the fortifications and headed for the edge of the forest. She didn't get why they weren't allowed out during the day. That was one of the muse king's rules. It was all very well to have allies, but why should some old man who never came near the fairy camp get to make all the rules? Just because he'd been fighting the vamps for centuries.

Stupid vamp invasion.

Her scowl deepened. She retraced her steps from last night, along the white road, past the stumps, over the broken sign that used to be the entrance to her village.

A glimmering line of web crossed the path. Hippy traced it with one gentle finger, followed it off the road and over to a rock. "Fluffy Ducky!" she cried, overjoyed to finally be reunited with her best friend.

Fluffy Ducky sprawled on the rock, soaking up the sun. Hippy put her hand out. "Come on Fluffy Ducky, I'll catch you some nice flies. You were a good spider, jumping on that vamp last night."

The hairs on Fluffy Ducky's legs quivered. He scuttled onto Hippy's fingers. She lifted her hand up, but he kept going, jumped off and ran down the side of the rock.

"Fluffy Ducky!" She set off in pursuit.

The spider darted to the road and ran along the white rocks.

"Where are we going?" Hippy ran to keep up. "Come on Fluffy Ducky, we need to get back before we're missed!" She bent over and swiped, once, twice. On the third go she fell on her face. Fluffy Ducky stopped in front of her outstretched hands, scuttled in a circle and came to rest on her fingers.

Hippy scowled at him. "Ow."

Fluffy Ducky crept all the way onto her palm and blinked at her with all eight eyes.

Hippy sighed. "Oh, alright." She got to her feet, leaving the spider cradled in her hand. "It's time to go home now."

A branch cracked in the forest.

She peered into the darkness behind the tree line. "What was that?" she whispered. "Can't be a vamp, they're all sleeping."

Something tall moved in the shadows. Fluffy Ducky's third leg on the right twitched, which decided her. "Alright Fluffy Ducky, we'll check it out."

Her bare feet made hardly a noise on the grass under the trees. Any Bloody Fairy worthy of the name knew how to creep. Hippy slipped in past the first of the trees, but no further. Fairies didn't normally venture too far into the forest. Forest people weren't nearly as nasty as vamps, but their hooves could do a fair bit of damage if they thought you were in their territory.

She crept along just inside the tree line. There, just ahead, a shadow in the shape of a person lurked under that big old tree with the knobbly trunk. She stood very still and peeked through a curtain of drooping fig leaves. Snatches of decay rose from the rotting mulch underfoot.

The figure under the tree wore a cloak that went all the way to the ground and a hood that completely concealed the face. Hippy's eyes widened. A spy. A real live spy.

But who would spy for vamps?

By the time she heard somebody else coming up behind her, it was too late. Her head collided with a branch and a violent shove in the back sent her reeling into the sunlight. She landed on her face for the second time that day and said several bad words before spitting grass from her mouth. Fluffy Ducky trembled in her hand. No wonder, there were three pairs of boots surrounding her.

Hippy jumped to her feet. "Hey! Did you do that?"

Her words faded into the morning. She looked up and up and up into the faces of three rather surprised muses. Her heart skipped a beat. She barely noticed the other two. The tallest muse, the one in the centre with the top hat and the long dark blue coat, he was the muse king. She'd never got within shouting distance of him before. She closed her mouth when she realised her jaw had fallen open.

"Do what?" the muse king asked. "You appear to have been ejected from the forest, my dear."

Hippy's cheeks burned bright red. She cleared her throat, but couldn't quite make her voice work.

The muse king chuckled. "Don't look so frightened, my dear girl. I'm not going to eat you."

"Somebody pushed me!" Hippy burst out. "There was somebody in the trees there and they hit me on the head and pushed me! The vamps have sent people to spy on us during the day!"

The king motioned to one of the muses with him. "Investigate, Nikifor."

Nikifor strode into the forest.

The king made a deep bow to her. "I am Pierus," he said. "Pleased to make your acquaintance."

Hippy stared, lost for words. The muse king had just bowed to her. Ishtar was never going to believe this.

Pierus seemed to be waiting for something. After a moment he spoke to the other muse with him, a tall woman with curling brown hair and a smattering of freckles across her nose who wore a leather bodice, a flowing skirt and a sword strapped to her belt. "Flower, you know all the Bloody Fairies. Is there something wrong with this one?"

Flower gave Hippy a kind smile. "Nothing at all. She's just shy. This is Hippy Ishtar."

Hippy blinked. She had to say something. Her voice came out as a squeak, so she cleared her throat and tried again. "Pleased to meet you." Curiosity overcame her. "Are you really the king? Do people call you king? Or just Pierus? Is it true you're as old as Shadow?"

"I think she just overcame her shyness," Pierus said to Flower. "Come my dear, walk with us." He put an arm around Hippy's shoulders and began to stroll along the track. Flower walked ahead of them. "You may call me Pierus."

Hippy looked up at him. The hair that curled down from under his hat was a rich, dark brown, the same as his eyes. He had the oddest face she'd ever seen. A full lower lip made him seem boyish, but his overhanging brows and hooked nose made him look as though he could erupt into temper at any moment. All the fairies said the muse king had a bad temper.

"Pierus," she echoed.

He gave her an indulgent smile. "And tell me, what are you doing out here on your own? I thought all the young fairies were confined to camp during the day. You can't be too careful, you know."

"I'm not a young fairy," she said with dignity. "I'm twenty years old. I'm allowed out." She paused. "But you won't tell my mum, will you?"

His grin got bigger. "Twenty years old? Positively venerable. But you still haven't told me what you were doing out here."

"I was looking for my Fluffy Ducky." Hippy opened her hand to show him the spider. "I found him."

Pierus shuddered. "Oh, how dreadful. What did you call it?"

"Fluffy Ducky! He's my friend."

"Can't you put it away?"

"Alright." Hippy deposited Fluffy Ducky into his pouch at her belt. "There. He won't hurt you, you know. I trained him to only attack vamps."

"Bloody Fairies," Pierus muttered under his breath. Then, louder, "and has he attacked any vampires lately?"

"Oh yes." Hippy gave him a cheerful grin. "Last night he jumped on one's face."

"Last night?" Pierus stopped walking. "You were attacked?"

"Yes. When I was looking for Fluffy Ducky."

"All attacks are supposed to be reported." Pierus's brows drew together, turning his whole face fearsome.

Hippy shrank away from his arm. "I'm sorry. I didn't know."

Flower rejoined them at that moment and laid a hand on her shoulder. "Don't be afraid, Hippy. You've done nothing wrong. Why don't you tell us all about what happened?"

Pierus's features relaxed. His smile turned everything sunny once again. "Quite right, my dear. Forgive an old man."

"You don't seem old," Hippy said.

He chuckled. "You know, I think I'm going to like you."

"Why don't you show us where it happened?" Flower said.

Hippy skipped ahead of the two muses, leaving them to a muted conversation about vamps and statistics and something about a plan. When she came to the tree where Fluffy Ducky had been hiding last night, she skirted the bloodstains on the grass and told them the whole story, except for the part with Ishtar and the blood. No Bloody Fairy worth the name would admit to being terrified of blood.

Pierus and Flower both looked very serious after she'd finished. Flower knelt to investigate the pile of sparkling ash, but did not touch. The other vamp, the one Ishtar had skewered, had disintegrated at sunrise, leaving nothing but dried blood. "It was probably a standard patrol," she said.

"Agreed." Pierus stayed by Hippy and watched Flower's progress. "There were just the two, you say?"

"Just two." Hippy looked at Pierus rather than the blood. "My father said we should be worried about the vamps being this quiet lately. He said they're getting ready for something. Is it true?"

"We believe so." Pierus's brows dipped. The motion changed the whole shape of his face. "The scouts say they've been holding their position at the Bitter Tower and building their numbers. Believe me, if that's the case, we intend to be ready."

"There's not much more we can do here." Flower got to her feet. "Why don't I take Hippy home and you can go and meet Nikifor?"

"Yes. Off you go my dear," Pierus said. "Stay out of trouble." He gave Hippy a little nod and then strode back toward the forest.

Hippy watched after him until Flower put an arm around her shoulders and started walking in the direction of the camp. She sighed.

"What's the matter?" Flower asked.

"He seems very nice," Hippy said. "Not at all like I expected."

Flower laughed. "What did you expect?"

"Someone really, really, old. Is it true he's been around as long as Shadow?"

"Of course it is." Flower swept her arm around to indicate the forest, the road, the fortifications in the distance. "When the world of Dream was plunged into chaos by the dreams of humans, Pierus helped to create all this, to save them from their own imaginings and give their phantoms somewhere to go. When all of the chaos became the world of Shadow, he carved out places of light and order for all our kinds to live in. That's why he's our king."

Hippy shrugged. "Everyone knows all that. I want to know how old he really is."

Flower leaned closer. "About three thousand," she said. "Give or take a few decades."

Hippy's eyes widened. She didn't talk all the rest of the way home, trying to imagine what it must be like to be three thousand years old.

Only when they went through the gates in the fortifications and then entered the Bloody Fairy camp did Hippy remember she wasn't supposed to talk to muses. She quickly moved away from Flower's arm.

Flower didn't seem to notice. She beamed around at the staring fairies. "Where's Leaf Ishtar?"

Hippy winced and backed away. "Do you have to?" she hissed.

"I've been meaning to talk to him anyway, you know."

"Well I'll just be-" Hippy bumped into someone. She knew who it was without turning around. She sighed. "Right here."

Leaf laid a hand on Hippy's shoulder. "Now what's she done?"

Flower gave him a sunny smile. "Nothing, my friend. We just found her out and about, looking for her pet."

Hippy sidled away. Her father scrunched up his nose and gave her a puzzled look. "You have a pet?"

"Fluffy Ducky," Hippy said. "My spider. You said I could keep him. Remember?"

Leaf shrugged at Flower and motioned for her to follow him. "You mustn't mind young Hippy," he said. "Her mother dropped her on her head as a kid. Never been the same since. Now what news do you have?"

Hippy scowled at her father for a full minute. When he completely ignored her, she turned on her heel and stalked away. She scooped Fluffy Ducky out of his pouch, cradled him near her chest and sniffed loudly. "He always has to tell that story. I don't think it's even true. There's nothing wrong with me." She plonked herself down on a rock and raised the spider to eye level. "Pierus liked me. I bet he wouldn't like any of the others."

"Talking to yourself?"

Hippy hurriedly slipped her spider into his pouch. She screwed up her face and glared at Ishtar, who stood in front of her, arms folded and eyes narrowed. "Go away."

"Oh, I suppose you were talking to that nasty spider?" Ishtar grinned. "It talk back yet?"

"Get lost!" Hippy clenched her fists.

"Where were you this morning? You were supposed to be spear throwing with us."

Hippy got to her feet. She drew herself up and gave Ishtar a haughty look. "I was reporting those two vampires from last night." She paused, to make the next bit sound impressive. "To the muse king. He said he liked me."

Ishtar stared. Her lip curled back. "Liar."

"Am not."

"Are too!"

"You ask Flower! She's over there with Dad!"

"Liar, liar pants on fire!"

Hippy sprang at Ishtar and knocked her to the ground. Ishtar lashed out with her fists. Hippy grabbed chunks of hair and yanked. The sisters rolled around and around on the ground, clawing and scratching at each other.

A straggly circle of fairies gathered to watch the fun. Nobody bothered to break it up for a good ten minutes, until Willow Ishtar strode into the circle, hauled them apart and clouted them both around the head with an over-large fish.

She stuck her finger in Hippy's face. "How many times have I told you not to pick fights with your sister?"

Ishtar made a gruesome face behind Willow's shoulder.

"But Mum-"

"Enough! You're both on sentry duty tonight. Go get cleaned up." Willow Ishtar rolled her eyes at the nearest fairy and shrugged. "Honestly," she said. "The things I put up with. You know that girl hasn't been right since I dropped her on her head as a kid."

CHAPTER TWO

Hippy balanced on top of the wall around the Bloody Fairy camp. Darkness blanketed the muse camp, the outer fortifications, everything. The moon hid behind thick, wet clouds. She patted her belt to make sure Fluffy Ducky was safe.

Ishtar balanced beside her, bare feet wobbling on the blunted spikes. A wolf's tooth tied into her hair bumped against her face. A bunch of crow feathers dangled over her eyes.

Hippy pushed back her numerous thin plaits to hide the shiny beads threaded through them. No wonder vamps didn't take her seriously. She didn't have a single feather, or even a tooth.

Ishtar eyed her. "Ready?"

She nodded.

"Let's go."

Hippy jumped. The air rushed past her face. She landed lightly ten feet below, Ishtar beside her, and started walking.

At least four of their brothers patrolled the tops of the outer fortifications tonight, watching for any sign of vamp activity. The muses patrolled the ground, because they couldn't climb or jump like fairies.

Hippy wondered if Pierus patrolled, or if he didn't have to because he was king. She tried to make out the muse camp, but it was too dark. Her foot caught on a branch and she stumbled into Ishtar.

Ishtar pushed her away. "Pay attention!" she hissed.

Hippy made a face at her back. Ishtar was going too fast. They'd already done a circuit of almost half the outer fortifications and seen nothing. She sighed and went back to looking at the tents.

Something moved in the darkness.

"Ishtar," Hippy whispered.

Ishtar stopped and held her finger to her lips. She'd seen it too. She beckoned Hippy forward.

The fairies crept toward where the movement had been, their bare feet making no sound on the lush grass. Hippy kept a firm grasp on her spear. If a vampire had made it through the walls there would be big trouble.

Ishtar paused at the spot where they'd seen the movement. There was nothing there.

Hippy found a murder hole and peered out through the wall. "Out there," she whispered.

Ishtar felt around the wall until a bolt clicked under her hand. "Come on, let's follow."

Hippy ducked through the low door after her. Out here, the walls didn't make things quite so dark. The moon peeked out from behind a grey cloud. A tall figure disappeared into the night.

She didn't wait for Ishtar. She ran after the spy, just because she could, and because she knew Ishtar couldn't keep up. She closed the distance fast. Her heart hammered like the drums at midwinter. The spy wore a cloak and hood just like the spy she'd followed earlier. If she could only catch up and find out who it was, maybe she could tell Pierus. She could take her sister and then Ishtar would believe her.

Her foot hit a rock and Hippy went flying face first into the ground. She spat grass, said several bad words and lifted her head to see the figure had completely disappeared.

Ishtar caught up a few seconds later and hauled her to her feet. She snickered. "Nice trip."

Hippy scowled. "Shut up."

"I bet the vamps just shake in their boots when they see you coming. In case you fall on them!"

"Shut up!" Hippy's voice rose.

"You can't help it though," Ishtar said. "What with being dropped on your head and all."

Hippy dropped her spear, tackled Ishtar to the ground and slapped her in the face.

Ishtar slapped her in return. Hippy gave a furious hiss, determined to show Ishtar she was–she was–she couldn't even think of anything, so she pummelled her in the ribs while Ishtar held her down and dug her knuckles into her head.

Someone cleared their throat above them.

Hippy and Ishtar paused mid-fight and looked up.

Hippy squeaked. Four pairs of pink eyes glittered down at them. Pale skin glowed in the darkness.

"Bloody Fairies," said one, sounding bemused.

Ishtar went for her spear. Hippy did the same, but neither fairy got anywhere near their weapon. A hand grabbed Hippy by the hair and hauled her to her feet. Two vamps grabbed Ishtar's arms. These guys didn't waste time. The fangs were already out.

Hippy jammed her elbow backward into soft flesh and was rewarded with an "oof" of pain. She kicked the nearest vamp in the shins, balled her fists and punched anything within reach until her hair was released. Then she went into her pouch, grabbed a handful of fairy dust and threw it in the face of the nearest vamp.

The distraction gave Ishtar enough time to plant her fist in her attacker's nose. Both fairies dived for their spears and went back to back. The remaining three vamps regrouped.

"Feisty little fairies," one of the vamps said. "I'm working up an appetite." He licked his lips.

Ishtar shook her spear at him. "You know what I'm going to do?"

"What?" the vamp sounded bored.

"I'm going to make you into a blood fountain."

Hippy shuddered.

"I think you're going to die," the vamp said. "Slowly."

"Why do they always say that right before we kill them?" Hippy tightened her grip on her spear.

"Dunno." Ishtar snickered. "Maybe that's the only way these sparklers know how to die."

There was a second's icy silence.

"What did you call us?" the vamp said.

Ishtar drew the word out and made it hiss at the end. "Sparklers."

The vamps dived for them. Ishtar impaled one on her spear. Hippy made a wild swing, missed and accidentally sliced a vamp right down the side of the face, before Ishtar skewered the last one.

Blood spurted in every direction. Fountains of red poured down Hippy's spear and onto her hands. She screamed and dropped the spear. Her stomach revolted. She froze to the spot, staring at her wet red hands. Her head pounded.

"Hey Hippy," Ishtar said into the sudden silence.

Hippy turned her head.

Ishtar plunged her hands into the now subsiding fountain of blood flowing from one of the dead vamps. She ran them over her face, turning it red, and grinned. Her teeth glowed white.

Hippy gagged.

"It's good for the skin. You should try it." Ishtar reached for her with dripping hands.

Hippy ran. Her breath came in sobs under each convulsive dry retch. Ishtar's feet pounded behind her.

"Come on Hippy!" Ishtar yelled. "It's just a little vamp blood!"

Hippy threw herself through the door in the fortification and kept running. She stumbled to her knees in the darkness and frantically wiped her bloody hands on the grass. She could smell it. She could almost taste it. Her own blood pounded. She couldn't even remember where she was.

"Hippy!" Ishtar's voice purred through the darkness, low and soft. "I'm going to paint your face with blood. Come out, come out. You can't get away from me."

Hippy stumbled to her feet and ran for a dim light shining ahead. Her feet made no sound. She slowed down when she came up to the silk walls of a row of tents and flattened herself between the nearest two.

Ishtar prowled the darkness behind her. She could smell the blood on her. Her stomach heaved again.

Hippy slipped down the side of the tents and peered around the edge. Her eyes widened. She'd never been into the muse camp. The tents surrounded a big open area where there was a huge central table and a fire pit. Shiny banners of purple and green were hung from all the tents, making pretty, pretty walls that flickered and glowed in the firelight. A group of muses sat around the fire talking in low voices. Soup bubbled in a huge cauldron, sending clouds of fragrant steam into the air.

The sound of footsteps sent her darting into the shadows around the edge of the clearing and then down a passage between a row of larger tents. She slowed and trod carefully over the taut ropes.

More voices, closer this time. Any minute now they'd see her and she'd be in trouble. She dropped to the ground, lifted the silk wall of the nearest tent and rolled underneath just in time to see a pair of feet go past.

Safe. She lay on her back, eyes closed, and took a few deep breaths. She couldn't smell blood any more. Her stomach unclenched. The fog in her head cleared and she opened her eyes.

Hippy stared. This tent was huge. The walls were hung with shiny, shiny mirrors everywhere, some big, some small, one very long with a gilt frame. Little tables gleamed here and there, and on them shiny statues stood watch. Most of the statues were of a woman holding a mirror, except for one little one of a woman with snakes coming from her head. A huge bed was draped with purple and red sheets in one corner. In the centre of the space was a gleaming, polished wooden table.

Hippy cautiously sat up and looked around. She was alone. She got to her feet and brushed her fingertips over the mirror with the gilt frame. It reflected a big-eyed girl with dirt on her face and wild hair back at her. She scrubbed at a spatter of blood on her forehead.

She crept around the edge of the tent towards the door. She would just go before anyone came in. Of course she would. She had no business being here.

She glanced at the table and stopped. It was covered with a huge map of Shadow. Hills and mountains were sketched out around Shadow City. Below the city was the forest and next to that, a little purple flag marked the spot where the camp was. Hippy drifted closer, intrigued. She'd never seen a map of Shadow.

Something shiny caught the edge of her vision. She left the table and touched a crystal hanging around the neck of a tall statue of the woman with the mirror. It sparkled in her hand. So pretty. She picked up a little sparkly figurine of a horse with wings from the base of the statue, studied it and put it down again.

Behind the statue there was a curtain. Unlike all the rest of the hangings in here it was plain black, with just a little sheen to it. Hippy twitched it open. Her eyes got very wide.

There was no room behind the curtain. She couldn't quite figure out what she was looking at, except that it was a dark space and it was somehow torn. Light gleamed through jagged edges going from the roof to the floor, shimmered and moved like water. It was so shiny.

Hippy reached her hand toward the light. The rip widened.

A voice right outside the tent made her freeze. She ducked behind the curtain and flattened herself in the corner.

Footsteps entered. Three different voices. Hippy crammed herself further into the corner, away from the rip. She shoved her knuckles in her mouth to keep from making a noise. That was Pierus out there, with Flower and Nikifor from the sound of it. Holy Shadow, she'd be in deep trouble if they found her here.

"More incursions." Pierus's voice filled the tent. He didn't sound pleased at all. "Vampires are pouring past the Bitter Tower now.

We're sitting targets out here with nothing but a pack of fairies and an untried Champion. These raids are just distractions. We can't delay any longer."

"But it's madness!" Flower sounded even less happy. "Even if it did have a chance of working, who's to say you'd even find it? We're talking about a legend here!"

"My dear girl, Shadow is made of legends," Pierus said. "And I can assure you this one is very real."

"I may be untried," said Nikifor, "but I swear to you I can defend Shadow as my father did before me."

"My dear boy, your father spent one hundred and fifty years defending Shadow, and he still got himself killed. What chance does a librarian barely out of Muse College have against this horde?"

There was a brief, raw silence. Hippy winced in sympathy for Nikifor.

"That's why we need it," Pierus said into the silence.

"But did you not say you cannot wield it alone?"

"There's the rub, Nikifor my boy. The ancients didn't trust anyone with it, not even me."

"Then one of us should go with you," Flower said.

"Not a muse." Pierus paused. "It has to be someone of the blood of the first guardian."

"What does that mean?" Nikifor asked.

"Wait," Pierus said. "Something's not right."

Silence. Something moved. Hippy held her breath. The quiet stretched out.

She closed her eyes and pretended to be invisible, but that only lasted until Pierus yanked the curtain open and glared down at her. His eyebrows met like the wings of an angry bird. He reached down and hauled her out by the front of her tunic.

Hippy squeaked. "I'm sorry! I didn't mean to come in here! I was hiding from my sister and then someone came along so I hid under the silk and I just ended up here and I didn't touch anything, honest!" She blinked at Pierus, who still had hold of her shoulder.

Flower and Nikifor looked stunned.

The corner of Pierus's mouth twitched. His brows receded the merest millimetre.

"Why were you hiding from your sister?" Flower's voice was gentle, but there was a flicker of amusement behind it.

Hippy's cheeks grew hot. She couldn't look away from Pierus. "I-

" she stopped.

"Leave us." Pierus never took his eyes off her.

Relief made Hippy's knees weak. She went to move, but he didn't let go of her. "Not you."

Hippy gulped. Flower and Nikifor left the tent without another word.

Pierus steered her to a low-slung chair covered in furs and unceremoniously dropped her into it. Then he went over to a table and poured two glasses of pink wine from a tall, slim bottle.

Hippy watched his every move. She cautiously accepted the glass when he came back and sat across from her.

Pierus fixed her with a stern look. "Why were you hiding from your sister?"

"I-" Hippy looked away. She clutched her glass. "I can't tell you."

"Why not?"

"I just can't."

"Have a drink, my dear."

Hippy obediently gulped a mouthful of wine. It was very nice and sweet and it made her feel more relaxed.

"I need to know what you were doing behind that curtain," Pierus said. "If you won't tell me why you were hiding from your sister, I'm going to start thinking you're a spy."

"I'm not a spy!" Hippy flushed a deep crimson. "It's just–I mean–"

"Just tell me."

"I'm scared of blood," Hippy burst out. "It's horrible, it makes me want to throw up and I can't think or move and Ishtar knows, so every time we kill a vamp she stabs them and you know how much blood that means, and tonight she smeared it all over her face and chased me." She closed her mouth abruptly, mortified.

Pierus went bright red. Then he went white. His lips trembled. He snorted. Then he burst into gales of laughter.

Hippy folded her arms and glared. "It's not funny!"

"I know my dear, it's just–you Bloody Fairies–" he leaned back in his chair and grinned at her like she'd grown a second head and told a joke with it.

Hippy got to her feet, cheeks flaming. "Don't you dare tell anyone!" She burst into tears and ran for the door.

For a three thousand year old muse, Pierus was fast. He made it there first and barred the way. Laughter lines still creased the corners of his eyes, but he was serious again. "Not so fast there, I haven't finished with you yet. Oh, are you crying?" He thrust a handkerchief at her. "Do stop."

Hippy slouched back to the chair and sank into it. She dried her face with the handkerchief and took another gulp of the wine. There, she felt better again.

Pierus resumed his seat.

She sniffed. "What? What else do you want, now you've had a good laugh at my expense?"

"I apologise, my dear."

He said it so seriously Hippy felt mollified. "I'm sorry I hid in your tent," she said. "I didn't mean to."

"Why did you go behind that curtain?"

She shifted in her chair. "I heard someone coming, it seemed like the best place to hide."

He leaned forward and rested his elbows on his knees. "And what did you see there?"

"I don't know. It was kind of a rip or something. What was it?"

"If I tell you, you must swear to me to keep it a secret." He frowned. "Fairies are not very good at keeping secrets, in my experience."

"I won't tell a soul," Hippy said. "Honest, and if I did they wouldn't believe me anyway. Ishtar wouldn't even believe me when I told her I met you. I swear you can trust me."

"Indeed." He regarded her intently. "What you saw behind the curtain is a rip in the fabric of Shadow. It is effectively a doorway into the world of Dream."

Hippy's eyes grew bigger than ever. "Dream?" she whispered. "Really? Where the humans live?"

"Really." He moved closer. All Hippy could see now was his eyes. "I must go on a journey into Dream to seek out an ancient treasure. It is our only hope of defeating the vampires and driving them back into the Darkness where they belong. If we allow the vampires to overrun us, Shadow will be lost."

Hippy stared. "When do you go?"

"Very soon," he said. "But perhaps you're wondering why I haven't gone already, when we know an attack is imminent."

"Not really," Hippy said. "I mean, yes."

"I cannot find this treasure alone. I need a descendant of the treasure's first guardian."

"What does that mean?"

"I asked myself that same question for many, many years. And only now, when I found you hiding behind my curtain, did I figure it out. I need you."

"Me?" Hippy's mouth fell open. She quickly closed it.

"Yes my dear, you. A fairy. A fairy who is willing to go on a quest with a muse to help save Shadow."

"But–but I–" Hippy put a hand to her head. There was no way. Mum and Dad would never allow it. The elders would be intractable. She'd risk banishment at the very suggestion. But to go away with the muse king, hunting for a treasure? Ishtar would never laugh at her again.

"Perhaps you need some time to think it over," he said. "You seem unsure."

"I want to do it more than anything," Hippy burst out. "But the elders will never allow it."

Pierus gave her a thin smile and patted her hand. "You just leave the elders to me, my dear."

CHAPTER THREE

The spiked fortifications of the fairy camp brooded like black teeth against a blacker sky. Nikifor and Flower each carried a smoky gas lamp on the end of a tall pole, shedding a cold blue light the sentries would see a mile off. Hippy dug her nails into her palms and chewed on her lower lip. Never mind how bad it looked being escorted home by not one, but three muses. She would not let Pierus know how much trouble he was going to get her in. No way. He was the first person to ever ask her to do something real.

"Hey!" A muscular fairy with a blood-smeared face barred their way when they approached the gates of the fairy camp. "You can't come in here!"

Hippy sighed. "It's me, Ishtar," she said.

"Oh, well you can come in. You other three get lost!" Ishtar shook her spear at them.

Pierus sniffed. "Who is this?"

Suddenly, the whole night was worth it. "Ishtar Ishtar, meet Pierus, King of the Muses," Hippy said.

Ishtar dropped her spear. She cursed and dived for it.

"Give me a moment, my dear." Pierus patted Hippy on the shoulder and then strode over to Ishtar.

She glared up at him. "You're not my king."

Pierus put an arm around Ishtar's shoulder and drew her away from the light. He bent down to speak to her. Hippy couldn't hear what he said, but he came back alone. "Come along," he said, and they all started walking again. "I don't think your sister will be giving you any more trouble," he added in an undertone.

Hippy grinned at her feet. She felt foolishly, dizzyingly, absurdly happy.

The gates swung open to admit them. Hippy took a deep breath. Time to face the music. Oh, hell. The elders were already waiting, arms folded, scowls on. Behind them lurked Ishtar and all eight of her brothers, spears planted at their sides. Flaming torches tied to the walls overhead cast leaping, chaotic lights over everyone's faces.

Leaf Ishtar strode forward. His grey-streaked black dreadlocks, each decorated with the claw of something that had left him with a few choice scars when he killed it, hung over his shoulders like snakes. He curled his hand around Hippy's sleeve, jerked her away from Pierus and hustled her back to stand with the elders. Only then did he deign to speak to Pierus. "Thanks," he said. "You can go now."

Pierus raised an overhanging eyebrow and looked at Leaf down the length of his hooked nose. Then he turned to leave.

Hippy almost squeaked in dismay. He wasn't going to ask!

Pierus turned back. "Oh," he said. "I'll need her back the day after tomorrow."

Leaf was so shocked he let go of Hippy's sleeve. His voice was deadly stern. "What do you mean, you'll need her back? What do you want with my daughter?"

"She's to assist me on a secret mission." Pierus's voice echoed through the deathly silent camp.

"What secret mission?"

"If I told you that it wouldn't be a secret."

"Look, Muse." Leaf took a step forward, fists balled. "I don't care if you're the king or a vamp's bootlace, my daughter's not going anywhere with the likes of you!"

This was going about as well as she'd expected. Hippy sidled away from her father, but she didn't get far. Her eldest brother's hand landed on her shoulder and kept her in place.

"Naturally that's entirely up to you," Pierus said. "But I should warn you, if she does not accompany me on this very dangerous mission, you're all quite sure to lose the war."

There was another silence. Score. Hippy's eyes widened. Pierus really did know how to deal with the elders.

"Well why her?" Leaf gestured at Hippy. "She was dropped on her head as a kid, she's no good for anything except throwing fairy dust."

Hippy clenched her teeth and balled her fists. One of these days-

Pierus's lazy words rolled around the camp. "I should think that reflects more on your parenting skills than her current capabilities. Hippy, I will expect you at sunrise, day after tomorrow. Don't be late." His coat flared out when he spun on his heel and strode away, trailed by Flower and Nikifor.

The gates closed after them. All the fairies stared. Hippy couldn't get the big stupid grin off her face.

Hippy sat alone on a bench, her back to the bonfire that always burned in the fairy camp through the night. She folded her hands in her lap and refused to look up from them. Her brothers and Ishtar jostled around them for the best seats. Her mother stood to one side, glaring. Everyone else, from the pint-sized children to the warrior mothers, the giggling teens to the old women, watched from the shadows. There was even a whole family of Feathertips from the next village here tonight, who would no doubt go home and blab all about her.

It was the singular most excruciating moment of her life. If only somebody would say something.

Her father finally broke the silence. "You're not going."

Hippy scowled. "Am too."

"Tell us what the mission is," one of the elders said.

"Can't." Hippy folded her arms. "I promised."

"Then how do we know he's not leading you into mischief?" demanded her mother.

"You just have to trust me."

"Trust you?" her father snorted. "You're just a ditsy little girl who's not right in the head. You're hardly even a proper fairy, and all this consorting with muses just proves it!"

"How do you know you can trust him?" one of her brothers said.

Hippy straightened. "He's the muse king! Who else should we trust?"

There was a smattering of derisive laughter.

"You can't trust any muse, least of all the king," an elder said.

"How would you know, when you never even talk to them?" Hippy shot back. "I don't know why you have to be so rude to them, what would we do if they weren't helping us?"

"They have to help us, it's their fault the vampires are even here!"

"What?"

Leaf snorted and raked dreadlocks from his face. "You think the muses are good, hardworking, decent people? Do you think they're handsome? Kind?"

"Flower's never been anything but kind to us," Hippy said.

Leaf waved a hand as though that were of no consequence. "We tolerate Flower," he said. "We don't tolerate any other muse. They are responsible for every vamp that attacks us. Why?" He leaned forward and shook a finger at her. "Because they created them. Every single one. They have free rein to inspire anything in those good for nothing artists and writers in the world of Dream. No rules, no boundaries, that's how they work. And we're the ones that get left with veiny, big-toothed bloodsuckers on our doorstep!"

Hippy shuddered. "But we wouldn't even be here if it wasn't for them! Didn't they inspire us into existence too?"

"That's still up for debate!" Leaf yelled.

"And didn't they carve out a place in Shadow for us to live?"

"She's already spent too much time with them," an elder declared.

"Stop arguing and listen, girl!" Leaf's dreadlocks quivered under the force of the words. "That muse king is the worst of all of them! The things he's done-"

Hippy looked pointedly away. "What's he done that's so bad then?"

Apparently, they'd all been waiting for this question. More fairies gathered in around the elders and sat on the ground in expectant silence. Hippy would have groaned under her breath if she'd dared.

Leaf cleared his throat. His mouth settled in a smug line. "Oh, he's done plenty," he said. "Ten thousand years is a long time to get up to mischief."

"Three thousand," Hippy corrected.

"Quiet you," an elder snapped.

Hippy stuck out her tongue at him.

"Back in what they called the Middle Ages, the humans in Dream did a lot of fighting." Leaf settled himself more comfortably in his seat, got out his pipe and lit it.

Ishtar, who was at his feet, sat up straighter. "I like fighting."

Leaf chuckled. "So did the humans. But they got so busy fighting each other they created nothing for a long time. They were all either fighting, or dying, or being miserable. They had no cause and nothing to live for–and the muses were getting bored, because no matter how hard they tried, the humans were blind to inspiration. Now this course of events would no doubt have sorted itself out, these things always do. But the muse king, he decided to interfere. He broke the rules and crossed into Dream."

Hippy jerked to attention. "Why? What did he do there?"

Leaf smirked. "He stirred up the humans. Messed with their politics. Next thing you know it was no longer peasants fighting their rulers and each other, it was religion fighting religion. That got the muses going and the artists, too. Simple creatures, humans. Give them a cause and they'll paint, they'll write, they'll bleed and they'll die for it."

"So he did a good thing," Hippy said.

"Will you stop interrupting!" Leaf took a long draw on his pipe. "That was only the beginning, see. You won't hear this from a muse, because they all think the sun shines out of his nostrils, but the fairies, we watched him."

"We weren't alive," Hippy objected.

"Your father's fathers were. And their father's fathers, and their father's fathers-"

"Oh and I suppose the mothers were just standing about doing nothing?" Willow interrupted. "It wasn't all the men, you know."

"Quiet, woman!" Leaf clenched his teeth over his pipe. "I happen to know good and well the women were too busy having their little wars to do any watching. As I was saying, the fairies kept an eye on Pierus. We saw that he wasn't quite right." He tapped his head. "While the other muses went about their business, he went off and disappeared for years on end. Came back more loony every time, raving about clocks, or frogs, or steam engines. And things got steadily worse in Dream, too. More wars. More chaos. Giant machines that poured smoke and filth into their water and their sky. And you know what that meant?"

A cricket chirped in the silence.

"More horrors for Shadow," Leaf said. "The worse things got in Dream, the more awful they got here. The vamps got crankier. The werewolves got bigger. Even the bearflies bit harder."

"We haven't been on a bearfly hunt in ages," Ishtar said.

"There's no such thing as werewolves," Willow cut in.

"Quiet! I'm telling the story, aren't I?" Leaf took a long draw of his pipe. His face grew grim. "Then came the worst thing of all. Pierus began to inspire a certain scientist who should have been left to his own devices. Dangerous men, scientists."

"And women," Willow interjected.

"Thanks to Pierus, this scientist invented a bomb." Leaf's words were so low everyone had to inch closer to hear him. "When they built this bomb and used it, millions of humans were killed in one single moment. The land was poisoned and diseased for generations. Then the humans took this invention and used it, again and again, even though they knew the dangers. Parts of Dream became so toxic that once again we suffered here in Shadow. Nobody knows if the poison seeped through a doorway left open by the king, or if it was just another echo from Dream, but a whole village of Fire Elves near the borders got sick. One of your Feathertip aunties went to help them. Don't know why."

"Because she was more interested in medicine than assassination is why," Willow said.

Leaf grunted. "She should've stuck to assassination, that's what the Feathertips are good at. She came back looking like a skeleton and said the Fire Elves died screaming. Nothing she could do. Then she died screaming too." He eyeballed Hippy. "The muse king visited that nightmare on Dream and on Shadow because he was bored. Is that the kind of man you want to trust?"

Hippy's eyes were like saucers. She put her hands over her face. "It's not true."

"It is true." Leaf's voice was stern. "And you'll do well to remember that's why no fairy consorts with a muse. Pierus, muse king, is no better than Rustam Badora himself."

Silence descended at the sound of the vampire king's name. Fairies shuffled off to their homes and beds. Nobody was in any mood to hear more stories. Gossip about Pierus might be juicy, but the mere mention of Rustam Badora was enough to send a fairy into a growling, frightened rage.

Hippy bowed her head and reached for Fluffy Ducky. His hairy legs tickled her fingers. A hot, fat tear fell onto her tunic.

Leaf's hand rested on her shoulder. "There now girl." His voice was gentle. "Don't take on like this. It's not your fault you got bamboozled by a muse. You're not the brightest spark in the bonfire, after all. Why don't you go off to bed?"

Hippy kicked her father in the shin, cupped Fluffy Ducky in her hands and flounced away. She made it all the way to the door of the hut before Ishtar caught up with her.

Ishtar blocked her way inside. She'd washed her face and hands. Her skin gleamed, no trace of blood on it, and she smelled of bitter herb soap. She struggled to say something.

"Spit it out," Hippy said.

Ishtar took a deep breath. "Sorry," she mumbled. Then, louder, "Don't go with that muse king. I don't like him." She disappeared inside.

Hippy sighed, disconsolate, and went in to bed. It was very hard to sleep when the two choices she was faced with chased each other around and around in her head like bearflies on a hot day. Leave for an adventure with a muse who had inspired nightmares? Or stay, fight vampires and be the fairy who wasn't like a fairy at all because she got dropped on her head as a kid?

CHAPTER FOUR

Hippy got stuck with scrubbing pots all the next day. The big cauldron that hung over the bonfire to make rabbit stew for the whole camp turned her hands greasy and black. The hot water she boiled in the cauldron to wash all the smaller pots dissolved the grease, but turned her hands bright red and made her skin raw. If this was her punishment for wanting to go off and save Shadow, well, all she could really say was nuts to Bloody Fairies. And a lot of other bad words.

Sometime during the afternoon Ishtar came back from target practice and plonked herself down on an upturned cauldron to watch her. Hippy scowled and ditched a pot at her head.

Ishtar ducked, caught it and wordlessly deposited it back on the pile of gleaming pots and pans.

Hippy stopped scrubbing and stared at her. "What in Shadow's wrong with you?"

Ishtar shrugged. She put her chin in her hands and continued to watch.

Hippy went back to scrubbing. "You've got a pointy head."

Ishtar's reply was automatic. "Your toenails smell."

"You run like a human."

"You've got bearfly breath."

"You've got a nose like a cabbage."

Ishtar sighed. "You're not going to run off with that muse, are you?"

Hippy scowled and scrubbed the pot so hard a shiny spot appeared on the metal.

"He's bad," Ishtar said. "Really, really bad."

"They're just stories. You know half the stories Dad tells aren't even true."

"And the other half are. But it's not that."

Hippy paused in her scrubbing. "Then what? He's been perfectly nice to me. Nicer than any of you."

"See, that's the problem. People are only nice when they want something. He creeps me out." Ishtar shook herself.

"What did he say to you last night?"

Ishtar looked away. "Nothing."

"What?" Hippy gave her sister her full attention. "Tell me."

"He said if he caught me being nasty to you again he'd send me dreams every night about being dropped in a big black hole, alright?" Ishtar jumped to her feet and walked away.

Hippy dropped her pot and ran after her. "What? Why?"

Ishtar swung around and faced her. "How did he know?"

"How did he know what?" Hippy's eyes widened. "Oh." She'd almost forgotten Ishtar's little secret. Her sister had promised not to tell the other fairies about her fear of blood, and Hippy had promised not to tell anyone Ishtar was deathly afraid of being trapped underground.

"Did you tell him?"

"No." Hippy slipped her arm through Ishtar's. "Look, I'm sorry he scared you, but he was really just trying to protect me. He's actually very sweet."

Ishtar jerked away. "Sweet? You're joking, right? He's way too old for you!"

Hippy blushed bright red. "That's not what I was talking about!"

"Yeah well for all we know, his big secret mission to save Shadow is all going to take place in his tent. He tell you to leave your clothes behind?"

Hippy's whole face burned with mortification. "You're just jealous!" she burst out.

"Am not!"

"Are too!"

"You're just a silly little baby with the brains of a bearfly! Any fairy with half a spear's sense could see you won't survive a day with him!" Ishtar went scarlet with the effort of shouting.

"Oh yeah?"

"Yeah!"

"Well-" Hippy couldn't think of a reply. "You are!" She made the rudest gesture she knew at Ishtar and bolted from the camp.

Obviously her eldest brother had been told to keep an eye on her, because he made a flying tackle the minute she got within shouting distance of the gate. Idiot. He knew she was faster. Hippy dodged and he ploughed face first into the ground behind her.

She ducked out of the gate and looked longingly toward the muse camp. No, she couldn't. She'd end up washing pots until she had grey hair.

Instead, Hippy ran for the outer fortifications and slipped through the first gate she could find. She pelted down the white road until she was quite sure she'd lost anyone dumb enough to chase her, then flung herself down under a tree and buried her head in her hands.

She could have cried. There was nobody there to see her. But her teeth were clenched too hard and her blood raced like ants before a storm. She was so tired of being the stupid one, of everybody else knowing better. She'd show them. She'd go. She'd save Shadow and then they'd stop talking about how she was dropped on her head.

Hippy dropped her hands and took a deep breath of fresh forest air. She scooped Fluffy Ducky out of his pouch and raised him to eye level. "We're going to Dream, you and me."

Fluffy Ducky blinked at her. A breeze stirred the hairs on his legs. "Are you excited?"

Fluffy Ducky raised one leg and waved it in the air.

"Yeah! Me too. You, me and the muse king, who would have thought?" Hippy smiled for the first time that day.

Fluffy Ducky ducked. A cold wind sliced past Hippy's face and an arrow embedded itself in the tree behind her. She shrieked, jumped to her feet and went for her fairy dust.

But there was nobody in sight.

Hippy said several very bad words. She carefully put Fluffy Ducky away and pressed her back to the tree. "You'd better not do that again, or I'll send my Fluffy Ducky after you!" she yelled.

Silence. Her voice echoed. Hippy edged around the tree until she came to the arrow. Her eyes widened. There was a piece of paper wrapped around the shaft. She didn't recognise the arrow at all. It didn't belong to a muse or a fairy and vampires didn't use arrows. They relied on swords and fangs.

This arrow was made of thin, pliable metal, not wood, and it had an odd symbol carved into the shaft, a nine-pointed star inside a circle. She yanked the arrow from the tree, unwrapped the paper and frowned at it.

You must not go, the message said. At least she thought it did, reading wasn't her strong point. Plus the pictograms were scrawled as though whoever wrote them was unfamiliar with writing in Fairy.

Hippy looked around again, but the road was still empty as far as she could see. Of course there could be anyone in the forest. She slowly folded up the piece of paper and stuck it in one of her bags, along with the arrow. Then with a glance at the sinking sun, she set off back towards the fortifications.

She walked with her head down, deep in thought. How weird was this? It definitely wasn't one of the fairies playing tricks on her, none of them had ever had an arrow like that. Could it be one of the forest people? Why would they care?

Hippy was so deep in thought she walked head-first into a muse outside the fortifications. She scowled and shoved him. "Watch where you're going!"

Nikifor reached out to steady her. "Hippy Ishtar?"

She scowled. "What?" She took a closer look at him, because he seemed a little bit pale around the mouth. She hadn't really spoken to him before, but it wasn't hard to tell he was scared. She softened her tone. "Are you okay?"

"But of course." Nikifor shook off whatever was bothering him. "The king sent me to find you. Your family were in the camp demanding your return earlier and wouldn't leave until he swore you were not there." Worry clouded his face. "Perhaps you should return to your family first and assure them you are safe and well?"

Hippy squared her shoulders. "No. I want to see Pierus and no fairy can stop me." She moved closer to Nikifor. "Can you hide me from them?"

He chuckled. "Not on your life, Fairy. Your father is positively frightening. Come on."

They ducked through a gate in the fortification and set off toward the muse camp. Hippy had to run to keep up with Nikifor's stride. She watched his fists clench and unclench.

"Seriously, what's the matter?" she said. "It's not you my dad's mad at, so it can't be that."

"No, little friend," Nikifor said. "It's nothing."

"Are you really a librarian?"

"What?"

"Pierus called you a librarian."

Something in the muse sparked. "I could have been. Do you know there are books at the Muse College thousands of years old? I was going to look after them. I would have been the guardian of all the knowledge of the muses." The spark died away. "But not anymore."

Hippy trotted at his side, curious. She'd never seen a library.

Fairies didn't write things in books, they told stories. "Why not?"

"Because my father was murdered and I was called to take his place. Come now." The words were short and somewhat bitter. He guided her in silence down a wide path between two graceful white tents. They skirted the little courtyard, where she attracted curious stares from three muses gathered around the fire pit. Hippy tossed her head and ignored them.

Pierus's tent was bigger than the others. Big purple and green banners hung down either side of the door. Nikifor struck a gong before they entered.

Pierus leaned over the map on the big table, his hands splayed over the mountains that bordered the Darkness. His hair made a curtain around his face. When he looked up at the arrivals, his brows were knitted together. The corner of his mouth lifted just the slightest bit when he saw Hippy. "Thank you Nikifor," he said. "You may go."

"My king-"

"I said go." Pierus looked back at the map.

Nikifor bowed and left.

Hippy stood for a minute looking at Pierus, but he was absorbed in the map. She shrugged and studied the lady with the mirror instead. Her metallic fingers were very finely wrought. Her eyes were blank and sightless. "If you ask me, something's bothering him," she said.

"What makes you say that?" Pierus's knobbly finger traced a line along the map.

"He's all twitchy."

"My dear girl, all that's bothering Nikifor is that he's afraid of his destiny. He'll get over it soon enough."

"His destiny?"

"He's our new Champion." Pierus frowned at the mountains. "To every generation is born a Muse Champion to protect Shadow from the Darkness. The gift falls to the eldest child in the line. Our last Champion, Valentin, was perhaps the greatest warrior Shadow ever saw. Until he got himself stabbed in the back by Rustam Badora. So now I have a vampire invasion and an untrained boy on my hands who'd rather have his nose in a book than his sword on the battlefield."

Hippy scowled. "It's not easy being scared, you know."

"I suppose you know. Where were you all afternoon? Your

dreadful father was here looking for you."

"I was out." Hippy went to the table and leaned over it. "Thinking. The elders have forbidden me from going with you."

Pierus chuckled, but still didn't look up from the map. "Surprise, surprise. Staying home then, are you?"

"No."

"Good." He sounded quite satisfied with the answer. "We leave at dawn. You'd best stay here till then."

Hippy grinned. She liked that idea. She had no desire to go home and wash more pots or listen to the elders yell again. But at the same time, she really wasn't impressed with him apparently finding the map more interesting than her. She took the arrow out of her pocket and dropped it in front of him.

That got his attention. At the very least, it made his forehead wrinkle. "Where did you get that?"

"I don't know," Hippy said. "It just kind of smacked into the tree next to my head while I was talking to Fluffy Ducky about whether or not to go with you. This was wrapped around it." She dropped the message next to the arrow.

Pierus scanned it. Then he chuckled.

"Well? Who's it from?"

"Nobody you need to worry about."

"But they shot an arrow at my head."

"They missed, didn't they? I'm very much afraid one cannot live for three thousand years without enjoying a little notoriety." Pierus pushed the map and the arrow out of her reach. "Does that worry you?"

"No." Actually it really did, but being the absolute centre of the muse king's attention was far more interesting than a few niggling worries about his misdeeds. "What does the star mean?"

Pierus raised an eyebrow at her. "Star?"

"The star in the circle. It had nine points." Hippy pointed at the arrow.

"You don't need to worry about that." Pierus walked around the table, leaned against it and folded his arms. "What's this awful knotted thing in your hair?"

"My dreadlock. I got that when I won the running races last year." Hippy played with the dreadlock, which was decorated with three shiny beads. "Ishtar won the spear throwing. She's got three."

"It's ugly. You should brush it out."

Hippy scowled. "I don't want to."

Pierus tugged on the dreadlock. "You Bloody Fairies and your knots."

Hippy was distracted by the tickle of Fluffy Ducky scuttling up her arm. "What are you doing out, Fluffy Ducky?" She grabbed for him, but he wasn't interested in going back in the pouch. He darted over her shoulder and leaped for Pierus's face.

Pierus yelled in fright and vaulted onto the table. "Get it off!" He swiped at the spider and missed. Fluffy Ducky hung onto his long hair by two back legs and waved two front legs in front of his eyes.

Hippy scrambled onto the table and scooped Fluffy Ducky off Pierus's hair. "Bad Fluffy Ducky!" she scolded. "What are you doing? Pierus is a nice muse, not a nasty vamp!"

Fluffy Ducky squatted low in her hand. A tremor ran through his body. He waved a foreleg at her.

"Put it away," Pierus said. "For Shadow's sake. Dreadful thing."

Hippy's lip trembled. "He's really very nice when you get to know him. Here, just let him sniff you." She stuck out her hand.

Pierus backed away and almost fell off the table. "Put it away!"

Hippy shrugged, scratched Fluffy Ducky under the chin and secured him in her pouch.

Pierus wiped a hand across his sweating forehead and uttered two ragged words. "Bloody Fairies!"

A distant, terrified shout split the quiet outside the tent.

CHAPTER FIVE

A discordant, metallic crash followed the shouts. Pierus leaped from the table.

A muse stumbled through the door and dropped to his knees in a motion that could have been a bow, but looked more like a collapse. Nikifor's lips moved in a bloodless face, but he was unable to form a word.

Pierus grabbed his hair and jerked his head back. "Out with it boy, what is it?"

"Vampires."

Pierus grabbed a curved knife from a low table and stuck it through his belt. "How many?"

"Thousands."

Pierus said a very, very bad word and glanced at Hippy, quite as though he'd forgotten who she was. "Protect the fairy," he said. "Don't let her leave. I'll be back." He strode away.

Hippy checked her fairy dust and made sure Fluffy Ducky was safe and sound. When she was satisfied, she slid down from the table, approached the young muse and clicked her fingers in front of his face. "Hey. Hey you, snap out of it. It's just a few vamps."

Nikifor buried his face in his hands.

Hippy shrugged and started searching the tent for a good weapon, since she'd left her spear at home. She thought the big statue might do in a pinch, although it would be a pity to break something so shiny on a vamp's head.

"What are you thinking?" Nikifor's voice was ragged.

"I'm thinking this mirror lady's head would probably do more damage than her feet," Hippy said. She hefted the statue.

"No." Nikifor shook his head. "I mean, what were you doing on the table? What's going on?"

"Fluffy Ducky mistook Pierus for a vamp and jumped on his face. I think maybe he's scared of spiders, because he jumped on the table." Hippy considered the possibility Pierus might be mad if she broke his statues and put the fighting lady down. She found a stout metal staff with an axe head at one end leaning in a corner. There, that was much better.

Nikifor breathed what sounded distinctly like a sigh of relief.

"What did you think was going on?"

He cleared his throat. "Nothing."

Hippy screwed up her nose. "Ew! You're as bad as my sister!"

"What? I said nothing!"

"Same nothing she said." Hippy leaned against the staff and scowled at him. "You people all have filthy minds. I'm here to fight vamps. That's all."

Nikifor got to his feet. He paced up and down the tent, throwing increasingly nervous glances at the door. "I'm sorry," he said. "You just seem so very young."

"I'm twenty!" Hippy took up a guard position at the door and watched the muses outside gathering weapons and strapping on armour. They were grim, but not in nearly the state Nikifor was in. "Aren't you going out to fight the vamps? How come you have to look after me? I can kill any vamps that come in here."

The pacing sped up. "Yes. No. I don't know!"

Hippy scowled. "What do you mean?"

Nikifor spoke so quietly she had to move closer to hear him. "My father fought the vampires at the borders of the Darkness for more years than I have been alive. I went out there one night as a child. I saw how he lost himself in the battle, how when he was done, vampires lay dead around him for miles." He curled one hand into a fist and pressed his knuckles into his own forehead.

Hippy flattened herself against the door, unsure whether to pat him on the shoulder or run away.

"I knew the moment he died," Nikifor said. "I felt the knife that stabbed him in the back as though it stabbed me. I felt his power leave him and come to me, just as though his death meant nothing. As though he meant nothing. And if I am the Champion now, if I am the one with all the power, then I am nothing too. Nothing but a vessel for death!"

Hippy frowned, bewildered. "What are you doing in here if you have that much power? You should be out there fighting!"

He flung himself away from her. "Don't you see? I can't! I can't lose myself like he did! Of course the vampires must be driven back, but I don't want to kill. Not them. Not anybody! My father was-" he fell against a wall. "He was a monster, and I must do what he did. I am afraid of myself, Fairy. They laugh at me. A muse afraid of his own shadow."

Hippy took a tentative step closer. "It's not so bad."

"It's terrible!"

"I'm a Bloody Fairy who's terrified of blood."

Nikifor looked back at her. The corner of his mouth quirked up. "Really?"

"Tell anyone and I'll take out your kneecaps." Hippy returned to the door and peered out, trying to make out words in the distant shouting. All the muses had gone. The darkness was lit by an orange glow in the direction of the fairy camp. Her heart thumped at her ribs in sickening certainty about what might be on fire out there. She started from the door.

Nikifor hurried after her. "Come back! Pierus said you were to stay here!"

"My home is on fire!" Hippy threw the words over her shoulder and ran.

The darkness crawled with muses running for the outer fortifications in rigid, square formations that bristled with spears. Hippy gave them a wide berth and headed for where flames leaped from the walls of her village into the sky. She dodged the rapidly decaying forms of three dead vamps on the ground.

Knots of fairies fought hand to hand with vamps around the gates. Hippy took stock quickly. There weren't that many vamps here, just enough to be a pain in the rear end. The boys had the bulk of them pinned. Ishtar fought two at once under the walls, but they were pushing her dangerously close to the flames.

Hippy bolted over, swung her staff in a wide arc and buried it in the nearest vamp's back. Blood exploded into the air. Her stomach revolted. She jumped out of the way in time to avoid being splattered.

Ishtar impaled the other one on her spear. Then, with barely a pause for breath, she grabbed Hippy by the front of her tunic. "Where in Shadow have you been?"

"With Pierus. What's going on?"

Ishtar let her go. "I knew it. I just knew it! What's going on is the entire vamp army is out there with siege weapons. Some of them already got in and set our camp on fire. Obviously. And they're throwing things at us!"

A ball of flame sailed overhead, fell in a graceless arc and pounded into the ground between the two camps.

"Ishtar listen to me," Hippy said. "You mustn't tell anyone else. Pierus and I are going to find something that will drive out the vamps. It's our only hope."

Ishtar's habitual scowl deepened. "What is it?"

"I don't know! You've just got to hold them off until we get back, okay?"

"No!" Ishtar grabbed her wrist. "Your place is with us. Let him get it on his own."

"He can't, he needs a fairy! He needs me!" Hippy yanked her wrist away. "Just do it, alright? Hold them off."

"You've no more sense than a bearfly in winter, Hippy Ishtar!" Ishtar hefted her spear and charged back into the fray.

Hippy remained where she was. There was another shape in the darkness behind Ishtar, someone in a cloak and hood. The spy!

No time to pursue him. Hippy ran to the outer fortifications and peered through the first murder hole she could find. Her jaw dropped. The vamp army was vast. It was more than vast, the vamps stretched to the horizon like a legion of pale, hideous ghosts. When the fairies on top of the fortifications sent a hail of arrows over them, they raised their shields and returned fire with more balls of molten metal from the enormous trebuchet that squatted like a giant amongst them.

A pair of bright red eyes peered at her through the hole. Hippy squeaked and scrambled back. She really, really hoped this treasure thing wasn't going to be difficult to find. She ran for the muse camp. The whistling of fireballs deafened her. Flashes of light in every direction confused her until she couldn't remember which way she was going.

A whistling sound went overhead, followed by a loud roar. Hippy looked up. Wow. She'd never realised fire could be shiny. It had such pretty colours when you watched the flames get closer and closer and closer.

A hand grabbed her by the back of the tunic and dragged her out of the way. The fireball slammed into the ground where she'd been standing.

"Didn't I tell you to stay put?" Pierus demanded.

Hippy pointed at the fairy camp. "They set our walls on fire."

His voice was low and angry. "I know. Come on." Without letting go of her, he started walking.

Hippy ran to keep up, since she didn't fancy being dragged. "What's going on? Why are there so many?"

"They've been breeding. We have to go get the Apple of Chaos right now."

"What's the Apple of Chaos? Will an apple stop the vamps? They don't eat fruit-"

Pierus jerked her aside when another flaming ball slammed into the ground directly in their path.

Hippy yelped. They all but ran the last few yards to the tents. She glanced over her shoulder before they made it, just in case she never saw home again.

Home was a wall of flames. Shadows struggled in a background of leaping fire. Tall, pale shapes dogged their every step. "We're not alone," she said.

Pierus said a bad word and yanked her into the tent.

Nikifor sat by the door, curled into a ball. He was so white he looked like he was going to faint.

"For Shadow's sake." Pierus prodded him with his shoe. "Get up, boy."

"I'm sorry my king," Nikifor whispered. "I just can't."

"Your father would turn in his grave if he knew his son and heir was a coward and a weakling."

Nikifor flinched.

Pierus went to a corner table and slammed a glass onto it. He picked up a bottle and poured from it a stream of smooth, clear green liquid. "If he had a grave," he added after a thoughtful pause. "We couldn't find anything to bury when the vampires were done with him."

Hippy shot Pierus a glare. "You don't have to be so cruel to him."

"Don't interfere, Hippy. I don't know you fairies raise your young, but I don't believe in mollycoddling." Pierus took the glass to Nikifor.

Nikifor looked at the glass as though it might be poison and shook his head. "I will not go down that path."

Pierus thrust the glass in his face. "You are needed out there, and this will help. This will free you. Drink, damn you!"

Nikifor stared at the glass for another long minute. Then he took it and drained it in one breath. When he finished, the glass slipped from his fingers and smashed on the floor. His eyes closed.

"Is he okay?" Hippy reached out to shake his shoulder.

Nikifor raised his head and looked through her. He sprang to his feet like a feral cat scenting a fight. His sword sang from its scabbard, and he left without another word.

"Finally. Valentin never gave me this much trouble. We have to leave." Pierus hurried from one table to another, gathering up small crystals from each. "I need five minutes, Hippy, to open a door to the right place. Can you hold them off?"

"I've got enough Bloody Fairy in me for that." Hippy barred the door with her staff.

"Good. When I call, you must join me straight away, no matter what." He disappeared behind the black curtain.

The first vamp to appear in the doorway was tall and pale like all of his kind. White-blonde hair rippled over his shoulders. His veins glowed sickly blue in the gaslight. He tilted his head to one side and studied her. "What a treat," he said. "A nice, ripe little fairy, all for me."

"I'm going to make you sparkle," Hippy said. "Like a sunbeam."

The smile dropped from the vamp's face. He lunged.

No time for sparkling then. Hippy swiped with the blade on her staff, but he dodged and knocked her back into the tent. She leaped to her feet, swung the staff in a wild arc and clipped the side of his head. His ear flew off and landed on the table. Blood poured from his head.

The vamp put a hand to the wound and said some very bad words in Vampish.

Hippy swallowed the sickness rising in her stomach. "Maybe your mum won't think you're so ugly now." She ran at him and impaled him on the pointy blade, just like Ishtar always did. Blood sprayed the tent walls. The vamp staggered, clutched the staff and pulled it out.

Hippy yelped and backed toward the nearest table. That should have *killed* him!

The vamp followed. Blood poured out of his mouth. She was going to be sick. She was already dizzy. She felt around behind her and found the statue of the lady with the mirror. She hefted it.

"You're going to die slowly." The vamp spat blood with every word.

"Gross. Would you go and bleed on someone else?" Hippy swung the statue in a vicious, tight circle and smashed it over his head. The mirror snapped off.

The vamp fell to the floor, but not before five more burst through the door. Hippy leaped onto the table top and went for her fairy dust.

Then she froze.

The last and the tallest of the vamps held her eyes. White blonde hair waved over his face, past bright red eyes and down his back. Purple veins forked from his jaw to his cheekbones. Bloodless lips curved. "You give a lot of trouble for a fairy."

Hippy took a step back on the table. Superstitious terror made her hands shake so much she could barely keep a hold of the broken statue. "Rustam Badora," she said, even though her lips had gone numb.

The other vamps stepped aside. He bowed. "Pleased to make your acquaintance, Fairy." He bared long, gleaming white fangs at her.

"Pierus!" Hippy's voice rose on the word.

"Now!" Pierus roared.

Hippy threw the statue at the vamp king, vaulted backwards off the table and ran for the black curtain, the vamps right behind her. When she dived through, Pierus caught her hand. Lightning crackled in the shape of a star between nine crystals. Shadows pulsed in the rip.

"Now." Pierus ran for the lightning.

Hippy gripped his hand. Her feet only hit the ground twice before she hurtled through something cold and tingly for the space of three quick breaths. She landed on her feet in complete darkness.

CHAPTER SIX

Hippy couldn't see her hand, even when she waved it right in front of her face. The air was stale and musty. Several large somethings landed with uneven thumps on the floor behind them.

Absolute silence. A quick, indrawn breath from Pierus. In the distance a rhythmic metallic clang, like a hammer striking rock.

Then, a whisper. "Where in Shadow are we?"

The words hadn't come from either of them. Hippy and Pierus automatically went back to back. Neither of them had a useful weapon.

A deep, silky voice penetrated the darkness. "They're in here somewhere. Find them. Kill them both."

A female voice, with an edge that sent a shiver down Hippy's spine. "But my Lord, don't they say if he dies, Shadow dies too?"

Skin hit skin. A heavy form made a dull thud against a rock wall. "Anybody else have a question?"

Hippy stayed perfectly still. She hardly dared breathe. Vamps could see well in the dark, but this was really, really thick underground darkness, the kind that made Ishtar freak out. Maybe they had a chance.

Footsteps crunched on rocks. All five vamps must have followed her through the rip. But who had spoken first? That hadn't been a vamp, she was sure of it.

Sparks danced. They flared, caught and became a sputtering fire held in an upraised hand. The bluish flames cast a sickly pall over Badora's face, then turned red and flared up, lighting the inside of a small cavern.

The vamp's lips curved into a thin line when he saw Hippy. "There you are."

Another four vamps circled them. This was absolutely no time to be frozen with the primordial terror only the vamp king could inspire in a fairy. No time at all. Think. Pierus must have a plan. He must. But he wasn't doing anything, Shadow's sake, Ishtar was right, she had no more sense than a bearfly in winter and she wasn't going to last a day.

Hippy slowly eased open Fluffy Ducky's pouch. He ran over her hand and scuttled down her leg. She opened another pouch and took out a handful of fairy dust.

"Very quiet, aren't you?" Badora advanced. The vamps closed in with him.

"I was just thinking about shiny things," Hippy said. "You know. Moons and stars and crystals and vamps covered in fairy dust. Did you hear? Five sparkly vamps walked into a cave-"

Badora's eyes flashed in the firelight. He bared his fangs. "Vampires. Don't. Shine."

"I didn't say you were shiny, I said you were sparkly."

"I don't think insulting them is going to help us," Pierus muttered.

"Are you crazy? We always insult vamps. It's the best way to start a fight."

One of the vamps screamed, clutched at something on his face and began a frenzied struggle before falling to the ground.

Hippy never took her eyes off Badora. "I wonder who Fluffy Ducky will decide to make friends with next?"

"I really hate Bloody Fairies." The vamp leaped at her.

Hippy ducked. Behind her, Pierus went down low and took out another vamp at the legs. An arrow that came from neither of them whistled through the air and a third vamp dropped to the ground.

Badora crouched, poised to spring, just out of reach of any fairy dust she could throw. The scuffle behind her intensified.

Then an explosion shook the cavern. Hippy threw her arms over her head while rocks pounded the floor. Sunlight poured through a man-sized hole in the roof and the vamp Pierus was fending off screamed and burst into flames.

A single figure bearing a bright, bright light descended on a rope through the dust and debris. She landed on both feet in the middle of the cavern and flashed the light all around her. "Holy hell!" she yelled. She dropped the light, yanked a big metal cylinder from the pack on her back and mounted it on her shoulder. "Nobody move!"

The vamp king's laughter filled the cavern with rumbling echoes and sent a spinning vortex of dust through the shafts of sunlight.

The woman whirled in his direction. "Who the hell are you people?"

Badora got to his feet. "A human," he said. "Congratulations,

Muse King, you have granted my dearest, longest held wish. The only thing I like better than fairy is the taste of human. You've just given me back their world." He motioned to the one remaining vamp. They both leaped, clung to a ledge high on the wall and leaped again.

Hippy thought they were going to go through the hole in the roof and be burned up by the sunlight, but they veered off another way and disappeared. She said a bad word, bent to scoop up Fluffy Ducky, ran for the wall and scrambled straight up it.

The human yelled in fright. "How is she doing that?"

"Hippy!" Pierus yelled. "Get back here!"

Hippy clung to the wall and looked over her shoulder. "We can't let them get into Dream!"

"My dear girl, you are no match for Rustam Badora!"

"You're just going to let him go?" Hippy's voice rose to a squeak.

"No you silly little fairy, we are going to get the Apple of Chaos and deal with all of the vampires at once!"

"But I want to fight the vamp king." Hippy let go, dropped through ten feet of air, landed lightly on both feet and pouted at him.

The human yelled in fright again. "How did you do that?"

"What?" Hippy scowled at her, then walked over to one of the piles of ashes. She removed the slender metal arrow from it and placed it in her pouch.

Why were vamp spies killing vamps?

"Hey!" The woman's voice rose an octave. "Don't ignore me little girl! I've got a gun here! What the hell is going on? What are you people doing at my dig site?"

Pierus made a deep, disgusted noise. "Young woman, do you have even the vaguest conception of what you have just done?"

The woman pressed some kind of button on her metal thing. A loud click echoed through the cavern. "I'm asking the questions here."

"Come here Hippy," Pierus said.

"Don't you call me a hippy!" The woman turned her metal thing on Pierus.

Hippy stared at the thing. "What does that do?"

The woman aimed it at the hole in the roof. Her finger moved and an explosion came from the metal cylinder. "That's what it does."

Hippy's eyes shone. "It goes bang." She took several steps forward. "Can I try?"

"Are you people completely insane?" The woman went red in the face.

"I think you need to calm down, young woman," Pierus said.

"Stop calling me young woman! I've got more grey hairs than you have, sonny!"

"You mustn't mind him," Hippy said. "He's three thousand years old."

The woman rubbed her head. "This must be the most absolutely ridiculous conversation I've ever had."

"You're right, it's a complete waste of time, which I'm afraid is a precious commodity now you've allowed the vampire king to escape into your world," Pierus said.

"You're insane."

"And you're wasting our time." Pierus peered intently around the cavern. "I'm sure the Apple was hidden not far from here."

"Apple?" the woman said. "You're here for an apple?"

"You, human woman, where are we?"

"At my dig site." The gun, which had been dropping, raised again. "Clear off."

"She's worse than a fairy," Pierus muttered.

"Hey!" Hippy scowled. "If you want my help you can just stop fairy bashing, alright?"

"Who's bashing fairies?" the woman's voice rose on a note that hovered somewhere between panic and disbelief.

"Pierus," Hippy said.

"Pierus?" The woman tilted her head. "Funny, I came across that name a while back." She gave Pierus a stern, hard look over the rim of her glasses. "Rather an obscure Greek myth. King Pierus had nine daughters and went around saying they were better than the nine muses. Ended badly."

Pierus sniffed. "I never heard such rubbish. I assure you, nothing of that sort ever happened."

She glared for a bit longer. Hippy began to fidget and wonder if she should let Fluffy Ducky sort it out when the woman abruptly lowered her weapon and returned it to her pack. "I suppose we really should calm down and remember our manners." She grabbed Pierus's hand and shook it. "Poppy Praeconius, archaeologist. Pleased to meet you." She took Hippy's hand. "And you are?"

Hippy shook her hand vigorously, since that seemed to be expected. "Hippy Ishtar." The woman was only a little taller than her, so she didn't have to crane her neck like she did with Pierus to see her face. Poppy looked as though she were in her forties. She had a few lines around her grey eyes, and otherwise rather stern features, which were currently smudged with dirt. Her glasses were crooked and her long, sandy, grey-sprinkled hair was pulled back into a severe bun. She wore the most curious trousers and tailored dress, all in khaki. "You're the first human I've ever met," Hippy added.

"Really? You're the first lunatic I've ever found in a cave. I'm sure we'll get along famously." Poppy shouldered her pack.

"What's a lunatic?"

"Someone who believes in fairies." Poppy scanned the cavern.

"But I *am* a fairy." Hippy's lower lip trembled.

"Of course you are, dear."

Pierus put a hand on Hippy's shoulder and bent down to her level. "Humans don't know about us," he said in a low voice. "Try and be a little more circumspect, my dear."

"Circum what?"

Pierus sighed. "Never mind. Come along, we've wasted enough time. If my calculations were correct, we shouldn't have far to go. You, human, bring me your bright light, would you?"

"Why not?" Poppy picked up her light and followed him to the walls.

Hippy trotted behind while Pierus studied the rock. She was far more interested in the human. Really, she could have passed for a fairy if she was shorter, or a muse if she was a lot taller. But something bothered her. She couldn't quite put her finger on what it was.

"Here," Pierus said.

The light stopped over a series of markings on the wall. Next to the markings, a tunnel branched away.

"These are fascinating." Poppy leaned forward. "This is a Greek script, but I'm not familiar with it at all."

"Of course you're not, women have no place reading the ancient texts," Pierus snapped. "Would you keep that light steady?"

Poppy glanced over her shoulder at Hippy. "Is he always this pleasant?"

Hippy barely heard her because underneath the unfamiliar letters, she saw an etching of a lady with snakes on her head. "Hey, that's like the statue in your tent! The little one. I smashed the big one over a vamp's head."

"You broke my statue?" Pierus scowled.

"That's Medusa," Poppy said. "She could turn men to stone just by looking at them. You're very small to be smashing heads, aren't you?"

Pierus strode down the tunnel. Hippy hurried to keep up. Poppy walked beside her, her light bobbing around their feet.

"He your boyfriend?" Poppy whispered.

"Ew! He's way too old." Hippy screwed up her nose in disgust.

"Your dad?"

"No, he's a muse. My dad's fighting vamps."

"A muse?" Poppy flashed her light at Pierus's silhouette. "In what respect? Are you an artist?"

"Don't be silly, I'm a Bloody Fairy."

"No need to snap dear, you could be a bloody garbage collector for all I care, I'm just trying to understand how a pack of lunatics came to be in a cave that's supposedly been sealed off for thousands of years."

"We came through the rip."

"Through the what?" Poppy's question was cut off when they followed Pierus around a bend in the passage and almost stumbled into him.

"You, human woman." Pierus motioned her forward.

"Call me Poppy," Poppy said. "It makes you sound less like an ass."

"How many years have elapsed since the sorcerers separated the dimensions?"

"How many years since who did what now?" Poppy pushed her glasses up on her nose and shone the light on Pierus's face.

He put a hand up to shield his eyes and squinted. "Would you stop that, you dreadful creature?"

"Didn't you say she doesn't know anything about Shadow?" Hippy said.

"Oh, yes of course." Pierus sighed. "What number do you put on the lapsing of time?"

Poppy blinked. "Are you asking me what year it is?"

"Yes!"

"It's 1982."

"One thousand nine hundred and eighty two years since what?" Pierus scowled. "I know for a fact Dream is older than that. From which catastrophic event are you counting?"

"The birth of Christ," Poppy said. "Where are you people from?"

Pierus walked up and down the tunnel. He counted on his fingers and muttered to himself.

"What's he doing?" Poppy whispered.

"I don't know." Hippy decided not to admit she'd lost track of the conversation. She wasn't that good with numbers.

"Ah, religion," Pierus said out loud. "How like humans to use it as a marker of time. I know where we are now. Human woman-"

"Poppy," Poppy said.

Pierus made an impatient noise. "Where are we, geographically?"

"In the tunnels under the old city of Thebes in Boetia. At least, it's where *I* believe old Thebes is located, even if-"

"And what exactly are you doing here?"

"Looking for my hat."

"Irritating woman. Why are you here?"

Poppy folded her arms. "You first."

"We are seeking an ancient treasure with the power to send an army of vampires back into the Darkness from whence they came," Pierus said.

"That's fascinating. I'm looking for a herd of unicorns to ride around in the moonlight."

"What's a unicorn?" Hippy asked.

"It's a horse. With a horn coming out of its head."

"They live down here?"

Poppy groaned. "Honestly, is there something wrong with her?"

"Apparently she was dropped on her head as a child," Pierus said.

"Hey!" Hippy kicked him in the ankle.

Pierus ignored her. He spoke through clenched teeth, as though dealing with two particularly fractious children. "Now young woman, you strike me as an intelligent sort, who wouldn't blow holes in caves for nothing. Tell me why you're here."

Poppy straightened her back. "Pandora's Box," she said.

Pierus went a step closer to her. A tic jumped in his forehead. "Is that what they call it now? What makes you think it's here?"

Something changed in Poppy's demeanour. Her eyes sparked. She paced up and down on the spot, using her hands to emphasise her words. "I've been following the trail for a while," she said. "I happened to have the opportunity to read a very, very, ancient fragment of text that led me to believe Pandora's Box was not in fact an analogy for the dangers of arcane knowledge, or the loss of innocence, or whatever else, but in fact an actual physical object of immense value. According to what I read, the myth about Pandora opening the box was all wrong. It was a cautionary tale. The box was in fact created to hold something the ancients feared, and she guarded it. Of course I searched in all the wrong places, until I found irrefutable evidence that led me to believe Medusa was invoked to guard the treasure. I knew there was a temple to Medusa in ancient Thebes, so naturally I came here. To a sealed cave. And found you two and your acrobatic friends."

Pierus scowled. "You were nearly right," he said. "We are in fact in search of the same artefact. And it is indeed hidden here."

"How do you know?"

"Because I helped to hide it. And if I have my bearings right-" he turned in a slow circle. "We must be close. Now tell me young woman, what did you intend to do with what you call Pandora's Box once you obtained it?"

Poppy straightened her glasses. Her voice was perfectly friendly and even. "It would have to go to the museum, of course. It would be a national treasure."

Pierus gave a low, deep chuckle and walked on down the tunnel. "Really. So you are not down here for any kind of personal gain?"

"I absolutely resent what you are implying," Poppy said. "I'm trying to build a professional reputation as an archaeologist here."

"And what do you intend to do when the fairy and I return to Shadow with it and leave you here?"

"Well seeing as you're obviously both insane I'm not all that worried about you disappearing."

"Then you won't mind accompanying us for the moment."

Hippy trotted alongside the two of them, only half-listening to the conversation. Somewhere nearby she could hear the unmistakable sound of water trickling over rock. She wandered away from them, seeking the source of the sound. The tunnel dipped down and the sound grew louder. All at once she teetered on the edge of a hole in the path. She yelped and jumped back.

"Hippy?" Pierus called from somewhere nearby.

"I found water!" Hippy dropped to her stomach and looked in the hole. Three feet below, a shallow, dark stream rushed past. She shuddered. She didn't want to fall in that.

Pierus and Poppy caught up and leaned over the hole.

"Well done my dear," Pierus said. "This is exactly what we were looking for."

Hippy beamed.

"We'll need to go down there."

Her smile vanished. "Down there? Into the water?"

"Is that a problem?"

Hippy scooted back from the edge. "You go. I'll wait here."

Pierus raised an eyebrow. "I thought you came to help me, not sit around while I did all the work."

"Oh for Heaven's sake, you two." Poppy put her hands on the edge of the hole and dropped down into it.

"Come along my dear," Pierus said.

Hippy pouted. "I don't like water."

"Now."

Hippy heaved a sigh, stalked back to the hole and dropped into it. She landed with barely a splash in icy cold water that went right up to her waist. She screamed.

Poppy, just a few feet away, put her hands over her ears. "Would you not do that? It echoes in here!"

Hippy quickly hiked up her belt to keep Fluffy Ducky dry and put her arms out to get her balance. "Yuck, yuck, yuck!"

Pierus swung himself down from the hole and slid into the water behind her. He had to bend his head to avoid hitting the roof of the tunnel. He looked both ways. "In which direction are we from the temple?"

"Just south," Poppy replied.

"Upstream," he said, and started walking against the current.

Hippy followed him. Walking against the swift flow of the water was difficult enough to start with. The wetter her leggings and dress got, the more difficult it became. Her bare feet slid on the slick rocks. Poppy's torch lit up the black water just enough to make it look murkier and more dangerous. Hippy tried not to think about water monsters. Huge fish with sharp teeth. Swimming vamps. Eels with lights on their heads. Dragons. It was harder and harder to keep her balance when she started to shake.

Poppy grabbed the back of her dress and kept her upright when she almost slipped. "Steady on."

Hippy grabbed her arm and held on tight.

"So let me get this straight," Poppy said. "You can scale a vertical wall and drop ridiculous heights without batting an eyelash–I haven't figured those out, but I will–but you're afraid of water?"

Hippy nodded.

"What are you, a cat?"

She shook her head.

"You're an odd one."

"I'm a Bloody Fairy."

"Yes, you said that before. What is that, some kind of circus cult?"

"No, it's my family. We're all afraid of water."

"Why?"

Hippy blinked. "I don't know! It's just the way things are!" She flinched when the water lapped up to her ribs.

"I think you're very brave to be facing your fear like this." Hippy beamed. "Really?"

"Really. Any idea where your lunatic friend is taking us?"

"No."

"Wonderful."

They walked in silence for a few more minutes. Each trickle and drip of water echoed in the tunnel. Pierus forged ahead, bending lower and lower when the tunnel narrowed. "Here," he finally said, stepped out of the water and disappeared.

Hippy hurried to pull herself onto the rocks, where a set of crooked, dilapidated stone steps wound up into another passage. She took them two at a time to put distance between herself and the water. Poppy followed close on her heels.

They came out in a huge cavern, where a still, glassy lake mirrored tiny glowing lights on the roof. The air was so cold Hippy was quite sure icicles were forming on her wet skin.

Poppy swept her torch over the lake. The beam found a stone bridge so old it looked like part of the cave arching over to the other side. Pierus was already halfway across it.

They hurried after him. Fine granules of stone skittered away under Hippy's bare feet. Behind her, Poppy's heavy, wet boots crunched with every step.

Hippy tried not to look at the water below. She focused instead on Pierus's back. There was a tear in his dark blue coat. When she caught up with him, he put his arm around her shoulders.

"Now is your time to shine, my dear."

"Good. I like shiny things."

Pierus stopped at the edge of the bridge. "Light please, young woman."

Poppy shone her torch ahead over a big, empty sandy floor.

Pierus made the tiniest sound, perhaps a sigh of relief. "Up a little."

The torchlight moved up and illuminated an enormous stone statue of Medusa. Hippy's eyes widened in awe. The stone was pitted with age. A chunk missing from her mouth made it look like she was snarling. Her blank stone eyes looked right through them all. Her hands were cupped in front of her. The snakes that curled from her head writhed in frozen fury.

Hippy smiled. She liked snakes.

Poppy said what sounded like a bad word.

Hippy repeated the word, intrigued. "What does that mean?"

"It means I find that thing incredibly disconcerting, dear."

"Hippy you must go up to the statue," Pierus said. "And bring me back what you find in those hands. Do not be afraid."

Hippy tentatively took a step off the bridge. Then another. The statue didn't move, so she gained confidence.

"Why her?" Poppy asked. "Why not you or me?"

"It has to be her," Pierus said. "Nobody else can touch it."

Hippy walked barefoot to the statue. Water dripped from her tunic, making tiny craters in the cold, fine sand. The statue's hands were too high for her to reach, so she found all the tiny little niches nobody but a fairy could see and scrambled up the rock wall next to it. When she reached elbow height she hung onto the wall and leaned over to look in the cupped hands, but it was too dark to see anything. "I need light!"

The torchlight flooded over the stone hands, lighting up ancient fingers, stone palms, an empty bowl.

Hippy bit her lip. Pierus was going to be very cross. She gave a disconsolate sigh. "It's not here."

Pierus was very, very quiet. "What?"

"I said it's not here."

"Are you sure?"

"It's completely empty."

CHAPTER SEVEN

Pierus's voice could have chilled a bearfly in the hive. "Look again."

"There's nothing there," Hippy said.

"Look again!"

Hippy made a face at him and leaned across once again. It was very awkward to hang onto the rock with one hand and reach across a stone shoulder with the other, but she didn't feel it would be very respectful to climb on the statue itself. She reached into the cupped hands and felt around. Nope, still nothing. She checked all of the fingers, in case it was a very small treasure, with no success. Pierus was just going to have to accept it, the thing was gone.

Something sharp scraped the palm of her hand.

Hippy scrabbled for the object. She picked it up between two fingers and studied it in Poppy's light. She blinked. "Freakin Fairies!" she yelled, and promptly fell backwards off the wall. She heard Poppy shriek just before she flipped, rolled on her back and landed at Pierus's feet.

"What do you mean, Freakin Fairies?" Pierus's voice was positively icy.

Hippy stood up and opened her hand. Poppy shone her torch on the object in it.

"It's a snake tooth," Hippy said. "Like the ones the Freakin Fairies who live in Quicksilver Forest wear in their hair."

Pierus cursed black and blue, turned on his heel and stormed back over the bridge.

Hippy ran after him. "What does it mean? How do the Freakin Fairies even know about the treasure? What do we do now?"

"We find them," Pierus said.

Poppy followed close behind them. "Are you two saying fairies took Pandora's Box from a cave that's been sealed for three thousand years?"

"Who else?" Pierus demanded. "Three thousand years ago

Pandora was the only one who could touch the Apple of Chaos. Now that gift lies with her descendants. I knew that traitorous creature was going to come back to haunt me."

"My God, you two really believe all this stuff," Poppy said.

Pierus whirled on her. "You! Did you have anything to do with this? Are you in cahoots with the Freakin Fairies?"

"Back off!" Poppy planted a hand on his chest and shoved him. "See this? This is my personal space. I'm very particular about it. Don't get in it. I'll have you know I'm also very upset about coming all the way down here, at great personal risk, for nothing at all." She pushed her glasses up on her nose, shoved past Pierus and stalked ahead.

Hippy giggled. "I like her. She's just like a fairy."

Pierus put a hand on her shoulder and matched his pace to hers. "If I were you my dear, I wouldn't trust her."

"Why not?"

"Just take my word for it. I know humans, and this one is not what she says she is."

"Oh." Hippy's eyes widened, considering this. "Can we keep her anyway?"

Pierus chuckled. "She's not a pet."

"But she's fun. And she knows stuff."

"You have a point there. She does indeed appear to know things."

They descended the steps together. Hippy balked at the sight of the stream. "Isn't there another way out?"

Poppy, who had just lowered herself into the water, looked back. "Actually no," she said. "In fact the water may be our only way out, depending on whether your so-called vampire friends decided to cut my rope or not once we were gone."

Silence greeted this statement. Hippy shuddered. She'd forgotten, briefly, about the vamps.

Poppy waded downstream.

"Go on," Pierus said. "I'm right behind you."

Hippy wasn't quite sure if he was trying to be comforting or scary, but she splashed disconsolately into the water anyway and waded after Poppy. It was no easier going downstream than up, because now the water pushed her off balance the other way. She gritted her teeth and kept going.

When Poppy went right past the hole in the rock overhead, Hippy's nerves tightened like screws in a cooking pot. "You were serious about the rope being cut?" She eyed the roof, which sloped down to meet the surface of the water. The rock was dark and slick with slimy condensation. Something with a lot of legs crawled on the rough surface, oblivious to the current below.

"In my experience it's best never to leave a site the same way you went in," Poppy said. "Can you swim?"

"Swim? No!" Hippy's voice rose to a squeak.

"Probably a good time to learn, then." Poppy dived and disappeared.

"Oh for Shadow's sake." Pierus put one arm around her waist. "Just hold your breath."

Hippy had just enough time to grab Fluffy Ducky's pouch and hold it above the surface before Pierus dived, taking her under.

The water deafened and blinded her. She was wet. All wet. Panic flashed through her brain. Surely no Bloody Fairy in history had ever, ever been this wet. The only thing that stopped her from complete terror was the fact her hand was dry, even if her knuckles did keep scraping rock, so Fluffy Ducky must be okay.

Bubbles escaped from her mouth. Pierus kicked his legs and propelled them through the water with his free arm. Stars burst in front of her eyes. Her lungs strained. Her brain threatened to explode out of her skull.

Then all at once they shot out into sunlit water and surfaced in open, empty countryside.

Hippy opened her mouth to scream because the experience had been so awful, but the sound only lasted a second before Poppy clapped a hand over her mouth and kept it there until she stopped.

"Not a good idea," Poppy said in a low voice. "Just relax. It's only water. Okay?"

Hippy nodded.

Poppy took her hand away. "Come on."

Hippy was only too glad to get out of the water, flop onto the grassy bank and do her best to wring out her sodden clothes while still wearing them. First though she took out Fluffy Ducky to check on him. He sat on her hand trembling. Droplets of water shone on his hairs. He blinked at her with all eight eyes.

Poppy crouched down next to her. "What do you have there?"

"Fluffy Ducky." Hippy held him up for her inspection.

"Cute. In a frightening sort of way." Poppy studied him closely. "Looks like some breed of tarantula. Does he bite?"

"Only vamps. Well, mostly only vamps. He doesn't like Pierus, which is weird. He's normally such a good judge of character."

Poppy snorted. "I'd say he's perfectly accurate. You know I saw spiders like that in the Central American jungles a couple of years ago. Woke up with one hanging in a brand new web right across my bed."

Hippy stared at her, impressed. "Did you bring him home for a friend?"

"'Fraid not, love. Thought he was better off in his natural environment."

Hippy put Fluffy Ducky in his pouch. The hot sun was already drying her clothes off. She unpinned her hair and squeezed the water out of it, which was quite an operation, considering she could barely reach portions of it.

A footstep crunched on the grass nearby. Hippy looked up to see Pierus, his hair and clothes clinging to his skin, watching her. He had a funny tilt to his mouth that unsettled her.

"What is it?" Hippy wrung the last of her hair out and pinned it back into place.

Pierus muttered something and stalked away.

"That sounded like `just like Pandora.'" Poppy sounded amused.

Hippy stared after him. "You two keep talking about her," she said. "Who is she?"

"Come on." Poppy helped her to her feet and they followed Pierus through the long grass and up a sloping hillside. "Pandora was said to be the first woman created by the Greek Gods, long, long ago. Zeus, the king of the Gods, gave her a box to keep and told her not to open it. But of course she did and all the bad things that ever were–you know, greed, hate, envy–all came flying out into the world. The only thing left in the box was hope."

"Sounds nasty," Hippy said. "Why do you want such a box?"

"Can't you imagine? Something so old and fabled would be infinitely valuable."

"What happened to her?"

"Who, Pandora?" Poppy shrugged. "The usual myths don't really say. Of course the ones I've been pursuing have been lost for so many years, it's difficult to translate, but I've gathered she suffered some kind of punishment. Banished in darkness was the literal translation, but I've really no idea what that means."

They gained the top of the slope and stopped. Ahead lay a flat grassy area strewn with rectangular rocks. To one side pillars rose from the ground, but supported no roof. Pierus crouched in the centre of the ruins. His coat flared out around him.

Hippy went and crouched down beside him. She plucked a blade of grass and twirled it in her fingers. "It's a nice hill," she said. "But the house is all broken."

"Three thousand years will do that," Pierus said in a low voice. "I had no idea it would affect me so much."

"What would?"

"I lived over there." He pointed to the south. "I used to come here often. This was a temple then, a beautiful stone temple."

Hippy tried to imagine it, but she'd never seen a temple.

Pierus patted her hand. "Forgive an old man for getting maudlin," he said. "I've been back to Dream from time to time, but never to my home. I had no idea it would be like this. It must be all this talk of Pandora. I brought her here once." He brushed a lock of wet hair out of Hippy's face and tucked it behind her ear. "You remind me of her."

Hippy quickly stood up and stepped out of reach. She wasn't sure why the look on his face made her nervous, but it did. "Poppy said Pandora opened a box and let all the bad things out."

Pierus chuckled. "It didn't quite happen like that."

"How do you know?"

"Of all people, I should know. She was my wife."

Poppy cleared her throat behind them. "Sorry to interrupt, you two," she said. "Where's your transport?"

"Transport?" Hippy looked at Pierus.

"Given we weren't anticipating the theft of the Apple of Chaos, transport was not my first consideration when we arrived," Pierus said.

"If talking like a pompous ass gave you wheels, you'd go miles. You'd better follow me. You don't want to stay here." Poppy turned around and walked down the slope toward a road that wound beneath the hillside.

Hippy skipped after her. Pierus followed a minute later. She thought maybe he was saying his goodbyes first. How odd, to think of Pierus as a young man with a wife. She wondered what Pandora had been like.

By the time they reached the road Hippy was hot and thirsty. She re-pinned her hair to lift it off her neck while they walked. The fabric of her tunic had dried all stiff and was gritty against her skin. Poppy seemed to know where she was going, even though the road was completely empty and wound on for miles and miles and miles.

After a while Poppy headed away from the road and towards a stand of trees where a black vehicle was parked. It was similar to cars Hippy had glimpsed in Shadow City the one time she'd been there, but it had the oddest dents all over it, a little round hole in the windscreen and no sleek shiny horns or buttons or dials to be seen. It was shrouded in foliage.

Poppy gave an apologetic shrug. "You can never be too careful." She lifted a camouflaging branch off the bonnet and took a key from her pocket.

"How right you are, Miss Praeconius," said an unfamiliar voice.

Something cold and metallic pressed into Hippy's neck. She looked around in surprise.

Three men in black and white suits had appeared out of nowhere. One was short and bald, the other two were very big and had shoulders like tree branches. One pointed a gun at Poppy's head, the other at Pierus.

Poppy slowly raised her hands in the air. She gave a nervous laugh. "Gentlemen, really, it's so nice of you to come out and meet me here! I'm sure we can dispense with the hardware."

"Dispense with the hardware? Really?" The bald guy made a wheezing noise low in his throat that could have been a laugh. "That's my insurance. Where is it?"

"Gone." Poppy looked steadily into his eyes and never flinched.

"Gone? Now why don't I believe you?"

"She's telling the truth!" Hippy scowled at him.

"Shut up Hippy." Poppy kept a smile pasted on her face, but spoke through clenched teeth.

"Hippy is it?" Bald guy grabbed Hippy's chin and twisted her face one way and then the other. "Yeah, she looks like a hippy. What do you know about the box, little girl?"

"I'm not a little girl," Hippy said.

"Seriously she's got nothing to do with it," Poppy said. "Her and the old guy, I just met them up on the hill. They're tourists. Now Tony I'm sure we can talk about this like civilised people."

"Sure we can." Tony jerked his head at a long black car that had just pulled up on the road behind them. "Get in. All three of you. No funny business or the hippy gets it, alright?"

CHAPTER EIGHT

It was all very well climbing into the back seat and looking to see if there was anything shiny in there, but when the doors locked them in and the countryside rushed past faster than the wind, Hippy started to feel sick. She'd never actually been inside a car, not even in Shadow City. Bloody Fairies didn't trust any mode of transportation that lacked visible feet.

It was very cramped on the two facing bench seats. Poppy sat on one side, in between Tony and one of the big men. The other big man sat between her and Pierus.

"Now isn't this cosy?" Tony plucked a small white box out of his pocket, took a little white tube from that and applied a flaming match to the end. The most foul-smelling smoke curled from the stick and filled the car.

Hippy couldn't quite believe what she was seeing. "Do you know that thing in your hand is on fire?"

Poppy muttered something under her breath.

Tony chuckled. "It's a cigarette, sweetie." He sucked on the thing and exhaled a cloud of smoke around her head. "What's wrong with her?"

Hippy winced and waited for someone to say it.

"Nothing's wrong with her," Poppy snapped. "She's just not from around here."

Hippy beamed, then coughed when she inhaled a lungful of smoke.

"See I have a problem with this," Tony said. "I could almost swear you told me you were going after this box alone, and I've got a very good memory." He tapped his head. "But then you go underground and you come up with two new friends. What gives?"

"You know I've been asking myself just that," Poppy said.

"I could just about see my way clear to getting over that little hurdle," Tony continued, "if you had of come back with the box. Like you promised. But you didn't, so we're going to have a problem."

"Damn right we're going to have a problem." Poppy took a deep breath. "Someone else got there first. I'm going to need more money if you want me to keep chasing this, Tony. A woman can't live on air."

Pierus made a sharp movement. The big man planted a hand on his chest.

Tony glared at him. "Don't you worry mister, you'll get your turn to talk. Mostly because I just don't like you. Unlike you-" he looked at Hippy. "You I could get used to." He paused a moment and sucked on his cigarette. "You're not getting another cent, Miss Praeconius, till you give us something solid. I'm starting to think there is no treasure. You don't want to me to think that, because you know what'll happen." He drew a finger across his throat.

"Now Tony, have I ever given you cause not to trust me?" Poppy looked at him over her glasses.

Hippy lost interest in the conversation. She reached in to check on Fluffy Ducky.

"I don't trust anybody." Tony dragged on his cigarette. "I don't trust you. You're too smart for a woman. I don't trust your man friend here, he walks around looking like he's smelled something bad. I could maybe trust the little girl here, but it'd probably get me in deep trouble. You see where I'm coming from?"

"Little girl?" Hippy scowled. Fluffy Ducky ran up over her arm, paused on her shoulder and launched himself straight at Tony's face.

The two big guys went for their guns. Tony screamed.

Pierus gave a low, deep chuckle. "That's the first time I've had any use for that creature."

Poppy moved faster than the men. She seized their guns right out of their hands and pointed each one at their owners. "Hippy just make sure that spider doesn't bite him, will you? You, Ugly, stop the car."

The big guy next to Hippy snarled and thumped on the glass that separated the cabin from the driver. Hippy reached across and plucked Fluffy Ducky off Tony's face, but held him just about two inches away to keep the man cowed. "I'm not a little girl." She gave him her most ferocious scowl.

The car slowed to a halt.

"You two, get out." Poppy jerked her head at the door.

The big guys got out of the car.

Poppy reached across and locked the doors. Then she extended one leg and thumped the floor twice. The car moved off again. "Alright Hippy, put the spider away."

Hippy tucked Fluffy Ducky safely away.

Tony said a whole string of bad words.

Hippy's jaw dropped in astonishment. "Do rabbits do that kind of thing over here?"

Tony spluttered.

"There," Poppy said, when he subsided. "Now we're on more even terms, perhaps we can all be a little bit more friendly."

"You're going to regret this." Tony made a nasty face at both Pierus and Hippy. "And you two as well. Those are my good friends you left back there!"

"They're big boys, they'll be fine." Poppy handed a gun to Hippy. "Here love, hold this. No not like that, that's where the bullet comes out. Point it at Tony–that's it–and don't squeeze the trigger unless I tell you to."

"Which bit's the trigger?"

"Don't give it to her, she's psycho!" Tony yelled.

Hippy broke into a big grin. "Really? That's almost the nicest thing anyone ever said to me." She wiped a tear from one eye.

Tony dropped his face in his hands. "I knew it was gonna be one of those days. Alright Praeconius, what do you want?"

"You off my back would be a good start." Poppy took a slim metal file out of her pocket and started scraping dirt from underneath her nails. "I mean really, I'm doing my very best to be a serious archaeologist here, but it's very difficult when you and your goons overreact at every little setback."

Tony scoffed. "You're not a serious archaeologist, you're a thief!"

"I would be a serious archaeologist if you'd get off my back, give me the space to pay you your money back and move on!"

"I knew it," Pierus said between clenched teeth. "I knew you weren't to be trusted."

"You think?" Tony glared at all of them.

"Shut up, or I'll put you out of the car too, and keep your friend," Poppy said.

Pierus turned bright red. Then he went white. "You wouldn't dare."

"I'm doing the fandango with organised crime here, you want to try me? Now shut up, I'm trying to close a deal." Poppy returned her attention to her nails.

"Seriously, who is this guy?" Tony said.

"Never you mind. Now here's the deal, Tony. Pandora's Box was gone, but we have a lead on who took it. I'm going to need time to chase that up and some cash to cover expenses. Not a lot mind, but you understand it'll all be worth it in the end."

"You're crazy," Tony said. "You think I'm going to give you more money and let you run off with the box?"

"I don't care what you think. I'm sure you don't want me to teach young Hippy here how to shoot that gun, do you?"

"Oh!" Hippy exclaimed. "I think I found the trigger!"

"Alright, alright!" Tony put his hands up. "But you got a week, alright? And then I'm coming to check up. And you'd better not have these two jokers with you when I get there, either."

"Good man." Poppy stuck out her hand and the two shook. "Are we in Athens yet?" She peered out of the window.

"What makes you think that's where we're going?"

"That's where you always go. Ah, good. Let us out here."

Tony leaned forward, giving Hippy a wide berth. He knocked on the glass. The car slowed to a halt.

Poppy unlocked the doors and pushed them open. "Come on team."

"One week Praeconius!" Tony yelled.

Poppy slammed the door shut.

Hippy stared all around her with big eyes while the car pulled away. More cars rushed past on a big, wide road. Tall, dirty buildings loomed over them, their rows of windows climbing up and streaming across for miles. In, around and behind them crowded far more ancient buildings, most crumbling and in ruins. People swarmed everywhere. Most of them stared at her. She moved closer to Pierus.

Pierus put an arm around her shoulder and shook his head. "This is Athens?"

"You sound disappointed. What's the matter, you two never been in a city before?"

"I was here briefly, three thousand years ago." Pierus set off after Poppy when she strode off down the path. Hippy had to run to keep up.

"Oh yes, I forgot, you're from another world, blah, blah, blah.

Hippy don't look so frightened."

"Fairies tend to be isolated," Pierus said. "I'd wager she's never even seen Shadow City."

"Yes I have," Hippy said. "I went there once with my Dad and Ishtar and all my brothers to see a play about war at the Shadow Theatre. It was a good play. There were fairies in it. And their costumes were shiny."

"Where's Shadow City then?" Poppy turned a corner and headed along a row of shops and cafes, skirting tables and chairs and people drinking from little white cups.

"East of the mountains, beyond the forest," Hippy said.

"Which mountains? The Pindus?"

"No. The Great Western Peak of Impossible Doom. But then, everything's East of that except the Darkness."

Poppy halted in the middle of the footpath, turned around and glared at them over her glasses. "There's no such place."

"How narrow human minds are," Pierus said.

Poppy made a noise of disgust. "Come on, we're almost there."

"Almost where?" Hippy broke away from Pierus and trotted along next to her. "Where are we going? Will there be food there?"

"The Library. And no, you'll have to wait till later." Poppy turned into a street that was much wider and emptier than the others and went up a set of white stone stairs that curved up to a huge building fronted by six enormous stone pillars.

Hippy followed her, struck dumb by the size of the building. Pierus, not far behind, muttered to himself about modern architecture.

Inside it was dark and much cooler. Poppy hurried them past a long desk and deep, deep into the shadowy recesses of the library, until they reached a shelf packed with books so old and dusty Hippy had a sneezing fit.

There Poppy stopped and looked Pierus square in the eye. "I'm not stupid," she said. "I know you're linked to Pandora's Box, I just don't know how. I don't believe in fairies or vampires, but the legends I read mentioned someone named Pierus. That's the only reason I didn't leave you underground. I want to know the truth. Who are you?"

"Why?" Pierus ran his finger along the spine of a book. "So you can steal the Apple from under my nose and sell it to your friend Tony?"

"Look, that's all very complicated." Poppy straightened her glasses. "But believe you me, I have no intention of letting Tony anywhere near anything so valuable."

"You have someone who'll pay more?"

Poppy folded her arms. "None of your business."

"Oh, but it is, young woman." Pierus lifted a dusty mirror from the end of a bookshelf, laid it on the nearest table and polished it with his sleeve. "What you call Pandora's Box is nothing. What it held, the Apple of Chaos, is everything. We need it."

"What for?"

"To drive out the vamps." Hippy slumped down in the chair next to Pierus and put her head in her hands. Now everything was quiet, the images she'd turned her back on such a short time ago poured into her mind. "When we left, they'd set my village on fire. There were so many of them. They filled the night for as far as I could see."

Poppy leaned over, her balled fists resting on the table. "Hippy I can see you think you're telling the truth, but there is no such thing as vampires."

"Of course there are. I've killed like a hundred in the last year alone."

"Don't be silly. You're such a little thing, you couldn't kill anybody."

Pierus chuckled. "Never underestimate a Bloody Fairy, my dear. They live for war. Now come here. Look into this mirror." He passed his hand over it.

"Why?" Poppy leaned over to look in. Her eyes widened.

"Witness, young woman, the other side of your world. The reflection humans never see. What you see is our world, the world of Shadow, where all your nightmares were once given life."

Poppy stared, transfixed.

Hippy closed her eyes and put her hands over her ears to block out the sounds of home: the sounds of fairies and vampires at war.

CHAPTER NINE

"So let me get this straight." Poppy pushed her glasses up on her nose. A strand of hair had escaped from her coif and her glasses were crooked. The library around them was deserted and silent. "You're a real life, honest to God muse. Your job is to inspire people."

"Correct." Pierus sat opposite her, one hand splayed on the table, the other turning the pages of a book he paid no attention to.

"And she's a fairy."

"A Bloody Fairy," Hippy interrupted.

"How? What makes you a Bloody Fairy?"

"That's her clan," Pierus said.

"So when you said a freaking fairy got to the box first, you were actually being quite literal."

"Yeah." Hippy scowled. "I hate Freakin Fairies."

Poppy ran an agitated hand through her hair. "You understand this is a lot for me to take in. Were those other men really vampires?"

"One of them was Rustam Badora, king of the vampires," Pierus said. "Oldest and strongest of them all. He will wreak havoc on your world if we cannot find the Apple of Chaos and stop him."

Poppy said several bad words, put her face in her hands and rubbed her temples. "I'm in over my head here."

"On the contrary my dear, you are far better equipped to help us than most humans."

Poppy took her hands away from her face. Her voice had a sharp edge. "What makes you think I'm going to help you?"

A smile played around the edges of Pierus's mouth. His words held more than a tinge of arrogance. "I am the king of the muses. I've been watching and inspiring humans for three thousand years. You are like open books to me. You can hide nothing."

Poppy's cheeks flamed bright red, but she said nothing.

"I knew your type the moment I saw you," Pierus continued.

"You're a liar. A cheat, a manipulator and a liar."

Hippy's eyes widened. She moved closer to Pierus, but Poppy had all her attention. She couldn't see any of what he was talking about. *And* Fluffy Ducky liked her.

Poppy slumped back in her chair. "I suppose I should defend myself."

"I'm not judging you," Pierus said. "On reflection, you may be very useful. But I must know everything you know about what you call Pandora's Box and why you're searching for it. If you lie, I will know."

"Just like that, huh?" Poppy got out of her chair and paced from shelf to shelf. "Just like that, I find out there's a whole other world full of nightmares, you're from it, and I'm supposed to divulge all my deep dark secrets."

"I could find out for myself," Pierus said. "But you wouldn't find it a pleasant experience."

Poppy looked at him askance. "I don't think I want to know about that."

"Then talk. We're running out of time. The moment darkness falls the vampires will begin their reign of terror."

Hippy glanced up at the high windows, but it was hard to tell from those what time of day it was. Her stomach growled. She moved up and down the shelves, watching for people who might be listening. Poppy's voice floated after her.

"I became acquainted with an elderly gentleman some time ago," Poppy said. "Originally the whole point was to gain his trust and–er– relieve him of some of his considerable fortune." She cleared her throat. "Not all of it, you understand, but I had some debts to clear and to be honest he could afford it. Now this gentleman had an extensive library and was very knowledgeable about ancient history, so we ended up having some rather interesting conversations. I mean really, when it came down to it, I rather liked him. I try to avoid that, but there it is."

Hippy wandered back towards the table. "Why did you avoid liking him?"

"Because she was going to cheat him of his money, my dear," Pierus said. "Keep up."

Poppy scowled. "Only a little of it. Anyway, he had a theory about Pandora's Box. He used to say he thought the story was an allegory for something that existed, something that had magic powers. He was a bit whacky that way. At least I thought he was a bit whacky, until–" she winced. "Well, it all went a bit pear-shaped, didn't it? Some random thugs came and smashed up the house. At first I thought they were for me, but they were all over him. Right before they came in he gave me this book and told me to hide it and get out if I could. So I did. I got out of the house and I called the cops."

"And you never went back, naturally." Pierus sounded amused.

"Not once I found out what was in the book." Poppy reached into her pack and brought out a battered volume. She opened it up and slid it across the table.

Hippy went over to the desk to see.

Inside the book was a sheet of paper so old it was almost crumbling. On it was etched a faded map, on which notes were made in letters Hippy couldn't for the life of her read. Besides, she was hungry. She lost interest and went to poke at a spider web on a top shelf in case there were any dead flies in it for Fluffy Ducky.

Pierus, however, studied the map intently. "These are the caves we were just in."

"Damn right they are," Poppy said. "I figured all that out, but not in time to clear my debts. So naturally Tony came looking for me and I had to promise to cut him in to get him off my back."

"And what was your real plan?"

"Get the box and disappear. Set myself up for life."

"You're lying."

Poppy sighed. "Look, I have a son, okay? He's very young and there are a lot of people out there who'd use him against me if they knew. I was going to make sure he was safe. Then I was going to disappear and set myself up for life."

Pierus seemed satisfied with this. "Tell me about the people who attacked your elderly gentleman."

Poppy shrugged. "Garden variety thugs, I thought. Long-haired louts."

"Did you notice anything else about them?"

"They did seem a trifle on the short side. And vicious."

"Hippy," Pierus said.

Hippy came back to the table.

"Short and vicious," Pierus said. "I'd say that was a good description of a fairy, wouldn't you?"

"Vicious, yes, but I wouldn't call us short. I'd call you

unnecessarily tall." She scowled. "I'm hungry. So is Fluffy Ducky."

"Hippy take another look at this map." Pierus pointed to an illegible scrawl in one corner. "Do you recognise this?"

Hippy's stomach growled again. "No."

A note of impatience entered Pierus's voice. "You haven't even looked. I need to know if this map was made by a Freakin Fairy."

Hippy took a pinch of fairy dust and threw it on the map.

Pierus jumped back and said a bad word. "What did you do that for?"

The paper sparkled. It didn't crumble.

"Yes, the map was made by a Freakin Fairy."

"How can you tell?" Poppy reached for the paper.

Pierus caught her wrist. "Don't touch, unless you want to lose your fingers."

Hippy shook the dust off the map and put it back in the book, which she closed and thrust at Poppy. "Please can we go and have something to eat now?"

"Sure." Poppy didn't sound convinced. Her eyes were glued to the table, where every bit of wood hit by fairy dust crumbled to fine white ash, leaving ragged holes in the surface.

"Fairies," Pierus said. "Like I said, vicious. And short."

The sun sank rapidly outside the windows of a dingy cafe. Hippy was in a much better mood, having consumed two of something called a burger and a very big, thick, milky drink, all under Poppy's bemused gaze. Pierus had eaten very little. Maybe that was why he was always in such a bad mood, Hippy thought. He was permanently hungry. "What now?" she said.

"I suppose if we find the Freakin Fairies, we find the box," Poppy said.

"There's not much point in finding the box." Pierus toyed with a glass.

"What?" Poppy wiped her fingers on a napkin and pushed her plate away from her.

"The box was nothing more than a box. It's what was in the box that's important. It's the Apple of Chaos we need to find."

"See, I told you my story," Poppy said. "You still haven't told me what this Apple of Chaos actually is."

"All in good time." Pierus rose to his feet. "Come along now." He strode out of the cafe.

Hippy and Poppy followed. The evening air was sultry with heat and petrol fumes. Electric lights flickered on up and down the busy road.

Poppy linked her arm with Hippy's. "How do you keep from knocking his teeth out?"

Hippy was taken aback. "He's the muse king. I wouldn't dare."

"Is there a fairy king?"

Hippy giggled. "No."

"Why not?"

"If anyone tried to be our king we'd probably put a sack over their head and hang them from the fortifications by their toes. The elders would never stand for it."

"But you're scared of this muse king?"

Hippy scoffed. "Scared? Of a muse?"

"You're scared of knocking his teeth out."

Hippy frowned. The conversation seemed to be going in a circle, so she changed the subject. "How old is your son?"

"He's two." Poppy fished in her pocket and took out a battered photograph of a smiling toddler with sticky-out hair. "That's him. His name's Drew."

"Who looks after him?"

"His dad." The picture disappeared back into the pocket.

"Your husband?" Hippy understood this much better. Most fairy husbands took turns looking after the children when there was a war on. Everyone knew women got more done on the battlefield.

Poppy chuckled. "God no. I'd never marry a man named Bob Smithers. The very idea." She stared off into space for a minute. "It was all quite foolish, really. He was a good deal younger than me, so I was rather flattered by the attention. We had a romance, I got pregnant and had the baby, and all of a sudden he seemed to think I was going to clean his house and cook his dinner all the time. Never mind someone rather unpleasant was hounding me for money I'd borrowed and making threats against the child. I left before things got ugly. All in all it worked well. Bob met a nice young girl and got married within the year, giving Drew a nice normal mother and me the freedom to make a lot of money the best way I know how."

Hippy cast a worried glance at the horizon. The sun had halfway disappeared. "Seems a complicated way to do things."

"What would you do?"

"Throw fairy dust on the bad guys."

"Yes, well, we have some rather inconvenient laws about turning people to dust here. Does that muse even know where he's going?"

Pierus, who had been striding ahead, stopped abruptly and turned back. "Did you say something?"

"I was just wondering if you knew where we were going. I presume we're looking for Freakin Fairies."

"Hippy, tell her the best way to look for a Freakin Fairy," Pierus said.

"Oh, that's easy." Hippy gestured at the opulent neighbourhood they were passing through. "You just look for the biggest, most ostentatious, ugliest place you can find."

"I see. That's very interesting, but how do you know they're in Athens? Or even in Greece? My elderly gentleman was in Venice. The thugs could have come from anywhere in the world."

"That's mildly inconvenient." Pierus looked up and down the street. "Hippy? See anything?"

Hippy shook her head. "I don't think there's a fairy for miles. Can I go hunt vamps now? They'll be waking up soon."

"I told you, you're no match for Rustam Badora on your own!"

"Then come with me."

Poppy cleared her throat. "I have a hotel room not far from here. For the record, I'm all for steering clear of the vampires and figuring out a more useful way of searching than wandering the streets of every city in the world looking for a flash house with a Freakin Fairy in it."

CHAPTER TEN

Hippy sat on the edge of the narrow balcony railing, leaning against the brick wall. She tossed the knife she'd stolen from the kitchen into the air and caught it. Then she did it again. And again. There was nothing else to do.

To her left, through the glass door into Poppy's hotel room, Poppy and Pierus were still arguing about the best way to track down the Freakin Fairy. To her right was the longest drop to the ground she'd ever seen, and down there, lots of shiny lights and cars and ladies in pretty dresses. Another hotel rose up on the other side of the street, facing all the balconies and windows with mirror images of themselves.

She knew where she'd rather be. But no, Pierus had expressly forbidden her from going vamp hunting. Never mind that with every hour they wasted, Rustam Badora was building another army. Never mind if they killed him now, the vamp army on Shadow would fall apart. No, she had to sit here and do nothing because blah, blah, blah.

She caught the knife and jammed it into the wooden balcony rail. Maybe Poppy was right. Maybe she should just knock Pierus's teeth out.

Hippy jerked the knife out of the wood and secured it inside her pinned-up hair, where she knew it wouldn't fall out. Pierus and Poppy could be busy arguing for ages. She curled her feet around the thin railing and slowly stood up, arms out for balance. She'd never jumped from anything so high the people below looked like ants before. Nothing in Shadow was this high except the mountains, and you couldn't really jump off them.

She looked over her shoulder. Pierus had his back to the door. Poppy was waving a book around. Good. She turned back.

Hippy almost shrieked in surprise. She clapped her hand over her mouth just in time. There, on the balcony directly across the street, a hooded, cloaked figure leaned on the balcony rail watching her. He pulled back his hood.

In the dim light Hippy could see a dark face framed with long black hair, plaits and dreadlocks. He put his hands on the rail and leaped up to balance on it, just like she was doing.

Hippy eyeballed the figure for a whole ten seconds. She could call Pierus. Or she could do things her way and liven up an otherwise dull night. She pointed down.

The figure nodded.

Hippy jumped. It wasn't like jumping off the fortifications at all. She plummeted down, down, down through the air. Wind rushed past her face, stung her eyes, whipped her hair. She never took her eyes off the fairy plummeting with her.

They landed at the same time on opposite sides of the road. Hippy's knees buckled slightly, but that was the only sign she'd jumped from a greater height than usual.

The fairy waited only long enough for her to cross the road before he took off.

Hippy gave chase. She pushed her way through knots of women in sparkly dresses and men in black and white suits, dodged people on bicycles and crowds flowing out of cafes and bars.

The fairy just kept going. Every time she thought she'd catch him, he ducked down another corner. Every time she thought she'd lost him, there he'd be, right ahead.

Hippy was about ready to give up and go back to look at the sparkly dresses when she rounded a corner and smacked right into him in a dead-end street that smelled like rotten cabbage. Walls towered on three sides and the only light spilled from a few windows overhead.

She shoved him hard. "Freakin Fairy!"

He tilted his head to one side and studied her with a lively curiosity that made her want to shove him again. "Bloody Fairy. I wouldn't have believed it if I hadn't seen it with my own eyes."

"Believed what?" Hippy raised her hands to her hair to make sure the knife was still there.

Another two figures emerged from the shadows, both cloaked. They were taller than the fairy, but not tall enough to be muses.

"Who are you people?" Hippy closed her hand around the hilt of the knife. Just in case.

"There's no need for weapons. We only wanted to talk to you," one said.

"Then show me your faces."

The other one snorted. "To a fairy who consorts with the muse king? Unlikely." She made an impatient movement. "Get on with it. This has taken too much time already."

"Get on with what?" Hippy moved her hands away from her hair.

"We want you to give a message to your friend the muse king," the fairy said.

"What message?"

"Tell him to go back to Shadow. He'll never find the Apple of Chaos."

Hippy drew herself up. "Want to bet?"

"Yeah." The fairy folded his arms. "Even if it wasn't safe from him, he's hardly going to get anywhere with only a Bloody Fairy for help."

Hippy leaped, tackled the fairy and pinned him to the ground by the throat. "Say that again!"

"That again!" The Freakin Fairy used the bewildered second Hippy took to figure out his response to gain the upper hand and push her off.

Hippy only got in one good smack to his face before the tall couple dragged them apart.

"This achieves nothing." The man's voice was stern.

"This is what you get when you deal with fairies," the woman muttered.

The Freakin Fairy looked at his feet and kicked at a rock. "Sorry," he muttered.

The hood turned in Hippy's direction.

She scowled. "We need the Apple of Chaos," she said. "It's the only way to drive the vamps back!"

"We know the situation and sympathise, but you must find another way," the hood said. "We will not allow the Apple of Chaos to fall into the muse king's hands. You have no idea what he could do with it."

"Nothing, without my cooperation."

"Is that what he told you?"

Hippy glowered at all three of them and brushed dirt off her arms from the scuffle. "Rustam Badora is running around right now making new vamps. Maybe the three of you should think about helping, instead of playing games." She turned her back and walked away.

"We know about the situation with Badora," the hood said.

Hippy looked over her shoulder. "Do you know where he is? I for one am not planning on sitting around waiting for him to come knocking." She gave the fairy a pointed look. "Bloody Fairies aren't afraid to go on the hunt."

The Freakin Fairy lunged. The hood grabbed him by the back of the shirt and held him back. "Don't forget to give the muse king our message."

"Whatever." Hippy left the alley. She was halfway down the next street before she realised she was completely lost and had no idea how to get back to Poppy's hotel. No big deal, she wanted to find the sparkly dresses again anyway.

She followed the streetlights until she came to busier roads, where lights from the overflowing bars made it almost as bright as day. She slowed and stared around her with big eyes. Ladies in sparkly dresses leaned on the arms of men in black and white. They sat at tables and crowded into small spaces drinking sparkling liquid out of shiny, shiny glasses. This was nothing like Shadow at all. She liked it. She wondered where she could get a sparkly dress and a shiny glass, but she was too shy to go up to a human and ask. The ladies looked forbidding in their painted faces and the men who noticed her looked at her like she was a piece of meat.

Hippy stuck her tongue out and squashed up her face at a man who was doing just that. He went bright red and hurried away.

She strolled down the street and kept admiring the sights. The pointy letters she didn't understand were scrawled on almost every building. Some of the cars had the most interesting little metal animals on their hoods. She wanted to break one off and take it home, but that might have been impolite, she wasn't sure.

She sighed. She liked looking at the shiny things, but she really needed to start looking for signs of Rustam Badora. So far the necks of all the humans she'd seen had been fairly intact, so he obviously wasn't here.

A car that had been meandering down the street through the crowds of pedestrians braked sharply next to her.

Hippy looked around in time to see a man jump out of the back door and head toward her. Oh! She knew that car. She waved. "Hi Tony!"

"You!" Tony grabbed her by the shoulder. "I want to talk to you. And don't you try anything with that damn spider of yours either.

Get in the car. Come on."

Hippy folded her arms. "I don't want to."

"I said get in the car. Don't argue. You and me, we're just going to have a friendly chat." He tightened his hand around her shoulder and shoved her in the back door.

Hippy tripped and almost fell into the car. She saved herself from an undignified face-first sprawl by catching the back of the seat. Tony shut the doors and the car moved off.

Hippy scowled at him. "What? I wasn't doing anything." "Oh, I'm sure you weren't. Just wandering the streets at nine o'clock at night dressed like Robin Hood or something. Shouldn't good little girls be at home in bed?"

"I'm not good, and I'm not a little girl."

Tony chuckled, but the sound held no mirth. "See, I suspected that. What you doing with a crook like Praeconius and that other geezer anyway?"

"Hunting vamps."

"Huh. You don't have to tell me, I'm not your father." Tony leaned forward. "What's your real name?"

"Hippy."

"Figures. Well Hippy, I've got a problem. I've been looking for my friends all day, the ones Praeconius kicked out of the car. Now they're big blokes who can look after themselves, see? And they know what to do if they get separated from the team. But they haven't checked in and I can't find them anywhere. I didn't really think Praeconius was the vicious type, she's just after money, see? But I got nothing else. So you tell me where my men are."

Hippy felt a finger of cold seep into her chest. So that's where Rustam Badora had started. What had he done, followed their trail as soon as the sun went down? Followed them underground somehow? Had Tony's friends strayed into a cave, or crossed his path after dark?

"I don't like the way you're looking at me," Tony said.

"Vamps," Hippy said.

"What do you mean, vamps?"

Hippy twisted her fingers together. She didn't know how to explain it to him.

Pierus had said humans knew nothing of Shadow. It had taken a long time for Poppy to believe them. How was she supposed to convince Tony? "There's a very bad man," she said, hoping Tony would be happy with a half-explanation. "Pierus and I are trying to stop him, but he followed us here. Your friends may have met him."

"Sweetheart, I'm a very bad man." Tony smirked at her. "My friends are very bad men. What's this geezer going to do?"

"Drink their blood."

Tony screwed his face up. But he didn't laugh, as she'd feared he would. "You're serious?"

Hippy nodded. "I'm trying to find him," she said. "Before he can kill too many people."

"You? What're you going to do? You're nothing more than a little piece of jail bait."

"I don't know what jail bait is, but I've killed hundreds of his kind."

"Well then you're the youngest psycho I ever met." Tony ran his hand over his bald head. "Fine, I'm game. How do we find him?"

Hippy stared. "You want to help me hunt Rustam Badora?"

"Sure, why not?"

Hippy drew her legs up under her and thought hard. Tony's friends had had hours to be killed, wake up and come back. If Rustam stayed with them they could be anywhere. If not, they might not know what had happened. "Where were they supposed to go?"

"We got a rendezvous point," Tony said. "But I checked in twice already. They weren't there."

"Try it again," Hippy said.

CHAPTER ELEVEN

"This is your rendezvous?" Hippy walked on her toes around a busted table to avoid treading on anything nasty with her bare feet. Two long fluorescent lights flickered and blinked overhead, picking out jagged shadows and not much else in a really, really big room full of broken furniture and bits of glass.

"Well it ain't exactly a romantic dinner for two, but something tells me you're not that kind of girl," Tony said.

Hippy shrugged. "I just like nice wide open spaces better."

"Hippy."

"What?"

"Nothing, I was just calling you a hippy."

Hippy screwed up her nose at him. These humans didn't make a whole lot of sense.

"This way." Tony headed for a big steel door and pushed it open. "You first sweetie."

Hippy brushed past him and entered the next room. She stopped short. This one was lit by gas lamps hanging from the walls, just like the muses used back home. And sometimes the vamps. Tony came in behind her and closed the door.

Hippy looked over her shoulder. "Why'd you close the door?"

Tony chuckled and curled his hand over the back of her neck. His fingers were cold.

Icy cold.

Hippy said a bad word she'd heard Poppy use earlier. Now he was so close she could see a mark on his neck that had been concealed by his collar.

"They told me you were dumb, sweetie, but I had no idea just how dumb. What happened, you get dropped on your head as a kid?"

Hippy balled a fist, twisted around and punched him in the nose. "You're a vamp!"

"Ow!" Tony stumbled back, clutching his nose.

A low laugh rumbled through the room. Footsteps paced toward her from the shadows in the far corners. "Close," a voice said. "He's close. I'll give him the gift of blood soon enough, but for now I need someone who can pass for human."

Hippy bolted for the door. There was a rush of wind at her back. Rustam Badora slammed into her, pinning her to the cold metal. His fingers were so cold they burned her skin. He leaned close and inhaled near her neck.

"Ah, fresh fairy. You make me homesick."

Hippy reached for her belt.

Badora's free hand closed around her wrist and pinned that to the door too. "Tut, tut, tut. You keep that spider safely locked away or I'll squash it."

Hippy scowled. "Let me go."

Badora leaned in close and breathed on her neck again. "Oh, I will, my dear. I have humans enough and more to satisfy me here. But I do intend to kill you the moment we both set foot in Shadow again. I'm saving you for last. I'm anticipating the bouquet of your blood with every breath." He made a growling noise in her ear and then licked the side of her face.

"Eeeeewwwww!" Hippy wriggled out of his grip and broke away. She madly scrubbed at her face, stumbled backwards and almost fell over Tony, whose nose was bleeding. She lashed out in revulsion and punched him in the side of the head, which sent him crashing into the wall. "Ew ew ew! That was disgusting!"

Badora lounged against the door. His mouth crooked up. "You must make the muse king a very amusing pet."

Hippy stopped jumping around and scrubbing her face. "I'm not a pet."

"Of course you are. What else would he want with you?"

"I'm helping him find-" Hippy clapped her hands over her mouth.

"Find what?" Badora pushed himself off the door and paced toward her, hands behind his back. "Find what, Fairy?"

"His, um, shoes." Hippy backed away as fast as he approached.

"Find Pandora's Box, perhaps?" Badora's red eyes looked her up and down hungrily. "Tell me, what does he want with that?"

Hippy had reached Tony's position again. He was curled up against the wall, still clutching his nose. Blood seeped through his fingers. Ew. She felt sick. Her head started to spin, but there was no time for that. She clenched her teeth hard and kicked him in the ribs. "You told him about Pandora's Box?"

"Would you stop hitting me?" Tony yelled through his hands. "Boss make her stop!"

Badora didn't even spare him a glance. He just kept moving closer. "I know a legend about Pandora's Box," he said. "It's not a pretty story."

"You're not that pretty either, but do I go on about it?" Hippy kept moving, even though now they were just circling the room.

The vamp king's fangs made shallow indents in his lower lip. His white skin looked almost blue in the gaslight. "Vampire legend says we came from Pandora. But it was Pierus himself who made us what we are, when he stole something she guarded."

"That's the biggest load of bearfly droppings I ever heard." Hippy dodged around a table. "Is that why you brought me here, to tell me vamp bedtime stories?"

"Ask the muse king," Badora said. "He'll tell you. Or maybe he'll tell you a lie instead, to keep you from leaving."

Then he disappeared. Hippy flattened her back to the wall and was preparing to run for the door again when he reappeared in a blur of speed in front of her. One long, curved, manicured nail traced the length of her face. "Pandora was madder than a bearfly at full moon, you know. I don't care about her box."

Hippy thought he probably should, but she decided not to say anything.

"I have a message for Pierus." Badora leaned in closer.

She screwed up her nose and inched away. "I hope it's that you've found yourself a cure for bad breath, because you really need it."

The vamp's shoulders dropped. "Well really, if you're not going to take any of this seriously I don't see how we're going to get along."

Hippy rolled her eyes. "Don't get all twitchy. What's the message?"

"I'm proposing a truce. Obviously Pierus can open a door between the worlds. Tell him if he opens a door to allow my army into Dream, the Bloody Fairies will be left alone. We won't bother anyone in Shadow again."

Hippy edged along the wall away from him. "I don't think he'll go for it."

"He'd better." Badora stalked her every step. "Because if he doesn't I'll raise an army here and return to Shadow and crush muses and fairies alike. It's really very simple. All we want is our own land, with a ready food source. It's his choice whether that's going to be on Dream or Shadow." He reached out and curled his fingers around her arm. "If I were you, Fairy, I'd convince him to let us have Dream. Purely in your own interests. You're quite safe until the day I set foot back in Shadow."

Hippy glared. "One day I'm going to make you sparkle."

"Your threats are pointless. I am Rustam Badora." The vamp released her arm. "Get out of here."

Hippy ran for the door. When she got to it, she stopped short and said a bad word.

"What is it?" Badora stalked her.

"I don't even know where we are," Hippy said. "I don't know how to get home."

He chuckled. "Tony can take you back. He knows the way, he's been following the three of you most of the day." He whirled around, strode to where Tony was still curled against the wall and hauled him to his feet.

A few drops of blood from Tony's nose got onto Badora's fingers. He licked them.

Hippy hid her eyes and shuddered.

When both men approached, Badora's smile was thin and Tony was bleeding less. "Don't worry," he said. "I told him to take you straight home."

Hippy backed through the door. "I thought you were going to vamp him. What if he runs off?"

"Oh, I am. He'll return to me. He can't help himself. Of course if he doesn't return to me–" Vamp fingers fastened around Hippy's throat. "I'll be very upset."

Hippy nodded emphatically.

He released her. "I will expect an answer from Pierus tomorrow night. We will find you both." He turned to go back into the room.

"Wait!" Hippy steadied Tony, who was swaying next to her. "Where are Tony's friends?"

Badora licked his lips. "Where do you think?" He closed the door behind them.

Hippy sat in the back seat of the car, as far away from Tony as she could get. She'd never seen anyone in the early stages of vamp before and had no idea when he'd start wanting blood. Of course she should just set Fluffy Ducky on him, but then Rustam would be cross. She buried her face in her hands. What kind of a fairy was she? She'd gone there to kill him and ended up his messenger fairy. Maybe she should just go back and turn him into a blood fountain that would make Ishtar proud.

"Hey, don't you go passing out in my car," Tony said.

Hippy took her hands away from her face. "Huh?"

"Boss said you had too much to drink and to take you home," Tony said. "Don't you pass out. I'm not carrying you."

Hippy scowled. "You even touch me, vamp, and I'll break your nose again."

Tony snickered. "A little thing like you? Break my nose? I'd like to see you try. Alright girly, here's your hotel."

Hippy looked out of the window at the hotel she'd jumped from several hours earlier. She breathed a sigh of relief, but that was quickly chased away by nerves. Pierus was probably going to be a little bit upset. "I don't want to go in."

"Boss said I was to walk you to the door," Tony said.

"No!"

"Come on. Let's go." Tony grabbed her by the scruff of the neck and dragged her with him out of the car, across the footpath and through the front door.

Hippy said several bad words and kicked him in the ankle. They stopped in front of the elevator and waited for the light to reach the ground floor.

"Where'd you learn language like that?" Tony hustled her inside as soon as the door slid open.

"From Poppy." Hippy watched the light move from floor to floor with a growing sense of dread. How Tony knew exactly which floor to go to she didn't know. At least, when they got off on the twenty-second floor, he didn't know which door to go to.

Until she showed him. She couldn't help but feel she shouldn't have done that.

Tony thumped on the door.

A few seconds later Poppy thrust it open and brandished a gun the length of her arm in his face. "What do you want?"

Tony grabbed Hippy by the scruff of the neck and thrust her at Poppy. "I believe you lost this." He paused, blinked rapidly and looked closer at Poppy. "Praeconius?"

"No, it's the Easter Bunny." Poppy grabbed Hippy and pulled her inside.

"You got that box thing yet?"

"Back off Tony, you said I had a week!" Poppy shut the door in his face, turned her back and leaned against it. A muscle in her jaw quivered. She laid the gun on the table next to the door and turned on Hippy. "Where in the blazing hell have you been?"

Hippy quailed. Poppy angry was a sight to behold, and she'd had her share of frightening creatures already tonight. She backed up fast.

Pierus thrust a chair under her. "Sit." His voice was dry and cold.

She collapsed into it.

Hippy looked up at the both of them with wide eyes. Yep, they were both pretty mad. Her first attempt at talking came out in a squeak, so she tried again. "Did you know Tony was a vamp?"

CHAPTER TWELVE

Hippy sat in the chair with her hands folded in her lap. Poppy and Pierus towered over her. This was worse than when the elders told her off after Pierus asked if she could go to Dream with him. Much worse, because they were both much taller and she was getting a crick in her neck.

"Tony's not a vamp," Poppy said. "It's impossible."

"But he got bit by Rustam Badora."

"That's the vampire king?"

Hippy nodded.

Pierus spoke through clenched teeth, his face white with fury. "I told you not to go hunting vampires on your own!"

"I wasn't on my own, I was with Tony."

"Since when?" Poppy demanded. "Last thing we saw you were on the balcony. We were worried sick when you disappeared! We didn't know what happened to you!"

"Oh, that's easy. I saw a Freakin Fairy on the other balcony, so we both jumped off and then played chase."

Pierus went from white to bright red. "You saw a Freakin Fairy?"

"Saw him? We got in a fight! It was lots of fun."

Pierus put a hand over his eyes. His voice was strangled. "All of Shadow is at stake and I'm stuck with a Bloody Fairy!"

Hippy scowled at him. "What else was I supposed to do? Tell him I'm not allowed out? Hang around here and argue while Rustam Badora is out killing Tony's friends?"

Pierus sighed. "Poppy, would you excuse us for one moment?"

"I'll make some coffee." Poppy stomped into the other room.

"What's coffee?" Hippy eyed Pierus, nervous. He had a funny look on his face.

"Hippy." Pierus crouched down in front of her, bringing himself to eye level. He placed his hands on either side of the chair. His brow was wrinkled just enough to create all sorts of fascinating lines and furrows. His dark hair tangled over his ears. "I need you to listen to me very carefully. I know it's not in your nature to pay attention, or obey orders, but this is important."

"Alright." Hippy tried not to let him see how her blood was pumping overtime from nerves. She absolutely did not want the muse king to know he made her nervous by being so close.

"You are too important to take these kinds of risks."

Hippy blinked. "I am?"

"Yes, you are." He leaned in a little closer. "I can't retrieve the Apple of Chaos without you."

"Oh." Of course that was why. No need to be unaccountably disappointed.

"And-" he paused, apparently struggling to frame the next words. "Well, the thing is, my dear girl, you've become–that is–" he paused. "Perhaps it's because you're so like her."

"Huh? Who?"

"Pandora." He dragged another chair over and sat opposite her, this time not quite so close. He looked directly into her eyes. "Hippy Ishtar, you have become important to me. For more than just the mission."

Hippy tilted her head to one side. She felt like she should say something sensible, or profound. "Rustam Badora licked my face. It was really disgusting."

Pierus tensed, closed his eyes, looked away and took a lot of deep breaths.

Poppy walked back in, dragged a table over, set three hot cups on it and sat with them.

Hippy sniffed her cup. The most intriguing aroma came out of it. "What's this?"

"Coffee. Drink up, it's going to be a long night." Poppy took a sip.

Hippy took a cautious sip of her coffee and burned her tongue. "Ow!"

Poppy grinned. "Let it cool a little, dear. Now where were we?"

"I think it would be best if Hippy told us everything that happened tonight." Pierus appeared to have composed himself.

Hippy thought about it for a minute. "Well, first I chased the fairy into an alley that smelled nasty. There were two other people from Shadow there and they said to tell you you'd never find the Apple of Chaos. They said to find another way to deal with the vamps."

Pierus's upper lip took on a disdainful curl. "What did they look like?"

Hippy shrugged. "They wore cloaks. They were tall, but not like you. And the Freakin Fairy did what they told him to. Weird, huh?"

Poppy gave Pierus a sharp look. "Well? Sounds like you have enemies."

He snorted. "Nothing worth worrying about. If they're all that stands between us and the Apple we'll be home by tomorrow."

"Who are they?" Hippy thought about the arrow safely hidden in one of the pouches at her belt, but she didn't take it out in case he just took it away again.

"Nobody," Pierus said.

Poppy's voice was sharp. "Look buddy, if we're going to be a team and find this thing you need to start sharing. Answer the goddamn question."

Pierus arched an eyebrow at her. "Literally, nobody," he said. "You don't live for three thousand years without attracting a few fringe lunatics. They call themselves the Invisible Army and they make it their business to follow me around and generally be irritating. Apparently now they've decided they don't want me making their homes and families safe from the vampires."

"They seemed nice." Hippy took a sip of her coffee. This time it didn't burn. It was bitter, but it made her feel good.

Pierus's voice turned acid. "Of course they seemed nice. They want to win you to their cause. If they got their hands on you for longer than five minutes, mark my words, they'd say or do anything to turn you against me."

Hippy felt like he'd slapped her. She buried her face in her coffee and sniffed loudly.

"See, now you're sounding like a giant ass again," Poppy said. "Lay off her, would you?"

There was silence. When Hippy looked up from her cup again, Pierus's eyes were on her.

"Continue," he said. "What happened next?"

"I left them there and I went to look at the sparkly dresses," Hippy said. She stared into her coffee. "I like sparkly things. Like vamps covered with fairy dust, right before they turn to petrified ash."

"Focus, dear." Poppy tapped the table with her index finger. "How'd you hook up with Tony?"

"Oh!" Hippy took another sip of coffee. She felt really good.

Energetic. Her words tumbled out faster. "He pushed me into his car and was going on about his missing friends, so we went to the rendezvous point to look for them, but Rustam Badora was there so I broke Tony's nose, then Rustam licked my face and it was really really gross, so I hit Tony again and he got upset." She paused for breath, but went on before Pierus or Poppy could respond. "You know, Badora's not nearly as scary as I always thought, he's just another vamp and he said he wasn't going to kill me until we were both back in Shadow but I told him I'd make him sparkle first and then he said I should tell Pierus he wants a truce but it was a stupid truce. Is it true you stole something from Pandora and made the vamps?" She blinked rapidly and stared at Pierus.

His mouth twitched. "Poppy, take the coffee away from her."

Hippy grabbed the mug and tipped the rest down her throat before Poppy could respond. "Is it true?" she repeated.

There was a long silence. Pierus tapped his fingers on the table. Hippy twitched.

"It's true I had a hand in creating the vampires," Pierus finally said. "To my eternal regret."

"You're responsible for vampires?" Poppy rubbed her forehead. She looked tired.

Pierus looked away from them both. "Believe you me, if I'd had any idea what would become of it, I'd never have allowed Pandora-" he broke off.

"People must want to smack you in the head a lot, huh?" Poppy said.

Hippy giggled and bounced up and down in her chair.

Pierus gave a weary sigh. "Hippy, tell me about this truce. And do try to slow down a bit."

Hippy stared at the roof and tried to gather her rather scattered thoughts. "Well." She drew the word out. "He said if you opened the rip and let the vamp army into Dream he'd leave Shadow alone forever but if you didn't he'd raise an army here and take them back to Shadow to crush us all forever and all he wants is a home for his army and a reliable food supply." She stopped and panted for breath.

Pierus snorted. "What makes him think he'll get an army back into Shadow without my help?"

"This sounds like a really nasty guy," Poppy said. "Maybe Hippy's right. Maybe we need to stop him first."

Hippy got up out of her chair and paced around the room. She had so much energy right now. She considered for a moment, then walked right up a wall and onto the nice high roof. From her upside down position she saw Poppy go pale.

"Get down!" Poppy yelled. "My God, if anybody saw you!"

"Okay." Hippy let go and dropped to the floor. At the last minute she rolled, jumped to her feet and walked up the wall again.

Poppy buried her face in her hands.

"You did give her coffee," Pierus said. "What did you think was going to happen?"

"I don't know. I'm not used to Bloody Fairies!"

Hippy dropped from the roof and rolled again. Before she could head back to the wall a third time Pierus grabbed the back of her shirt and held her in place. "Hippy."

"What?" She jumped up and down on the spot.

"When am I to give Badora his answer?"

"He's coming to find us tomorrow night."

Poppy groaned. "If you don't make her stop that I'm going to feed her to the vampires myself."

"Can I go hunt vamps?" Hippy stopped jumping and turned around. "Please? Please can I? I promise I'll be good for a whole day, honest." She bolted for the door.

"Hippy Ishtar."

Pierus's sharp voice stopped her in her tracks.

"Come back here and sit down."

Hippy scowled, stomped back to the table and sat.

"Is there any way to counteract the effects of this drug?"

"Caffeine's not a drug." Poppy yawned and eyed Hippy. "Well, maybe if you're a Bloody Fairy. But you know what? I can't function on no sleep. Unlike you two, apparently. She's just got to wear it off. Take her up on the roof and let her jump off it a few times. Or even better, try a depressant." She went over to a small cupboard, took out a bottle of amber-coloured liquid and plonked it on the table. "Brandy. I'm going to bed. Make any more noise and I'll shoot you both." She left the room and firmly closed the door behind her.

Hippy sat still for a whole two seconds. Her heart thudded uncomfortably fast. Her skin itched. She felt like she was going to burst. She really, really needed to keep moving. "Roof," she said. "I feel weird."

Pierus gestured at the door. "After you, my dear."

Hippy didn't look back. She left the room, found the stairs and ran up eight flights. The final door led to the roof of the hotel, a bare concrete expanse. Pierus hadn't even caught up yet. She jogged to the edge of the roof and looked down. From up here she couldn't even see the ground. Wow. She wondered if the Freakin Fairy was watching.

Hippy gulped some air and jumped. She rushed down, down, down through stinging, biting wind, past window after window, then a streetlight. The pavement jarred her ankles when she landed in a crouch. It was awfully tempting to run into the city again. She considered it.

Wait, no, that jump was fun.

Hippy went back into the hotel, ran up thirty flights of stairs and onto the roof.

Pierus sat on the ledge bordering the roof and raised an eyebrow at her. "You fairies never cease to amaze me."

"Yeah? Well watch this." Hippy stepped onto the ledge and dived.

She somersaulted in midair, plummeted again and landed neatly on her feet in front of a startled pedestrian. "Wow," she said. "I'm getting better at this."

She ran up the stairs and jumped again three more times.

By the fourth time she reached the roof her heartbeat had slowed and she was out of breath. It was a curious sensation. She flopped down next to Pierus.

"Better, my dear?" He uncapped the bottle of brandy. "Have some of this."

Hippy took a swig of brandy. It burned her throat and made her cough and hack. When the burning subsided, she spoke. "Dream has weird drinks. But I'm starting to like it here." She handed the bottle back.

Pierus took a swig, coughed and thumped a fist on the wall.

Hippy giggled. Everything was returning to normal, except she now felt a pleasant fuzzy sensation inside her skull. She slid down to sit on the floor with the wall at her back.

Pierus joined her and handed her the bottle again. "My dear girl, Dream's intoxicants are no better or worse than some of the frightening concoctions you fairies come up with."

Hippy took a swig and handed the bottle back. "Yeah." She sighed. "I miss my mum's cooking."

Pierus curled his fingers around hers. "Dream food will make you forget your mother's cooking."

Hippy moved closer to him for warmth. "Pierus?"

He looked down into her face and seemed at a loss. "Yes?"

"Tell me about Pandora."

CHAPTER THIRTEEN

Pierus downed another mouthful of brandy. His voice mellowed so much he sounded almost relaxed. Hippy wondered if it was the drink, which seemed to be having a similar effect on her. Dream really did have some wonderful things. She honestly couldn't understand why everyone didn't drink brandy and coffee all the time.

"Pandora was the most beautiful woman in Thebes," Pierus said. "Maybe in all of Greece."

"How do you know?"

He chuckled. "Perhaps it was a matter of opinion, but I never saw a woman to rival her until I met you."

"Me?"

"My dear girl, don't be coy. You may not be terribly bright, but I suspect if you scrubbed away a layer or two of dirt and brushed your hair properly you could take Dream by storm. Humans valued beauty above all else three thousand years ago. Not much changes."

Hippy scowled. "I don't see as how it does me any good. It doesn't help me fight vamps or be more like a proper fairy."

Pierus pulled her closer and wrapped his arm around her shoulders. "I think the fairies are fools." He tipped her face up with his free hand and gently smoothed the lines out of her forehead with one finger. "There. I like you better when you're smiling and pretty."

"Better than what?" Hippy pouted. "I wouldn't be much help to you if all I did was smile and look pretty."

Pierus shook his head. "And that's where you and Pandora are so very different."

"How?"

Pierus leaned his head against the wall and closed his eyes. "She knew how beautiful she was," he said. "She was vain and distractible, but when she wanted something, she got it. She wanted me." A smile played around the corner of his mouth.

"What for?"

Pierus snorted. "What do you think? Or have the fairies kept you a complete innocent?"

Hippy blushed and looked away. "Oh. That."

"When I first met her she was married to a man who cared nothing for her," Pierus said. "He was the richest and almost the most powerful man in Thebes, but had little interest in women. She carried on an affair with me and he never even protested." He was silent for a moment. "Twice I saved her life, for she was a foolish girl who used to put herself in danger."

"And then what happened?" Hippy watched the stars, entranced. They were different in Dream. Even listening to stories felt different. It felt like she could step into it and be there.

"He died."

"How?"

"I'd rather not talk about that." Pierus lazily brushed a lock of hair from her face and took another swig of brandy. "Suffice it to say it was his own fault, and just the first of many unpleasant things."

"Is this going to be a scary story?" She accepted the bottle. It didn't burn quite so badly now she was used to it.

"Very." Pierus took the bottle from her and set it on the ground. "After her husband died Pandora was left in the care of her brother, a man both evil and mad. She married me to escape him, and because we loved each other. But it was only then the devious creature showed me the Apple of Chaos."

"Was it shiny?" Hippy asked.

He leaned closer and whispered into her ear. "Very shiny."

She grinned. "I like shiny things."

Pierus gave a low sigh. "They used to say Pandora was created by the Gods as a gift to mankind. I still don't know whether that story was true, but she was most certainly the guardian of something extraordinary. She possessed a box, which she guarded jealously and would rarely be parted from. Nor would she open it, until she knew she was safe. With me. After we were married she allowed me to see what was inside."

Hippy caught her breath. "You opened Pandora's Box? You let the bad things out?"

Pierus shook his head. "Poppy told me that pile of rot. It's a silly little myth and nothing like what really happened."

"Then what really happened?"

"Inside the box was a glass sphere. It called to me almost as much as it called to her. She said it was a sacred apple tossed into a volcano by the Goddess of Chaos, and there turned to glass filled with the most potent magic known to man, chaos itself. As the guardian, all she had to do was place her hands on it, and things would happen." Pierus paused. "I warned her it was dangerous, but she wouldn't listen."

Hippy couldn't take her eyes off him. This was one of the best stories she'd ever heard. She hardly dared breathe, in case she missed what happened next.

"For a time I convinced her to put it away, but she was still under the sway of her brother. He knew about the Apple of Chaos too, and he made her use it to gain him power. He was insatiable. He wanted people to worship him, but when they did, he would drive them to madness with his evil ways."

A poison entered his voice that made Hippy want to shift away, but she couldn't. His arm was like a dead weight on her shoulders. "You stopped him, right?"

A thin smile curved his lips. "I tried, but it was too late for Pandora. Perhaps the madness took her long before I knew her. Perhaps it was the Apple of Chaos that tipped her over the edge. She began to have nightmares. Then her nightmares spilled over into her waking life, and at the end, they became real. And I, I who was the closest person to her, was not immune either. My nightmares of pale men who drank blood and killed indiscriminately began to haunt my waking life. Our terrors laid siege to all of Thebes." His head dropped forward and he squeezed his eyes shut. A shudder went through his wiry frame.

Hippy gave his arm an awkward pat. "Then what happened?"

"I took her to a sorcerer," he said. "We asked him to help us find a way to mend what we had done. He told us it could be done, but the price would be a terrible one. We agreed, of course. We had no choice."

"What did he do?"

"He took the Apple," Pierus said. "He worked his magic on it and made it into a doorway. Beyond the doorway he made a new world, and into that world he banished every creature we had created. Finally, and last of all, he banished Pandora, myself, my sisters, her brother and all his followers, in fact most of Thebes, for nobody was untouched by chaos. I was the last to go. He made me hide the Apple of Chaos deep underground and then he cast spells so I could never remove it. The thing was so powerful he couldn't simply render it useless, you see. But he made it so it could not be worked by anybody but a descendant of Pandora. Then he ensured Pandora was trapped in Shadow and made me Shadow's guardian. Since the chaos inside the Apple had to go somewhere, he channelled its power through me and my sisters, which was how we became muses. We use the chaos to inspire writers and artists here in Dream."

Hippy blinked. She was getting sleepy, but she wanted to stay awake for the end of the story.

"The sorcerers gave one final gift." Pierus's voice grew very, very quiet. "Or perhaps a curse. I've never been quite sure."

"What was it?"

"That I should live as long as Shadow does. Or that Shadow should live as long as I. I am Shadow's guardian. If I die, so does everything you and I have ever held dear or fought for."

That woke her up. Hippy's eyes were like saucers. "You mean, if you die-"

"Shadow ceases to exist."

She dropped her head against his chest. Her brain was spinning like the clunky old waterwheel in the river near home.

"What happened to Pandora?"

Pierus stroked her hair. "My dear girl, she went quite mad. She left me and ran off with some creature she found living in a tree. Together they bred a race of silly little creatures who spread all over Shadow, split off into clans and spent all their time fighting each other."

Hippy sat bolt upright. "The forest people?"

Pierus chuckled. "No. Fairies."

"I'm descended from Pandora? She's like my great, great, great grandmother?"

"Add another three thousand years' worth of greats, and yes, she was."

Hippy blinked, trying to understand exactly what this meant. "Were you sad when she left?"

Pierus's mouth curved, but there was something rather cruel in his smile. "No."

Hippy wriggled out of his grasp and jumped to her feet. She stood there a moment, swayed and put a hand to her head. "I feel really strange."

Pierus got to his feet and put an arm around her waist. "You're drunk. So am I, or I wouldn't have told you all that. With any luck you won't remember in the morning."

Hippy blinked at him. Then she giggled. "I don't know what drunk means, but you're a lot nicer when you are."

This time his grin was genuine. He grabbed her waist and pulled her close. "I know it's wrong," he said into her ear. "I know I'll regret it, but you're the most amusing creature I've encountered in a long time and I intend to keep you."

"Keep me where? Now you're just being silly."

He tangled his hand in her hair, lifted her onto the wall so they were the same height and put his mouth on hers.

Hippy's eyes widened. She'd kissed a boy fairy once and they'd both agreed it was a ridiculous kind of thing to do. But this was the muse king kissing her. Ishtar would be furious. The muse king had chosen *her*. A thousand nonsensical thoughts flitted through her head.

Pierus broke away, looked into her astonished eyes, scooped a hand under her knees and lifted her into his arms. "You, my dear, are drunk and need to get some sleep."

"I like being drunk." Hippy buried her face in his shoulder and closed her eyes while he crossed the roof and descended the stairs. By the time they reached Poppy's rooms, she'd passed out.

CHAPTER FOURTEEN

Hippy squeezed her eyes shut tight. She felt like a bearfly had crawled down her throat and died. Her head pounded. Something tickled her face and a very large form pressed her into the back of the couch she'd been sleeping on.

She opened her eyes to slits and discovered it was Pierus taking up all that room. He was fast asleep. She put her hand on her face and found Fluffy Ducky nestled there, eyeballing Pierus with all eight eyes. "Fluffy Ducky." She tickled the spider's back. "What are you doing?"

Two metallic clicks above her head made her open her eyes all the way. She looked straight into the barrel of Poppy's gun, which was pointed at Pierus's head. Behind it, Poppy glowered from under a chaotic mess of wild, knotted hair.

Hippy grabbed Fluffy Ducky and shielded him on her chest. "Don't shoot my spider!"

"I wasn't going to shoot your spider," Poppy said. "I was going to find out what the hell's going on here and then shoot the muse."

"Oh." Hippy tried to push him so she could move away, but he didn't budge. "Why?"

Pierus stirred and opened his eyes. Then he sat bolt upright and put both his arms out to shield Hippy. "What in Shadow are you doing, human?"

Hippy squeaked in outrage, since she and Fluffy Ducky were now pinned to the back of the couch.

"I was about to ask you the same thing." Poppy's scowl made her look doubly frightening under all that hair.

Pierus's voice went very, very cold. "It's none of your business."

Poppy's eyes flicked to Hippy. "I'm making it my business. Hippy, are you alright?"

"I can't breathe!" Hippy wheezed.

"Get off the poor girl before she suffocates, would you?"

Hippy squirmed out from behind Pierus when he shifted to give her some space.

Poppy kept the gun firmly pointed at his head. "You need to keep your hands to yourself. She's too young for you."

"I'm twenty!" Hippy protested.

"And he's three thousand. That is not okay."

Hippy looked from one to the other, utterly mystified as to where all the tension had come from.

Pierus's mouth tightened into a thin line. The air around him turned so cold it felt like there was a blizzard in the room. "Remove your gun from my face, woman." He got slowly to his feet. "And do not presume to interfere with either me or my fairy." He brushed over Poppy's eyes with his long, thin fingers. The very room might have iced over.

Poppy had opened her mouth to reply, but she didn't say anything. She blinked a couple of times.

"I expect you need some coffee," Pierus said, his tone quite normal and friendly again. The cold eased.

Poppy lowered the gun and scowled at them both. "I need coffee." She stomped off to the kitchen.

Hippy stared after her, utterly bewildered. "Can I have coffee too?"

"Absolutely not," Pierus said. "You'd drive the humans mad, jumping off the hotel in broad daylight. And would you put away that awful spider?"

Hippy pouted and placed Fluffy Ducky in his pouch. Her head hurt too much to try and puzzle out what had just happened. "I feel horrible." She rubbed her pounding forehead.

Pierus laid his hands on either side of her face and gently massaged her temples. "It's called a hangover."

Hippy closed her eyes and dropped her head forward. The pain drained away under his fingers. "Ishtar and I used to hang over the fortifications all the time and drop fairy dust bombs on vamps, but it never made me feel nasty like this."

His reply was patient. "A hangover is what humans call the sick feeling they get the morning after drinking half a bottle of brandy."

"A drink did this to me?'

"One must be very careful in Dream."

"Why would they want to drink anything that makes them feel this bad?"

"Because humans are not all that concerned with the

consequences of their actions. I should know, I used to be one." His fingers stilled, but remained on her temples. "Hippy how much do you remember of last night?"

Hippy raised her eyes to his. She couldn't quite fathom his expression. It lurked somewhere between fear and an odd, possessive, fascination. "Everything."

"You don't hate me?"

"Why would I hate you?" She tilted her head, puzzled. "It was a very nice kiss."

Some tension left his frame. "I was thinking more of the story I told you. I hadn't told it in a very long time. I'm not proud of my human life."

Hippy shrugged. "It was a good story. It had shiny things in it."

Pierus shook his head, but his lips twitched with amusement. "Bloody Fairies." He leaned forward and kissed her affectionately on the forehead. "Do you feel better now?"

She nodded. "I'm hungry."

Poppy chose that moment to storm back into the room. "So am I," she said. She thrust a handful at money at Pierus. "I want you to go buy us some food."

He looked at the money and then back at her. "Why me?"

"Because Hippy will get lost or distracted and because I'm not a morning person."

Pierus glanced pointedly at the clock behind her. "It's two in the afternoon."

"Like I said, I'm not a morning person. There's a cafe on the corner. Go, before I change my mind and shoot you after all."

Pierus took the money. "To think I'm a king in my own land." He slammed out of the room.

"Ass." Poppy stomped into the bedroom and slammed the door behind her.

Hippy sat down and took Fluffy Ducky back out of his pouch. She laid her hand flat so he could sit there and blink at her. "Everybody's in a funny mood this morning," she said.

Fluffy Ducky blinked four of his eight eyes.

She lowered her voice. "The muse king kissed me, Fluffy Ducky."

He waved a hairy foreleg in the air.

"Do you think he *likes* me?"

This time he waved two forelegs at her.

Hippy nodded. "I think so too. I know it's going to get you and me in big trouble, but it's kind of exciting."

Fluffy Ducky's hairs stood on end and he shuddered.

"You're hungry, right?"

He blinked twice.

Hippy went in search of dead flies and other bugs. She hit pay dirt on a window sill so high she had to climb a few feet up the wall to get to it, and left Fluffy Ducky up there to gorge himself.

After she came back down, Poppy reappeared. Her hair was neatly coifed, her glasses were straight and she wore a tailored grey skirt suit. There was no sign of a gun at all. She smiled at Hippy. "Come on, I'll get you a glass of milk. I'm sure that'll be quite safe."

Hippy followed her cautiously into the kitchen, a tiny room with a fridge, a rusty cook top and a narrow bench. She sat on the bench and swung her legs. "Are you feeling better?"

"Much, now I'm awake." Poppy poured milk from a glass bottle into a chipped cup and handed it to Hippy. "There. Fairies like milk, don't they?"

Hippy shrugged and sipped at the drink. "I like coffee better."

"I know dear, but I'm not prepared to have a hyperactive child climbing my walls."

Hippy narrowed her eyes. "I'm not a child. I'm twenty years old, like I told you."

Poppy leaned against the fridge and folded her arms. "You are a child, compared to him."

Hippy scowled into her milk. "Everyone's a child compared to him."

"Fair point, I suppose." Poppy heaved a deep sigh. "Look, I know good and well it's none of my business, I've barely known you for a day, but you seem like a nice kid and he seems like–well–" she paused, at a loss for words. "I'm just saying be careful, alright? Men are all nice when they want something, but later on they can get mean."

"My sister Ishtar had a boyfriend who was mean to her once."

"Really? What did she do?"

"She tied a rock to his head and dropped him from the fortifications." Hippy giggled. "It was funny."

"Yeah well, if Pierus is ever mean to you, you just follow her example, alright?"

"I don't understand why you're so upset." Hippy set her empty cup down. "It was just a kiss."

"Just a kiss?" Poppy looked faintly relieved and disapproving at the same time. "When I saw you on the couch together I thought– you know–"

Hippy knew. Poppy thought the same thing Ishtar and Nikifor both thought. Maybe they were all right. She didn't really want to consider that. Kissing was one thing, anything else with Pierus – ew. But she didn't want Poppy to get her gun out again, so she didn't say anything. She slid off the bench at the sound of Pierus's footsteps outside the kitchen. "The vamps are coming to find us tonight. I can't wait." She skipped from the room.

Right after they'd all eaten, Poppy started packing up her belongings. Hippy watched the frenetic activity for a few minutes. She scooped Fluffy Ducky off the floor after Poppy very nearly trod on him and never even noticed.

"What are you doing?" Pierus asked.

"Leaving this hotel. Obviously. It was probably unwise to stay here a second after Tony brought Hippy back last night, but getting a room that late is murder. We need new digs." Poppy shoved some clothes and the gun into a big bag and zipped it up. "You ready?"

"Rustam Badora said he had Tony following us all day yesterday," Hippy said. "What if he just follows us again?"

"Ah. Good thinking." Poppy's forehead wrinkled. "You two can act as a diversion. I'll come meet you later."

"Indeed." Pierus stretched his legs out and studied her face. "And what happens if you don't come to meet us? You're not thinking of losing us and going after the Apple of Chaos on your own?"

"As a matter of fact I would like nothing more than to lose you, in particular, in a very deep hole," Poppy said. "Unfortunately I have no leads without the two of you and you two haven't got a hope in hell of making it without me, so let's not quibble. Oh, and for the record, I'm after the box, not the Apple of goddamn Chaos. So I suggest you go and be conspicuous and meet me in three hours at– ah–"

"The Acropolis," Pierus said. "I should like to show it to Hippy."

"Fine." Poppy hoisted her bags.

"I should come armed if I were you, that close to sunset."

"Right. Wooden stakes at dusk. You two go ahead so I can get out unnoticed."

Pierus put a hand on Hippy's back. They left the room and headed for the elevators. "What did she mean wooden stakes?" Hippy whispered.

"Humans have some foolish ideas about a stake to the heart killing vampires."

Hippy tilted her head and considered this while she watched the elevator light travel up to them before the doors rattled open. She hung on to Pierus during the quick, rapid descent in the metal box. "I suppose it would work, if you could get that close. Fairy dust is better. Or a spear. That works well."

"Since neither of us has a spear, I trust you have your fairy dust handy." Pierus slipped his hand into hers when they left the hotel and walked out into the afternoon sunshine. A few lines smoothed from his face and his shoulders relaxed when they put distance between themselves and the hotel.

Hippy had to walk very fast to keep up with his long strides, but she didn't mind. It was a warm day and she was exploring Dream, hand in hand with the muse king. Things were really going very well. If only the fairies could see her now, they wouldn't make fun anymore.

Pierus hesitated on the edge of a busy footpath, in full view of all the traffic and pedestrians, looking around. Hippy had no idea if he'd seen anything, but a moment later he plunged them into the city. They hurried across busy roads, dodged traffic and wove their way through road after road bordered by towering buildings.

"Do you know where we're going?" she asked after the tenth dizzying corner. "All these streets look the same!"

"It's very different to what I remember," he said. "But I'd know my way to the Acropolis blindfolded. It was the one place in Athens I was able to visit."

"Did you go there with Pandora?"

"Never."

They crossed another road, walked past some older houses and into a stand of trees. Hippy skipped along at Pierus's side. She liked it under the dense green canopy. It reminded her of the forest near home.

Pierus gave her an indulgent smile. "Now look."

At the edge of the trees the ground sloped away beneath them to a descending pathway of forest. Beyond that rose a hillside covered in white stone ruins. The afternoon sun cast a distant building lined with pillars in bars of light and shadow.

Hippy's breath caught in her chest. She stared. "It's beautiful."

"Come on. I'll show you everything." He tugged on her hand.

Hippy followed him, amazed he could look so much younger in this place. She glanced over her shoulder, half-expecting to see Pandora following behind, but all she could see was a Freakin Fairy-shaped shadow flicker into the trees. She gave a cheery wave, then turned all of her attention to the muse king.

CHAPTER FIFTEEN

Late afternoon sunlight slanted across the stone floors of the Parthenon, the huge temple at the peak of the Acropolis. The sun shining between the pillars patterned the stone in light and shadow so intense you could have tripped over it. A few tourists still straggled around, looking at the carvings, talking about Zeus, laughing with each other.

Hippy stood in a warm, golden slant of sunlight. She closed her eyes and tipped her head back. The sun made lights behind her eyelids and warmed her skin. The air carried a faint aroma of flowers and smoke. Dream was so strange and exotic and busy. She hadn't realised until this moment just how much she liked it. There was always something going on, but no boundaries. Here she could do anything she wanted to, if only she could stay.

Soft footfalls approached. A hand slid around her waist and something soft and smooth brushed her face. Hippy opened her eyes and smiled at the purple daisy in Pierus's fingers.

He tucked the stem behind her ear and smoothed her hair back. "It's almost sunset."

"I know." Hippy curled her fingers into his long coat.

"We don't seem to have done much in the way of preparing to meet the vampires." Pierus's mouth crooked up.

"What's to prepare for?" Hippy turned in his arm and leaned against him so she could watch the sun turning the ruins pretty shades of orange. His arms wrapped around her. "Poppy should be here soon."

"Indeed." Pierus sounded like he didn't think she'd turn up at all. "I wouldn't count on her too much, my dear."

The sunset deepened to red on the horizon and spread across the curling blanket of clouds.

"I like the sunset," Hippy said. "It's so shiny."

"Fairies and shiny things. It's going to be the death of you all one day."

Hippy giggled. "That's just silly. Shiny things could never hurt anyone."

"I stood once outside Thebes with Pandora and watched the sunset," Pierus said. "I remember the colours vividly. She thought there was blood in the sky."

Hippy turned around in the circle of his arms. "Were you mad when Pandora left you?"

He cupped her face in his hands. "Furious." He bent down and kissed her lips.

This was a different kind of kiss from last night. Hippy's eyes widened. Her blood raced. She should really break away, but for the first time ever somebody was treating her like an adult and it was exciting. What other Bloody Fairy had ever caught the eye of the muse king? She let her eyes close, giving herself up to the experience. She didn't realise how much time passed until a now familiar voice spoke right next to them.

"Don't stop on our account, will you?"

They broke apart. The sunset had given way to full night. A few weak electric lights outside were all that remained to see by.

Rustam Badora paced a slow circle around them. His eyes picked up every spark of light and mirrored it back at them in bright red. Ten more vamps waited like sentries at the base each pillar. They were all new vamps, Hippy noted. They retained, for now, their pink human colouring. In another few days they would pale and eventually turn as blue-white as Badora himself. Tony, standing in their midst, was the only one with a tinge of paleness, the colour beginning to leach from his waxy skin.

"It's not like you to keep a fairy around for that sort of thing, Muse King." Badora's footsteps echoed on the stone. He slowed and reached a finger towards Hippy's face. She batted his hand away.

The vamp's laughter rolled around the stone pillars.

"Are you here to play games, Badora?" Pierus pulled Hippy closer.

She scowled. There went the whole being treated like an adult thing.

"Really." Badora, who had watched the exchange with interest, drew the word out. "Games are one of my favourite things. But the muse king is all business." He resumed pacing. "I presume the Bloody Fairy has conveyed to you my terms?"

"She did." Pierus's voice remained even. "Quite out of the question. I cannot allow you to farm fairies for food."

Badora disappeared. He reappeared inches from Pierus. Their faces were so close they almost touched. "Then you will open a door for my army into Dream."

"Your kind always were unrealistic."

Badora bared his fangs. "I prefer to think of it as taking our destiny into our own hands. You called us out, Muse King. You cannot stop us. If you will not accede I will simply take my human army back into Shadow and overrun the pitiful territory you defend there."

Pierus gave a low laugh that sent more chills down Hippy's spine than anything Badora could have produced. "And how do you propose to return without my help?"

Without taking his eyes off Pierus, Badora reached out for Hippy. His fingers closed around her neck. "How do you think?"

"That's my fairy you've got your hands on."

Hippy decided she'd had enough when the vamp's fingers cut off her air flow. She loosened Fluffy Ducky's pouch with one hand, lifted the spider out and flung him at Badora's face. He ducked. Fluffy Ducky flew through the air and grabbed onto Tony's face. Tony screamed, swatted at him, stumbled back and tumbled down the stairs.

Badora sighed. "He's not going to make any kind of vampire." His fingers squeezed. "You know I'm actually missing Shadow? Humans are very rich. I need some good, plain, fairy in my diet."

Pierus leaped for him. Badora jerked his head. The remaining nine vamps swarmed, closed in, swept him under.

The vamp king drove Hippy up against a pillar and pinned her there by the neck. "It's just you and me now, sweetie."

Hippy cast about for a weapon. Spots danced in front of her eyes from the lack of oxygen and she couldn't seem to find her fairy dust. One flailing hand brushed something sharp in her knotted up hair and she remembered Poppy's kitchen knife. She tore it from her hair and stabbed wildly at the nearest target. The knife sliced into something soft and jelly-like.

Badora's scream sounded like talons scraping down a metal pipe. The hand around her neck disappeared. Hippy gulped air and jerked her knife back with a pop. The vamp stumbled away, one hand clutched to his right eye. He bellowed several incredibly filthy words in Vampish.

Hippy checked the end of her knife and found a slightly squished eyeball on there with slicks of blood all over it. "Eeeewww!" she shook the knife to try and get rid of the thing before the sight made her throw up.

The eyeball flew off, hit the next pillar and exploded.

Badora crouched on the ground, still clutching his face. "You'll pay for that Fairy!" he roared. "I'll give you the slowest death you ever experienced! I'll make you beg for mercy! I'll drain every last drop and then bring you back and do it all again!"

Hippy took a deep breath and overcame the nausea. There, she was definitely getting better with blood. "That looks nasty. You should probably keep an eye on it." She swung her leg around and kicked him in the head as hard as she could.

Badora toppled over.

"You're not so tough." Hippy tossed the knife into her other hand and grabbed a handful of fairy dust to finish him off, but another vamp dived at her. She shoved the fairy dust into his face, ground it in and pushed him aside, only to find herself in the thick of the fight around Pierus. She would much have preferred a spear to the little kitchen knife, but there was nothing for it. She slashed at the next vamp to attack. Her knife sliced into soft flesh over the chest. Blood spurted over her face. She spat madly and tried to hold herself together.

Pierus loomed over her. "Hippy, run," he said. "Now."

"You can't fight these by yourself!" Hippy flung fairy dust in a vamp's eyes.

"As a matter of fact, I can. I said run." He shoved her so hard she reeled out of the fight and collided with another body.

As she instinctively brought the knife around in a wide arc, Poppy grabbed her arms and yanked her behind a pillar. "What the hell?" she hissed. "I just got here and I saw you stab that guy! What kind of a violent psycho are you?"

"That's very sweet of you to say, but they're all vamps." Hippy leaned around the pole to see what Pierus was doing. With any luck he was offering his throat to a vamp. Bastard. How dare he push her out of a good fight?

Pierus had gone very still. He stood in the centre of the circle of vamps, a thin smile curving his mouth. He slowly raised his hands and pressed them to his temples.

"What's he doing?" Poppy kept a firm grip on Hippy's tunic while she struggled to dart out there and help him.

"Getting himself killed!"

"No, he's doing something."

Pierus said a word. It sounded like a really, really bad word, but it wasn't anything Hippy had ever heard before. He said it so forcefully it seemed even the ground beneath them vibrated, and then the vamps around him stopped closing in. One clutched his head and made a strangled noise. Another dropped to the ground. One by one, the vamps contorted in pain and fell.

Hippy shrank back towards Poppy. She shuddered when the air iced around them. "Is he doing that?"

"Apparently." There was a tremor in Poppy's voice.

Pierus's words made the ground tremble a second time. "You are cursed creatures," he said. "Go. Put an end to yourselves."

The vamps disappeared from around him so fast they seemed little more than blurs of light. Poppy said a lot of bad words under her breath.

Hippy looked around for Badora to see how he'd taken this, but he was gone. Damn. She should've killed him while she had the chance.

Pierus sank to his knees on the stones. Exhaustion lined his face. His colour was almost grey. "Hippy," he said.

Hippy broke away from Poppy's grip, ran to him and crouched down. "Are you okay? What just happened? What did you do? Where did Rustam Badora go? Why did you push me?"

Pierus held up a hand. "My dear girl, patience. It's the old magic– it's been so long, I can only work them like that in Dream, and only because they were not quite full vampire–" he swayed. "I didn't realise it would take so much. Give me your hand. I'm sorry my love, I must ask a little more of you if we are to survive the night."

"What are you talking about? They're all gone!" Hippy gave him her hand, only to find it crushed in a death grip.

He pulled her closer and gripped the back of her head with the other hand. "Do you trust me?"

Hippy blinked. "Well, I suppose so."

"Then trust that this is necessary, and that I am grateful." He put his lips on hers.

It wasn't like a kiss at all. It hurt in ways she couldn't describe. Her blood slowed. Her fingertips and her feet grew icy cold. Her skull ached. Dark, brittle fingers clutched her ribcage from the inside and squeezed.

Hippy struggled against Pierus's grip. When he wouldn't let go she balled a fist and punched him in the chest with her free hand, which broke his hold. She scrambled away. She felt as though she'd run a marathon after that small exertion. She panted. Her head pounded. She staggered to Poppy and got behind her. "What did he do?" Her voice came out in little more than a whisper.

Poppy's hands moved. Her pack opened. She aimed her gun at Pierus. "Yeah. What the hell did you just do to her?"

Pierus got to his feet in one fluid motion. "This is getting tiresome, Poppy," he said. "Put that thing away. I didn't hurt her. At least not much."

"You know this whole thing just got a little too weird for me," Poppy said. "Hippy let's go." She backed away, pushing Hippy with her.

Hippy burst into sudden, uncontrollable tears.

"Hippy-" Pierus held a hand out. "Hippy come back. Just let me explain."

"I really don't think she wants to." Poppy backed them up past the line of pillars. "But we'd both like to know exactly what you just did to her. In plain language."

"I used ancient magic to push back the vampires," Pierus said. "It's been so long since I've been able to summon that power, it left me drained to the point of death. If more come, we would be lost. I needed energy from someone who had plenty to give."

"It didn't occur to you to explain this to her before you just sucked it out of her?" Poppy's fury made her voice shake.

Hippy gulped and tried to swallow her sobs. All she managed was a hiccup. The stones looked like a really comfortable bed.

"There was no time!" Pierus stalked their retreat, both hands reached toward Hippy. "I'm sorry it went so badly. Hippy, look at me. It had to be you. It had to be someone as close to me as you."

Hippy peered around Poppy's shoulder at the urgency of his plea and hiccupped again. "Why?"

"Because only love can replenish like that."

"Love?" Hippy took a step away from Poppy.

"Seriously, you're not buying this?" Poppy said.

"I tried not to," Pierus said. "A muse and a fairy, it's unheard of, but from the first moment I saw you, so much like Pandora, yet so much more–I'm sorry I scared you."

Hippy took a step towards him. "Do you mean it?"

"I love you, Hippy Ishtar."

"Oh for Pete's sake. Somebody get me a bucket!" Poppy exclaimed.

Hippy took another step towards him. "Then don't ever do that again."

"Come to me." Pierus held out his hand. "Thanks to you, I am restored. I can make you better now."

"Don't do it Hippy," Poppy said.

Hippy took another hesitant step toward him.

Pierus smiled. His whole face softened. "Do not be afraid, my love."

"Definitely going to throw up." Poppy made a disgusted noise, put away her gun and turned to walk away, but before she'd gone two steps, a slim metal arrow whistled past her head. She yelled and threw herself to the ground.

A second arrow sliced open the sleeve of Pierus's coat. A third barrelled toward his chest.

Hippy yelled a warning and Pierus jumped out of the way. A cloaked shape clattered into the Parthenon with a sound like a galloping horse, seized Hippy around the waist and threw her over his shoulder.

"Pierus!" she screamed, but her captor had already thundered down the steps and into the trees beyond. She hammered on his back with her fists, but Pierus had left her with little energy to do anything more.

In the thick of the darkness under the trees, her captor dropped her on the ground. Hippy tried to jump to her feet and run, but a second cloaked figure pinned her there with something sharp and heavy. A hoof. It was a hoof, these really were forest people from Shadow that had been following them everywhere. She'd never met one before, only heard about them, terrible stories about what happened to fairy children who wandered too far into the forest. Fluffy Ducky would save her. Where was Fluffy Ducky? Her hand went to her belt, but the pouch was empty.

Footsteps crashed through the undergrowth. Pierus called her name in a voice edged with fury.

Hippy screamed again, but the sound was cut off by a third figure who clapped a hand over her mouth.

"Do it," said the one pinning her to the ground. "There's no time to explain."

"Sweet dreams," said the Freakin Fairy in her ear. Then he removed his hand and clapped a rag over her mouth.

Hippy took a deep breath to scream again. An acrid smell assailed her nostrils and burning fumes hit her lungs. The voices disappeared and she fell into darkness.

CHAPTER SIXTEEN

Gaslight flickered over Pierus's face and gave his skin a bluish tinge. His grey eyes sparked.

Hippy reached up to touch his face. She felt overwhelmingly happy, even though she had no idea at all how he came to be kneeling over her. He loved her. The muse king was in love with her, the least of the Bloody Fairies.

Pierus's lips curved in a thin smile. "I told you this was a bad idea."

"What was a bad idea?" Hippy turned her head to the side and discovered her hair was loose. It covered the ground around her head like a great creeping shadow. His hands pinned it to the stone.

"What were we supposed to do, just let him use her up?"

"What are you talking about?" Hippy tried to move, but she was quite stuck.

Pierus leaned down closer. His lips drew back and a set of fangs gleamed in the gaslight. Then it wasn't Pierus at all, it was Rustam Badora. Blood dribbled from an empty eye socket. "Wake her up," he said.

The bleeding one-eyed vampire face got closer and closer. Hippy tried to scream, but no sound came out. She couldn't move a single limb. She needed her spider.

A bucket load of ice cold water hit her in the face. Badora vanished. Hippy sat bolt upright, but it was still pitch black. "Where's my Fluffy Ducky?" she yelled.

Silence. The mattress beneath her was hard and lumpy. Rough blankets scratched her legs. Water soaked into her hair and dripped down her back. She turned her head this way and that, trying to see anything at all. It took her a minute to realise there was a piece of heavy cloth tied around her eyes. It made her skin itch. She raised her hands to remove it.

A female voice cut through the darkness. "Not so fast there, Fairy."

Hippy's hands froze in midair. She knew that voice. That was the woman in the hood she'd met in the alley after chasing the Freakin Fairy. Wait. She'd been in the Parthenon with Pierus and Poppy, and then–and then–

Hippy let out a long, tense breath. She'd been kidnapped by forest people. She remembered now. The sound of hooves clattering over stone. The flash of terror. She'd never be seen alive again. Pierus would find her bones up a tree. She'd be fed to a bearfly by dusk. "You people so much as touch me and I'll be playing kick with the dust of your corpses before you can say feet," she said.

"Charming," the woman replied. "Remind me whose idea it was to kidnap the fairy?"

"Mine," rang out the cheerful voice of the Freakin Fairy. "I think. No. Wait. Hey if that was my idea, what was I thinking? I can't stand Bloody Fairies!"

"Quiet, both of you. As for you, we took the precaution of removing your fairy dust."

Ah. The man in the cloak. Hippy turned her head towards his voice. "You'd better let me go," she said. "Picrus will be looking for me."

"No doubt." The click of hooves moved toward her. "I promise you we are not going to harm you, Fairy. But I must ask you to give your word you will extend us the same courtesy."

"Huh?"

"He said be good and you won't get hurt," the Freakin Fairy said.

The forest man sighed. His voice was right over her head. "That was not quite the intent, but close enough."

Fingers on the side of her head peeled the blindfold away. She squeezed her eyes shut against the bright light. When her vision adjusted, she looked up into the face of the first forest person she'd ever seen up close. He had short dark hair, a v-shaped goatee, sharp cheekbones and eyebrows that came to points at the top, making him look permanently sceptical. The cloak and hood had gone. He wore black pants and a blue collared shirt, clothes he must have obtained here in Dream. The pants were almost long enough to cover the hooves. Hippy tried not to stare.

The man smiled and his whole face suddenly looked really quite friendly. "I apologise if we frightened you."

"I wasn't frightened." Hippy raised herself to a crouching position and glanced around. They were in a small room lit by a bare electric bulb. The Freakin Fairy skulked by a sink and the forest woman lounged against the opposite wall, arms folded. Her face was all pointy like the man, but her hair was long and straight and tied neatly at the back.

The forest man's eyes crinkled in amusement. "Of course you weren't." He stuck his hand out. "I'm Fitz Falls. That's my sister Ana, and your fellow fairy over there is called Clockwork Silver."

"That's a stupid name for a fairy."

"Yeah?" Clockwork made a face at her. "Bet yours isn't any better."

Hippy tossed her hair. "I'm Hippy Ishtar. It's a *much* better name."

Clockwork grinned. "Hey, I've heard about you. Aren't you the Ishtar who got dropped on her head as a kid?"

Hippy dodged past Fitz and leaped for Clockwork, but before she could get anywhere Fitz grabbed her by the back of the dress, lifted her in the air and dumped her bodily back on the bed. An impatient tic developed near his right eye. "I said be good and you won't get hurt."

Hippy scowled.

"Why don't you just let them have it out?" Ana said. "They're going to sooner or later, they can't help themselves."

"Because that's not how we conduct ourselves!" Fitz's voice lashed through the room, silencing everyone. "Fighting amongst ourselves achieves nothing. Now Hippy." He turned on her so suddenly Hippy scuttled back against the wall. "I promise you it is not our intent to harm you in any way. Believe it or not, we are your friends."

"Yeah? Well Rustam Badora promised not to harm me until I returned to Shadow, but he still tried to kill me the first chance he got. Why should I trust you?"

"We are not vampires, for starters." Fitz's voice returned to its former calm tones. He hesitated. "How did you get away from Badora, if you don't mind my asking?"

"I stuck my knife in his eye." Hippy mimed the action and made a popping noise.

Ana winced. Clockwork looked mildly impressed.

Hippy looked from one to the other and folded her arms. "What do you want with me? I want to go back. Fluffy Ducky is missing."

"There are more important things at stake than your duck," Fitz said. Then he blinked. "Wait. What's a fairy doing with a duck?"

"He's not a duck, he's a spider." Hippy spread her hands out. "He's this big. And he's all alone in a strange place with nobody to feed him, unless he's chasing the vamps, and sooner or later he'll run out of them."

"You have a vamp-eating spider?" Clockwork gave an envious sigh.

Hippy's lower lip trembled. "How would you feel if you were just a little face-sized spider all alone in a strange place with nobody to take care of you?"

"I'm sorry Hippy," Fitz said. "We can't go back for your spider. It's simply impossible. In fact we've stayed in one place too long already, the muse king could have traced us by now." Ana snorted. "Who'd have thought *we'd* be the ones doing the running? No wait, I forgot. You stole his fairy." She pushed herself off the wall and began gathering bits of clothing up from around the room.

Hippy jumped to her feet. "Pierus is coming here?"

"Doubtless," Fitz said. "But don't get your hopes up, we'll be long gone. Come on."

"No." Hippy sat down, folded her arms and glared. "I'll wait for him. He might have rescued Fluffy Ducky."

Fitz sighed. "Move."

Hippy glared harder.

"Please move?"

"Oh for Shadow's sake," Ana said. "I hate fairies. I really do." She slung a bag over her shoulder, strode across the room, grabbed Hippy by the ear and pulled.

Hippy yelped and got to her feet. "Ow! Ow, ow, ow!"

Ana propelled her across the room. Clockwork opened the door, a grin splitting his face from ear to ear. Fitz followed.

They went along a dingy hall, clattered down a staircase and stopped in front of a door that had rude words scratched into it before Ana let go of Hippy's ear. "Now, Fairy," she said. "We're going to walk nice and quietly outside. You can either behave or be carried by the ankles."

Hippy took a second to figure out what Ana was talking about. Then she scowled. "Fine. I'll behave."

Ana's hand landed on her right shoulder. Fitz gripped her left. Clockwork opened the door and they walked out into a hotel lobby as dingy as the room and stairs had been.

The room had a reception desk, a few plastic potted plants and a scratched up table and chairs in it. A group of men sitting around the table playing cards stared at the group passing by. Hippy stared back. Fitz and Ana whisked her past too fast to be able see much else.

Hippy twirled a lock of hair between her fingers. She kept twirling, working her way back and forth until she found a bead. She yanked and it came loose. Then, very slowly, she dropped her hand to her side. When they pushed out through the swinging doors she dropped it on the footpath. She mentally apologised to Pierus that there was not much more of a trail she could leave. She checked up and down the road. It was a busy afternoon. Cars whizzed by at their usual startling rate and pedestrians crowded the footpaths. Hardly anyone appeared to take any notice of them. She calculated her odds. She was fast. The forest people would never keep up, but Clockwork had managed to stay ahead of her last time they met. She needed a distraction to get a lead on him.

"Hey." Hippy pointed up at a building across the road. "That's really shiny."

"What's shiny?" Clockwork craned his neck to look.

Hippy kicked Fitz in the shin, elbowed Ana and bolted down the street.

This was more like it. The wind in her hair, the stench of petrol in her lungs, crowds of gaping humans blurring past. Galloping footsteps pounded the pavement behind her. She pushed her way through a knot of pedestrians at a crossing, dodged a chip vendor and leaped a bicycle abandoned on the footpath. Cars tooted at her when she raced across the road in front of them. The hoof beats faded.

Hippy couldn't get the grin off her face. Pierus would be so proud of her, escaping his enemies. When she found him. If she found him. She slowed. Wait. How the hell was she supposed to find him? Maybe she should ask someone directions back to the Acropolis and look for Fluffy Ducky first. Maybe he'd find her there.

A dazzling sparkle in a shop window caught her eye. Hippy stopped, entirely mesmerised. Behind the glass, rings, necklaces, bracelets and a tiara made entirely of glittering cut diamonds were laid out on mirrored shelves. A million points of light sparkled like stars in the night sky. She laid a hand flat against the window and pressed her nose to the glass. They were so very, very, shiny. Who even cared about some old Apple of Chaos when there were things this sparkly to look at?

Another form joined her at the window. "Fitz planned for this," he said. "It was a good plan. You stopped just where he said you would."

"Huh?" Hippy tore her gaze away from the shiny things.

Clockwork grinned at her.

She pouted. "How did you catch up?"

He leaned forward. "I'm faster."

Behind them a car horn tooted. Clockwork grabbed Hippy's waist and shoved her into Ana, who lifted her bodily into the back of a rusty old van. It was all done so fast she didn't even have time to kick anyone.

Clockwork and Ana followed her in and closed the doors. The car moved into the traffic.

"I thought I told you to behave," Ana said.

Hippy, who was still trying to recover from her undignified face-first sprawl, folded her arms, sat up and kicked the inside wall. "Yeah, but you never said *how* I should behave."

CHAPTER SEVENTEEN

They'd been driving for hours. At least it felt like hours. Hippy didn't normally deal well with enforced inactivity for two minutes, let alone the space of time it took to drive a long, long way. Athens had dwindled and faded from cluttered suburbs to scattered farmhouses some time ago. She had no idea how Pierus and Poppy were supposed to find her now.

Poor Fluffy Ducky, all alone. She gave a despondent sigh. Through the window she could see vineyards and farmland rolling by. Every so often the van hit a pothole and everyone bounced. If she'd had her fairy dust she could have made a hole in the wall and jumped out.

Clockwork had been clicking his tongue for the last ten minutes non-stop. It was driving her mad. She scowled at him.

He grinned and clicked louder.

"Shut up Clockwork," Ana said. "I'm trying to concentrate." She returned to scribbling in a big notebook.

The grin dropped from his face. Clockwork stopped clicking. He tilted his head to one side, crossed his eyes and stuck out his tongue.

Hippy smothered a giggle. She couldn't help herself. She scrunched up her nose and cheeks and bared her teeth.

Clockwork gave a muffled snort. He peeled his eyelids back and squashed his face in.

Hippy swallowed a giggle, choked momentarily and hiccupped. The sound came out like a squeaking hinge.

Ana gave them both a dirty look. "Shh."

Clockwork rolled his eyes, put a finger to his lips and pretended to choke himself.

Hippy couldn't hold it in any longer. The laugh exploded from her chest in a strangled snort. Once it started, she couldn't stop. Then Clockwork started too, which was doubly funny.

"For Shadow's sake!" Ana slammed her book down. "What are the two of you laughing at? Aren't you meant to be mortal enemies?"

Both fairies laughed harder.

"Fitz!" Ana yelled. "I'm going to strangle the fairies!"

The van pulled over to the side of the road and crunched to a halt on a gravel shoulder. Fitz climbed into the back of the van. "You drive Ana," he said. "I could use a break anyway."

"Good luck getting a break with these two." Ana climbed into the driver's seat. The van skidded over the gravel, fishtailed down the road and then straightened at a considerably faster speed than Fitz had been driving at.

"Hippy. Clockwork." Fitz sat on the floor between them. "Now that you've decided to get along, how about we have a little talk?

The effect of his voice was instant. Hippy and Clockwork both stopped giggling and paid attention. Hippy had no idea why, except that he seemed very calm. Maybe calm was contagious.

"That's better." The barest smile dimpled Fitz's cheeks.

"We're not getting along." Clockwork's mouth settled in a sulky pout.

"Are you really a forest person?" Hippy couldn't help asking. She could see the grey, ragged hooves peeping out beneath Fitz's pant legs.

"Yes I am." Fitz smiled at her. "I am Fitz Falls of the Fish-Tailed Green Dragon Dancer Tribe."

Hippy blinked. "Long name."

"It's not my real one," Fitz said. "Just in case you get any ideas."

"Did you shoot an arrow at my head when I was outside the fortifications?"

"No." Fitz gave her a level, measuring look. "I shot it at the tree. The idea was to scare you off what you were doing. Obviously it didn't work."

"But how would you know what I was doing?" Hippy frowned and made an effort to put it all together. "You were the one I saw in the forest, standing under the tree-"

"Yes." Fitz's reply was patient.

"Then someone hit me over the head. But it wasn't you." Hippy blinked. "Ana hit me over the head?"

"To my deep regret," Fitz said. "Considering she pitched you at the feet of the pretender king and set you on your current course."

"The who?"

"The pretender." Clockwork plucked at threads on his shirt. "The so-called muse king."

Hippy folded her arms. "What's he pretending, then?"

Fitz and Clockwork glanced at each other. They both shrugged.

"Well?" Hippy demanded.

"It's a long story," Fitz said.

"Is it a story with shiny things in it?"

"Not really."

Hippy shrugged. "Boring." She studied her fingernails. There was dried blood encrusted under them. Ew. "Where are we going?"

Another silence. Then Fitz spoke, his voice low. "We're taking you home."

The van screeched to a halt beside the road. Ana leaned around the seat. "Home?" she yelled. "What do you mean? We can't take her home! That's not part of the plan!"

"Ana," Fitz said. "Keep driving."

Ana muttered under her breath. The van pulled back onto the road.

"I don't want to go home," Hippy said. "I like it here in Dream."

Fitz glanced at Clockwork and raised an eyebrow.

Clockwork shook his head vigorously. "No way," he said. "My dad would never allow it. Even I'm only here on trial."

Hippy pretended to ignore them while she cleaned the blood from her fingernails.

Fitz sighed. "Look Hippy, I'm sorry, but I don't see any other choice. You shouldn't be here. He shouldn't have brought you. You'll be much safer with your family than with Pierus."

"My family are under siege from an army of vamps so vast they stretch as far as the eye can see." Hippy tried to make her voice calm, like Fitz's, in the hopes of making him see sense.

"You will suffer less at the hands of that army then you will with the muse king."

"You don't understand. Pierus and I are on a mission. The only way to drive back the vamps is with the Apple of Chaos and he needs me to do it."

Clockwork made an impatient noise. "Do you know we thought the Apple was safe because no fairy would ever agree to help him?"

Hippy set her jaw. "It's your home too that's under threat. Where do you think they'll go when they've drained every Bloody Fairy dry? Quicksilver Forest, that's where! Why won't you help us?"

"Because the price is too high." Fitz's voice was hard.

Hippy grimaced. "No need to get all twitchy."

Fitz wiped sweat from his forehead and took a deep breath. "I'm sorry," he said. "I just find it frustrating that you won't understand."

"Of course she won't," Clockwork said. "He did that thing you warned us about." He wiggled his fingers at Hippy. "He voodooed you."

"He did what?"

Fitz put his face in his hands for a minute, thinking. Finally, he sat up straight. "I need you to listen to me carefully."

"Okay." Hippy wondered what Fluffy Ducky was doing, and if he'd found any shiny webs to play in.

"We are members of the Invisible Army."

Hippy shrugged. "Pierus told me all about that." She thought for a minute. "How many of you are there?"

"We are legion," Fitz said.

Clockwork snorted. "A legion of four."

Fitz gave him a look. "Fine, there are four of us. We watch the muse king, Hippy. We've been watching him for generations, ever since our forefathers noticed something was off about him."

"You have four fathers?"

"Pay attention." Fitz knitted his fingers together. "Tell me, has he told you the great lie yet?"

"What great lie?"

"That if he dies, so does Shadow."

"Yes, he told me that."

Fitz leaned forward. "In the beginning, when Shadow was new and the muses had just discovered their immortality, he told the same story. My ancestor heard it. He talked to the other muses. They said it was rubbish, to be blunt. But then, one by one, those muses met with fatal accidents. Every original muse, except Pierus. The children were raised to eat up his lies. The parents were murdered."

Hippy frowned, troubled by this. "Murdered by vamps?"

Fitz sighed. "No, I don't believe so. All I know is from that time my ancestors watched Pierus to see what he would do. For many centuries he did what he claimed was his task. He kept the citizens of Shadow safe. He carved out areas for the many tribes to live. But then he got bored. He found ways to return to Dream and interfere in human affairs. He stirred up wars and inspired darker and darker things into our world. Then he inspired a bomb. A bomb so big it killed millions of humans." Fitz splayed his fingers and mimed an explosion.

Hippy folded her arms and leaned back into the wall. She tried to ignore the growing discomfort Fitz's words caused. "My dad told that story way better than you."

Fitz fixed her with an unwavering stare. "Did he tell you what the Apple of Chaos would do in the wrong hands?"

"He didn't know about the Apple."

"You must understand, Hippy, the Apple of Chaos is ancient magic the likes of which you and I cannot comprehend, but we know this much: it cannot be destroyed. Even in pieces, it generates power. It allows those who wish it to pass through the barrier between Dream and Shadow, if used correctly. But if it is used to hold a doorway open for too long, then the two worlds will collapse into each other and the darkness will overwhelm both. Shadow will disappear and Dream will be devastated by ancient nightmares."

Hippy shrugged. "He doesn't need it for a doorway. Anyway, he wouldn't do that."

"But what would he do, given free rein?"

"Drive back the vamps."

"And then?"

Hippy looked into Fitz's eyes and saw herself reflected there. *It called to me,* Pierus had said. *The most potent power known to man.*

"I can see by the look in your eyes you have an inkling," Fitz said. "You are not completely lost."

Hippy snapped back to herself. "I'm not lost at all. He said you'd do this. He said you'd try and turn me against him." She returned her attention to her fingernails, only to find her hands were shaking.

"That's not why you're here," Fitz said.

"Then why? I was just starting to have fun when you turned up, you know."

"I made it my business to study the ancient magic Pierus learned," Fitz said. "We were watching. I saw what he did to the new vampires. I hoped he would be so exhausted we could take him back to Shadow unconscious and trap him there. But then you went to him."

Hippy shuddered. The thought of that still made her fingers and toes go cold. But then he'd said he loved her. Didn't that make it better?

"He stole your energy," Fitz said, "Just like a vampire would steal your blood."

Hippy tried to ignore the words, but he was merciless.

"When he stole your energy, he linked you to him," Fitz said. "He does that. How do you think he commands such loyalty from the other muses? He possesses something of them, and now of you. He can sense you. He can follow you. He will use it to manipulate you. You would have been lost forever had we not intervened."

Hippy felt queasy. "But-but he wouldn't," she said in a small voice. "He loves me." Her face burned as soon as she'd said the words, because of the look Fitz and Clockwork exchanged.

"It's too late," Clockwork said. "You weren't in time. Maybe we should just pitch her out of the van and return to plan A."

"No." Fitz continued to scrutinise Hippy. "No, there's still a chance. Your father may be able to talk some sense into her before they come."

Clockwork chortled. "Good luck there." He grinned at Hippy. "My dad eats Bloody Fairies for breakfast."

CHAPTER EIGHTEEN

Enormous wrought iron gates swung inwards at the approach of the van. Hippy pressed up against the window and wondered how they moved all by themselves. The gates were so pretty. The iron bent, twisted and curled in graceful patterns, framing three big stars, each with nine sharp silver points.

Ana drove the van down a long, winding driveway, through tall trees, neatly trimmed hedges and gardens planted with masses of bright yellow and orange flowers. Hippy glimpsed a shiny blue bird wandering the gardens. It was half as high as her and had a long sweeping tail that looked like it was made up of hundreds of tiny eyes. "What's that?" she asked, startled.

Clockwork peered out of the window. "Oh, that's Ralph."

"That's a Ralph?"

"No, it's Ralph the peacock. My dad likes to collect his tail feathers when they fall out. He says it makes people feel like they're being watched, so they behave in his house. He's smart like that." Clockwork grabbed onto the back of the seat to keep from sliding when the van screeched to a halt. "We're here!"

"I noticed." Hippy, who had lost her grip and landed on the floor, scowled.

Fitz opened the back doors and hopped out. "It's alright Hippy," he said. "You have nothing to fear here."

"Except my dad," Clockwork hissed in her ear.

Hippy gulped and climbed out into the sunlight. She might have had nothing to fear, but she didn't miss the fact her three new companions formed a tight group around her. Not one of them actually laid a hand on her, but she had a good idea if she ran that would change pretty quickly.

They went straight up the driveway to the towering house that sprawled before them, as wide as a whole street would have been back in Athens. Balconies with white wrought iron railings fanned gracefully from all of the upper floor windows. Mirrored tiles embedded in the dark brown bricks between every window and balcony made the whole house sparkle. Looming from the corner of the sweeping stairs at the front was a six foot tall statue of a woman wearing nothing but her hair, standing in a big shell and looking into a mirror.

You just look for the biggest, most ostentatious, ugliest place you can find, Pierus said in her head.

Hippy sighed. Those had been her words, not his, but she could hear him clear as day. Actually she kind of liked the house. It was shiny. She looked askance at the naked lady when they climbed the gleaming white marble steps, then studied the imposing double doors. On them was a big brass knocker shaped like a dragon's head with huge teeth. The eyes were made of gleaming stones that watched every step she took. The knocker itself was an iron ring that extended just below the teeth.

She put her hands behind her back. She wouldn't have touched that in a million years. Just in case.

Fitz lifted the knocker and gave two sharp strikes with it. The thumps echoed inside. When he pushed, the door opened silently and they all went in.

Hippy stared at the polished floors, the huge crystal chandelier, the winding stairs. The walls were lined with paintings in ornate brass frames depicting all kinds of things, from tiny little girls with wings to grim-faced humans in stiff dresses and lacy collars.

"See that?" Clockwork pointed at one of the winged girls. "That's what humans think of when they talk about fairies."

Hippy studied them. "They're kind of pretty."

"Come on." Fitz went through a door over which was set two crossed golden swords attached to a silver shield. They walked down a long hall where every inch of space was covered with shimmering tapestries and shiny cloth stitched with the most intricate water-like patterns. Ana prodded Hippy in the back every time she slowed down to stare at something new.

Fitz finally stopped in front of a closed door with a big brass handle. He paused and frowned at Hippy.

She narrowed her eyes. "What?"

"I think the word he's looking for is behave," Ana said. "Nicely."

"Or else," Clockwork said in her ear. He drew a hand across his neck.

"My dad would drop your dad off the fortifications," Hippy

hissed.

"Wanna bet? My dad would break his nose before they were halfway up."

Fitz turned a pained expression on them both. "Would you two shut up for five minutes? Hippy, you have nothing to fear. Just answer any questions Mr Silver puts to you and try not to say anything else."

Hippy made a face at Clockwork. "Mr Silver?" she hissed.

Ana tapped her on the back of the head. "Weren't you just told to shut up?"

Fitz rapped on the door, then pushed it open. He took a firm grip of Hippy's shoulder and guided her inside. The other two followed.

Inside, a huge fire crackled in one corner, adding a bright orange glow to electric lights that were muted by coloured glass lightshades. Here, too, every inch of the wall was covered, but not with shiny things or artwork. Instead there were pieces of paper with writing scribbled over them, some in pictograms, some in the letters she'd seen in Athens, some in other letters altogether. There were maps of Dream and maps of Athens and maps of somewhere called Greece. There were sketches, too. When she looked closer, she realised one of them was of Nikifor. Her eyes widened. She found another one that looked like Flower. There was a detailed sketch of Pierus, with notes made in letters all around it. There was a very new-looking sketch of Poppy and under that one of herself marked with red words under the picture. She pointed. "What does that say?"

Fitz scowled at her and shook his head.

Silence descended. A chair scraped the floor at the other end of the room, where a big heavy desk was strewn with papers and lit only by a single electric lamp.

Once her eyes adjusted to the shadows, Hippy made out a man standing there watching them. She gulped and wished Clockwork hadn't spent so much time trying to freak her out.

Mr Silver went around the desk and walked towards them. He was tall for a fairy. He could have measured over five foot. Long black hair decorated with only one plait and a bead framed a face with wide cheekbones and a square jaw. A streak of grey went from one temple to his shoulder. Apart from the hair, he wasn't like any fairy she'd ever seen. He looked more serious than a muse about to walk into a pit of fairy dust. He looked hard, too, as though he'd been fighting for a very long time and had no idea how to stop.

When he looked down on Hippy, his heavy eyebrows drew together. "What's this?"

"A Bloody Fairy, Mr Silver," Fitz said.

"I know it's a Bloody Fairy. Why is it in my house?"

Hippy scowled. She didn't much like being referred to as 'it.'

"She was in danger," Fitz said. "I couldn't leave her in his hands."

"I wasn't in danger," Hippy burst out. "I was perfectly alright. You *kid*-" she trailed off when Mr Silver's gaze fell on her. "Hello," she finished, in a small voice. "I'm Hippy Ishtar."

Mr Silver studied her closely. "Who are your parents?"

"Willow and Leaf Ishtar."

"The only two Bloody Fairies I know of who come close to being remotely sensible. What were they thinking letting you come here?"

"They didn't exactly know," Hippy said.

Mr Silver raised an eyebrow. The effect was enough to make Hippy's cheeks burn scarlet. "What were *you* thinking?"

Hippy straightened her back. "The vamps were about to overwhelm us. There was an opportunity to find something that would drive them back. I took it."

"You mean you ran off with the muse king to help him find the Apple of Chaos."

"Well, sort of."

The eyebrow went up again.

Hippy looked at her feet. "Yes," she mumbled.

"And what made you think anything he told you was the truth?"

"He's the muse king!" Hippy couldn't hold down her outrage, even though Clockwork's dad was every bit as terrifying as Clockwork had said. "He was there helping us fight the vamps all along. Why shouldn't I trust him?"

Mr Silver looked at Fitz.

Fitz shrugged. "We tried to tell her. She wouldn't listen. She thinks she's in love."

Hippy's cheeks burned. "I do not!"

Mr Silver tapped her on the forehead. "Quiet."

"Okay." She edged back behind Fitz.

"Clockwork," Mr Silver said. "Come here."

Clockwork trotted forward, keeping his head slightly bent. "Yes Dad?"

"Take the Bloody Fairy out of here. I wish to talk to Fitz and Ana alone."

Hippy peered out from behind Fitz. "Can we go see Ralph the peacock?"

Mr Silver's mouth twitched. "Of course," he said. "But don't leave Clockwork's sight. There are some things in my gardens you wouldn't like to encounter." The corners of his eyes crinkled.

At the sight of that crinkle Hippy was only too glad to leave.

Clockwork scowled. "It's all your fault. If you'd stopped yammering we could have stayed and listened to what he was talking about with Fitz and Ana."

Hippy teetered on the edge of a marble step, trying to decide which part of the garden looked the most interesting. "Where's Ralph?" she said. "What's in the garden I wouldn't like? Is it a vamp? It can't be, they can't come out during the day. Who's that lady?" She pointed at the statue.

Clockwork straightened his back and puffed out his chest. "That's Aphrodite," he said. "She was one of the Goddesses in Ancient Greece. As for what's in the garden-" A wicked grin curved his mouth. "Wanna see?"

"Alright." Hippy bounded down the steps after him. "But can we see Ralph first?"

Clockwork glanced over his shoulder, then slowed to wait for her. "You'd better stick close," he said. "You don't want to fall into the snake pit."

"A snake pit?" Hippy did a little delighted jump in the air. "What kind of snakes?"

Clockwork set a quick pace down a path made of flat stones embedded into lush green grass. "Big snakes," he said. "With two heads and fangs the size of a bearfly's bottom. They'll crush you as soon as look at you and then chew you up and eat you whole."

"Will not!" Hippy skipped over the stones behind him. "How can they eat you whole if they already chewed you up?"

Clockwork stopped and spoke in an ominous voice. "You don't want to find out."

Hippy stared at him. Then she giggled.

Clockwork's serious face only lasted for two seconds. Then he grinned. "Fine, no two-headed snakes. Just stick to the paths, okay?"

He headed off.

She followed for a few minutes and almost bumped into him when he stopped.

Clockwork crouched down and put a finger to his lips. "Ralph's over there."

Hippy sat next to him and watched the blue bird peck at a bug in the grass.

"Wait for it," Clockwork whispered.

Ralph threw back his head and uttered a harsh, deafening screech. Then he fanned out his tail in an explosion of layered, gleaming eyes. Hippy's jaw dropped. She'd never seen anything so perfect. "Wow," she whispered.

Clockwork looked satisfied that she was suitably impressed. He leaned forward and made a clicking noise with his tongue. "Ralph," he called.

The peacock turned his head their way. He took a few steps forward.

"Ralph!" Clockwork clicked his tongue again. "Come here!"

Hippy leaned forward and stuck out her hand too. "Ralph," she called.

The peacock turned his head to the side and eyed her. Then he ran toward them, head down.

"Uh oh." Clockwork jumped to his feet.

Ralph made straight for Clockwork, screeched and pecked his trousers. Hippy shrieked and jumped away. Clockwork grabbed her hand. "Run!"

The pair bolted, the peacock in hot pursuit. They ran from stone to stone, leaped a low, bushy hedge and then clambered onto the high marble rim of a tall fountain.

Ralph stayed on the grass and screeched at them for a full minute before walking away, never taking his eyes off them until he was out of sight.

"Yeah you'd better leave!" Clockwork yelled after him. Then he chuckled. "Actually he always does that."

Hippy balanced on the fountain wall and walked around it. Crystal-clear water welled just under her feet from a huge shell in the centre. A statue of a woman with no arms rose from the water. Clockwork watched her intently.

"I want to see the snake pit," she said.

CHAPTER NINETEEN

"It's not really a snake pit." Clockwork switched paths and headed off down a line of red flagstones. "Actually she doesn't live in a pit at all."

Hippy followed. The fountain was soon obscured behind them by a garden of hibiscus trees so tall a muse could have hidden in them.

She glanced over her shoulder at the thought, but of course there was nothing there. She honestly didn't see how Pierus was supposed to find her out here at all.

Clockwork ducked under an arch made out of roses and skirted a garden choked with thick, woody lavender and straggling thyme. He beckoned madly. "Over here!"

Hippy ran up behind him. "Wow," she said. "She's pretty."

They leaned on a steel fence that ran a complete circle around lush grass and a murky pool. Beside the pool, the most enormous reptile Hippy had ever seen lay in the sun. She was yellow and white. Her body, at least as thick as a good-sized tree, lay coiled all around the pool in intricate tangles. She eyed them sleepily.

"Her name's Doris," Clockwork said. "She's not poisonous, but she eats stuff whole. She's pretty sleepy at the moment because two vamps got in here the other night. Dad fed them both to her."

Hippy's eyes widened. "No way."

"Actually it's true." Clockwork leaned so far over the fence his feet almost left the ground. "My dad doesn't tolerate vamps. At all."

"I wish I had a vamp-eating snake," Hippy said. "I wonder if my dad would let me have one when I get home."

Clockwork turned his back to the fence and gave her an odd look. "You're going to go home?"

"Not yet." Hippy couldn't take her eyes off Doris. She was the most beautiful creature she'd ever seen, except for Fluffy Ducky. "I like it here in Dream."

"What about your family? What about the war?"

"That's why I'm here. To stop the vamps. You know that. You

Freakin Fairies might not be at war with them yet, but if they overrun us you'll be next."

"I thought you were here because you thought the muse king was in love with you."

Hippy scowled. "That's none of your business."

Clockwork hugged himself and pursed his lips. "Oh Pierus," he said. "My one true love. You're so–so–so old!" He made a loud kissing noise.

"Shut up!" Hippy tackled him, knocked him to the ground and brandished a fist in his face. "You take it back!"

Clockwork laughed. "Or what?"

"Or I'll slap that grin onto the other side of your face!"

"You couldn't slap a bearfly into a waterfall."

Hippy cracked her palm across his face. Clockwork yanked her hair so hard it brought tears to her eyes, then pushed her. Hippy kept hold of his ear with one hand and hit him with the other while they rolled down the grassy slope, right into a row of grape vines trained along low wire runners.

Clockwork landed on top and put a knee in her stomach. "Is that all the fight you've got?" he crowed. "I could get a better fight out of the peacock!"

Hippy narrowed her eyes. "Weren't you the one who ran away from the peacock?" She clenched her fist and punched him in the leg.

"Ow!" Clockwork lost his balance and rolled into a grape vine. Three grapes dropped on his head.

Hippy sprang, but she'd barely had a chance to punch him in the ribs when a low growl sounded on the other side of the garden.

Both fairies froze.

"What's that?" Hippy whispered.

"That's the reason we were supposed to stay on the path."

Hippy looked up, and up, and up. Over the tops of the vines she could see what looked like a brown, furry hump. The next minute, a big head attached to a snake-like neck thrust through the leaves and sniffed at them. It drew its lips back over teeth the size of daggers and snarled.

"We should go now." Clockwork grabbed Hippy's hand and bolted. They ran through garden beds and trees and bushes, skirted the snake pit and finally picked up the footpath.

The thing churned up the grass behind them in an ungainly

pursuit, snarling and making horrible noises the whole way. Hippy ran as hard as she could. The spit from its mouth hit the path behind her like rain.

"This way!" Clockwork dived over a bush, rolled on the grass and ducked under a stone sculpture of a man with a broken head rising from an ocean wave.

Hippy pressed in there with him. "What is it?" she whispered.

"That's Crunchy the Camel," Clockwork whispered back. "The singular most terrifying animal in all Dream. My dad keeps him because–well, I'm not sure why."

Crunchy snorted and snarled behind the sculpture. His hooves dug at the grass and he let out several irritated brays, then walked away.

Clockwork let out a long breath. "Don't tell my dad we went off the path."

"Okay." Hippy punched him in the shoulder.

They both burst into muffled giggles, which were interrupted by the loud clang of a bell.

Clockwork rolled his eyes. "That means we have to go inside."

They came out from their hiding place, checked for any signs of the camel, then ran back to the house, up the white steps and straight through the double doors.

Clockwork skidded to a halt on the polished floor. Hippy ran straight into him, then jumped back at the sight of Mr Silver.

Mr Silver looked them both up and down. He walked in a circle all around them, inspecting them more closely. "Have you two been fighting?"

Clockwork nodded emphatically.

"Good. I'm glad you're getting along. Go and get cleaned up for dinner, both of you. Hippy, I want to see you in my study in fifteen minutes. I imagine it'll take that long for you to scrub off all that dirt."

Clockwork grabbed her arm and they left the room at a more dignified pace. "You're in trouble now," he hissed as soon as they were out of earshot.

Fifteen minutes later, Hippy was scrubbed and cleaner than she'd been since the war started. She'd just experienced her very first hot shower, something she'd enjoyed despite the fact it was so wet.

Now, however, little winged bugs did a crazy dance in her stomach. She felt sick. She'd thought her own father was scary before she met Mr Silver, but now she knew better. Not that she'd ever admit it to Clockwork.

She stood to attention in front of Mr Silver's desk and tried to keep her eyes down like Ana had warned her when she brought her back here, but it was really difficult. She wanted to look at the fire, because it was the only shiny thing in the room. And Mr Silver had just sat there staring at her for a whole minute now, was she supposed to say something?

"Sit down, Hippy."

Hippy dropped into the nearest chair. Mr Silver looked very, very serious. But then he probably always did.

"Do you know who we are?"

"You're the Invisible Army," she replied. "Fitz told me."

"Do you know why we do what we do?"

She shook her head. "I don't believe any of that stuff about Pierus. He's really very nice when you get to know him." She hesitated, because the words felt untrue, even to her. "...And even if he did do bad things, he's sorry now. He's trying to help us get rid of the vamps."

"And you really believe this?"

She nodded.

"It never occurred to you that you were being manipulated?"

Hippy twisted her fingers together and shrugged. "Why would he do that?"

"Why, indeed?" Mr Silver studied her. "Why did he choose you to help him?"

"Because I look like Pandora." The words were out before she could stop them. She scowled. She should have said something better, like because I had a vamp-killing spider.

"Pandora?" Mr Silver's cheeks dimpled. He got out of his chair, came around the desk and sat facing her. "What do you know about Pandora?"

"She was his wife," Hippy said. "The Apple of Chaos sent her mad and they got banished to Shadow."

"That's not entirely untrue, I suppose. What about after that? How much did he tell you?"

"He said she ran off with someone else and started the fairy tribes."

"Also not a lie. And then?"

Hippy shrugged.

"You know Pandora was our ancestress," Mr Silver said. "In fact the Freakin Fairies are her direct descendants. The other clans, including your own, are offshoots of ours."

Hippy scowled, but didn't think it was a good time to argue.

"Only we know the real story of what happened to Pandora." Mr Silver rested his chin on his hands.

Hippy finally returned his gaze, her interest piqued. "What happened to her?"

"As you say, she ran off with another man. She freed herself from him the moment she set foot in Shadow." He paused. "It is said before they went to Shadow, she and Pierus were almost always at war with each other. He insisted on controlling every aspect of her life. The women of our tribe would tell you she was hoping to have more freedom in her new world than she'd been allowed in Greece, but I wouldn't know about that." He gave an expansive shrug. "So she ran off with a wild man she met in the forest. He didn't care what she did so long as she stuck around. They went deep into Shadow and lived together for about twenty years. She bore him twenty children."

Hippy nodded. Twenty was a lot, but fairies tended to have big families. She was one of ten herself.

"But." Mr Silver lifted a finger. "Pierus, it was said, was furious when she left."

Hippy nodded again. He'd said that.

"He searched for her. In fact he never stopped searching for Pandora. Twenty years later he found her, older and wiser and mother of a tribe. He of course had not aged at all, for he and his companions had become the muses. The story says he couldn't understand at first why she'd aged and lost her beauty, but he nevertheless begged her to return. She refused."

Mr Silver looked at the back of his own hand for so long Hippy began to squirm, wondering if that was the end of the story.

"Then what happened?" she finally asked.

"Her family had welcomed him into their midst, for they were hospitable," Mr Silver said. "He ate and drank with them. On the day he left, he wished them all long lives and the best of health. He himself served Pandora a cup of wine, which she drank. She told him she hoped he would find happiness. Only when she'd drained that cup did he walk away."

Hippy's heart beat an uncomfortable tattoo. She had a very unpleasant feeling about this.

"His seat was barely cold when the cup fell from her hand and she choked and went grey. Then she fell to the ground, utterly dead, in front of her husband and all of her children. The cup she had been holding began to smoke. A hole was burned into the very wood where the liquid remained."

Hippy pressed a hand to her mouth to muffle the strangled sob that tried to escape.

Mr Silver continued mercilessly. "They went after him, of course, but he was gone. Muses can make themselves scarce when they wish it. If you've ever wondered why fairies do not trust muses, that is why. That is where it all started. As for you, if you wish to ally yourself with such a man, I cannot stop you. I have little doubt he is on his way here at this very moment. But you should walk into this thing with your eyes wide open, little girl. Pandora was the only woman the muse king ever loved. He has never looked twice at a woman since her. That is until now, if what my people tell me is true. I hope you're prepared for what such an attachment with the muse king will bring you."

Hippy buried her face in her hands and took several deep breaths. She tried to compose herself. "How do I know what you're saying is true?" she asked from behind her hands.

Mr Silver got up from his desk and went to a bookshelf in the far corner. He returned with a small box, which he placed on her lap before returning to his seat on the desk.

Hippy uncovered her eyes. The box resting on her lap was very, very old. Pieces were chipped away and broken, but it looked as though it had once been incredibly beautiful. Faint shapes were all that remained of carvings of women dancing and men with spears. Old, rotted leather straps and rusted brass buckles held it together. She took a sharp breath in. She knew exactly what this was without being told.

"Open it," Mr Silver said.

Hippy very, very gently eased off the buckles and opened the box. Inside she found an equally ancient wooden goblet. The wood was so old it had turned dark, dark brown. On one side of it there was a hole surrounded by thin, burned edges.

"This is all we have left of Pandora," Mr Silver said. "The box that cursed her and the cup that killed her. They've been treated with fairy dust to halt any further decay."

Hippy gently closed the box and handed it back to him. When he took it, she went and crouched in front of the fire. She held her hands out to the warmth and tried to stop them from shaking.

Mr Silver put the box away before he returned and crouched beside her. He said nothing.

Hippy stared into the flames. Her thoughts chased each other around and around. Pierus lurked in the back of her mind, boring a hole in her thoughts with the intensity of his gaze. All the times she'd been frightened by a mere look or a word and ignored it. Ishtar was right, she was no kind of a fairy, to be so close to someone with fairy blood on his hands and not know it.

"I'm sorry," Mr Silver said, after a long silence. "I can see by your face you're finally convinced."

Hippy said nothing. She wondered if the flames could burn away her disgust with herself.

"You seem a pleasant, happy-go-lucky kind of creature," he continued. "It wasn't my intention to destroy any part of that. But I fear for your fate if you were to continue with the muse king. I fear even now, if you return to him, he will draw you back in. He has already forged a link with you that you will find hard to break." He sighed and touched her shoulder. "Hippy?"

She looked up at him.

"I do not believe you are either as innocent or as young as you appear."

"Oh?" the word was cautious.

"I think you are strong," Mr Silver said. "If I didn't, I wouldn't ask you what I'm about to ask you."

Hippy shifted to a sitting position in front of the fire. "Ask me what?"

Mr Silver sat too, so he was at eye level. "The muse king must not be allowed to possess the Apple of Chaos," he said. "But he is coming here and he will sense its presence."

"It's here?" Hippy was startled.

"If the worst happens and he finds it, you will be all that stands between Shadow and an unstoppable tyrant. If he gets hold of the Apple of Chaos I want you to go with him and use it to drive back the vamps. But do not let him keep it."

Hippy stared. Then she slowly nodded.

Mr Silver looked into the fire, then back at her. "The Apple can be broken, but not destroyed," he said. "With any part of it, he will gain power. With all of it, ultimate power. But if even one piece is missing, and cannot be found-" He held up a finger. "One piece, Hippy." He rose to his feet and held out a hand. "Come. We've kept the others waiting long enough."

CHAPTER TWENTY

After dinner Ana escorted Hippy upstairs, then down a long hall decorated with scarves onto which hundreds of tiny mirrors were sewn. They were shiny and caught the electric lights, but even that wasn't enough to distract her. Hippy walked slowly, her eyes on her feet. She couldn't stop the thoughts going round and round in circles in her mind.

Ana opened a door at the far end of the hall and flicked on a light. "You can sleep here," she said. "Don't try and leave. There'll be one of us around all night."

Hippy nodded and went into the room.

When Ana closed the door behind her, she looked around. It was really very nice. The walls were covered in patterns of leaves and a full length mirror hung in one corner. The four poster bed was enormous and made up with crisp white and blue sheets. Big double doors led out to a balcony. She went over to the mirror, curious to see what the glass would tell her.

The glass reflected back a pair of over-large eyes in a face tanned brown by years in the outdoors. Her hair, still wet from the earlier shower, clung to her skin. Her clothes looked outlandish after days of walking around in Dream. No wonder people stared.

Disturbed by the doubt in her own eyes, Hippy turned on her heel and went to the doors. They opened at a touch onto the balcony. The polished tiles were smooth under her bare feet. She leaned over the cold railing. It was only two storeys up; that jump was nothing. She could be out of here in minutes if she wanted to. She suspected Mr Silver knew it. But then, she'd have to negotiate the garden.

A full moon rose in the east into a clear, starry sky. The stars told different stories here. At home, she could have climbed the fortifications, balanced right at the top and picked out the Big Bearfly, the Lovers, and all the other constellations. But at home, nobody would be safe and warm and tucked up in enormous beds. They were all fighting and dying. Ishtar could be hurt, or worse.

The stars here were too peaceful.

Hippy sighed and went back inside. She left the balcony doors open so she could feel the breeze, changed into the long cotton night dress lying on the bed, turned out the light and got under the sheets. She hadn't realised she was so tired. She closed her eyes and fell asleep almost instantly.

At first she dreamed of Pandora. At least, she thought it was Pandora, until she realised it was herself drinking out of a wooden cup. Pierus watched from the shadows. The liquid burned her tongue, her throat, spread like acid through her blood and-

Hippy woke up with a start. She took a deep breath. The room was empty. Of course it was. She closed her eyes.

She stood outside the gates of Mr Silver's house with Pierus. He was little more than a tall, thin shadow in the dark, staring through the bars with a cold, hungry fury that made the shadows press in around them. "I can feel it," he said. "It calls to me. It has always called to me."

Hippy pressed her back against the bars, wishing she were on the other side. "Is it true?" she said. "Did you murder Pandora?"

His eyes flashed white in the darkness. They bored into her. "I warned you they would try to turn you against me. Don't listen to their lies. You're with me now. Forever." He reached out for her.

Hippy discovered she had Pandora's cup in her hand. She held it out to him.

Pierus took the cup, but it fell from his hand and clattered on the road. Then his face stretched into a soundless scream and he turned to ash.

Hippy sat bolt upright, this time gasping for breath. She scrambled out of bed and slapped herself in the face a couple of times to make sure she was awake. She ran out onto the balcony.

The moon had risen all the way into the sky, bathing the garden in eerie silver light. Far below, she heard Crunchy paw the ground and cough. A gentle breeze stirred the leaves.

She leaned on her balcony, put her face in her hands and breathed deeply to calm herself. It was just a dream. Just a dream, even if it was vivid and creepy and horrible. What if Fitz was right? What if Pierus had done something to her? What if he could be in her head?

No. No, he wouldn't do anything so invasive. He loved her. He'd said so. He needed her. She had to get back to him.

But what about Pandora?

No. That was thousands of years ago. He was different now. He was helping her tribe fight the vamps, didn't that show he'd changed?

"Pssst," said a voice.

Hippy jumped so hard she almost tumbled over the railing. "Clockwork!" she hissed.

Clockwork leaned on the next balcony, separated from hers by only a few feet. "What are you doing?"

"I couldn't sleep." Hippy clamped her teeth over her lower lip to stop it trembling in a very unfairylike manner. "Well, I could sleep, I could sleep for a week, but I keep having these dreams."

"What kinds of dreams?" Clockwork jumped onto the edge of the railing and leaped the space between the balconies. He balanced on Hippy's railing, then slid down and sat on it.

Hippy shrugged and looked away.

"You've been acting weird since dinner," Clockwork said. "What did my dad say to you?"

She shrugged a second time. "Just stuff."

"My dad never says just stuff." Clockwork tilted his head. "I had a dream earlier. I dreamed we were running away from Crunchy, and Ralph the Peacock landed on my head. Then we saw this shiny ribbon in the sky and sparks fell out of it. Then there was this kind of crack in the air and all these vamps came out of it. We threw fairy dust at them all and then played kick with their ashes."

Hippy giggled. "That was a good dream."

"What did you dream about?" Clockwork's eyes were bright and curious.

Hippy looked away. "I dreamed about Pierus standing outside the gate. He said the Apple of Chaos called to him. Then he said I was with him forever. It was so real."

"You must have thought that was a good dream." All the humour had bleached from his voice.

Hippy shook her head vigorously. "It was scary."

"Come on." He glanced over the garden, put a hand in the small of her back and steered her inside. He closed and locked the balcony doors. "Go to bed."

Hippy sat on the bed, but she didn't get in. "I don't want to have any more dreams."

"I can help with that. Just wait a minute." Clockwork disappeared into the hall.

Hippy listened to the sound of low voices and then footsteps hurrying away.

Clockwork slipped back into the room and sat on the end of the bed. "I just told Fitz about your dream," he said. "He's going to check the grounds to make sure Pierus isn't here."

"Do you really think he did that thing?" Hippy said. "Voodooed me?"

"If that's what Fitz said, then that's what he did. But I can stop you from having any more dreams tonight."

"How?"

Clockwork grinned. "That's a Freakin Fairy secret. You just lie down and go to sleep."

Hippy lay down and closed her eyes. Sleep crept into her mind like a drug. At first it came with an image of Pierus's eyes burning into her brain, but then there was a movement from the end of the bed, and a light.

The dream disappeared.

When Hippy woke up the next morning, Clockwork was stretched across the end of her bed, snoring. She giggled at the sight. She felt rested and refreshed.

She got out of bed and dressed quickly before he woke up. Then she went over and tugged on his hair.

Clockwork blinked. "Huh?"

"Rise and shine, sleepyhead." Hippy went over to the mirror, since it was a novelty, and poked at her hair until all the braids fell into place.

Clockwork stretched, yawned and ambled toward the door. "Come on," he said. "Or we'll be late for breakfast."

Hippy's stomach growled. She followed Clockwork out of the room, skipped down the hall and took the steps two at a time. They raced each other into the dining room, where they skidded to a halt at the sight of Mr Silver seated around the table with Fitz and Ana.

He looked from one to the other. "Overslept, did we?"

"Yes," said Hippy.

"No," said Clockwork.

She poked him. "You did too."

Mr Silver cleared his throat. "Sit. Eat."

Hippy and Clockwork sat at their places, where plates of food lay waiting. Hippy devoured toast and eggs and reached for the mug next to the plate, hoping it was coffee. She was disappointed to find only a weak, milky tea.

When they'd finished eating, Mr Silver spoke. "Fitz informed me of your dream last night, Hippy."

Hippy's cheeks burned. She nodded.

"I checked the grounds and the perimeter, but there were no intruders," Fitz said.

"Nevertheless, I have little doubt the pretender is nearby," Mr Silver said. "Did you have any more dreams?"

"No." Hippy glanced at Clockwork and smiled.

He smiled back, then dropped his fork on the floor when his father's thoughtful gaze fell on him.

"Well Clockwork," Mr Silver said. "Since you and Hippy seem to be getting along so well, you can take first patrol this morning. Any sign of anything at all, I want to know about it. Ana, you take the streets, see if there's any sign of strangers in the neighbourhood. Fitz, you're with me."

Just like that, they were dismissed. Hippy and Clockwork headed out into the gardens.

Hippy looked around for any sign of Crunchy, but the garden was as serene as could be. They headed down the wide driveway together.

Ana overtook them and gave Hippy a hard stare. "I'm watching you," she said, then disappeared in the direction of the gate.

Hippy stuck out her tongue at Ana's retreating back.

Clockwork chuckled. "Wait till you see her in a bad mood."

"Are you telling me that's her happy face?"

"Pretty much. She doesn't like it here. She just kind of hangs around to make sure Fitz doesn't get into too much trouble. She wants to go home and get married to some guy. I heard her telling Fitz."

Hippy watched Ana disappear down the road and thought about her own sister. She wondered how things would have gone if Ishtar had come to Dream with her. "How many brothers and sisters have you got?"

Clockwork scaled the perimeter wall and balanced on top of it. "Fifteen sisters," he said. "No brothers. I was kind of glad when Dad said he needed me here for a while. You?"

"Eight brothers and a sister." Hippy scrambled up behind him. She looked out over the street. She hadn't been able to see much on the drive in. It was just a quiet street really, plenty of trees, lots of houses behind big walls. Anyone could be hiding anywhere. She averted her eyes and followed Clockwork along the wall. "I'm the youngest."

Clockwork laughed. "That explains a lot."

"That explains what?" Hippy caught up, ready to clout him if necessary.

"That explains why you're kind of dumb about stuff. Everyone knows the youngest kid gets protected the most."

Hippy dropped her hand just before she made contact with the back of his head and knocked him off the wall. "Protected?" She sighed. "I guess. It's not much fun though."

Clockwork glanced over his shoulder. "You miss them." He said it in a matter of fact way.

She shrugged. "Maybe a bit."

He stopped and took her hand.

Hippy glanced at their interlinked fingers, puzzled.

"Don't go with him," he said, with a peculiar intensity. "I like you."

Hippy's eyes widened in puzzlement. Something about the way he looked at her made her tingle. "Really?"

"Really." Clockwork tugged on her hand. "Come on, we're supposed to be patrolling."

They continued along the wall, hand in hand. Clockwork set a quick pace. The gardens flashed by underneath on one side, the street on the other. Hippy glimpsed Crunchy the Camel and the snake pit, but she barely noticed them because her cheeks had gone so hot trying to figure out exactly what Clockwork meant when he said he liked her.

When she looked at the back of his head and realised she liked *him,* she was so shocked she slipped and fell off the wall. Clockwork tumbled down with her and landed a few paces away.

Hippy crouched under a thick vine with stems the size of her arm and eyed him. "Freakin Fairies aren't allowed to like Bloody Fairies."

He shrugged. "I don't care. Do you?"

She shook her head. "No." She gave him a little smile. "No I don't."

Clockwork broke into a big grin. Just as quickly, the grin dropped from his face and his eyes widened. "You won't tell my dad?"

Hippy shook her head emphatically. "No way. He scares me."

He closed the gap between them hesitantly and wrapped his arms around her.

Hippy buried her face in his shoulder and smiled. Somehow it felt so right to be here. She felt like she'd been pretending to be someone she wasn't with Pierus all along.

The thought of Pierus made her stiffen. Guilt squeezed her gut. Her neck prickled as if he was watching her. Watching her betray him. Her blood began to pound. What if he was watching? What if he was angry?

"Hey," Clockwork said. "Check out that big spider."

CHAPTER TWENTY-ONE

Hippy tipped her head back and squealed. There, balanced on a branch right above her head, was a spider the size of her face. "Fluffy Ducky!"

"Fluffy Ducky?" Clockwork sounded dubious. "Your vamp-eating spider? Are you sure?"

"I'd know Fluffy Ducky anywhere." Hippy wiggled her fingers. Fluffy Ducky scuttled onto them, down her arm and settled happily on her shoulder.

Clockwork swarmed up the wall, balanced on top of it and let out a piercing whistle. When it was returned from somewhere down the street, he jumped and landed back beside Hippy.

"Why'd you do that?" She only gave Clockwork half her attention, because she was busy scratching Fluffy Ducky on the back while he blinked at her with three eyes.

"To let Ana know they're here. Come on." Clockwork grabbed her hand and sprinted down the nearest path.

"What? Who's here?" Hippy grabbed Fluffy Ducky and secured him in his pouch so he wouldn't get lost again.

"Who do you think?" Clockwork picked up the pace when they ran past the place they'd encountered Crunchy yesterday, but he wasn't there. Ralph the Peacock sat in the branches of a tree and ignored them.

Hippy had trouble thinking and running at the same time, but she figured it out by the time the house came into sight. The idea made her cold all over. "Do you mean Pierus and Poppy? How do you know?"

"The spider! How do you think?" Clockwork stopped on the stairs leading up to the front door so they could catch their breath.

"But Fluffy Ducky doesn't need them to find me."

Clockwork shook his head. "We can't take that chance. Come on." He pushed open the doors. They hurried inside and down the hall to Mr Silver's study, where Clockwork rapped on the door.

Fitz opened it. "News?" He stood back to let them in.

Hippy followed Clockwork inside. She slowed, reluctant to be in here again. Her eyes strayed to the bookshelf where she knew Pandora's Box rested.

"Well?" Mr Silver rose from behind the desk.

"It's Fluffy Ducky," Clockwork said.

Mr Silver blinked. "You've lost me, son."

"Hippy show him."

Hippy took Fluffy Ducky out, balanced him carefully in her hand and went to the desk. She held him out. "Fluffy Ducky came back to me. I lost him at the Acropolis when he was eating vamps and Fitz kidnapped me."

"You have a vamp-eating spider?" Mr Silver reached a finger toward Fluffy Ducky. Fluffy Ducky waved a foreleg.

Clockwork leaned in too. He stroked the hairs on the spider's back.

Fluffy Ducky blinked all eight eyes and waved the other foreleg.

"He likes you both," Hippy said, impressed.

Fitz cleared his throat. "I'm sure the spider's very nice, but are we missing the point here?"

"What?" Mr Silver had one finger underneath one of Fluffy Ducky's feet.

Fitz muttered something that sounded distinctly like a bad word. "How did the spider get here?"

"Ah. Yes." Mr Silver detached himself and sat down. "How did the spider get here, Hippy?" He gave her a stern look.

"He must have followed me," Hippy said. "Or he could have been following vamps, if they're looking for me. I don't think Rustam Badora was very happy when I poked his eye out."

"Or the pretender brought him," Clockwork said.

"Is that likely?" Mr Silver asked.

Hippy thought about it. She would have liked to think Pierus would bring Fluffy Ducky back to her, but Fluffy Ducky didn't like him very much. Before she could answer, there was a rap at the door.

"I would imagine that's Ana with the answer to that question." Mr Silver gave her a thin smile.

Hippy's heart thumped. She glanced at Clockwork, but he was pale and silent.

Fitz opened the door.

Ana hustled a woman wearing khaki pants, a black shirt and a backpack across the room and deposited her in front of the desk. "Found her lurking around the gates. She said she knows you," she said.

"Poppy!" Hippy launched herself at the woman.

Poppy, who was still rubbing her arms ruefully where Ana had manhandled her, was almost thrown off balance. She grabbed Hippy and hugged her. "You have no idea how glad I am to see you. Are you okay?"

"Of course I'm okay. Fluffy Ducky came back and there's a camel here and-" Hippy stopped short at a look from Mr Silver. "Sorry." She took a few steps back.

"Poppy Praeconius," Mr Silver said.

"Ratchet Silver." Poppy patted her hair into place. "How nice to see you again."

"You really do know her?" Ana said. "You know she's the human who's been helping Pierus?"

"Helping is really not the best term," Poppy said.

Mr Silver leaned back in his chair and studied her. "I suspected it was you. You have a talent for falling in with unfortunate company."

"Unlike you, I suppose. Do you mind if I sit down? Your friend here made me rather dizzy dragging me off the street like that." Poppy sat down without waiting for an answer. "I'm getting too old for this kind of thing."

Mr Silver smirked. "I had rather expected Tony to bring you in."

"Tony?" Poppy's surprise was palpable. "It was you who put Tony on me? I wondered."

"As soon as I heard you were looking for Pandora's Box I had him stick to you like glue. When will you learn to keep your nose out of places it doesn't belong?"

Poppy grinned. "When will you learn to pick your people better?"

Mr Silver scowled. "What have you done with Tony?"

"She didn't do anything," Hippy said. "Rustam Badora made him a vamp. Then Fluffy Ducky got him."

"That spider's growing on me," Poppy said. "I found him asleep in a pile of ash at the Parthenon and kept him with me ever since in case we found Hippy. He's handy in a fight, and we've been in a couple the last two nights."

"'We' as in you and the pretender?" Mr Silver said.

"If you mean Pierus, yes. Unpleasant sort of fellow, but I was worried about young Hippy here, so I decided to stick it out."

"How very noble of you." Mr Silver clasped his hands and leaned his chin on them. "Hippy is perfectly safe with us. Swear to me you will abandon your search and you may go."

Poppy chuckled. "Really? Just like that?" She shook her head. "I'm afraid it's not that simple."

"Oh?"

"The vampires have been on our trail every night. I don't know how, because we've been on the move. To be honest I don't even know how Pierus knew how to find you, but the man's like a dog with a bone. The thing is, if things go according to pattern, you're going to find a lot of vampires here tonight whether we're here or not." Poppy paused and rubbed her head. "You know, if those words had come out of my mouth a week ago I'd have slapped myself."

"Vamps we can handle," Mr Silver said.

Poppy sighed. "I'm not keen on sitting here playing games. Pierus asked me to come in and talk to you. He's outside the gates. He wants to negotiate."

"For what?"

"For Hippy."

Hippy slipped her hand into Clockwork's. He squeezed it.

Mr Silver glanced at her. "No."

"Look," Poppy said. "Don't shoot me, I'm just the messenger, but he said if you refused to negotiate he'd find another way in. If you want my honest opinion the guys an ass, but he's desperate. He wants to see Hippy and he wants to get back and stop this vampire war thing in Shadow before it gets any worse."

"A word to the wise, Poppy," Mr Silver said. "Appearances can be deceiving, and your honest opinion means nothing to me. I have never hired you for your honesty." He appeared to be deep in thought. "Fitz, Ana, bring the Pretender in. Don't take your eyes off him for one second."

"Is that really a good idea?" Fitz glanced at Hippy, then back to Mr Silver.

Mr Silver's look turned cold. "Are you questioning my judgement?"

"Come on." Ana grabbed Fitz's shoulder and steered him out of the room.

"Clockwork," Mr Silver said. "Take Poppy to a room so she can freshen up. I'd like to talk to Hippy for a moment."

Clockwork let Hippy's hand go and headed for the door.

Poppy rose and looked pointedly at Hippy. "Will you be okay?"

Hippy nodded and watched Clockwork leave the room. Nerves jumped around like little bugs in her belly.

"Sit down," Mr Silver said.

Hippy sat in the seat Poppy had vacated.

Mr Silver frowned. "I'm sorry Hippy, I'd hoped to have longer before you had to face him again."

Hippy laced her fingers together and looked at her nails. They were dirty. She wondered what Pandora's nails had been like when she died, and if Pierus even cared.

"I have no intention of allowing him to take the Apple," he continued, when it became evident she wasn't going to reply. "But I'm also aware things can go very wrong around him. If they do, you will be Shadow's only hope."

Hippy raised her eyes to his. "Me?"

"You." Mr Silver leaned forward. "I don't know what's going on in that head of yours, if you believe me or not, but I'm going to ask you to make a choice, right now, and cling to it, even when things are at their darkest and it seems there is no hope. Decide where your loyalties lie, Hippy Ishtar. With Pierus, or with yourself?"

"I don't understand."

"If your loyalties lie with Pierus, then so be it," Mr Silver said. "You will do as he tells you to and that will be the end of it. If your loyalties lie with yourself, then you will do what you think is right. Right for your own future and for all of Shadow."

Hippy nodded slowly. Now he was beginning to make sense. "I don't want to go with him," she said in a small voice. "I want to stay here. With Clockwork."

Mr Silver raised an eyebrow. "With Clockwork?"

Hippy's cheeks burned. She muttered a bad word. She'd promised not to tell and now she'd blown it. She nodded.

He gave a deep sigh. "I had an idea things were like that with you two. It is regrettable. You would have made a fine Freakin Fairy. But right now Hippy, the stakes are too high. Nobody else is in a position to watch Pierus or to stop him. We need you. Shadow needs you."

Hippy gripped the edges of her chair. "What are you saying, Mr Silver? You're going to make me go with him?"

He made a helpless gesture with one hand. "If I could see another way, I'd take it."

Hippy bowed her head. For once, her thoughts did not tumble

around like birds in a blizzard. Her mind was crystal clear and she knew he was right. "What will I tell Clockwork?"

"Nothing. Pierus must not suspect you of being anything other than a ditsy little girl ready to blow wherever the wind takes her."

Hippy flinched. "Is that what you think of me?"

Footsteps approached the door. Mr Silver glanced toward it. "I think you are far more than he will ever realise. Go and stand over there now." He motioned her to the corner of the room. "The game begins, Hippy Ishtar. Be sure to play it well."

There was a sharp rap on the door. Mr Silver's thoughtful, worried eyes pinned her in her corner. Hippy couldn't decide if this was a bargain struck between them or if she was just a piece to be moved around a board in a game she didn't understand.

CHAPTER TWENTY-TWO

Pierus strode into the study like he owned it. He did not appear to notice Fitz and Ana had slim metal arrows set taut in silver crossbows trained on his every step. Clockwork and Poppy followed behind.

Hippy couldn't take her eyes off him. He seemed to take up the whole room. There were so many little things she noticed for the first time, like the fact he looked no more than a man in his thirties, the way his dark hair curled over the lapels of his coat, the way his full lower lip gave him the look of an overgrown boy and the way a muscle quivered in his jaw. She watched his right hand clench and unclench. She wondered what expression he'd worn on his face when Pandora died.

When he looked at her nothing in his face changed. He didn't even smile. He'd never given her such a hard, cold look. Hippy stared back, wide-eyed and silent.

He went straight to the desk, leaned over and planted two fists on it. "What do you think you're doing, Silver?"

Mr Silver didn't rise. He merely tilted his head. "Your diplomatic skills haven't improved any, Muse. If this is your tactic for negotiation I'm surprised the Bloody Fairies didn't use your head for target practice weeks ago."

Pierus's hand slashed through the air. "You are wasting time. Your foolish actions have given Rustam Badora an extra two nights to amass his army."

"I imagine they'll have something far more painful planned for you when you do go back," Mr Silver said. "I wouldn't be surprised if they used your blood to paint their walls." He waved a hand. "Sit down, you're making my office look crowded."

Pierus seated himself in the chair in front of the desk and glowered. Fitz and Ana backed up a few steps, but did not dip their arrows.

"Well," Mr Silver said. "Now that the pleasantries are out of the way I suppose we should talk business. What do you want?"

"You have something of mine."

Mr Silver leaned closer to the muse. The gleam in his eyes suggested he was actually enjoying himself. "And what might that be?"

"Don't play games, Silver."

"No really, I'm curious. Over which of my possessions are you claiming ownership?"

"Freakin Fairies," Pierus said in a venomous undertone, "are impossible to deal with." Then he dropped his head into his hands and took a deep breath. When he looked up and spoke again, his anger had been replaced by nervous tension. His voice was even. "Let me explain things to you," he said. "There is very little time. The Bloody Fairies are hours away from being overrun by the vampire army on Shadow. They will all be killed." He glanced at Hippy. "Every last one. Meanwhile, Rustam Badora grows a second army here in Dream nightly. Miss Praeconius and I have been attempting to stem the tide, but there are already too many. If we are to prevent disaster in both worlds I must return to Shadow tonight, with the fairy and the Apple of Chaos. I must also find a way to take Badora with me, to prevent any more vampires being created here. It is imperative we stem the tide now, or all of Shadow and Dream could be overrun. I never thought I would say it, Silver, but I need your help."

"See, that's where I have a problem," Mr Silver said. "I happen to have personal experience of the fact you are a cheat, a manipulator and a liar. I've no reason to believe anything you tell me. And I wouldn't trust you with the Apple as far as I could kick you."

"Perhaps I have changed." Pierus kept a steady gaze on the Freakin Fairy.

Mr Silver gave a dry chuckle. "Really."

"One does not inspire a bomb that takes millions of lives and come out unscathed." Pierus raked a hand through his hair. "I swear to you I have dedicated myself to Shadow. I rallied the muses to aid the Bloody Fairies against the vampires after we lost the Bitter Tower. I will not rest until every one of them is back in the Darkness where they belong."

"Very noble of you." Mr Silver rolled a pen along the desk under his fingers. "But my position remains unchanged. You are the king of lies."

"You will allow me to prove to you, at least, the desperate situation in Shadow," Pierus said. "All I need is a mirror."

Mr Silver glanced toward the door. "Clockwork," he said.

Clockwork pulled aside a heavy curtain that hung beside the door. Behind it was a full length mirror.

Pierus went straight to the mirror and stood in front of it. He passed his hand over the surface, muttered under his breath and then moved away.

Hippy moved closer. The surface of the mirror shimmered, brightened, hardened. Shapes took form. Blackened stumps poked like rotten teeth into a rosy sunrise. The fortifications, no more than a burned shell, mounted weary guard over a field of bloodless corpses. The living lifted the dead onto carts already piled high. She glimpsed Ishtar, her face grey with exhaustion, dragging the body of their eldest brother by the shoulders.

Hippy pressed a hand to her mouth, but she couldn't strangle the cry that tore from deep in her gut. The sound echoed through the room. "Stop it," she said. "Stop it, Pierus!"

Pierus waved his hand over the glass. The images disappeared, but the room felt cold and alien. "Hippy." He went toward her.

Clockwork got between them. His voice was as fierce as the fist he brandished at Pierus. "Haven't you done enough?"

Pierus looked down on him as though he were a gnat.

Hippy turned to Mr Silver, already suppressing her unfairylike outburst. "That's my family," she said. "My sister. You have to help them."

"She's right," Pierus said. "Silver, there are only a few more hours until dark, and then the vampires will descend on us. We must be ready for them."

Mr Silver gave a thin smile. "Vamps we can handle. You-" he shrugged. "That remains to be seen. Fitz, Ana, I think you can put away the weapons. We can trust the king of lies to behave himself for a little while. Ana, I suggest you prepare the traps. Take the human and see she is armed. Fitz, you will see this muse is adequately prepared and does not leave your sight. Clockwork, Hippy, you will also arm yourselves. You're all dismissed."

"I would like a few moments alone with Hippy," Pierus said.

Hippy's heart thumped. She could not take her eyes from the bookshelf and the box and cup it held.

Mr Silver spoke a single, cold word. "No."

Pierus's lips compressed to a thin line. "Hippy," he said. "Come to me."

Hippy tore her gaze away from the box. She pushed past Clockwork, stormed to Pierus and shoved him with all her strength.

Pierus, who had not been expecting the attack, stumbled into Fitz.

"Did you murder Pandora?" Hippy yelled.

The look he gave her was stricken. His face went pale and something dark crossed his eyes.

She needed no more answer than that. "I thought so." Hippy stormed from the room, Clockwork on her heels.

Her anger cooled quickly when Pierus was out of sight. Clockwork took her up a flight of stairs and into a room packed with so many different kinds of weapons Hippy could barely speak for excitement. She walked slowly around the perimeter, her eyes shining, trailing her fingers over tall spears leaning against the wall, swords hanging from long wooden racks, wickedly curved axes, crossbows and daggers of every shape and size.

Along the next wall she found guns, shelves of ammunition and other things she didn't even know the names of. "Wow," she said. "Your dad sure knows how to be prepared."

Clockwork chuckled. "He's been getting ready for this for years."

"This? This right here? War with the vamps?" Hippy took a thin, sharp dagger from the wall and secured it in her hair.

"Not exactly. He's been getting ready for the pretender to come and try to take the Apple of Chaos." Clockwork stuck matching daggers in his boots. "I guess he didn't really think of him having an army of vamps on his back."

Hippy picked up a shiny silver instrument and weighed it in her hands. When she slipped it over her fingers it became a heavy, spiky, very nasty thing to punch people with. She put it into her pocket for easy access. "I don't want to go back with him," she said in a low voice. "Just so you know. No matter what happens."

Clockwork secured the straps of a scabbard across his chest to brace it against his back. He slid a long sword into it. His voice was bright and confident. "Don't worry. My dad would never allow it."

Hippy strapped throwing daggers to her ankles and wrists. She ignored Clockwork's eyes widening when she lifted her skirt to strap another set to her thighs. "What makes you so sure?"

"He likes you," Clockwork said. "If he didn't, you wouldn't have been allowed to stay here. He wouldn't send anyone he liked to be killed." He planted several short daggers and a handgun securely in his belt.

"Killed?" Hippy swallowed hard and filled her other pocket with a handful of little sharp blades she presumed were for throwing at vamp's heads. "Really?"

"Of course." Clockwork wound a long, metal-tipped bullwhip around his shoulders and torso. "I wouldn't give two chances to the fairy dumb enough to stick around once the Pretender had the Apple of Chaos."

Hippy ran her palm along the shaft of a spear that was just the right size for her. It reached only an inch or two above her head, not too long, not too short. She wrapped her fingers around it. A heavy weight settled in her chest where her heart should have been. "How well do you know your father, Clockwork?"

He gave her an odd look while strapping a double-headed axe to one shoulder. "Well enough to know he'd always do the right thing."

Hippy sighed and looked down. Under her fingers, leaning against the wall, was a black gun half as tall as she was and a belt bristling with ammunition underneath it. She slung the bandolier across her torso and then hoisted the gun over one shoulder by a rather handy strap.

Clockwork went to her and raised a hand gently to her cheek. "It's going to be okay," he said. "Don't worry."

"No," Hippy said. It was very difficult to keep her promise to Mr Silver and not tell when Clockwork was this close, and her breath was mingling with his, and he looked so very concerned. "It's not going to be okay, Clockwork. My family are dying. My tribe are being decimated. I can't sit here in this house and keep the Apple from Pierus if it means they become vamp food. I have to do what I can to save them. Do you understand that?"

Clockwork's lower lip trembled. Then he leaned forward and very, very gently kissed her lips.

Hippy's eyes widened. This wasn't like kissing Pierus at all. She didn't feel the least bit out of her depth. She did have a fleeting urge to pin Clockwork to the nearest wall and kiss him until she forgot her own name.

He took his mouth off hers and whispered into her ear. "I don't care where you have to go or what you have to do. I'll find you."

The door opened and they sprang apart.

Poppy strode in, closely followed by Ana, who looked the fairies over with deep suspicion. "What are you two doing?"

"Arming ourselves." Clockwork gave her an insolent look and stuck a flat disc with jagged edges in his shirt pocket.

Poppy gave them a huge grin. She nudged Hippy on her way to the row of guns. "Much more like it," she whispered. "Good girl."

Hippy scowled. She didn't want to be reminded this wouldn't last much longer. She lifted the gun with one hand. "How does this thing work?"

"Oh! Easy. Nice choice." Poppy showed her how to open the chamber and load it with bullets. "You're going to have to do this a lot, so I'd practise if I were you. You'll also find you can't kill the bastards with one of these, but you sure can slow them down." She put an arm around Hippy's shoulders and guided her hands to hold the instrument properly. "There, now you've got it. Look down the length, that's it, and aim at something. Aim at the middle of the door there."

Hippy closed one eye and squinted down the barrel. She thought she could probably be good at this.

"Right," Poppy said. "To shoot it, squeeze the trigger. Don't pull it, just put your finger around it like that and squeeze. No don't actually squeeze now-"

The door opened mid-squeeze. The gun fired. Hippy jumped back a step with the kickback, just as Pierus threw himself to the ground and Fitz leaped out of the way. A tiny little hole appeared in the wall right behind where Pierus had been standing.

There was absolute silence.

"Good shot," Poppy said, sounding impressed.

Clockwork snorted. Then he chuckled. Then he started laughing so hard he had to sit down and clutch his stomach.

Behind them, Hippy could have sworn she heard Ana giggle. Fitz scowled at them all and helped Pierus to his feet. "Hippy, try not to shoot unless you see a vampire," he said. "Please."

Hippy pressed her fingers to her mouth. She stared at Pierus with wide eyes. "I didn't know you were there," she said. "Honest." She tried to swallow a giggle, but it came out as a snort.

"Fairies, out," Ana snapped. "Now!"

Clockwork and Hippy edged around Pierus and fled down the

hall, still laughing.

CHAPTER TWENTY-THREE

From the roof of Mr Silver's house Hippy watched the streets wind away, languid orange, into the gathering evening. Every leaf and fence post shone and every shadow blurred just so into the light. It was perhaps the most beautiful sunset she'd seen in Dream yet.

Behind her Clockwork paced the perimeter of the roof, impatient for battle. He hadn't stood still for an hour.

She tried to focus on vamps and vamps alone. It was just too hard to think about what would come after that, if they all survived. There was no kind of choice. Mr Silver was right about that.

Beside her, Poppy had an inscrutable expression and a semi-automatic hitched on one shoulder. Her glasses were askew and a few hairs escaped from her hastily pinned bun.

Hippy felt another ache in her ribs. She was going to miss Poppy. She blinked rapidly, glad Ishtar wasn't around to see her get all emotional about a human.

Poppy glanced at her. "I was going to ask if you were nervous," she said. "But I guess this is your thing."

Hippy shrugged. "Usually the odds are more in our favour. At least, they were before the whole vamp army turned up."

"You ever think about staying?"

She smiled. "All the time. I like it here. But you know I can't."

"I know." Poppy hesitated. "But if you ever wanted to come back, or if things go really badly with Pierus-"

Hippy flinched.

"-Then look me up," Poppy said. "Seriously. You and me could have some fun together. There are lots more shiny things to be found out there, you know."

"I like shiny things." Hippy watched a shape move in the streets, too far away to be distinct. The sunset deepened to red. "Are you going to keep looking for Pandora's Box?"

"Of course."

"I wouldn't. Mr Silver covered it in fairy dust. If you touch it now you'll lose your hands."

Poppy stared. "He what? It's here? Son of a bitch!"

Hippy shrugged. "I'm just saying."

Poppy sighed. "There goes that wild goose chase. Never mind. Maybe I'll just write a novel about this whole thing and make myself rich that way."

"I hope Pierus isn't your muse then."

They both giggled.

"How do you know Mr Silver?" Hippy said.

Poppy winked. "Let's just say like you, he likes shiny things and I'm good at obtaining them." She grabbed Hippy's hand and pressed it hard. "Listen, this might be the last time I see you for a while. Hippy, promise me you'll be careful of Pierus. He's dangerous."

"Do you think?" She gave Poppy a toothy grin. "Ever tangled with a Bloody Fairy?"

A bell clanged far below. Clockwork was by their side in a heartbeat, straining to see in the fading light. "They're here."

The streetlights flickered on up and down the street. Pale faces loomed out of the dark. The gates shook once before tall, lean shapes swarmed over them and into the garden.

Hippy tried to count them. She gave up quickly. Numbers had never been her strong point.

Clockwork kissed her on the cheek. "Bet you I get more vamps than you do."

"Oh yeah?" Hippy launched herself off the roof and dropped silently through the air, her gun clamped under her arm and her spear brandished and ready. The first of the vamps to reach the house broke her fall. She jumped up and down a couple of times, impaled him on her spear and dodged out of the way of the jet of blood that spurted from the wound.

Clockwork landed beside her, grinning. "Show off."

There was no more time for banter after that, because they were surrounded.

A vamp started toward her, lips drawn back over barely human teeth in a low snarl. His eyes had the pale pink tinge of a new vamp. Hippy drove her spear into his gut and didn't even care about all the blood this time. She took her gun in her hands and squeezed the trigger, just like Poppy had shown her. Another vamp staggered backward, blood spurting from a hole in his neck. She squeezed again and again until a path cleared through the crush.

"Gee Clockwork I'm so scared of these guys!" she yelled at the top of her voice.

Clockwork put a hand on his face and gave an exaggerated pout. "Me too. Let's run into the garden and hide."

The vamps pressed in, fangs bared. The path out narrowed. Hippy bolted through grasping white fingers, Clockwork following at her ankles. They barged into the garden, leaped hedges, dodged flowers and made as much noise as possible. The vamps rushed in on their trail.

Hippy crouched, tripped three vamps, slipped the shiny thing over her fingers and punched the next one in the face. "Suckers," she hissed.

Clockwork pulled the sword from the scabbard strapped to his back and slashed at anything that moved. Hippy skewered several more vamps with the throwing daggers, but they just kept coming.

There was a low, feral snort just above her head. A glob of saliva hit a wounded vamp in the face.

"Crunchy!" Hippy dived to the side.

Crunchy pawed the ground, snarled at the oncoming attackers and charged, flinging vamps in every direction.

Hippy and Clockwork fled further down the path, this time with only half as many vamps in pursuit. Clockwork skidded to a halt under a tree. In the lowest branch slept Ralph, his tail sweeping down to the ground. "Hey! Hey Ralph!" he shook the branch.

Ralph raised his head from under his wing and uttered a warning snarl.

The vamps burst into the glade, skidded to a halt and surrounded them. Hippy's eyes widened. "Tony! I thought Fluffy Ducky ate you!" She gave him a cheery wave.

Tony was terribly pale and his eyes had a reddish tinge. He pointed at her. "That's the one," he said. "Take her alive to the boss. Kill the other kid."

The vamps closed in.

Ralph stood up on his branch, stretched and gave a deafening screech. Then he launched himself, claws first, into Tony's face.

Tony screamed. Hippy and Clockwork ploughed into the group around them with drawn daggers.

"They don't put up much of a fight you know," Clockwork said when they met in the middle.

"New vamps." Hippy shrugged. "Hey, is that all there was?"

They looked around. Apart from Tony pinned to the ground by a peacock, there were no living vamps in sight. From across the garden drifted the dulcet sounds of somebody being kicked in the head.

Hippy and Clockwork set off through the bushes, Ralph at their heels. The garden swallowed everything. The paths wound and twisted. Trees cast shadows so deep they could have led into caves. Not another soul appeared.

Then they burst into a big clearing where a six foot high marble fountain rose like a dancer from a mob of angry vamps. On the fountain stood Mr Silver, with Doris wound around his shoulders and torso. Loops of her body coiled into the water. She slid like a lover across Mr Silver's shoulders, raised her head and hissed.

The vamps closest to the fountain quailed, but only for a second. They surged forward. Whenever one climbed the fountain, Doris reared her head back and struck faster than the eye could see.

"That looks like the fun place up there," Clockwork said.

Hippy still had her new favourite shiny thing over her knuckles. She stalked up to the back of the circle and punched a vamp in the kidneys. When he whirled around to face the attack, she punched him in the face.

Clockwork set to with his sword. They ploughed straight into the thick of the vamps. Hippy took the dagger from her belt, since she'd lost her spear and gun, and cut anything that came within reach. This happened to mostly be hands reaching out for her, so she left a trail of fingers in her wake, along with a few fangs that got too close to her shiny, shiny fist. Clockwork swarmed up the fountain and she would have followed, except for the crowd of angry vamps that dragged her back to the ground.

Hippy shrieked and struck out with renewed fury. Fangs crunched. Fingers yanked at her hair, bringing tears to her eyes. She snapped her head back and hoped the unmistakable sound of a skull cracking wasn't her own. She snap-kicked a vamp in the knees and smacked another one in the nose, but there were so many now she could barely breathe for the stink of metallic vamp-breath and the fingers crushing her face, digging into her arms, her back, forcing her head inexorably aside while those pale, predatorial faces descended like knives.

She found a throwing dagger on her wrist. Loosened it. Fangs scraped her neck and without a second thought she buried the blade in flesh all the way up to her hand. Warm, wet liquid oozed through her fingers. The vamp went blue and fell, only to be replaced by another and another. There were too many. She was going to die, which meant she'd never have to worry about Pierus again, and Ishtar would never know she'd been right.

"Hang on Hippy!"

The voice came from very far above. Something shiny and jagged and circular fell from the sky and buried itself in the forehead of a vamp who was inches off biting her. Then another and another.

Hippy balled a shiny, deadly fist and struck at everything that moved until two pairs of warm fairy hands grabbed her by the shoulders and the hair and hauled her onto the fountain.

She scowled, brushed her torn dress down and pushed her tangled hair out of her face. "Stupid vamps!"

"Are you okay? Did you get bit?" Clockwork grabbed her in a fierce hug. "I'm sorry, we couldn't find you for a minute there."

Hippy allowed herself exactly three seconds to bury her face in his shoulder, shudder and wish they could go off somewhere and kiss some more instead of all this fighting. She looked at Mr Silver over Clockwork's shoulder and thought she saw a peculiar look of regret in his face when he met her eyes. She raised her head. "What's the score?"

Mr Silver glanced over the garden, where the vamps had regrouped and once again clawed at the fountain. "The score is we're all still alive and this is the stupidest pack of vamps I ever met," he said. "Badora's either losing his touch or humans don't make very intelligent bloodsuckers."

Fluffy Ducky scuttled onto Hippy's arm. She gave him a stern look. "Where were you two minutes ago? You be sure to come right back to me, okay?"

Fluffy Ducky leaped, sailed over Doris's head and clamped onto a vamp's eyes. The vamp screamed, broke from the pack and ran into the bushes, clawing at his face.

Mr Silver's grin turned positively evil. "I like that spider a lot. What do you say we cull these vamps a bit faster, kids?"

Clockwork gave a little excited jump. "Have you brought what I think you've brought?"

Mr Silver crouched, since he couldn't bend with a twenty foot long snake on his shoulders, and picked up a bag. From it he took two grey items that were egg-shaped but as big as two fists, and handed one to each of them.

"What's this?" Hippy pulled a pin-shaped item from one end. "Oops. I think I broke it."

Clockwork's grin stretched from ear to ear. "Uh-"

Mr Silver's voice was dry. "It's a grenade. Throw it, Hippy. Into the vamps."

Hippy shrugged and ditched it into the thick of the vamps. The air split. A deafening blast almost threw her backwards into the welling fountain. Flames billowed and a cloud of black smoke engulfed the crowd. Vamp ash rose into the night air like leaves where the grenade had hit. Those nearby who'd caught fire screeched in terror and redoubled their efforts to climb the fountain.

Hippy kicked one off the marble rim, then jumped up and down and clapped her hands. "Yay! It went bang! You do it Clockwork!"

Clockwork whooped and ditched his grenade into a group that had escaped the first attack and were fleeing. The second explosion, every bit as loud as the first, set a tree on fire.

Hippy put out her hand. "Fluffy Ducky!" she yelled.

Fluffy Ducky swung out of the darkness, landed on her hand and scrambled onto her shoulder.

"Well-trained spider, that." Mr Silver scanned the damage. "I'd say that's a severely dented vamp army. Clockwork, get the hose and put that fire out. You can meet us at the house. Hippy, with me." He strode away.

Hippy trotted after him. The snake followed. She glanced over her shoulder once and saw Clockwork hosing down the burning tree. She wished she could go back to him instead. The flush and excitement of battle hammered through her blood and made her want things she'd never even thought about until that one little kiss with a Freakin Fairy. She could just imagine Ishtar's face if she knew.

They broke free of the garden and stopped. Doris kept going. Her sinuous coils slid over the path and the road and straight into the thick of a battle far fiercer than the one they'd just left.

Fitz and Ana fought for their lives on the marble steps. A circle of seven vamps surrounded them, all armed with steel poles. Other vamps lay dead and scattered around the road. From inside the house came the sound of smashing glass, a woman's yell, gunfire. A vampiric roar sent shudders down Hippy's spine. She knew that war cry. The Bloody Fairies had heard Rustam Badora's call to arms every night since the vamps first attacked.

Mr Silver laid a hand on her shoulder. "I cannot in good conscience keep you from the Apple of Chaos if it means the death of your tribe." His voice was thick, each reluctant word dragged from someplace he didn't like to go. "It's your choice, Hippy, if he takes it or not. Just remember, what happens after that depends on you. Go and find the muse king. I can help Fitz and Ana."

Hippy looked up at him and swallowed, hard. Her stomach coiled. There were a lot of things she wanted to say to Mr Silver right now, and some of those involved some very bad words.

She raised her shiny fist. "Can I keep this punching thing?"

CHAPTER TWENTY-FOUR

Hippy scaled the walls of the house with her eyes closed. It wasn't something she would normally do, but she could hear both Poppy and Pierus underneath Badora's periodic bellows and she needed to locate them both.

The wall vibrated beneath her fingers. Gunfire. That would be Poppy. Hippy clambered sideways to reach the nearest window and peer through.

Poppy was on her own in a huge kitchen fighting three vamps. She used her gun to fend off a blow and then ducked and dived instead of just killing them. Her hair had all fallen out of its bun and her nice suit was torn down the back. Her glasses barely clung to her grimy face.

Hippy lifted the window up, put Fluffy Ducky through and then swung in after him. "Hey!" she yelled.

The three vamps looked around. Poppy took the opportunity to kick one in the nether regions and clout a second in the head with her gun. There, that was more like it, although it didn't slow them down that much.

Hippy wiggled her shiny fingers at them. "I'm over here."

"So what?" The tallest of the vamps looked from Poppy to her. "You can wait until we're finished with this one." She motioned one of her companions to Hippy. "Hold the little girl. She's next."

"Oh, but my blood's so much more wholesome. I'm a Bloody Fairy, see." Hippy stalked toward them.

"Fairy?" the tall vamp looked around sharply. "She's the one he wants," she hissed.

"Oh yeah, that too. Rustam Badora wants to kill me himself. Blah, blah, blah. If you ask me, he should be keeping an eye on his army. Oh, but he can't, he's only got one left." She put her hand in her pocket, took a little sharp blade out of it and aimed for the nearest vamp's face.

The vamp caught her upraised arm in a vice-like grip. "We were warned about you," she said. "Secure her."

"Oh." Hippy gave her a mock pout. "Someone help me. I'm so frightened of the scary vamp."

Poppy raised her gun and fired. Half of the vamp's head disappeared and Hippy's face was sprayed with blood. She squeezed her eyes shut and shrieked. "Ewwwww! Did you have to?"

"What the hell's wrong with you?" Poppy shot a second vamp when he leaped at her.

Hippy buried her blade in the face of the third. "Wrong with me?"

"We're killing people!" Poppy yelled. "And you're taunting them!"

"They're not people, they're vamps." Fluffy Ducky scuttled back to her shoulder. Hippy grabbed Poppy's arm, took her to the door and peered out into the empty hall. "Poppy you have to get out of here. If you see any more vamps, just shoot them like you did there, that seemed to work. I have to get Pierus and get back to Shadow now. Do me a favour and tell Clockwork-" she stopped in the middle of the hall. "I don't know. Tell him something."

Poppy shoved her glasses more securely onto her nose, then looked at her over them. "Now Hippy Ishtar you listen to me-"

Hippy shook her head vigorously. "It's no good. I have to go back, I can't leave my tribe to be slaughtered. No matter how much I might want to stay." She blinked rapidly to hide her eyes tearing up.

Poppy tipped her chin up and looked sternly into her face. "You do what you have to do, but be careful. That is a very bad man you're throwing your lot in with."

"I know," Hippy whispered.

"My offer stands, if ever you want to come back." Poppy stayed one moment longer, looked like she wanted to say more, then changed her mind. She ran down the hall.

Hippy stood alone in the dark and listened to the click of her friend's boots retreating. She closed her eyes and took a deep breath. From the front of the house came the rumble and crash of battle. Behind her, nothing. Above and below, footsteps. Rustam Badora's bellow shook the walls, a sound to stir the remaining vamps into fever pitches of violence and blood lust. Maybe she should take out his voice box next. If she'd kept the eye, she could have had a vamp king souvenir collection.

Hippy's eyes snapped open. Wow. Now she was thinking like a Bloody Fairy. And she was covered in blood and didn't care. Today was a big day.

She made an excited squeak and did a little jump to celebrate, then set off down the hall at a run.

The roar came from above.

Hippy ran up the steps two at a time. She slowed and tip-toed through the hall, listening. At first there was nothing. Then a whisper of sound. She needed more than just the little blades she had left to take on Badora. She went into the weapons room, chose a spear and continued down the hall.

A door to her left reverberated under the force of a roar. Hippy jumped back, took a deep breath and went closer. It was closed. Locked. Weird. She spun a couple of times to work up some momentum and broke the lock with one blow of her foot before bursting into the room.

Gaslight gave a gloomy tint to a space that contained only a huge four-poster bed and a vampire. The light gave the vamp's white skin a bluish glow. He wore a patch over his missing eye. His other eye flashed bright red when he turned away from the window. He opened his mouth, roared again and sprang toward her, but then snapped back as though secured by some invisible bond to the bed post.

Hippy raised her spear and circled. "If you're practicing your singing, don't give up your day job."

Badora curled his lip back over his teeth and bared his fangs. "You. I expected *you* brought to me in chains."

Hippy shrugged. "Your army was too stupid. Now it's mostly dead. Shouldn't you be trying to kill me by now?"

Badora took a deep breath as though working himself up, then let out another roar. The window shook. He leaped at her again and this time almost swiped her before he was snapped back to the bed.

Hippy tilted her head. "Something's weird here."

The vamp leaned against a bedpost. His eyelids lowered. He smiled, which was a frighteningly toothy sight. "Little Hippy Ishtar. Not the brightest bug in the spotlight. He didn't send you then?"

"He? Pierus? What have you done with him?" Her eyes widened.

Badora's laugh was like a blunt axe chopping down a tree. "All I have to do," he said, "Is reach the right pitch of noise and I'll break it. I know the muse king's tricks. He can't keep me here long. I'm surprised he sent you. But then, maybe he knew I was hungry." He took a deep breath and roared again. This time the very walls shook and plaster showered over their heads. Hippy covered her ears and head, thinking the roof was going to fall in.

A resounding snap lashed through the room. Badora disappeared and the door slammed shut.

Hippy slowly turned around. He leaned against the door, still giving that nasty grin. "Came in here to kill me while I was captive, did you? Stupid Bloody Fairy. I'm going to make you pay for my eye." He leaped for her.

Hippy drove her spear at him, but it stabbed only thin air, taking her off her balance when it failed to find a target. She stumbled. A blow to the back of the head knocked her to the ground and the spear went flying from her hands. She rolled and landed on her back.

Badora landed on top. His fingers pressed into her face.

Hippy curled her shiny fist and punched him in the nose. Cartilage crunched. Blood spurted over his mouth.

The vamp king yelled a very bad word and pressed harder into her face. "I'm going to make you suffer," he hissed. "I'm going to keep you on a chain for the rest of your miserable life and feed from you."

Hippy grabbed his wrists and tried to remove his hands from her face before he put holes in it. "I'm going to make you sparkle like a rainbow."

"I'm going to kill your family while you watch."

"I'm going to tell the muses to inspire some writers to make vamps fall in love with humans and get all starry eyed and–and–chivalrous! You'll be all like, I can't drink blood I'm good now!"

Badora took his hands from her face and pinned her wrists and throat instead. "I'm going to drink your brains!" he roared.

"You can't drink my brains, they're not liquid!" That was all she had breath for once he started crushing her windpipe. Hippy struggled for air. There was nothing she could do. The one red eye burned into her, fierce, hungry, deadly, and she remembered why the fairies feared his very name. Shadows crept into her brain.

The door crashed open. Her spear clattered and was swept off the floor. A spark of fear in Badora's eye. A sickening crunch when the spear shaft made contact with his head. The weight left her ribs and throat. She rolled aside, gasping for breath, and got to her knees. Air flooded her lungs.

Badora bounced off the bed post. She got to her feet and staggered against the wall. Words coiled through the air. A low voice chanted sounds she didn't recognise or like. The room iced.

Hippy stumbled out of the room and into the brightness of the hall, where she collapsed, just breathing and savouring oxygen.

A roar echoed behind the closed door and finally she understood. It was the roar of a caged animal. A caged animal she'd almost set free.

The door opened and Pierus came out. He locked it, turned around and leaned on it. He looked Hippy up and down, but did not move toward her. "Tell me," he said. "Because I'm very uncertain. Are you my enemy or my ally?"

Hippy rubbed her fingers gingerly over her throat. "Ally," she said. "I'm your ally." She took a deep, shaky breath.

"Hippy." He crossed the hall, helped her to her feet and smoothed the hairs out of her face. He had a wild look about him, three thousand years of arrogance and cynicism stripped away by the night's battle. "Hippy, my love, what were you trying to do? He could have killed you!"

"I was looking for you," she said. "I thought from all the noise you must be fighting him."

A roar shook the door behind them.

"Come on." Pierus took her hand and led her further down the hall. He opened another door onto a similar room, again containing only a bed and a window. He closed and locked the door behind them and set Hippy on the edge of the bed. He knelt in front of her so they were at eye level. The wild look remained, but with it something cold and suspicious and knowing. Nobody else had ever looked at her like he knew all of her secrets, and she didn't like it one bit. "Why were you looking for me?"

"Because it's time to go back to Shadow. With the Apple of Chaos." Hippy fought to keep her voice steady. Butterflies jumped around her stomach. In just a few days she'd forgotten the effect the muse could have on her.

"So you are with me, at least that far." Pierus ran the back of his hand down her face. His voice went hard again. "And the fairy?"

"What fairy?"

"Don't be coy Hippy, it doesn't suit you. The Freakin Fairy. The boy. I saw you two together."

A tiny, in-drawn breath. She knew it gave her away. Her heart pounded as though she'd run a marathon. "You did?"

He leaned so close their breath mingled. "You were only gone from my side for three days. Is that all it takes for a Bloody Fairy to stray?"

"Stray?" He smelled of sweat and vampire blood and the amber that had spiced his tent in Shadow. She couldn't even think what he meant.

"Did you turn those eyes on him? Kiss him? Give him your body? Did you stray with one of my enemies?" Pierus's breath was hot on her ear.

Hippy shook her head. Her cheeks burned because she was about to lie. "No!"

"Are you with me and only me?" His voice softened the barest bit.

She nodded.

"Then prove it."

"How?" Hippy had a feeling she knew. Fear seeped through her blood like mercury, but it mixed with other sensations that confused her. The adrenalin of the battle running through her veins made it worse, or perhaps made it easier, to respond when Pierus kissed her. His eyes burned into her so fiercely she couldn't even think of Clockwork.

He lifted her up and deposited her squarely on the bed. His hands moved up her thighs. He knelt over her like a big black bird and shrugged off his coat. The gaslight in the room illuminated his profile. He had the face of a young man, but the eyes of someone three thousand years old. Someone bad. Someone who looked at her and saw something he both feared and wanted.

He bent down and ran his hands over her body. His breath heated the side of her face with one whispered word.

"Pandora."

CHAPTER TWENTY-FIVE

The room was dark and silent except for the sound of Pierus dressing.

Hippy sat on the edge of the bed, already dressed, Fluffy Ducky cupped in her hands. She'd found him roaming the floor, trembling. His tiny leg hairs fluttered against her palms.

She closed her eyes to shut out the dark. She thought about what Ishtar would say if she knew. What any fairy would say. Her cheeks burned. Her blood raced. She pushed away thoughts of Clockwork. There was no turning back now.

She just wished she didn't feel so un-shiny about it.

She wished he hadn't called her Pandora before he took the last shred of her innocence.

She wished she could go and shower and scrub the smell of the muse king out of her skin.

Pierus settled his coat over his shoulders. "Come," he said. "Time is short."

Hippy put Fluffy Ducky in his pouch, but didn't move from the bed.

Pierus crouched in front of her and took her hands. His face, little more than a shadow in the darkness, was too close. "Don't be afraid, my love."

"I'm not afraid." She had to clear her throat a few times for the words to come out right.

"Good. Because the greatest test is yet to come, and to succeed, you and I must be as one in thought and purpose. We have to be as two halves of a single being, the light and dark working together."

Her reply came out harsher than she'd intended. "Is that what you and Pandora were?"

His hands tightened around her fingers. "No," he said. "And that is why we failed. That was why we unleashed the vampires in the first place. But you and I are different. You are not Pandora."

"I'm glad you noticed."

Pierus chuckled. "My dear girl, I wouldn't have chosen just any fairy. It had to be you. Someone pure. Come now."

Hippy thought that was an odd word to use after what they'd just done, but she allowed him to pull her from the bed and lead her out of the room. She blinked in the light of the hall and was vaguely surprised to hear Rustam Badora bellow. It seemed like an eternity had passed, but there they were, still in the middle of a vamp attack.

Pierus unlocked Badora's door.

Hippy backed away. "What are you doing?"

"He must return with us."

"Can't we just kill him?"

Pierus looked over his shoulder at her. His lips curved in a thin smile. "And have another leader rise in his place? I prefer to know my enemy. Besides, I have plans for our friend. Wait here."

Hippy waited. She tapped her foot. She looked nervously up and down the hall, half-hoping one of the others would appear and try to talk her out of going with Pierus. But it was too late for that now. She closed her eyes and listened for the sounds of battle, but just then Badora roared so loud the door shook.

Silence followed.

Pierus pushed a figure out into the hall. The vamp king was hunched over, his head and torso covered by a sheet from the bed. His hands were crossed behind him as though bound, but there were no visible bonds.

Pierus grabbed his shoulder. Hippy darted into the room and retrieved her spear, then followed them down the hall.

"I can smell the fairy," Badora said from beneath the sheet.

Gross. Hippy sniffed her hair and wondered if she needed another shower.

"Quiet." Pierus hit him in the back of the head.

They clattered down two flights of stairs and onto the ground floor.

"Do you know where the Apple of Chaos is?" Hippy said.

Pierus gave her an indulgent smile. "Details, my dear. Did you only just think of that?"

She scowled. "I was occupied with killing vamps." She poked Badora in the back with her spear.

"I will exact revenge for every death," he growled.

"Shut up." Hippy felt more like herself again now she had something pointy to carry around. "Well? Do you know where it is?"

"It has called to me since we arrived in Dream," Pierus said. "Here, it is like a roar." He pointed at the floor.

Hippy looked at the tiles, then back at him. "It's on the floor?"

Badora snickered. "Didn't pick her for her brains, did you? When did she get dropped on her head?"

Pierus sighed and put a hand on Hippy's wrist to prevent her from driving the spear through his back. "It's underground," he said. "Come, this way. I found an entrance earlier."

He led them at a quick pace through the entrance room and down a hall Hippy hadn't seen before. This hall was lit for a way by long, flickering electric lights. Pictures of little winged girls lined it. They were all blue and pink and green, and there were so many bubbles and sparkles Hippy forgot what she was doing until they reached a cast iron door with five solid bolts. Fortunately every single one appeared to be quite broken.

Pierus pushed the vamp king through the door and flicked a switch on the other side. Fluorescent lights illuminated a stone staircase descending into darkness.

"I smell mould," Badora said. "Damp. I take it we're nearing your precious Apple, muse king. I hope you're planning on feeding me that fairy before you send me back to my army."

Pierus shoved the vamp in the back. He hit the wall, tumbled down the steep stairwell and cracked his head on the stone.

Hippy gave a delighted squeak. "Can I throw him down the next staircase?"

Pierus patted her shoulder. "Of course, dear. Come along."

They hurried down the stairs and found Badora in a crumpled heap in front of another door covered in broken locks.

"Did you break all these?" Hippy pushed the door open.

"Naturally. It was terribly good of Silver to keep the vamps so busy while I searched his house." Pierus hauled the vamp through the door by a shoulder.

Badora gave a long, low chuckle, followed by a groan of pain. "You were always famous for letting others fight your battles, Muse King."

Pierus grabbed the sheet, twisted it tighter around the vamp's head and neck and walked on.

Hippy had never heard a vamp choking before. In fact, she'd never even seen one taken prisoner. The whole thing could have been quite interesting, except she'd walked through a heavy velvet curtain and found Mr Silver's collection of shiny things.

She stood transfixed. She didn't know where to look first. There were statues twice her height of beautiful ladies with long hair and jewels in their hands. There were tables on which polished vases bearing pictures of dancing women were carefully arranged with bowls inset with sparkling stones, and other tables heaped with gleaming jewels. The walls were lined with gold and silver veils strung with coins. On one pedestal, inside a glass case, was a huge, sparkling diamond. Across the room in a similar case was an emerald the size of her fist. Everywhere she looked, things sparkled and shone.

Suspended from the ceiling in the centre of the room, the shiniest thing of all rested inside a glass case that sparkled with the unmistakable sheen of fairy dust. The shiny thing was nothing more than a glass sphere, a sphere shimmering with lights from within, a whole world in itself. Lights splayed across the glass case, danced around the roof, rippled on the floor. She couldn't look away.

Badora struggled to his feet and turned around like a blind man seeking the source of a sound. "That," he said. "I remember that. I don't know how, but I do. Muse King, what do you think you're doing?"

"Hippy." Pierus laid a hand on her shoulder. "Hippy." He clicked his fingers in front of her eyes.

"Oh. What?" Hippy looked around at him. "I like shiny things."

"I know you do, my dear." Pierus ran a finger down her cheek. "And I need you to get me the shiniest thing of all." He pointed at the roof.

Hippy's eyes widened. "Is that the Apple of Chaos?"

"Don't do it fairy," Badora said. "You and I might not get along now, but I'm telling you, if you get him that thing, my armies will be the least of your worries."

Hippy glanced at the vamp, disconcerted.

Pierus gently prised the spear from her grasp and patted her on the shoulder. "Come along my dear, time is short and the Bloody Fairies are dying. Get the Apple." He lifted the spear, swung it once and clubbed Badora in the side of the head with it. The vamp slumped into an unconscious heap.

Hippy hesitated. "What's he talking about?"

"Nothing. He's just trying to stop us from defeating his armies. Get the Apple for me, Hippy."

The edge to his voice made her want to back up a step, but she held her ground. "I don't think you're telling me everything. What's going to happen to the Apple after we get rid of the vamps?"

Pierus reached her in three steps. He put a hand under her chin and forced her to look into his eyes. "I didn't bring you with me to think," he said in a low, acid tone that made her flinch. She tried to move away, but his fingers curled around her arm and held her in place. His voice softened. "Now Hippy, my love, don't resist me like this. You are mine now. You belong to me, and you must do as I say. I promised you I would save your people, and I will. But I cannot do it until you get me the Apple of Chaos. Don't worry about the vampire. Forget his ravings. Forget them. It's me you trust. I'm looking after you. Don't you trust me?"

Hippy stared into eyes like coals. He filled the room, sucked up all the oxygen, left nothing else. Her head felt like cotton wool and deep down she knew something was wrong, badly wrong, but she couldn't get hold of it for fear of that vice-like grip hurting more than it already did, for fear of his fierce words descending into fury with her. He was like a wall she couldn't see past, dragging words from her soul she didn't think were true, to be spoken into ice cold air. "I trust you," she said.

The cold eased. He rewarded her with a smile and a kiss on the forehead. "That's my good girl. Now go get me the Apple." He let her go.

Hippy backed away, hesitant, unsure what had just happened or why she felt icky.

"Go on." He never took his eyes off her.

She climbed the nearest wall, crawled out onto the roof and looked down. Pierus stood over the prone vamp, watching her. Then the lights caught her attention. She let go of the roof with everything but her feet and walked, upside down, to the glass case.

Up close it was even brighter. She put her hands on the case. It was hot to the touch, like a light bulb. The very glass seemed to hum. Her breath caught. She recognised that feel. Glass didn't hum unless a fairy had put a curse on whatever was inside it. She'd only ever seen the Bloody Fairies do one curse and that had resulted in an interloper from the city running screaming from the village with his pants on fire. She giggled and wondered what kind of curses Freakin Fairies put on things.

"Hurry," Pierus urged. "You need to break the glass."

"I'm not breaking that," Hippy said. "It's got a curse on it."

He made an impatient noise. "Fairy curses are nothing. Break it."

"I don't want to. It's all sparkly." Hippy smoothed her hands over the glass.

Pierus's voice took on an edge. "Break it now, Hippy."

"Oh, alright then." Hippy took a dagger from her hair and cut the fine wires attaching the case to the roof. "Look out."

"No wait. Don't let it just drop!"

The case dropped through the air. Hippy released her hold on the roof, tumbled, flipped and landed at the same time as the case. It smashed at her feet. She grabbed the Apple before it ever hit the ground and lifted it slowly up, but shut her eyes before she could look at it properly. She held it out to Pierus. "Here. Whatever the curse is, you can have it. I'm not looking at it first."

There was the sound of fabric tearing before he took the weight from her hands. "My dear girl, I told you curses are nothing. You have done well."

She opened her eyes and watched him. Pierus held the Apple with a piece of torn fabric from the sheet covering Badora. He cupped it in his hands like it was the most precious thing in the world, a child he had regained after millennia. He turned toward the light and held it up. "Now I remember," he said. "I remember the way it felt. But what's this? It never happened this way before."

He went silent, staring into the Apple of Chaos as though into another world. The lines and shadows deepened on his face. When he finally did speak, his voice cracked. "No," he whispered. "No!"

Hippy took a tentative step toward him. "Pierus?"

His hands trembled. The Apple of Chaos flared a bright, angry red. His lips curled back over his teeth and angry lines marred his face.

"Pierus? What's wrong?"

He turned murderous eyes on her. Hippy saw herself reflected in those eyes, a tiny figure looking up, and up, and up. His face was hard and set with pure hatred. The hand he flung out clipped her in the face.

She tripped and fell hard in the shattered glass of the case. A shard sliced open her hand. When she lifted the hand out of the debris, blood ran over her skin and dripped onto the floor. A familiar panic squeezed her chest.

Pierus flung the Apple of Chaos against the wall so hard it

shattered on impact.

CHAPTER TWENTY-SIX

The silence that followed was broken only by the endless clink of a piece of Apple of Chaos rolling across the floor. Pierus collapsed to the ground, face in his hands. A harsh noise that could have been a sob erupted from him. His words came out like gravel. "What have I done?"

Hippy took deep breaths to keep panic at bay. Blood dripping from her hand made a sticky red pool on the floor. Badora twitched under his sheet. Her lip trembled, so she clamped down on it with her teeth, which only succeeded in drawing more blood. She inched further away from the muse. "You hit me."

Pierus took his hands from his face and looked at her. He looked really hard, searching her face for something. Then he shook his head. "It wasn't you," he said. "But she looked like you. No, it can't have been. Damn those Freakin Fairy curses!"

"It was me." Hippy wiped an errant tear that leaked from her eye and left a streak of blood on her face. "What kind of a muse are you, anyway? One minute you love me and the next you hit me, without even a reason for a fight." She sniffed. The clinking stopped next to her hand. She closed her fingers over a jagged shard of Apple.

"Hippy?" The hard look fled. Pierus crawled toward her. "Hippy, I'm sorry, I didn't mean to. I didn't know what I was doing."

Hippy moved away from him and dodged around the vamp. Blood dripped from her hand onto the sheet. "I want to go home." She blinked back more tears. "You hate me."

"No, Hippy. I don't hate you. I love you. It's just the Apple of Chaos showed me–I saw–"

Whatever he might have seen was lost when Rustam Badora leaped to his feet, hands still bound. The sheet slid from his shoulders. His head snapped toward Hippy and an animal snarl rolled from his throat. "Damn this infernal muse magic. You can't tease me with your blood and expect to live, Fairy." He leaped and knocked her to the ground.

Hippy yelped and rolled aside, but Badora had already sunk his teeth into her bleeding hand. That *hurt*. She curled her other fist, the shiny one, and planted it squarely in his eye patch.

Pierus hauled Badora off her, grabbed the sheet and once again wrapped it around the vampire king's head and neck.

"Ew!" Hippy shook her hand madly and sent more blood flying everywhere. "That was even grosser than when he licked me! Did you see what he did?" She jumped up and down to try and rid herself of the memory of teeth in her hand.

"My dear girl, I suggest you stop that before you make him any worse." Pierus spoke through set teeth while struggling to control the bucking and twisting vamp.

"Oh." Hippy stopped shaking her hand, which was now bleeding from two puncture wounds as well as the original cut. "Can I kill him? Please can I kill him?"

Badora groaned from beneath the sheet. "I'm so hungry Muse, you can't do this to me. Just give me the fairy and I'll do whatever you want."

Hippy wondered if she imagined the half-second hesitation before Pierus clouted him in the head. "Shut up," he said. "Touch my fairy and I'll hand you in chains to whatever is left of her clan."

She scowled. "Your fairy? Stop calling me that. I'm not anybody's fairy."

Pierus finally secured a hold on the vamp king that stopped him from struggling. His voice no longer shook. There was no sign of his earlier distress. "I'm sorry I hit you Hippy, that was not my intent. Now would you get the pieces of the Apple of Chaos for me, before anything else goes wrong? I don't even know if it'll work now, but we have to try."

Hippy went to the wall where the smashed Apple of Chaos lay and gathered up the remaining five chunks of glass. They felt cold and lifeless in her hands. "Of course it'll work. Mr Silver said the Apple could be broken but not destroyed."

"Did he now? And what other gems of wisdom did he impart to you, my dear?"

Something in his tone made Hippy wince. She kept her face averted from the muse. "Nothing much. What was the curse? What did you see?"

"Nothing to concern yourself with. Show me the pieces."

Hippy went to him and held out the pieces on her palms. A slick of blood was painted across the largest of them.

"Put them together," Pierus said. "I don't dare let go of this filth while you bleed like that."

Hippy crouched and gently set the pieces on the floor. She played with them, fit them together until she found matching shapes. When she put the right ones together they melded almost seamlessly, leaving only hairline fissures. The last piece to go in was a shard the size of her little finger.

"Good," Pierus said. "Good girl. Now bring it here."

Badora jerked under his hands. "Don't do it, Fairy. Once you give him that thing, he'll never stop."

Hippy held up the Apple of Chaos. Pierus laid one hand on top of hers, careful not to touch the glass. "Keep hold of it," he said. "And close your eyes, Hippy. Think about Shadow. Think about home. Think about the battlefield. Hold it in your mind."

Hippy squeezed her eyes shut and thought about how very much she wanted to go home and see Ishtar and Mum and Dad and her brothers.

A crash at the door jarred her thoughts.

"Hippy! Don't do it!"

Her eyes flew open. Clockwork burst through the door, looking stricken. She swallowed a lump in her throat and wondered how it was possible to tell him she was sorry with just a look.

Clockwork ran toward them. "Don't go with him!" he yelled. "We'll find another way, I swear we will!"

She almost pulled away from Pierus and ran to him, but the muse king spoke one of those words that sounded very bad. The very air around them ripped open. For a split second Hippy could see Clockwork reaching out for her, and at the same time, hear cries of battle in a night lit by flames.

Then the rip was gone and they were in the middle of a darkened battlefield. All around them fairies and muses engaged in pitched battles with vamps. Vamp hordes bellowed in the distance. Flames roared from the shattered fortifications and the night bled with fear and death.

Pierus reached out and grabbed a passing muse by the back of the shirt.

The muse skidded to a halt, his eyes wide and frightened. "My king! We thought you killed!"

"Fool. Would you be here to fight if I were dead?"

"N-No, my king."

Pierus thrust the prisoner at him. "This is the vampire king. See he is secured, then send me Flower, if she lives." He paused. His voice imperceptibly hardened. "And Nikifor."

"Yes, my king." The muse hauled Rustam Badora away.

"Now my dear, we put an end to this." Pierus pulled Hippy close. Once more they placed their hands around the Apple of Chaos.

"What do we do?" The Apple grew warm under her skin. The cuts on her hand tingled. The lights swirled.

"Think of a light," Pierus said. "The brightest light you've ever seen. Think of the sun rising at midnight and driving every vampire back into the Darkness where they belong. Keep this image in your mind and do not waver. Do not resist what you feel, for this is where we must truly work as one."

Hippy felt a momentary dizzying fear when a memory of a kiss where the life had seemed sucked from her soul flashed through her mind.

"No," Pierus said. His free hand curled around the side of her face. "You must not block me, Hippy, not now. You must give yourself into my hands as you did once already tonight."

That just wasn't fair, bringing that up. Hippy squeezed her eyes shut. The battle raged around them. The fingers on her face weighed like lead. Alien images flickered past her mind's eye. She saw the Acropolis again, but it was whole and sparkling and new. She saw people she didn't know, a world in the grip of night and terror, muses, so many muses. She saw a green-haired woman who looked like her, only older, embracing Nikifor. Pierus lay lifeless at their feet.

Fear darted through her body like lightning.

"Now." Pierus's fingers tightened their grip and he raised the Apple above their heads. "Now Hippy, the light!"

Hippy reined in her wandering concentration and imagined the sun bursting out of the ground beneath their feet. Then her mind was no longer her own and all she could see was light.

She opened her eyes. Blazing gold light streamed from the Apple of Chaos between their hands in living, pulsing waves. The light exploded through the battlefield, making the night brighter than the sun. Fairies and muses shielded their eyes, stunned. The vamps who did not flee the light burned to ashes where they stood.

Pierus and Hippy walked together across the battlefield, holding the Apple of Chaos high. The light grew stronger and stronger. The remains of the vast vamp army turned tail and ran. The light burned brighter and brighter until she could no longer see the vamp army or even her own hands. The Apple burned her skin. The energy that had rushed her body when she started flowed back into this thing of power she held. Her tingling blood turned sluggish and cold. Her fingertips and toes iced over. She shivered uncontrollably, but still the hand glued to the Apple burned and still Pierus did not let up. Her lips were cold. She felt so tired. The light enfolded her like a blanket. Somewhere in the back of her mind a warning stirred. She struggled to catch hold of it. Clockwork. She hung onto a picture of Clockwork, the last thread she had.

With an effort of will, Hippy tore her hands away from the Apple of Chaos. The moment she did so Pierus dropped it. The light flooded back into the orb, leaving the battleground in darkness. She swayed back and forth like a flower stalk in the breeze. Fluffy Ducky scuttled out of his pouch, up over her hand and arm and leaped down to the Apple. There he sat, every hair standing on end, all eight eyes glaring at Pierus. He gathered himself to leap again.

Pierus cringed. "You still have that dreadful spider? Get it off!"

She was beyond caring. She collapsed at his feet.

The grass was damp and fresh and smelled faintly of blood. Hippy blinked. She had fully expected to pass out or fall asleep. Maybe she had. Fluffy Ducky was nose to nose with her, firelight reflected in his eight eyes. The light disappeared and came back again when he blinked. She blinked back. Sleep pressed her into the ground like a huge, heavy blanket. She wiggled her fingers. Even that was an effort, but it was enough for Fluffy Ducky to scuttle onto her hand.

"Hippy? Hippy, I'm sorry, I got carried away. I forgot about the backlash." Pierus's voice sounded as though it were coming from underwater.

Hippy's skin crawled when he touched her. She made a half-hearted effort to fend him off, but her limbs were like stones. She lay in his arms like a raggedy doll when he lifted her off the ground.

His voice was closer now, but still distorted. "Hippy? No, stay with me, I can fix you, but you must stay open to me." His hand feverishly searched her face.

Hippy turned her head to try and escape the hand. Lights approached. Fire on sticks. Shiny, shiny fire. Flames danced and glinted off spear tips.

Pierus's hand stilled. Her head lolled.

A voice lashed out of the darkness. "What have you done to my daughter, Muse?"

The sound of that voice made her extraordinarily, ridiculously happy, but her words only came out in a croak. "Dad?"

Pierus's hold tightened. "There's nothing wrong with her," he said. "Nothing I cannot fix. Let us pass."

"There's plenty wrong," Leaf said. "First she got dropped on her head as a kid, then she went off with you. There's so many levels of wrong there I can't even count them."

"We just saved your entire miserable tribe." Pierus's voice was low and venomous. "You'd all be dead now if she hadn't agreed to help me."

"And that's possibly the only reason we don't dispatch you right now," Leaf said. "Ishtar, Rain, take her home."

Relief. Relief washed through her whole body. Hippy glimpsed the circle of spears surrounding Pierus, the savagery in the dear, familiar faces. Then her sister and brother took her from the muse and put her arms around each of their shoulders. She slumped forward. Even her brain felt heavy.

"Hippy," Pierus said behind her. "Hippy don't go."

"Get me away from him," she whispered.

Ishtar and Rain moved fast. Her feet barely hit the ground. The fairies moved from their circle and fell into a phalanx around her.

"I'll come for you," Pierus said.

"Over my dead body," Ishtar hissed in her ear.

Hippy closed her eyes. Only now could she give herself up to blissful sleep.

Now she was safe.

CHAPTER TWENTY-SEVEN

"Why's she all covered in blood? She hates blood."

"I don't know, Mum. I think it's her own. Look, she cut her hand."

"So she did. Pack some spider webs into that, would you?"

"Alright. Have we got any fresh ones? Wait, what's that?"

A silence.

"She got bit," Willow said.

Ishtar said a lot of bad words.

"Ishtar Ishtar, don't you use language like that!"

"Mum she never got bit in her life! How'd she let something like that happen?"

"Just clean it out and make sure there's no poison in there. You never know where those vamps have been. I'm going to use that muse king's head for a soup bowl if I catch him back here again."

"I don't understand what's wrong with her. Why's she blue like that? Why won't she wake up?"

A series of light slaps stung her wrists.

"Stop it, Ishtar. She's just exhausted is all. Who knows what that muse did to her?"

"If you're going to use his head for a soup bowl, does that mean we can't stick it on a spike on the gate?"

Willow chuckled. "You're right. It'd be better if he had two heads."

Hippy sighed and drifted deeper into sleep. The conversation made her feel safe. Her fingers and toes were still cold, but the rest of her body was pleasantly warm.

Pictures formed behind her eyes, images so vivid she wondered if this were real and her sister and mother the dream.

She stood under a tree with Nikifor and a fairy that looked like her, except taller and with green hair. She carried an odd sort of weapon, a wooden stick that was curved at one end. There was blood on her face. Nikifor wiped away the stain with a gentle touch and she looked at him like he was the only man in Shadow.

Something disturbed Hippy about this fairy. Something about the eyes. She was fairy all over, but she had Pierus's eyes.

The fairy looked at her. "I'm coming, Mum."

Hippy sat bolt upright, big-eyed and sweating. Her breath came short and fast. The room was dark and close. "No," she whispered. "No no no no no no no. Anything but that."

"Hippy?" Ishtar's voice was sleepy. She got up off a pallet on the floor and lit a gas lamp.

Hippy stared at her for a full minute before her brain would work. The walls were black and the room smelled of old smoke. A hole in the roof, hastily thatched, let a cold breeze in. She shivered. "Ishtar?"

"Yeah. It's me." Ishtar's voice had an edge. "Lie down. Mum said you had to sleep."

"I can't." Hippy grabbed her sister's hands and dragged her towards the raised pallet she lay on. "No. I'm never going to sleep again. It was horrible."

"What was horrible?"

The words spilled out before she could stop them. "I just had the dream."

"The dream? What dream?"

Hippy gave Ishtar a look.

Ishtar's eyes widened. "*The* dream? The baby dream?"

Hippy nodded.

Ishtar said an extremely bad word, stormed over to the wall and punched it. Burned wood crumbled under her fist, leaving a jagged hole. She stormed back to Hippy. "I can't believe you!" she hissed. "What are you thinking? What *were* you thinking? It was him, wasn't it? The muse king?"

Hippy gave a single miserable nod.

"You're going to be in so much trouble."

"Going to be? I already am!" Hippy buried her face in her hands.

Ishtar sat on the bed beside her. "What happened? And when?"

"It was only earlier today." The words sounded as miserable as she felt. "I was fighting Rustam Badora and he got the better of me. Pierus pulled him away and then we went into this room and he said–he said–" she sniffed. "He said I had to prove I was with him only, or something, and that I hadn't betrayed him with Clockwork-"

"Who's Clockwork?"

"Nobody." Hippy looked sidelong at her sister. "It just happened. What am I going to do? What's he going to say?"

"Say? I don't give a bearfly's backside what he says." Ishtar strode up and down the room, fists clenched. "Of all the stupid things you could have done! I told you this would happen, didn't I? I warned you! You could have stayed here and fought vamps and been safe, but instead you go off and get yourself pregnant to the muse king!" She whirled back to Hippy. "He manipulated you into this. I hope you see that. I hope you're over your little crush now, even if the damage is already done."

"Crush?" Hippy shuddered. She wrapped the blanket around herself. "I don't ever want to see him again. Even though I have to."

"You don't have to do anything you don't want to. I'll kill him. I swear I'll kill him. He'd look good impaled on the gates of the camp. When we rebuild them."

Hippy watched Ishtar's furious movements. She blinked back the urge to bawl her eyes out, because Ishtar would tease her mercilessly about it for days, no matter how mad she was right now. "It's not going to be that easy."

Ishtar gave her a sharp look. "What do you mean by that?"

"I mean there's more to this than just you or me. There were these Freakin Fairies-"

Ishtar snatched up a spear from the floor. "Freakin fairies? Where?"

Hippy sighed. "In Dream."

"There are Freakin Fairies in Dream? Did you fight them? You'd better have fought them."

Hippy groaned, buried her face in the pillow and pulled the blanket over her head. "How did I make things such a mess?"

Ishtar dropped the spear, approached the bed and patted her awkwardly on the shoulder. "Look, it was bound to happen, what with you being dropped on your head and all. Just go to sleep. I'm sure when we tell Dad in the morning, he'll understand."

The lines on Leaf Ishtar's face were so deep his face looked cracked in the early morning light. "I don't understand," he said.

Hippy took a deep breath to compose herself. She'd woken up feeling much better, but having to face the elders first thing in the morning wasn't much fun. She was appalled so many of them were missing. "I'm pregnant," she repeated.

The fairies closest to her inched away.

Hippy scowled. "It's only been a day, you don't have to duck and cover yet."

"A day, you say?" Leaf looked over at Willow and rubbed his forehead. "Is it just me or is that a little too much information from our youngest daughter?"

Willow folded her arms and glared in the general direction of the muse camp, which could be clearly seen, since there were no walls left around the fairy camp. She was apparently too furious to say anything at all.

"Are you sure?" There was a hint of desperation in Leaf's voice.

"Of course she's sure," Willow snapped. "She had the dream. Ishtar told me. Every fairy has the dream the first night."

"I know, I know." Leaf sat heavily on the nearest stump. The other elders shifted and avoided both his and Hippy's eyes. "What were you thinking?"

Hippy shrugged and studied her feet with great intensity. She really hadn't thought this through. She couldn't tell her father she intended to go with Pierus on the orders of a Freakin Fairy to prevent him from turning Shadow into some kind of nightmare nobody had yet explained to her. She couldn't tell him how much the thought terrified her. She couldn't even tell him how much she wanted to stay, bury herself here and try to figure out what it meant to be carrying a child who would be neither muse nor fairy, but something of both.

As though reading her thoughts, one of the elders spoke up. "What of the child? It can't stay here. It's not really a Bloody Fairy."

Hippy clenched her fists. "*She* is too a Bloody Fairy, and *she* will go wherever I say she goes!"

Leaf shook his head. "I'm sorry Hippy, but it's true. We have never had the child of a muse and a fairy here. As for a fairy who wilfully ran off with a muse and allowed him to get her with child— how can we allow you to stay?"

He might as well have slapped her in the face. Hippy swallowed hard to keep herself from bursting into tears. "Dad? What are you saying?"

Ishtar, who had been sitting at the edge of the gathering, leaped to her feet. "No." Her voice was low and angry, but it rose with each word. "This isn't right, you know it isn't. It's not her fault. He tricked her. You know she's got the brains of a box of bearfly droppings, she was easy pickings for him! He was up to something, he had to be, and he used her!"

"If that is true, perhaps there is a way," Leaf said.

Another elder cleared his throat. "If your daughter was to repudiate any and all loyalty to the muse king and agree to give the child up to the muses once it was born, she might clear this mark on your family name. Otherwise she must leave and make her way on her own."

A vein throbbed on Leaf's forehead, but there was no other sign of emotion. He looked at Hippy. "Well?"

Hippy looked back at him, desolate. It would be so easy to repudiate Pierus. So easy. But give the child to the muses? Never. And the elders had just given her a way to go and carry out Mr Silver's orders, even though it hurt more than anything she'd ever done.

"Hippy tell them," Ishtar said. "Tell them what you told me. You don't care about him! You told us to get you away from him yesterday! For Shadow's sake, say something!"

Hippy glanced across to the muse camp. Three tall figures made their way across the divide. Even from this distance she recognised Pierus at their centre. Her heart was a stone and her stomach like lead. Her voice came out just as cold and heavy as the rest of her. "I will not repudiate my loyalty to the muse king. And I will not allow my child to be brought up by muses. She is a Bloody Fairy, whether you like it or not."

The silence was so taut it should have snapped and broken like a spring stretched too far. Every face turned away from her, except for Ishtar's, which burned with outrage.

"You've chosen your path," Leaf said. "You must walk it, girl. Get your things and go."

Hippy swallowed hard. She turned on her heel and went back to the battered hut she'd slept in every night since she was born, until the day she left for Dream.

"You can't do this!" Ishtar yelled behind her. "This is wrong, Dad! Can't you see she's hiding something? Why are you banishing her when she most needs our help? There are Freakin Fairies involved in this, she said so last night!"

Ishtar's voice faded when Hippy went into the hut. She went to her pallet, tied on her belt and made sure Fluffy Ducky was in there safe and sound. She put a comb into an empty pouch, but left everything else that was hers. She didn't know if she could bear to take any reminders of home to wherever Pierus intended they should go. She had to leave her childhood behind. Start a new and probably unpleasant life with the muse king. Not think about Clockwork, ever.

A tear trickled from one eye.

Ishtar burst into the hut. "Hippy, please," she said. "Think about what you're doing!"

Hippy grabbed her around the neck and hugged her. "I'm sorry," she said. "But I have to. I hope you'll understand one day."

Ishtar pushed her away. "Make me understand now."

"I can't." Hippy raked her hair out of her face and pinned it back.

"But he's going to kill you! You were half dead already last night!"

Hippy shook her head. "Don't worry about me. I know what I'm doing."

Ishtar stalked across the hut and opened a chest. "No you don't. You've no more sense than a bearfly in winter, Hippy Ishtar, and you're going to get yourself killed. But if you insist on going, take these." She piled several bags into a rucksack and thrust it into Hippy's hands. "Fairy dust, you'll need that. White kelsite, green skink juice, meteorite powder, bearfly whiskers, a vial of choking syrup, be careful with that. You can put it in his breakfast when he makes you cross."

Hippy strapped the rucksack across her back. She didn't know what to say. She sniffed. "You're giving me your choking syrup?"

"I can't exactly use it on anyone around here." Ishtar shuffled her feet. "If things get too much, find a way to send me word. I'll be there faster than you can make a vamp sparkle."

"I'll miss you." Hippy gave her sister one more fierce hug. Then she hurried from the hut before she changed her mind and stayed.

Outside she slowed. The elders stood and parted into two groups. They bore silent witness when she walked through them, head high, eyes fixed on the three muses waiting for her outside the camp.

Willow planted herself in Hippy's path and embraced her. "Look after yourself, daughter," she whispered in her ear. Then she let her go and rejoined the elders.

Hippy looked around for her father, but he turned his face away.

"If it's any consolation," Willow said to nobody in particular,

"That muse king's going to get the worst of it, going off Shadow knows where with a pregnant fairy."

The elders started to snicker.

The sound followed Hippy from the camp.

CHAPTER TWENTY-EIGHT

Hippy didn't look over her shoulder, because she didn't want getting thrown out to be her last memory of her family. She fixed her gaze on Pierus instead. Fury coiled in her stomach. She clenched her jaw.

Flower put on a big welcoming smile, but it seemed forced. There was a new scar on Nikifor's cheekbone and a tremor in his fingers. Pierus looked fresh and groomed, as though he'd spent the last week resting instead of fighting, except for one little detail. Hippy stared. A whole lock of his hair had turned so white it seemed a streak of light rippled from his temple to his shoulders.

He smiled like a man welcoming a long lost love home and reached out his hands. "Hippy," he said. "I was afraid they would keep you."

"Keep me?" Hippy marched up to him, balled her right fist and punched him in the stomach. "I just got banished because of you!"

Pierus doubled over from the unexpected blow. "What?"

She shoved him. "Don't even talk to me right now!" She turned her back on him and headed for the muse camp.

Flower ran to catch up with her. "Hippy? What's going on?"

Hippy gave her a sidelong glance. She sighed. She couldn't be mad at Flower just for being a muse. "I'm glad you didn't get killed."

"So am I." Flower put an arm around her shoulder and matched her pace. They left Pierus and Nikifor behind. "I probably would have if it wasn't for Nikifor. None of us would even be here. You should have seen it, Hippy. The night you and Pierus left he held back the entire attack almost single-handed. I've never seen anyone kill so many vampires in one night. It was like his father had returned to defend us all again."

Hippy tried to remember that night. It was a relief to think about something other than her own problems. "Really? I thought he was afraid."

Flower shrugged. "He got over it. The vampires swarmed on us every night and every night we held them back, but only just, because of him. I think last night we would have been overwhelmed, but then you and Pierus came back with that light. I was so proud of you."

"Proud of me?" Hippy couldn't help her words sounding bitter.

"Of course. It must have taken a great deal of courage to go to Dream and aid Pierus in his quest."

Hippy looked away.

Flower continued, her voice calm. "Your sister was afraid for you. I wasn't able to speak to your parents, the elders wouldn't allow any muses near the camp after you left. They were furious."

"They were right to be furious," Hippy said. "They were right about everything." She grasped Flower's hand and dragged her into an empty, raggedy tent when they reached the border of the muse camp, so they could speak privately. The words tumbled out. "Flower I'm pregnant. I don't know how to tell him. What's he going to say?"

Flower blinked. "Pregnant? Who to, Hippy?"

Hippy let out an explosive breath. "To Pierus of course!"

Flower let go of her hand and moved a step back. "What?"

Hippy stomped her foot. "You heard me!"

"I know, I heard you, I just-" Flower made a helpless gesture. "I don't get it. What happened? He's a muse, you're a fairy-"

"Well yes, I did notice that, as I was getting banished from my tribe. This is useless. I'm sorry I brought it up." She turned to go.

"No wait!" Flower grabbed her hand and pulled her back. "I'm the one who should be sorry, Hippy. I'm just a little shocked. At him, not you. I thought better of his intentions." A line marred her forehead. "Is that why you hit him?"

"One of many reasons."

"It puzzled me when he was so determined to take you with him rather than return you to your family. I understand now."

"Tell me what to do." Hippy glanced nervously over her shoulder. "How do I tell him?"

"Honey just tell him," Flower said. "You're not afraid, are you?"

Hippy opened her mouth, but couldn't find the words to explain to Flower exactly how terrified she was. Or what she had to do before it became obvious she was pregnant. If he knew anything about fairies at all he would guess by the end of the week, and she didn't even know what he'd done with the Apple of Chaos.

"Just tell him." Flower's voice was firm. "Everything will be fine. Pierus is a great king, I'm sure he'll be a wonderful father."

Hippy bit her tongue. She'd got so used to people who thought Pierus was an ass, as Poppy had so succinctly put it. She'd forgotten the muses worshipped the ground he walked on. She couldn't talk to Flower. She couldn't talk to anyone. She was completely on her own.

"Tell him," Flower repeated, as though she'd argued.

"Tell him what?" Pierus ducked his head to enter the tent at that moment.

"I'll leave you two to talk." Flower backed out and left.

Pierus looked down on Hippy as though she were an angry snake in a corner. "Are you quite finished hitting me?"

Hippy nodded. He took up all the space in the tent. She wanted to back away, but now was not the time to set a precedent like that. There was a horrible icky feeling in the pit of her stomach. What if Flower was right and he was a good king? What if Mr Silver was right and he was just all bad?

Pierus took her hand. His voice gentled. "They banished you?"

"They said I had to repudiate you or leave forever."

He gave a short, sharp laugh. "My, that's a big word for a pack of fairies."

Hippy moved away. "That's all you have to say? Maybe I'll go back and tell them I changed my mind!"

"I'm sorry." Pierus put a finger under her chin and lifted her face. "You did the right thing, my love. I will never forget that you chose me over your tribe. It means everything."

Hippy closed her eyes and rested her face in his hand. Surely Mr Silver was wrong. Surely a man who could look at her like that was good.

"You have something to tell me," he said.

Without opening her eyes, Hippy took his hand and guided it to her belly, where she laid it flat.

He was still and silent.

She opened her eyes to find him regarding her with a mixture of curiosity and something cold. It was not a comforting look.

"A child?"

"Yes."

"Are you quite sure? It's awfully soon to know."

"Fairies always know. We have a dream."

"I see."

"You've never encountered a pregnant fairy, have you?"

"My dear girl, I've made a habit of avoiding fairies for thousands of years, so no, I can't say I have."

Hippy scowled. "If that's all you've got to say, I'm going home."

"No, you're not." Pierus put an arm around her shoulder and guided her through the battered, torn camp toward his tent. "Don't you worry about a thing, my love, I'm going to look after you better than anyone else could."

"Really?" Hippy looked at him doubtfully. "Have you ever had a baby before?"

"I should think not. Always seemed like a dreadfully awkward process." Pierus pushed aside a tattered curtain and they walked into his tent. Inside was a shambles. He sighed. "What in Shadow happened in here?"

"I killed some vamps while you set up the door into Dream," Hippy said. "Remember? I smashed one in the head with that statue there, which was kind of fun. Then Rustam Badora came in." She paused. "What did you do with him?"

"He's in the Gulakh," Pierus said. "He'll never find his way out of there without my express permission."

Hippy shuddered. No fairy liked to hear about Shadow's most infamous prison, the Gulakh. Sometimes some of her cousins from the Feathertip tribe disappeared into that dark, cold place after assassinating the wrong people. Nobody ever heard from them again.

Pierus picked up the broken statue and set it on the nearest pedestal. "Tell me about this dream of yours."

Hippy kicked some rubble on the floor into a pile. "All fairies have the dream when they get pregnant," she said. "The child visits you."

"How do you know it's your child?"

"She called me Mum. It was pretty obvious."

"She?"

Something in Pierus's voice made Hippy stop and look over at him. She scowled. "Yeah, she. What about it?"

"What did she look like?"

Hippy studied his profile. Definitely. Definitely Mr Silver was right. She should find the Apple of Chaos, steal it and run. A dart of panic went through her. Run where? Mr Silver hadn't said what she should do after upsetting the most powerful muse in Shadow.

"Hippy?" his voice took on an edge. "What did she look like?"

"Who?"

"The girl."

"Girl? You mean our daughter?" Hippy picked a curtain up off the floor, considered it and dropped it again. Cleaning up really wasn't her thing. "She looked like any other fairy baby. Small. Fat." There, the lie rolled off her tongue as easy as that. She stepped around the curtain and poked at a head broken off a statue with her toe.

"What colour was her hair?"

Hippy glanced at him sidelong. Green. Her hair had been green. That hadn't struck her as all that strange in the dream, but now it did. Something about it bothered her. Something else she'd seen. "That's an odd question," she said. "Babies don't generally have hair."

"Of course not." Pierus picked up the spear she'd used to hold off Rustam Badora and propped it against one wall. He brushed debris from the table and neatly rolled up the map that still lay there. "My dear girl, perhaps you would be so good as to help me pack some of these things up, rather than picking them up and dropping them. We leave within two hours."

Hippy sighed. She'd known they'd be leaving. The muses wouldn't stay now the vamps were gone. She'd be far, far from her family for a long time. "Where are we going?"

"To my home."

"Where's that?"

"Beyond the forest."

Hippy paused in the act of prodding at a gas lamp to see if it would pack itself into something. "The forest?"

"Yes."

"I don't like the forest."

"Why?"

"It's all dark and full of trees."

"I thought fairies liked trees?"

"Yes, trees are fine, but forests are not."

Pierus took a deep, patient breath. "You will have nothing to fear in the forest. You will be with me."

"Well that's comforting. The forest people like you even less than they like fairies."

Pierus left his organising and moved across the tent. He put his hands on Hippy's shoulders, pushed her into a chair and stood over her. "I do believe the so-called Invisible Army filled your head with all sorts of fantastical stories while they had you under their sway." His voice was soft and just the tiniest bit menacing. He looked right into her eyes. Hippy couldn't tear herself away. She clenched her fists so tight her nails dug into her palms. Any moment she would be swept under by something she didn't understand, his voice, his eyes, the way everything dropped away until there was nothing left but darkness waiting to suck her in.

"You need to forget all that," Pierus said. "You're with me now, not them. You trust me, don't you?"

It was pretty hard to argue with that piercing glare. "I–I guess."

He dropped into a crouch and placed his hands on her wrists. "No. You don't guess. There is no room for uncertainty. If you are with me, then you trust me and you are guided by me. I am your protector. I am the one keeping you and the child safe. Do you understand?"

Hippy nodded.

"Tell me you trust me."

"I trust you." She gripped the edges of the chair so hard her knuckles turned white.

"Good girl." Pierus leaned in and brushed her lips with his. "Now go, before you break something. Find Nikifor and tell him to prepare for a journey." He moved back to the table and busied himself.

Hippy scrambled out of the chair, left the tent and gulped fresh air outside, ignoring the curious stares of the other muses, themselves all making ready to leave. She hurried across the camp and hid herself between two tents where she could be alone, then jumped up and down and madly brushed down her skin and clothes trying to rid herself of the icky feeling Pierus had just left her with.

It didn't work. She stopped, crouched and buried her head in her hands. Bad. He was definitely bad. She knew it because she knew if she hadn't fought what he just did with every fibre of her being, she'd have been swept under like a fish in a tidal wave. She had a horrible feeling it wasn't even the first time he'd done it to her.

She took a few deep breaths to calm herself and wondered if this was what Pandora had run away from.

CHAPTER TWENTY-NINE

Hippy sat on the back of a cart and watched the ruins of the fortifications dwindle into the distance. There went her family, her life, her home.

Behind her, Nikifor was piled under the big domed roof along with boxes and boxes of Pierus's things. His skin was the colour of the clouds overhead; if it hadn't been full daylight, she'd have taken him for a vamp. Pierus rode at the front, holding the reins of the two sleepy-looking donkeys pulling them along. The cart swayed on every bend and corner as though it would topple over and take them all with it.

She watched everything she knew disappear with dry eyes. Some little part of her had hoped the fairies would change their minds. Someone would come running after her and find a way to make her stay. But nobody had. Not one fairy even left the camp to wave goodbye. And why would they? She'd rejected them in favour of a muse.

She sniffed loudly. She'd been doing that ever since Pierus told her Flower wasn't coming with them, he needed her in Shadow City. The sound didn't seem to bother him though, sitting all the way up the other end of the cart.

She gave a disconsolate sigh. They slowly trundled around a bend, and the fortifications disappeared. There, home was gone. She may as well put it out of her mind.

They slowed to a crawl at a sharp corner. The cart tilted, then landed on all four wheels and rocked. The rutted road wound through the forest like a lost snake. The donkeys plodded on, unconcerned. The wheels turned up clods of mud and flung them out onto the road behind. Ancient fig trees with twisty branches and thick, whispering clusters of leaves pressed in on both sides of the track. Anyone might have been in those branches, watching. She'd have been a lot happier if she'd thought Fitz and Ana were lurking there this time.

A pebble hit the side of the cart and bounced up near her hand. She scowled and threw it onto the road. Stupid flying pebbles.

They trundled on. It must have been a whole five minutes by now since they'd entered the forest. She was bored. Nikifor was asleep and talking to Pierus was about as much fun as poking herself in the eye.

Hippy glanced over her shoulder, disinterested, at the sound of a knock from amongst the boxes. Nikifor had probably bumped something. Pierus certainly hadn't noticed.

Fluffy Ducky ran out of his pouch and up her arm. He settled on her head and rested there, quivering.

Hippy tried to look up at him and almost toppled herself over in the process. "Fluffy Ducky? What's the matter?"

Another knock, followed by a rattle.

Hippy crawled over to the covered section of the cart, shoved Nikifor's arm out of the way and studied the haphazard stacks of boxes.

Fluffy Ducky leaped from her head to the top box, scuttled down and came to rest on a small steel box tucked into a corner. It shook underneath him.

"What is it Fluffy Ducky?" she whispered.

The box shook again. Fluffy Ducky waved a foreleg at her.

Hippy reached out very, very, carefully and eased the box free of the pile. She glanced sidelong at Nikifor to make sure he was still asleep. A thin film of sweat covered his upper lip. Wow, he really looked sick.

Fluffy Ducky clung to the box. His hairs all stood on end.

Hippy ran her fingers around the edges until she found the catch. She pouted. It was padlocked.

The box shuddered so violently Fluffy Ducky was thrown off. The movement caused another package to slide off the top of the pile and hit Nikifor in the face.

Nikifor turned over, buried his head in his hands and snored.

Hippy suppressed a giggle. She took the tiniest bit of fairy dust from her belt and sprinkled it on the padlock. The metal sparkled, then turned to dust. The catch popped open.

The box was still. Fluffy Ducky waited, poised, on the pile above it.

Hippy opened it up. Her eyes widened. The box contained a severed hand, so white and veiny it could only have belonged to a vamp. The little finger twitched.

Fluffy Ducky pounced. The hand jumped two feet in the air, fingers splayed, and attempted to grab the spider. Fluffy Ducky twisted in mid-air, wrapped all eight legs around the index finger and chomped.

Hippy squealed with delight. "Go Fluffy Ducky!"

Nikifor sat bolt upright and stared around in panic. "Vampires!"

"It's a vampire hand!" Hippy clapped madly.

"What's going on back there?" Pierus pulled sharply on the reins.

"Fluffy Ducky's fighting a vamp hand!" Hippy jumped up and down with excitement. The cart rocked.

Nikifor put out his hands to steady himself. His gaze fixed on the wrestling spider and hand. "What fresh horror is this?" his voice cracked.

Pierus uttered a whole string of bad words he'd obviously picked up from Poppy, scrambled off his seat and into the cart. "Don't let it get into the sunlight!"

Hippy squealed a second time. "Fluffy Ducky it's allergic to light!"

The hand convulsed violently and flew from one wall to the other in an attempt to throw off the spider, at the same time evading Pierus's attempts to grab it. Nikifor pressed himself into a corner and watched the whole thing in horror-struck awe. Maybe this cart ride was going to be fun after all.

Pierus didn't sound happy. "Hippy Ishtar, if you don't control that spider I'm going to squash it. I need that hand."

Hippy pouted. "Fluffy Ducky come back!"

Fluffy Ducky stretched his legs out and wound them around a second finger, strapping the two fingers together. The hand went into a redoubled frenzy. It hit the walls, the roof, smashed into the pile of boxes and sent them tumbling all over the place.

Hippy shrugged when Pierus glared at her. "He's busy. He'll come back when the hand's dead."

A particularly nasty jolt shook the spider free. The hand took swift advantage by curling into a fist that knocked Fluffy Ducky flying.

"Fluffy Ducky!" Hippy ran after the spider, caught him and teetered on the edge of the cart. When she regained her balance she saw that Pierus had leaped on the hand and was struggling to subdue it.

"Nikifor the box!" the muse king snapped.

Nikifor picked up the discarded box and held it at arm's length. Pierus shoved the hand in there, closed the box, wound a hastily found chain around it and then put it inside a bigger box.

There was silence in the cart. Outside, a bird cackled. Leaves rustled in the forest.

"Why do you have a vamp hand?" Hippy asked.

Pierus breathed heavily from the exertion. His eyebrows gathered like storm clouds. "I need it," he said. "I need vampire genetics if I am to discover a way to keep them from returning."

"Why is it alive?"

"Because I preserved it with magic. Dead genetics are no good to me."

"What are genetics?"

"Enough questions." Pierus pushed his way past the boxes and Nikifor.

Hippy backed up, but there wasn't anywhere to go unless she jumped into the mud.

Pierus grabbed her shoulders and pulled her close. He looked into her eyes in that intense way he had. "You would do well to keep your hands to yourself, Fairy. Do not touch my things. Some of them are very dangerous."

Hippy scowled. It was rude of him to call her Fairy like that. She stroked Fluffy Ducky's back to calm him. "But I'm bored."

"Then I suggest you occupy yourself." He reached into a coat pocket and took something out. "Here. Perhaps this will amuse you." He opened his hand.

Hippy's eyes widened. There in his palm lay a shiny, shiny crystal in the shape of a teardrop.

Pierus dropped it into her hand. "Do try to behave yourself." Then he went back to his seat, picked up the reins and started the donkeys walking again.

Hippy resumed her seat. She held the crystal up and watched the sunlight play in all the tiny little facets. It was a very pretty little thing. It would normally keep her amused for hours, but something bothered her. Maybe it was the way she'd been so neatly manoeuvred into being a nice, cooperative, well-behaved little fairy.

She closed her hand over the crystal and twisted around. Pierus's back was to her. Nikifor sat amongst the boxes, awake, staring off into his own little world. Hippy threw the crystal at him. It bounced off his arm and fell amongst the boxes. He flinched, but otherwise didn't seem to notice.

She sighed and went back to watching the mud. It would have been so much better if Flower had come too.

A pebble hit the side of the cart and bounced off. A few seconds later another pebble hit her foot. That stung.

Hippy scowled and scanned the trees. Nobody there. If she thought for a second someone was throwing rocks at her, she was going to jump off this cart and throw fairy dust at them.

A small, round pebble hit her in the arm. When another one whizzed through the air, Hippy raised her hand and caught it. Right. That was it. She jumped off the back of the cart, pulled her feet out of the mud they promptly sank into, then dashed into the trees as soon as she was on firm ground.

The forest was green and close. She could just hear the donkeys plodding away down the road. Huge leaves slapped against wooden trunks. A big black and white bird landed in a branch and made a noise like a rusty hinge.

"Right," Hippy said. "Whoever you are, you'd better come out right now and tell me why you're throwing rocks at me!"

Silence. A shadow flitted behind a tree. Yet another pebble flew through the air and bounced off her forehead.

"Ow! That's it, you're for it now!" Hippy bolted after the shadow.

The shadow darted from tree to tree, keeping just ahead of her. Hippy kept on it, determined, even though whoever it was disappeared every time she got close enough to reach out and grab hold.

Only when she realised they'd gone a long way into the forest did she stop. The figure had disappeared.

Hippy turned in a slow circle. Trees everywhere. The undergrowth was thick with spindly plants with little white flowers. She wasn't sure which way led back to the road. If the forest people caught her alone out here they might do anything. Fairies weren't supposed to stray this far into the forest. She gulped.

Twigs crunched. A rush of air. Someone knocked her to the ground. Hippy balled a fist and launched it, but she stopped an inch before making contact with her attacker's face. Her eyes widened when she saw who'd landed on top of her. "Clockwork!"

He didn't look the least bit happy to see her. "Yeah, it's me. Surprised?"

"You shouldn't have come." Hippy studied every detail of his face, from the little cut under his eye to the dreadlock that was plastered to his cheek with sweat. "How did you get here?"

"I followed you through the door Pierus opened. I've been following you ever since." Clockwork reached a hand toward her face. It trembled. He snatched it away before he touched her. "Maybe I shouldn't have. I don't understand. What are you doing with the pretender? I thought you liked me."

Hippy reached up and brushed the dreadlock away from his face. She blinked back tears. "This is bigger than just you and me. I'm sorry Clockwork, but–but something happened and it's too late to go back now."

"What happened?" Lines of confusion marred his smooth forehead. "I need to know Hippy, because I left my dad behind to follow you here. I thought you'd come back with me if I rescued you."

Clockwork was the last person she wanted to tell. Her cheeks burned. She looked away.

"What is it?" This time he did touch her face and his voice was so concerned she almost let a tear escape.

"It's complicated."

"Tell me."

Hippy took a deep breath. "Promise me you won't be mad?"

"Why? What have you done?" Clockwork slid off her, sat on the damp ground and helped her into a sitting position.

Hippy poked at the grass. "The thing is, your dad said I should go with Pierus if he took the Apple of Chaos, because somebody would have to take it from him again. He said I was the only one who could do it."

A grin blossomed on Clockwork's face. "Then you don't like him better than me?"

"Of course not! He's an ass, just like Poppy said."

The grin dropped from his face just as quickly. "What do you mean my dad said you should do this?"

"He said the future of Shadow could depend on it," Hippy said. "And he made me promise not to tell you."

"Not to tell me? Why?" Clockwork's lower lip trembled. "Why you?"

"Because–because he thinks–" Hippy gestured in the direction she thought the road might lie, then dropped her hand. "Please don't be mad, if we weren't mixed up in all this I would never have let him do it. At least I don't think I would have, I can hardly remember how it happened, except I had to prove to him I was loyal, so I could take back the Apple of Chaos later–I'm sorry–"

Clockwork laid his hand over hers, his eyes wide. "What? What did he do?"

"He made me pregnant," Hippy whispered. Her hand went involuntarily to her belly. "I'm sorry. But now you know why it's so complicated."

Clockwork stood up. He walked to the nearest tree, balled a fist and punched it. Then he leaned his forehead against the trunk. "Why in Shadow would my father send *you* up against *him*?"

"Because I can get close to him." Hippy rose to her feet.

"But you don't even know what you're doing!" Clockwork burst out. "You're no match for him on your own! And pregnant? No. You just can't. I'm taking you back to Dream, Dad will just have to send someone else!"

Hippy marched up to Clockwork and slapped him across the face. "No!" She put her hands on her hips and glared. "Don't even start on that rubbish, Clockwork Silver. I haven't come this far just to turn back. I didn't get banished by my family and put up with Pierus being so mean for all this time just to be told I'm not good enough! People have been saying that all my life, and you know what? I don't give a bearfly's butt cheek what you all think of me. This is my battle now and I intend to fight it, pregnant or not. You can either help me or you can go back to Dream, that's totally up to you, but I will not be told I'm not good enough!" She stopped, panting for breath.

Clockwork inched back into the tree. "Oops," he said. "I forgot about pregnant fairies."

"Don't you pregnant fairy me."

"I'm sorry." Clockwork let out a long breath. "I just wish it was different."

"So do I." Hippy held out her hands. "Maybe when all this is over it can be."

He moved cautiously forward and held her hands. "Maybe."

Hippy flung herself on him and buried her face in his shoulder. "I lied. I do care what you do. Please stay close, however you can manage it, I can't stand to think I'm all alone with him. I don't even know where we're going."

Clockwork put his arms around her shoulders and stroked her hair. "I promise," he said. "I'll be close, no matter what."

CHAPTER THIRTY

Hippy and Clockwork had outrun the donkeys strapped to the laden cart, got a good way ahead and climbed a tree to wait without even breaking a sweat. The vehicle swayed like a ship in a storm down the road below them.

Clockwork watched the cart like it was full of poisonous snakes. "I suppose there's nothing I can say to make you reconsider."

Hippy shook her head and eyed the donkeys. She had to time the jump just right.

"I'll find a way to see you once you get where you're going," he said. "I'll never be far."

"Be careful. Watch out for forest people." Hippy squeezed his hand, kissed him on the cheek and then leaped off the branch.

She rushed through the air. The cart trundled closer. Damn! She was off by half a cart's length.

She landed evenly on both feet on the bench seat right next to Pierus.

Pierus started violently and jerked on the reins. The donkeys broke into a clumsy trot, causing the cart to teeter to one side. A wheel hit a rut too fast, bounced off it and veered to the side.

Pierus pulled up hard. The donkeys made grunts that sounded distinctly like swear words. The cart shuddered to a halt. "Nikifor check for damage!"

Nikifor slid off the cart and went to look at the wheels.

The muse king gave Hippy a lethal look. "What are you doing?"

Hippy returned a sunny smile. She patted her belt. "Fluffy Ducky ran away after his fight with that big mean vamp hand of yours, so I had to go find him. I just got back."

Pierus looked startled. "You left the cart?"

She nodded.

"You went into the forest?"

"He does like to climb trees."

"On your own?"

"I'm hardly on my own if Fluffy Ducky's around."

"That spider has got to go."

Hippy scowled. "Touch my Fluffy Ducky and I'll kill your vamp hand."

"My king," Nikifor said from beside the wheel. "There is no damage, but I suggest we resume moving immediately." He climbed back onto the cart.

Pierus scanned the road, made a clicking noise with his tongue and started the donkeys moving again. "Hippy," he said. "Sit down."

Hippy pouted. She'd been enjoying balancing on the seat while the cart moved, and besides, it gave her a good view of the treetop where she could still see Clockwork watching them go. "But I like it up here."

"Sit." Pierus curled a hand around her arm and yanked her down next to him.

Hippy landed hard on her rear end on the wooden seat. "Ow!"

"You're going to learn to do as you're told if it kills you." Pierus said this with a pleasant smile on his face that struck Hippy as odd, until she realised they weren't alone. Her eyes widened. Forest people emerged from the trees everywhere she looked. They didn't step onto the road; they just stood and watched. Their hair and clothes were tangled with leaves. Their hooves were caked with moss and mud. Every single one of them was armed with a crossbow or an axe.

"You see my dear, I have only your best interests at heart when I give you an order," Pierus said, still with that pleasant smile on his face. "You make far too easy a target standing up there."

They trundled on down the road at what seemed a snail's pace. The further they went, the more forest people appeared from the trees.

"Are they going to attack us?" Hippy whispered.

"Only if we stop in their territory or venture into the forest without their permission."

"Do they know you're the muse king?"

"Of course they do. They know I live beyond their forest. We have a treaty, of course. They leave me alone. I return the favour."

Hippy gave a disconsolate sigh. "I miss Poppy."

"That dreadful woman? Why?"

"She made long rides like this interesting. How come you haven't got a car? There are cars in Shadow City."

"Because there is not enough silver in Shadow to run a car further than a short distance."

Hippy flinched. "Silver?"

"My, you are a provincial little creature, aren't you? Fairies really need to educate their children."

"Hey! I learned my pictograms."

"Pictograms?" He snorted. "Cars, my dear, need fuel to get anywhere, and that fuel is liquid silver. Which of course is so jealously guarded by your dear friends the Freakin Fairies that nobody can run a car outside of the city for fear of running out of fuel."

"I didn't know that."

"Of course you didn't. You'll find you don't know most things about your world, which is why you need to pay attention to what I tell you. First and foremost, between now and when we arrive home, do not leave the cart without my permission. The forest is dangerous for little pregnant fairies."

Hippy shrugged. "If you say so." She eyed the forest people. "But the cart is boring."

"Didn't I give you a nice shiny crystal to play with?"

"I'm not a child, Pierus."

"Yes you are. Your entire species is juvenile and distractible and has the combined intellect of a moth colony."

Hippy stared at him, stricken. "Yeah? Well you've got a face like a moth-eaten cabbage."

"What did you do with the crystal, Hippy?"

"I threw it at Nikifor." Hippy swung her legs over the seat and into the interior of the cart. "If this is how you talked to Pandora, no wonder she left you."

Pierus curled his fingers around her arm before she could move further away. He never took his eyes off the road. "Don't leave the cart under any circumstances."

Hippy made a face at him, pulled away and clambered over the pile of boxes. She scowled at Nikifor until he looked away, then threw herself onto her stomach at the back of the cart, where she could happily glower at the diminishing forms of the forest people until they were out of sight.

Hippy woke with a start from a very pleasant dream about Pierus punching himself in the head. She smiled sleepily and laid her cheek against the wood of the cart. The forest trundled by. No forest people to be seen. It was late afternoon, judging by the mellowing of the light. The road surface had hardened up, making the ride smoother.

Something sparkled in the trees.

She sat up and leaned over the side of the cart. There, it sparkled again. Wow. She'd never seen anything quite so shiny. She looked over her shoulder. Nikifor was asleep and Pierus had his back to her.

Don't leave the cart, he'd said.

Shiny white light sparkled through the trees.

Hippy glanced over her shoulder once more. Then back into the forest. The shiny light had a sprinkle of blue in it.

Blue *was* one of her favourite colours.

Hippy leaped off the cart, landed on the road and bolted into the trees. Nikifor yelled out almost as soon as she'd gone and the cart lurched to a halt.

Hippy tiptoed toward the shiny thing bouncing up and down in a low tree branch. When she got closer, she pulled the leaves out of the way so she could see what it was. Her eyes widened when she found a little glowing creature struggling on the branch. At first she thought it was a dragon, but it was no bigger than her forearm, and everyone knew dragons were at least as big as donkeys. Besides, its face was rounder and it had little pointed ears and weird, featherless wings. Its claw was tangled in a thorny plant growing up the tree. Drops of blood stained the bark.

"Oh, you poor thing." Hippy ignored the heavy footsteps in the foliage behind her and reached slowly for the trapped claw.

The creature looked up at her with big, sad eyes and made a little whining noise.

Nikifor's hand landed on her shoulder. "I'm sorry Hippy, but you must return to the cart."

She turned on her heel, balled a fist and punched him in the stomach. Nikifor doubled over and apparently lost all his wind, because his next attempt to speak didn't work.

"Not until I've rescued the shiny thing." She returned to the trapped creature, gently prised the thorns away from its foot and removed one thorn from the pad altogether. The creature sent up a thin howl.

"There, it's okay, you're free now." Hippy lifted it off the branch and held it up. "Fly away."

The creature stretched its wings. It lifted off her hand, flapped the wings once and made an ungainly leap for her shoulder. When it landed there it nuzzled her neck.

Hippy giggled. "What are you doing?"

Nikifor, who had got his wind back, approached her more cautiously this time. "Please Hippy, Pierus said you must return to the cart at once."

Hippy shrugged. "So?" She headed for the road while giving the creature her hand to sniff. It nibbled at her fingertips with a hooked beak. "Are you hungry, little fella? Are you a boy or a girl?"

"She's a girl, and what we call a fetch," Nikifor said.

Hippy glanced over her shoulder. The muse blocked any path back into the forest. "A fetch?"

"They're very rare. Unless you travel to the mountains where nobody lives and find a colony."

"Well, you're very pretty. I think I'll call you Fangs," Hippy said.

"You call your killer spider Fluffy Ducky and a harmless shiny fetch Fangs?" Nikifor herded her down to the road.

"Yeah. So what?" Hippy sighed when she saw Pierus leaning against the back of the cart waiting for them.

"I thought I told you to watch her," Pierus said, the moment they were in earshot.

"I'm sorry my king," Nikifor said. "She's fast."

"Bring her here."

"Touch me and I'll break your teeth." Hippy marched across the road, pulled herself onto the edge of the cart, sat there and gave Pierus an enquiring look. "Well?"

"I told you not to leave the cart."

"But I saw something shiny."

Pierus went to speak, changed his mind and rubbed his forehead instead. "Bloody Fairies," he said. "What is that on your shoulder?"

"The shiny thing."

"Forget I asked." He turned to walk away, then came back and put his hands on either side of her face. "What do I have to do to make you behave?"

Fangs stretched her leg out, hooked her claws and stabbed Pierus in the back of the hand.

He yelled and snatched his hand away.

Hippy giggled. "Pregnant fairies don't behave for anyone.

Weren't you warned?"

Pierus took a step away from her. He rubbed the wound on his hand and looked like he was working up some very nasty words.

Hippy gave a big, insolent yawn. Finally, this trip was starting to be fun again. "Are we there yet?"

CHAPTER THIRTY-ONE

The hooting didn't bother her. For as long as Hippy could remember, she'd lain awake in her bed in the darkest, most silent hours of the night and listened to the Thump Owls' night conversations.

It was the screeching she didn't like. She'd never heard a bird make that noise. The regular tap-tap-tapping in the tree tops that followed the cart along the road also made the hairs stand up on the back of her neck. She told herself not to be afraid. There would be no more vamp attacks for a very long time. Nothing in the forest would harm her.

She lay on her stomach with a gas lamp set beside her. The light it shed only went as far as the edge of the cart, making the road and trees around them all the darker. They trundled on. Pierus had decided they should travel through the night rather than camp in unfriendly territory.

Fangs made a pretty bluish glow by her left hand. Her scales glittered and glowed in the gaslight like they were made of fairy dust.

Fluffy Ducky sat by her right hand. Hippy had been trying to introduce them all day and this was the closest she'd gotten, after finally convincing Fluffy Ducky it wasn't nice to attack fetches. Fluffy Ducky's hairs were still on end and occasionally he trembled and gave Fangs an eight-eyed glare. Fangs returned the glares with withering glances and spent the rest of the time cleaning her scales with the tip of her beak.

After a while Nikifor joined her. Hippy made room for him, but didn't look away from Fangs and Fluffy Ducky.

Nikifor sat cross-legged next to her and handed her a chunk of bread and cheese. "Here," he said. "You must be hungry."

Hippy scrambled into a sitting position so fast both Fangs and Fluffy Ducky jumped, bringing them a quarter of an inch closer together. "Starving." She tore into the bread.

Nikifor studied Fangs and Fluffy Ducky. "Are they making friends?"

Hippy shrugged. "They're not trying to kill each other. It's a good start." She glanced over her shoulder, but could not see Pierus in the dark. "Is he really going to stay awake all night up there?"

"He sleeps where he is. The donkeys know where to go and you and I will alert him to any danger." Nikifor followed the direction of her gaze. "May I ask you a question? Without you hitting me?"

Hippy giggled. "Sorry about that. Ask away. I promise I won't hurt you."

"Why are you here?"

The question was so direct it took Hippy by surprise. She considered what to say. "I had nowhere else to go," she finally replied. "My tribe will not raise the child of a muse."

"Child?" Nikifor let out an explosive breath. "So it's true."

"Of course it's true. Why'd you think I was so cranky?"

He chuckled. "I had presumed it was your disposition."

Hippy beamed. "That's so sweet!"

There was silence. The darkness rolled by. Nikifor stared into the night and appeared to forget she was there.

Hippy stroked Fangs on the back, then Fluffy Ducky too, so he didn't feel left out. She jumped when Nikifor spoke again.

"Why do you make him angry?"

"Huh? Who?"

"The king. Why do you set out to make him angry?"

"Oh. Why not?" Hippy scratched Fluffy Ducky's head. "He's an ass."

Nikifor's voice was soft and shocked. "You must speak of the king with respect!"

"Why?"

"Because he's the king."

"He's not my king." Hippy gave Nikifor an enquiring look. "Has he always been an ass?"

Nikifor raked hair out of his face. "You must understand the king has greater wisdom and knowledge than any of us, and everything he does is in the best interests of Shadow."

"Really." Hippy could hardly keep the skepticism out of her voice. "Does he continually insult my people in the best interests of Shadow?"

"It's not always easy to understand or accept what he does,"

Nikifor said. "But believe me, it is all for a purpose. He sees much further than you or I."

She scowled. "What are you trying to say?"

"I'm trying to tell you to trust him. Things will be much easier on you if you do."

"If I do what? Fall into line? Jump every time he opens his mouth, like you muses do?" Hippy leaned closer to Nikifor and looked up at him. "It's more fun making him mad."

"I'm only trying to help." Nikifor sighed and leaned his arms on his knees.

Hippy looked at him sidelong. She hadn't meant to upset him. Nikifor wasn't that bad, for a muse. "Flower said you held off the vamps almost single-handed."

He sighed a second time and buried his face in his arms.

"She said if it wasn't for you, everyone would have died," she persisted. "What happened? You were so scared the night we left."

"My king helped me." His voice was muffled against his arms.

"Helped you how?" Hippy thought back to the chaos of the night they'd left Shadow. Pierus had given Nikifor a drink and sent him on his way. She'd thought nothing more of it. "Was it that green stuff? You argued with him about that. You didn't trust him then."

"But I should have," Nikifor said. "He was right. It overcame my fear and I held off the vampires. That's all that mattered. The results were more important than the consequences. And I will conquer this."

"Consequences?" Hippy surveyed Nikifor in the lamplight. His hands trembled, even though he'd clamped them tightly together. "What was that stuff?"

"Sometimes I think I see signs of the king's madness returning." Nikifor's voice was so low she had to strain to hear. "But it cannot be. The death of so many millions of humans sent a shockwave through Shadow. Every muse felt it, him more than any other, because he caused it. He inspired that bomb. He went away for a long time." Nikifor's breath was ragged. The silence stretched out into the night.

"When he came for me at the Muse College I was afraid," he said at last. "He told me my father was dead and I was needed to take his place as Champion, to aid the fairies against the vampire hordes. I saw then that the madness was gone. We had our king back and he was protecting all of Shadow once more. Surely it cannot happen the same way again. There are signs, but I must not–I must not–"

Hippy scooted closer to listen to the interesting babble. "What did he do when he went mad?"

Nikifor raised his head from his hands, looking surprised to see her there. He took his coat off and laid it over her shoulders. "Go to sleep," he said. "We'll be at Castle Arch by morning." Then he moved back to the boxes, slowly, as though he were in pain.

It was hard to get to sleep after that. Hippy was deeply disturbed by Nikifor's ramblings, but there wasn't much she could do about it. Still, with Fluffy Ducky curled into her neck, Fangs nestled in the crook of her arm and Nikifor's coat for warmth, she eventually drifted off into vivid dreams of the green-haired woman and Nikifor fighting vamps together.

When she woke up it was early morning. Mist drifted across the ground. To her infinite relief they were out of the forest and trundling across a grassy plain. She sat up, clutched the coat around her shoulders to keep out the cold and tipped her head back to study the massive stone arch towering over the road. The stone was black from age and chipped and broken in places. Its shadow was icy cold.

When the arch was behind them she turned her attention to the building ahead. Her eyes widened. It really was a castle. A beautiful one, with stones so neatly cut and polished, they shone in the rising light. Rows of windows reflected the colours of the mist, making them shiny shades of silver and grey. Slim turrets with pointed roofs swept towards the clouds. The roof was castellated in neat lines of light and shadow. When they got closer, she could see intricate carvings over doors and windows, all of them of fetches with outstretched wings. She squealed and clapped her hands. Then she walked over the cart, dropped Nikifor's coat over him because he was shivering in his sleep and seated herself beside Pierus on the bench.

The muse king calmly watched the approach of the castle. "Good morning."

"Is this where you live?" Hippy could hardly keep herself from bouncing up and down.

His mouth crooked up at the corner, an expression she hadn't seen in days. "Yes, this is my home. It's called Castle Arch."

"Are we staying here?"

"Yes, my love."

"It's beautiful!"

"I'm glad you like it." Pierus smoothed her hair behind her ear with one hand. "We'll be here for some time."

"Can I explore? Can I go anywhere I want?"

"There will be some places not entirely to your taste, my dear, but for the most part you will have the freedom of the castle and grounds." Pierus patted her shoulder. "Perhaps we shall get along better in all this space."

Hippy gave him a sidelong glance. "Maybe."

"I'm sorry I was so hard on you yesterday," he said. "The forest makes me nervous and I only wished to keep you safe."

She shrugged. "It wasn't that bad, for a forest."

"Why don't you go and explore? Nikifor and I will take care of the boxes."

Hippy glanced dubiously at Nikifor. "Are you sure? He's not very well."

"He's not?" Pierus looked around in surprise.

"You didn't even notice? He's all pale and shaky and babbling about stuff. I don't think he'll even make it inside, much less carry boxes for you."

"Oh. That." Pierus guided the donkeys around a big, walled fountain and toward the castle doors. "Don't you worry your pretty head about that, my dear girl. I'll make him well again later."

Hippy took Pierus at his word, since he insisted she wasn't to carry anything. With Fangs on her shoulder and Fluffy Ducky in her hair she explored every room of the castle.

She'd thought Mr Silver's house was big, but this castle was enormous. She was lost within minutes. There were rooms full of shiny, shiny, armour, and other rooms full of paintings of humans and scenes from Dream, like people driving cars and operating machinery. One room had shelves and shelves full of herbs and smelled like a damp, ancient forest floor. Another room was packed so tight with books they seemed to be holding up the very roof. She found a huge kitchen with a store room packed with fresh food. How it had got there she had no idea, because there certainly didn't seem to be anyone else about.

Up a huge, curving flight of stairs there was a hall and more rooms to explore. Most of these were bedrooms; perhaps Pierus liked to have people come to stay.

Up another flight of stairs Hippy discovered the whole floor was one enormous room, from which more stairs led to the roof. Here she found maps and star charts tacked to the walls, shelves full of books she couldn't read the titles of and tables covered with the most curious instruments, all of them shiny, some of them quite sharp. A skeleton of a forest person, hooves intact, repelled her. A hollow steel structure shaped like a man and tall enough to fit a vamp or muse inside made her skin creep. She moved away quickly to look at a hanging model of planets and stars that drifted in a slow circle with the breeze of her passing.

Footsteps entered the room. "There you are," Pierus said.

Hippy ducked out from the centre of the planets. "I like your castle."

Pierus set a box on a table and smiled at her. "Glad to hear it. Come here, my dear." He held out a hand.

Hippy went to him, but stopped just out of reach of his hand.

Pierus closed the last step between them and put his arm around her shoulder. "This is my laboratory," he said. "Here I conduct my research and experiments and watch over Shadow. Do you like it?"

"You have a lot of shiny things."

"I do indeed. But I will make sure there are other shiny things for you to play with, my love, for this is not a place for you. When I am working I must be undisturbed, and when I am not working, my work must be undisturbed. Do you understand?"

"Not really." Hippy gazed up at a huge light made of candles in glass holders. "That's a pretty light."

"Perhaps this will help you to understand." Pierus lit a candle on the table, then took a pinch of black powder from a bowl. He tossed the powder into the candle flame.

A small, sharp bang split the air. A black smoke cloud exploded over the table.

Hippy clapped her hands. "It went bang! Can I try?"

"No." Pierus drew her away from the desk and towards the stairs. "I was rather hoping you'd get the message that coming up here is likely to result in you blowing your pretty little hands off. You can go anywhere, my dear, except here. Understood?"

She sighed. "Alright."

They descended the stairs to the second floor, where Pierus led her to the third door on the left. He opened it to reveal one of the bedrooms she'd glanced at earlier. In fact it was the biggest one of them all and contained a huge bed made up with filmy white hangings and heavy blankets.

"You and I will sleep here," Pierus said.

"Really? But there are so many bedrooms, I thought–"

Pierus gave her a look. It was part disappointed, part sardonic, and it made Hippy's cheeks burn bright red.

"Oh," she said, and decided it was probably best not to pursue the conversation.

Fangs shook herself, looked at the fingers curling around Hippy's shoulder and pecked them.

Pierus snatched his hand back. "I hope you're planning on housebreaking these pets of yours," he said, his voice a trifle less pleasant than it had been.

Hippy giggled and petted Fangs. "I'm sure she'll get used to you. One day."

CHAPTER THIRTY-TWO

Pierus had already managed to tarnish the shine of the castle. Hippy headed outside so she didn't have to talk to him.

From the very edge of the steps, the garden was a labyrinth of leafy wild things hidden in a snarl of neglect. Wild shapes crouched, watchful, silent, within the tangled branches and straggling leaves of thick bushes that had once been clipped into a crouching horse here, a winged lion there.

Hippy found the big fountain soon enough. A wall rose out of the very centre, a clear pool on one side and bubbling fountain on the other. She perched on the edge of the pool, carefully keeping her feet clear of the water, and looked out across the plains.

The forest huddled beyond miles and miles of grass. Clockwork could be hiding anywhere out there.

She slowly rose to her feet. Pierus wasn't that interested in having her around. He wouldn't notice if she was gone for an hour or two. And wherever Clockwork was hiding, he was sure to see her if she ran across the plains. She glanced over her shoulder.

"I wouldn't," Nikifor said.

Hippy was so startled by his haggard face and the fact he'd been right there behind her, she slipped off the wall and fell on her backside. She scowled. "Wouldn't what?"

"Wouldn't go out there." Nikifor offered his hand to help her to her feet. "He said you were to stay near the castle."

"You both seem to be under the impression I'm going to do what he says." Hippy dusted herself off. "You're going to be very disappointed about that."

"Are you hungry?"

"Hungry?" She brightened. "Of course I'm hungry."

Nikifor motioned toward the castle. "The king has prepared dinner."

Hippy's mouth dropped open. "He cooks?" She trotted at Nikifor's side through the big entry way.

"He is the master of many arts." Nikifor said the words with a smile, but his voice was grey and faded. "Through here."

Hippy went into a big room where a long table was surrounded by many chairs. The walls were lined with candlesticks in brass holders shaped like hands. The candles were alight, even though it was day, giving the room a warm glow.

At the head of the table Pierus stirred soup in a big silver tureen. He gave Hippy a thin smile when she approached, stopped what he was doing and pulled out a chair for her next to him. "There you are, my dear."

Hippy sat down. Her stomach growled. "I didn't know you cooked. I thought kings had people to do that for them."

"Generally we do, but we're rather isolated here and I'm hardly going to let a fairy run my kitchen. You'd poison us all in the blink of an eye."

"Mmmm," Hippy said. "Fairy dust soup. I miss my mum's cooking."

Pierus put a bowl in front of her and ladled steaming red liquid from the tureen. It splashed down the sides and a droplet burned her hand.

Hippy looked doubtfully at the mixture. Liquid fat floated on the surface and globs of red congealed at the edges. Chunks of purplish meat floated in it. She sniffed at it and wrinkled her nose. "Did something die in there?"

"Blood soup," Pierus said. "Fresh from a wild rabbit. I understand such things are terribly good for a pregnant fairy."

Hippy gagged and pressed a hand over her mouth. Her stomach threatened to revolt. Her chair clattered backward and fell over when she ran for the nearest door.

Pierus's laughter cut into her raw nerves like razorblades.

Hippy didn't stop until she found her way outside again, where she fell to her hands and knees and threw up under the overgrown winged lion until she'd emptied the entire contents of her stomach.

Her hands trembled. She went to the fountain, cleaned her hands and face and rinsed her mouth. She shot a furious glance in the direction of the castle and thought about walking right back in there and emptying the blood soup tureen over the muse king's head.

Instead she turned her back on the whole thing and walked down the path. When she was safely on the other side of the bushes she ran across the plains. The late afternoon air was cool and refreshing on her skin. The wind of her passing whipped through her hair, lifting it off her neck. The deepening light made shadows in the dips in the grass while the sky slowly turned a deep shade of blue-purple overhead. The further away she got, the better she felt. The grass was soft on her bare feet. The space helped to clear her head.

She stopped and turned around when the castle was a tiny dot in the distance, just where it should be. It was going to take a lot of convincing to go back there.

When she turned her back on the castle again, Clockwork stood in the path. He took her hand and they kept running.

Hippy had thought they would go to the nearby forest. Instead Clockwork skirted the trees and headed for where the ground sloped upward, then followed a rock face until it opened into a narrow fissure. Here the two fairies squeezed through the opening and came out into a damp, mossy clearing sheltered on all four sides by steep rock and open to the sky. In one rock face there was a shallow cave.

Hippy put her feet down gently on the moss. She tip-toed around the bases of the tall trees growing in there. They had to reach up very far to feel the sun.

When she'd walked the whole clearing she sat down next to Clockwork in the cave. He'd lit a fire in a depression in the rock; the flames warmed her fingers and toes. The light faded outside and cold seeped in with the darkness.

"Are you hungry?" Clockwork asked.

She shuddered. "I don't know."

"Here." He handed her a basket filled with berries and small, rock-shaped cakes.

Hippy's very empty stomach growled. She tore into a cake. "Where did you get these?"

"The forest people gave them to me."

Hippy almost choked. She swallowed what she was eating while Clockwork clapped her on the back, and got her breath back. "Forest people? You talked to them? They didn't kill you?"

"Of course not. Fitz gave me a few things to tell them if I was ever caught. Really, they were very friendly. They mostly wanted to know what the pretender was doing with a fairy on his cart."

"What did you tell them?" Hippy bit into a second cake. She was starving and the cakes were really good.

Clockwork grinned. "I said you were my sweetheart and I was here to rescue you from the muse king, who was holding you against your will. It seemed more likely than the truth."

She ate a handful of berries. "Did they believe you?"

"They gave me food and showed me this place to stay," Clockwork said. "And an axe." He pointed to a stout, long-handled, double-headed axe with wickedly curved blades resting by the fire. "And they said we could go safely through the forest when I rescued you."

Hippy investigated the weapon. "Nice." She gave a disconsolate sigh and ate another cake.

"Is he starving you?" Clockwork demanded.

"I don't know. Maybe." Hippy blinked back errant tears. Even pregnant fairies didn't cry. "He tried to give me blood soup. The smell made me throw up and he laughed."

"Come on. We'll kill him right now, take the Apple and go." Clockwork reached for the axe.

"No!" Hippy put her hand on his arm. "We can't. What if we killed him and it was the end of all Shadow?"

"You heard Fitz. That's a lie."

"What if Fitz was wrong?"

Clockwork poked at the fire. A shower of sparks went up into the darkness. "Fitz is the smartest person I know."

"But are you prepared to take that risk?"

He sighed. "I don't know. I guess you're not."

Hippy shook her head. "Not really. But listen, as soon as I have a chance I'm going to find the Apple of Chaos. Then we have to get out of here. Really, really fast."

Clockwork chuckled. "He's going to be a little bit upset, is he?"

"He's going to be so mad he'll eat his own face."

The two fairies giggled. The fire crackled. Silence settled. Clockwork and Hippy laced their fingers together.

"Are you going to be okay?" Clockwork said.

"Of course I am. What can he possibly do, apart from play his mean little tricks and act like a complete ass?"

"I don't know. The forest people said he took one of them to live in the Arch once."

"Really? What happened?"

"They don't know. He never came back."

Hippy thought about the skeleton she'd seen. She felt ill again. But she didn't want to worry Clockwork, so she quickly changed the subject. "You know what's really weird? Nikifor. I think Pierus is doing something to him. He gave him this drink the night we left Shadow, to take away his fear. Now Nikifor's really sick and he babbles and says weird stuff about consequences."

The stick Clockwork had been playing with stilled. "What did the drink look like?"

"It was green. He didn't want it, but Pierus made him."

"Sounds like vibe."

"Vibe?"

"It's a Freakin Fairy drink." Clockwork raked his dreadlocks out of his face. "Completely harmless to fairies, of course. It just used to give us a little bit of a laugh and make our voices go funny. But it's a terrible thing for muses. It takes away all their fears, all their boundaries and rules. It's like they suddenly have a direct link to all that inspiration out there. It floods them and they can't handle it. But once they start drinking it they can't stop either, or they go crazy and die." He drew a line across his throat with his index finger. "Pierus stole the recipe from my grandfather when my dad was young. He was supposed to be trying to negotiate for more silver, but once he had that, he scarpered."

Hippy stared at Clockwork, her eyes wide. "Nikifor's going to go crazy and die?"

"If he's been drinking vibe, then yes, one way or another. He could survive for decades if he has a little now and then, but if he doesn't, he'll have another day or two, tops."

"There must be a way to help him!" Hippy buried her face in Clockwork's shoulder. He smelled like wood smoke and leaves. She didn't want to go back.

"If he went to my people, maybe." Clockwork sounded doubtful. "But I'm more worried about you, Hippy. Let me go find the Apple of Chaos."

She shook her head. "No. If you get caught there's no telling what he'll do. I'm going to find it tonight and come back."

Clockwork turned her face and looked into her eyes. He looked very serious. "And if you don't come back tonight? If something goes wrong?"

"Then I'll come back tomorrow and tell you what happened. Don't worry. I can leave anytime I want. He can't stop me." Hippy leaned forward and gently kissed his lips.

Clockwork closed his eyes and returned the kiss. Hippy let herself imagine, just for a minute, that this was her life and she could stay in the cave all night. It was a nice thought, but she felt worse when she ended the kiss. "You'd better think up a way to get us back to Dream. I'll see you soon." She hurried out of the cave before she could change her mind and stay.

She found the crevice and squeezed through it. It was a good thing she'd decided to end all this tonight. In another few weeks she'd start getting fat from the baby and wouldn't fit down here.

CHAPTER THIRTY-THREE

Iron weights dragged from her feet. The night wrapped icy fingers around her ribs and squeezed. It was so very dark she couldn't even scc the ground, but she knew she was going the right way by the unerring dread that gripped her shoulders with each step.

The moon peeped over the turrets. Hippy shivered. She usually liked the moon, but here even that looked cold and unfriendly, outlining harsh angles on the castle she hadn't seen during the day. When it rose higher, it flooded the plain with silver light.

That was when she spotted Pierus.

Hippy slowed her pace. Far across the plain he moved up and down in a regular pattern, dragging something over the ground, then returning down the same path, scattering things. She would have sworn he was gardening if his movements weren't so like a weird dance, the way he would turn, the way the skirt of his long coat flared out.

She picked up her pace. The distance to the castle lessened. She passed under the Arch, where it was now so bitterly cold her teeth chattered until she'd left it behind completely. She looked over her shoulder at Pierus.

He looked up at the same moment. Their eyes met. There was no change in his expression, but he did not break the eye contact. Hippy experienced a horrible sensation of being pinned to the spot for three eternal minutes. She gritted her teeth, broke away and turned her back on him, but the prickling in her spine told her he watched her all the way.

She bolted toward the castle, but skidded to a halt again at the fountain. "Nikifor?"

Nikifor stood on top of the wall that divided the fountain, hair tumbled around his face, naked sword high in the air, transfixed by the moon. His eyes snapped to her when she spoke. He stared right through her. "I fear nothing," he said. "Nothing. Not your dreams or illusions or lies. Not the blood spilled from the sky every time I open my hand." He paced across the wall and dropped to the ground in front of her.

Hippy backed up fast. "Would you put that sword away? You're going to hurt yourself. Or I'm going to hurt you. Either way you really should calm down."

He stalked her movements. "Do you think I'm fooled?" His voice rose to a shout. "I know mist when I see it! I haven't spent my life dragging your every vision kicking and screaming from the ether just to come to this! I know I was born to kill, to drive back the darkness, and that makes me just another foul creation of your twisted intellect!" He doubled over and uttered a hoarse, guttural roar.

Hippy fled inside. Gas lamps and candles burned in every room. She raced into the dining room, but it was clean. She checked the kitchen, but there was nothing there either. She didn't even know what she was looking for until she stumbled into a small room that contained only a round table in the centre and two chairs. She slowed her pace. On the table she found a silver pitcher and two empty glasses; in the bottom of the glasses there were drops of green liquid. She picked up the pitcher and sniffed it. It smelled of something intoxicating, more intoxicating than coffee or Poppy's brandy or anything she'd ever encountered. It confirmed her worst suspicion. At least Nikifor wouldn't die in the next two days.

She backed out of the room and glanced towards the doors of the castle. Pierus was busy. So was Nikifor. Maybe there was no better time to find the Apple of Chaos and go, while they were both whacked off their faces on Freakin Fairy juice. She'd left Fangs scratching in the garden, she'd find her on the way out.

Hippy headed for the stairs, but she stopped only halfway up the first flight when footsteps thumped through the front door. She turned around, one hand on the railing.

Pierus's hair, normally so neat and tidy, hung knotted over his face, the new white streak tangled into the black. There were shadows under his eyes and beads of sweat on his forehead. He removed his coat, but never took his eyes off her. "And just where have you been all this time, my love?" He walked toward the stairs.

Hippy backed away. "Out."

"You are not permitted to go out. I thought I made myself clear on that point." He mounted the steps one by one, like a cat stalking a little bird.

Hippy steeled herself. She was more than a match for the muse king. She wasn't going to be afraid. She freed Fluffy Ducky from his pouch and let him run into the palm of her hand. "You leave me alone," she said. "You're not thinking right. I saw those glasses. You and Nikifor both drank the vibe, didn't you? I don't want any part of your madness."

"You are my madness." He stalked closer still. "Where did you go, Hippy Ishtar? Do you have a friend? Did you lie to me when you swore you were loyal?" He reached out and grasped the back of her head. His breath held the same intoxicating scent she'd found in the pitcher in the other room, but now slightly rancid.

She wrinkled her nose and pulled away. "Take your hands off me or I'll smack you in the teeth."

He brought his face close to hers and breathed in. "You smell like wood smoke," he said. "Interesting little thing, my love. Bloody Fairies don't know about the vibe, because they don't talk to the Freakin Fairies. So how do you know?"

Hippy's cheeks grew painfully hot. "Leave me alone." She shoved him in the ribs with her free hand and ran past him down the stairs, only to find Nikifor blocking the doorway.

Pierus went after her, wrapped a hand in her hair and snapped her head back. "I asked you a question, Fairy."

Hippy flung Fluffy Ducky at his face. Fluffy Ducky, who had apparently been waiting for this chance, curled his legs around, ready to latch on.

Pierus ducked his head, raised a hand and caught Fluffy Ducky in his fist. Then he smiled.

Hippy didn't like that smile at all. She screamed so loud the gas lamps flickered. "You let go of my Fluffy Ducky!"

Pierus stalked over to a table and opened a wooden box. He put the struggling spider into it, closed the lid and locked it.

Hippy shoved Pierus away from the box and tried to tear it open. "Fluffy Ducky! Don't worry I'm going to get you out!"

"Nikifor," Pierus said.

Something in his voice made Hippy stop what she was doing. She looked from one muse to the other. "Oh, no you don't."

There was nothing of the Nikifor she knew in the muse who stalked her now. Hippy clutched the box to her ribs and backed away from them both. "Stop it, both of you. You're not thinking straight. And trust me, I will hurt you."

"But my dear girl, I always think straight. I plan everything."

Pierus closed in from her right, Nikifor from her left.

"Did you plan this?" She put her foot on the first step. Fine, she'd go all the way up and jump off the roof. There was always an escape.

"No. This is a diverting distraction. Put down the box."

"No." Hippy backed up three more steps. "I won't let you hurt Fluffy Ducky."

"Look." Pierus put his hand into his pocket, then opened it. A wisp of something sparkly rose into the air.

Hippy's eyes widened. "Oh, that's shiny."

Nikifor darted forward and knocked the box out of her hand.

"Fluffy Ducky!" Hippy leaped after the box, but both muses caught her by the arms. She kicked at the air, scratched any skin she could reach, even tried to bite the both of them, but it was like fighting air. The two muses carried her up the stairs and down the second floor hall.

Pierus kicked open the bedroom door. "Go play somewhere else, Nikifor," he said.

Nikifor let go and backed away.

Hippy wrenched free of Pierus's hold. He shoved her in the ribs so hard she stumbled into the bedroom and collided with a wall. For one terrifying moment she thought he was going to follow her in. If he did, she'd kill him, the future of Shadow be damned.

But he stayed in the doorway and just looked her up and down. "This is what happens when you forget you are *my* fairy," he said. "If you find a way to leave this room I'll feed you your spider for breakfast."

He closed the door. A lock turned on the other side. Then a bolt slammed home.

Hippy threw herself at the door and hammered on it with her fists. "I want my Fluffy Ducky!" she screamed.

It must have been the early hours of the morning when Hippy woke up. Her eyes were still sore. There was nobody there to see her, so she'd cried herself to sleep in the big bed after exhausting her voice and her fists hammering on the door.

Moonlight bathed the bed hangings in silver and the floor with white. The door was still closed, but Pierus was curled up on the floor muttering to himself.

She sat up and searched for a weapon. She could put an end to Pierus right now.

His back arched. His hair fell over his face and he whimpered.

Hippy slid off the bed and watched him, uncertain. "Pierus?"

He raised haunted eyes, but she didn't think he saw her. "Pandora," he said. "You're here. I knew you'd be here." He took a deep, ragged breath and reached out to her, but remained on his knees. "Pandora forgive me. Forgive me my love, free me from these chains of ice."

"I'm not Pandora." Hippy circled him, keeping out of reach.

"Don't you think I know you?" His voice cracked. "Don't you think I've seen you pursuing me across the centuries, wreaking your vengeance at my heels, my every step? But this, this last is the cruellest of all, my love, take this fairy curse off me!"

Hippy paused with her hand on the door. "What fairy curse?"

He stayed where he was, his back to her. His shoulders shook. "It was so neatly done, it could only have been you. To show me my death in the Apple, the one thing you and I shared."

"What death?"

"Cruel ghost," he breathed. "Must I relive it every time I close my eyes? Every time I see you? Is this how you punish me for my crimes?"

"Yes, absolutely. Tell me about your death." Hippy took a cautious step closer.

"She looked like you." His voice turned to a rasp. "But she had green hair and she was with Nikifor. They're going to kill me, Pandora. The darkness will finally take me. I will know the horrors, all of them. Forgive me. Save me." He dived forward, clutched her ankles and pressed his lips against her feet.

"Ew." Hippy tried to move away, but his hands were like manacles. "Stop it Pierus!"

"Forgive me Pandora," he said. "I beg you, forgive me."

Hippy considered kicking him in the head, but then he started to cry. She grimaced. She'd never seen a muse cry. The creature at her feet was not the powerful, cruel muse king at all, it was a wretched shadow of him. The black core of her rage escaped her grasp, to be replaced with only pity and contempt. She sighed, sank to the floor and patted him awkwardly on the head.

He released her ankles and laid his head in her lap. Sobs shook his whole body.

Hippy absently stroked his hair and looked out of the window at the moon. A woman with green hair who looked like Pandora. Who looked like her. Her daughter, the child even now growing in her belly, was going to kill Pierus. Her daughter and Nikifor. Did he know? He must suspect it.

"Pierus," she whispered. "If Nikifor is going to kill you, why do you keep him here?"

"I must keep my enemies closest of all," he said in a voice so low she could barely hear it. "Keep them close. Keep them weak."

Her hand stilled on his hair. Poor Nikifor. Poor, stupid Nikifor. She'd have to get him away from here when she was done punching him in the face.

CHAPTER THIRTY-FOUR

Hippy woke alone. Morning sunshine slanted across the bed, warming her legs. The door was ajar.

She jumped out of bed, ran down the stairs two at a time and made a beeline for where the wooden box lay on the floor. The lid was open. The box was empty. Fluffy Ducky had got away. Her heart pounded in relief and she started a search of the whole bottom floor, calling for him.

Hesitant footsteps approached when she neared the front doors. Nikifor stopped in the doorway of the dining room. He looked fresh and rested, but for the shadows under his eyes. "Good morning."

Hippy eyed him warily. "Where's Pierus?"

"He had to go away for the day. He'll be back by nightfall."

"Nikifor." She crooked her index finger to beckon him. "Come here."

He strode toward her. "What is it my little friend?"

"Closer." Hippy beckoned him down to her level.

Nikifor bent closer.

Hippy grabbed his ear in her fingertips, punched him in the mouth and then pushed him away.

Nikifor lost his balance and fell to the floor. He wiped blood from his lip and looked up at her with wounded surprise. "What did you do that for?"

"Just to remind you if you ever attempt to manhandle me again, I will beat you black and blue." Hippy shook a fist at him to punctuate the point.

Nikifor stared. "What are you talking about?"

"I'm talking about last night! Now where's Fluffy Ducky?"

He got to his feet and backed away from her. "I'm sorry Hippy, I don't know where Fluffy Ducky is, and I don't know what you're talking about. I would never cause you harm."

"Oh, you wouldn't?" Hippy advanced on him. "What did you call that last night then? You took Fluffy Ducky from me when he was in that box over there! Then you and Pierus dragged me upstairs and locked me in the bedroom! What's the matter, did that horrible vibe stuff damage your mind too much to remember?"

Nikifor stopped backing away. His mouth fell open. His eyes went wide and blank while memories tried to crack their way into his brain. His hand went to his head. "No," he said. "Oh no."

"You really don't remember." Hippy's anger drained away.

He shook his head. "I'm sorry."

"You both went crazy," she said. "I was scared, Nikifor."

He wouldn't meet her eyes. "There was no other way."

"Of course there's another way. The Freakin Fairies can help you."

"Nobody can help me. Nobody except my king."

"He's not trying to help you!" Hippy stopped herself. She had to be more careful than this. She took a deep breath.

"I made you breakfast," Nikifor said.

"You did?" She gave him a suspicious look. "Does it have blood in it?"

"No. It has eggs in it."

"Fine, I'll eat it, but only because I'm hungry. And then I'm going to find Fluffy Ducky. He must be terrified."

"Perhaps if I help you, you will forgive me for my behaviour?"

She glared. "Perhaps."

They searched every room in the castle except for Pierus's laboratory, where Nikifor refused to go. Then they searched the gardens outside, the fountain, everywhere. Hippy went around the entire perimeter calling for Fluffy Ducky, but he didn't come to her. She stopped to look out over the plain, bewildered. Where last night there had been only grass, this morning there were seedlings growing in long, neat rows, with two leaves each.

Fluffy Ducky wouldn't have gone that far.

She turned her back on them and investigated the bushes. Nikifor, who had either given up or was distracted, hacked at a few with his sword, teasing out the overgrown shapes hidden inside them.

"Nikifor wait."

He lowered his sword. "What is it?"

Hippy went closer to the bush he was working at. "There's a

web." She pointed to a thick mat of web just peeking out of the foliage. "See, there."

"Is it Fluffy Ducky's?" Nikifor bent closer to see.

Hippy eased aside the branches. "Fluffy Ducky? Fluffy Ducky it's me, are you hiding in here?"

The foliage trembled. Something inside shifted.

Hippy's heart hammered in excitement. "Fluffy Ducky! It's okay, you can come out now, the nasty old muse king isn't here!" She forced the branches aside.

Three eyes peered at her out of the leaves. A big, hairy leg slowly pressed a branch down.

Hippy frowned. Those eyes were the size of saucers and that leg was almost as big as her forearm. "Fluffy Ducky? What happened to you?"

There was a clicking noise from inside the bush.

Nikifor took a step back. "Are you sure that's your spider?"

"Of course it is. I'd know Fluffy Ducky anywhere. But he's–he's very big."

Hippy wiggled her fingers at Fluffy Ducky. "How'd you get so big? Did you eat a whole vamp or something?"

A branch cracked. The whole bush shivered. Then Fluffy Ducky scuttled out. Something gleamed behind him. He hissed.

Hippy's lower lip trembled. "There's no need to talk to me like that, Fluffy Ducky. It wasn't my fault he put you in that box. He locked me up too."

Two wickedly curved fangs twitched. He hissed again.

Nikifor's voice was unnaturally high. "Hippy I don't think he wants to play."

"Fluffy Ducky?" She blinked rapidly when tears formed in her eyes. "What are you doing?"

Fluffy Ducky leaped.

Nikifor hauled Hippy out of his path.

Fluffy Ducky landed where she'd been standing. He was almost the size of a small fairy. He scuttled in a circle to face them, hissed and pawed at the ground with thick, hairy feet.

Tears ran down her face unimpeded now. "Fluffy Ducky no," Hippy said. "It's me, don't you recognise me? We've been friends forever!"

Nikifor, who still had hold of the back of her dress, dragged her away from the giant spider.

Fluffy Ducky crept forward. He stalked them step for step until they'd reached the fountain. Only then did he scurry back to his bush.

"Fluffy Ducky!" Hippy wailed.

The branches shivered under his weight and settled.

Hippy ran towards it again, but Nikifor picked her up off the ground and hurried back to the castle while she kicked the air and pummelled him in the ribs.

He set her down in the big entry room. "I'm sorry, Hippy."

"Let me back out there!" Hippy yelled. "He knows it's me, he does! He just has to–to remember!"

"Hippy that spider will kill you if you go near it again." Nikifor crouched to be on eye level with her. "I'm so sorry. That's not your Fluffy Ducky anymore."

Hippy collapsed on the floor and sobbed furiously.

Nikifor disappeared into another room and returned with a small, shiny creature in his arms. "Look," he said. "I found Fangs earlier."

Hippy took Fangs from him and held her close. After a while, she calmed down enough to stop crying. She wiped her eyes. Fangs crawled onto her shoulder and cuddled into her neck.

"What happened to Fluffy Ducky?" She kept her voice steady with an effort.

Nikifor, still crouching in front of her, was silent. Hippy looked at the expression on his face. Right then, she knew.

"He did something."

"We must not jump to conclusions." There was doubt in his voice. "Pierus knows how important your spider is to you, he wouldn't-"

"What did he do last night after he locked me in?"

Fangs stretched her wings and backed a little way down Hippy's shoulder.

Nikifor rose to his feet. He closed his eyes and rubbed his head. "I can see images, hear sounds–at times today I have thought it was coming back, but–" he paced to the wall and back.

"Think Nikifor," Hippy said. "Think hard. You left us at the bedroom. What happened when he returned? Did he open the box?"

"Yes. Yes, he opened the box."

Hippy took a step toward him. "And then?"

"He–he took the spider up to his laboratory." The words died on Nikifor's lips almost before they were fully spoken. He looked aghast. "Hippy, please, I'm sure he wouldn't have done anything on purpose. Perhaps there was an accident."

Hippy turned on her heel and headed for the stairs.

Nikifor pursued. "No. You must not go up there, it is forbidden!"

"Back off, Nikifor."

"I must ask you to stop, or-"

"Or what?" Hippy whirled around and brandished a fist. "What are you going to do?"

"We will find another way! When he returns, I'm sure if we talk to him-"

"Talk? You want to talk? Tell you what, you talk. I'm going to kill something." Hippy bolted up the stairs. When she reached the third floor several paces ahead of Nikifor, she dragged the heavy double doors closed and locked them.

"Hippy!" Nikifor yelled from the other side. "Hippy please, don't make him angry with us!"

Hippy went into the laboratory. On the big table in the centre she found the vamp hand bound to a slab of steel with rope over each finger and the wrist. It twitched when she came near. There were tiny cuts all over it. Beside it, in a bloodstained bowl, were several black seeds.

Her stomach revolted. Her skin crawled. Behind her she could hear Nikifor scratching at the lock on the door. She reached into her belt, took a pinch of Ishtar's fairy dust and sprinkled it over both the hand and the seeds.

The fingers jerked and clawed at the slab. Then the skin turned grey and crumbled to dust, just like the seeds.

Hippy let out a long, shuddering breath, but she didn't feel much better. She investigated the shelves and the planets. She couldn't look at the skeleton. When she drew aside a heavy red curtain, she gasped. Behind that, suspended in midair, was the shiniest, brightest cage she'd ever seen. It appeared to be made of pure light, or maybe fire, it was hard to tell. The intricate egg-shaped network of lines enclosed the Apple of Chaos, but it was broken again. The pieces floated, each separate, each trying to join the rest.

She frowned. Two were missing, she was sure of it. There had been something shiny in Fluffy Ducky's branches, and Pierus was gone for a whole day. If he was hiding the pieces one by one, then she was already too late to rescue the whole thing.

But Mr Silver had said she only needed one piece. Just one.

She reached out for the cage. The lights were warm. They got hotter. Her fingertips hovered just underneath them. They buzzed. Her skin tingled. The hairs on the back of her fingers curled and smoked.

Hippy snatched her hand away. She backed up and reached for the nearest heavy object she could find, which was a thick, hard-covered book. She hurled it at the cage.

The book bounced off the lights and landed at her feet, a cross-hatch pattern burned into the cover.

She stamped her foot and screamed in rage. Nikifor crashed into the other side of the door.

Fangs, still on her shoulder, made a low whining noise.

"You're right," Hippy said. "We should just go." She ran up the stairs that wound from the centre of the room and came out on the roof. It was flat, damp and mouldy up there. She hurried across it and looked out across the plains.

The grass was dotted as far as she could see with tiny blotches of green. Pierus must have worked hard last night. How he'd planted so many seeds and why, she had no idea. She wondered if they were the same as the ones she'd found soaking in vamp blood.

There was no time to worry about that. She had to get out of here. She climbed onto the edge of the roof, jumped and landed in the garden below. Fangs took off from her shoulder halfway down and flew into the garden.

Hippy ran straight out onto the plain before she had too much time to think about leaving Fluffy Ducky behind. She hoped Fangs would follow.

Her feet barely touched the ground, she ran so fast. She ignored the seedlings, even though they'd all doubled in size since this morning, and now had several leaves apiece. She didn't slow down until she'd gone under the huge cold Arch. Then she only slowed a little bit. Running felt good. The wind whipped through her hair. She could forget about Fluffy Ducky while she ran.

There was a movement at the corner of her eye. Hippy tried to see what it was without stopping, tripped over and hit the ground.

The seedlings all around stretched and bent toward her like compasses. She drew her hand out of reach of one. They were only little plants.

Hippy got to her feet. The leaves followed her every movement. Her breath came in short, quick gasps. Her blood hammered. She walked through them on her toes. It was horrible. Her neck prickled. They were watching her, she could swear they were.

She picked up the pace. The distance to the forest gradually diminished. Soon she'd be with Clockwork and she'd never go back, not for anything, not even the Apple of Chaos. She'd tell Mr Silver she'd failed and he could find another way to save Shadow. She couldn't do it, not without Fluffy Ducky.

Her feet pounded over the ground. She just barely missed the seedlings with each step. She was almost in breathing distance of the grass and the forest when she felt a sharp sting on her heel. The pain hit her like an axe in the foot. She stumbled forward, fell and rolled until she was out of the seedlings.

She lurched to her feet and put more distance between herself and the horrible little plants. Everything went blurry. The grass looked like painted stripes on a wall. The distant trees swayed and bent like people. She turned in a circle. She couldn't find the slope.

"Clockwork?" Hippy tried again when her voice wouldn't come out right. "Clockwork?" She stumbled to her knees. Then she fell forward on her face and lay there on the grass, her open eyes turned towards the seedlings. Blood trickled from her foot. Her heart slowed. Insects rustled in the grass.

She couldn't move at all.

CHAPTER THIRTY-FIVE

Hippy couldn't blink. All she could see were a few blades of grass. There was no way to tell how much time passed. Once, a centipede crawled past and stopped to try and outstare her. Her fingertips and toes grew cold. After a while she couldn't even feel the pain in her foot.

Two sets of distant footfalls made the ground shiver against her cheek. Grass rustled under her ear. A bat swooped so low she could feel the wind on her face. The light faded. Night would fall and whoever was coming would miss her lying there in the darkness.

The footsteps crunched near her head. A shadow crossed her face. "Look, a dead fairy," a voice said.

If she could have, she would have jumped up and run away when she heard Pierus's reply. "Oh, Hippy." He stooped and picked her up. Her head fell onto his shoulder as though it belonged to a rag doll. He smelled like stone, sweat and fear. He'd walked a long way. Behind him, through locks of his hair, she glimpsed his companion.

The man was tall like Pierus. Every inch of his body was covered. He wore a long black coat with a high collar, black pants, tall boots, black gloves, a hood. A silver mask obscured his face. When he spoke the lips didn't move. "Your dead fairy is staring at me."

"She's not dead." Pierus's fingers rested briefly on the pulse at her neck. Her skin crawled, but she couldn't even flinch. "...Yet." His long strides took them straight back into the seedlings.

Hippy wanted to yell a warning. Both Pierus and the stranger were completely oblivious to the danger. Then, after a few minutes, she realised there was none. No leaves moved. Nothing stung them. Maybe they let people in but not out, like a spider luring flies into its web. Horror made little sick inroads into her stomach. Pierus's fingers rested carelessly across her cheek while he carried her back into her prison.

The stranger hurried to catch up with him. There was something familiar about him. Something she couldn't place. "You didn't tell me you still had the fairy around."

"Why would I tell you anything? You haven't proved to me you'll keep your end of the bargain."

"Oh, I'll do that, Muse King. You can count on it."

"Very well."

So why keep the fairy? You've never been able to stand them."

"She carries my child."

"A *pregnant* fairy?" the stranger sounded astonished. "Isn't that a little dangerous for you?"

"Desperate times call for desperate measures," Pierus said. "If I can't find a way to control this fairy, how am I meant to control the entire plague of them when the time comes? Besides, I've got used to having her around."

"Apparently she's not all that keen on being around," the stranger said.

"She'll learn." The two words were clipped and cold. "My rose garden will serve its purpose." He glanced over his shoulder at the stranger. "Perhaps now would be a good time to warn you not to leave without me. The roses do not discriminate."

The stranger looked around him at the seedlings. "These? These roses? What will they do? They're just a bunch of flowers."

"They're bloodthirsty little creatures who will poison anybody who tries to leave Castle Arch." Pierus sounded positively delighted. "Except for me."

"Are you telling me I'm to be trapped in a castle with you and a fairy for weeks on end? I know what I'll be doing for fun."

They passed through darkness. Hippy thought they must be under the arch. Pierus's voice was like a blizzard. "If you lay one finger on her without my permission, I will personally remove your liver and then feed it to you. This is *my* fairy."

The stranger chuckled. "Don't get your breeches in a bunch. I can wait. She's still staring at me. Are you sure she can't hear us?"

"Of course she can't." Pierus reached up and closed her eyes.

Darkness. Footsteps crunched on grass. Her brain went fuzzy. She knew that voice, knew that walk, but couldn't for the life of her figure out who the stranger was.

Pierus imperceptibly relaxed when they walked into the shadow of the castle. Doors opened. Heavy boots climbed the steps.

Pierus yelled for Nikifor, who ran in from Shadow knew where and skidded to a halt.

"My king, you found her–thank Shadow–" Nikifor's voice trailed off. "Is she dead?"

The contempt in Pierus's voice was palpable. "No, you pathetic excuse for a muse, she is not dead, no thanks to you. Prepare a room for my guest. I believe he would like something with no windows. Later perhaps he can give you lessons in how to stand up to a fairy half your size."

Then they went up three flights of stairs. He swept a table clean with one arm, then dropped her onto it.

He went away. Hippy fought the slowness of her brain. She couldn't lose touch now.

Something cold and wet dripped onto her foot. The sensation sent shudders all up her leg. The ice cold in her fingertips and toes receded.

Again, the liquid dripped onto her foot. Soft fabric cleaned the wound. She could think more clearly. She tried to remember if she'd seen a weapon in here, a knife, a sword, anything. Oh for Poppy with her gun right now.

She opened her eyelashes just the tiniest bit. Pierus bent over her foot, frowning in concentration. Oh. She could move. She waited until he'd finished binding a bandage around the wound. When he moved away again she wiggled her fingers, just to make sure. Then she sat up and rubbed her head. She felt fine. Pierus had his back to her at the other table.

Hippy put her hand into a pouch at her belt and found a slim metal arrow there. It would have to do. She crouched on the table, crept forward and leaped.

Her leap took her straight into Pierus when he turned towards her. She threw her whole weight into the motion, sent him crashing to the floor and pressed the tip of the arrow into the skin at his throat. "What did you do to my Fluffy Ducky?"

His ribcage vibrated under her knees when he laughed. "Did you miss me, my love?"

"If I did, my aim's about to improve." She raised the arrow into the air and stabbed downward.

"Tut, tut." He caught her wrist when the point of the arrow was a hairs breadth from his skin. "You know what will happen if you kill me. You kill everything. Besides, I didn't hurt Fluffy Ducky. I gave him a new purpose in life."

Hippy's hand trembled in his grip. She'd never actually fought

Pierus. She had no idea how strong he was. "I don't care," she said. "Maybe it's worth it. I hate you."

Pierus pushed on her wrist, rolled her onto her back and stuck his knee in her ribs. He took the arrow from her hand, snapped it and tossed the pieces away. Then he put a hand around her neck and squeezed lightly. "You don't hate me." He moved down until his face was just inches above hers. "I won't allow it. Although I have to wonder–" he traced a line down her cheek with his fingernail "-If you would still have been the sweet, innocent little thing I first took to Dream, had the Invisible Army not interfered. Would you, Hippy?"

Hippy forced her words out through clenched teeth. "Take your hands off me."

"But of course." He let her go, stood up and walked away.

Hippy lay on the floor, gasping for breath.

"What in Shadow made you try to leave the castle alone?" he said from across the room. "I know you were dropped on your head as a child, but really, any fool could figure out I wouldn't let you go that easily."

Hippy sat up. She rubbed at her neck and didn't look at him.

He returned to her and crouched down. "I'm sorry," he said, although he didn't look or sound the least bit like he meant it. "I had intended that we should get along better on my return. I brought you a gift." He put a pile of fabric in her lap.

Hippy stared at the fabric, dumbfounded. It was white. It was shiny. In fact it was so shiny, when she moved it patterns of rainbow colours played along the material. She unfolded it. Inside she found a row of sparkly gems sewn in a v-shape. She looked up at Pierus. "I don't understand."

"When I saw it I knew it was for you," he said. "I know how much you like shiny things."

"You knew how much I liked Fluffy Ducky, too."

He made an impatient gesture. "Forget the spider. Try it on."

She rose to her feet and shook out the fabric, to discover it was a dress. A little too long for her, but it was the shiniest, most beautiful dress she'd ever seen. The sparkly gems ran from the fitted bodice to the waist and met in a point. The skirt flared slightly at the hips. The sleeves were cut out at the shoulders, then ran sheer to the wrist, where more little gems sparkled.

"Well? Do you like it?" Pierus went behind her, took the dress from her hands and held it up against her. "A beautiful dress for a beautiful fairy."

"But what would I want a dress like this for?" She knew she should move away, but she was hypnotised by the colours in the fabric.

"Because in three days we are to be married."

Hippy experienced one terrifying moment of being unable to breathe. She broke away from the muse and backed up until she hit a table and could go no further. "Married? Ew! But you're old!"

A muscle ticked in his jaw. "Don't try my patience, Hippy."

"I don't *want* to get married!"

"What did you think was going to happen? You are carrying my child, my dear girl."

"But–but I don't–"

He slung the dress over one arm, went to her and put an arm around her shoulder. "It's quite alright, I know it's an emotional moment for you." He guided her toward the door and down the stairs. "Fear not, it will be a very special day for both of us. For all Shadow, in fact." He turned down the second floor hall and opened the door. "I suggest you get some sleep. You've had quite an ordeal today."

"But I don't want to sleep."

"Really, first you don't want to get married, now you don't want to sleep. What a reactionary Bloody Fairy you are. If I were you my dear, I'd be extremely careful at night time from now on. You never know what might be prowling the castle." He put the dress in her hands, shoved her into the room and locked the door.

Hippy was ready for the shove this time and she only stumbled a few steps. She glared every kind of hatred under the sun at the door. Outside, the sky was black. In here, a single gas lamp cast a dim light.

She laid the dress on the floor. It really was shiny. She was about to jump up and down on it with her dirty feet when she had an idea. She walked around the dress, considering it from every angle. After all, it wasn't a *proper* fairy wedding dress. Not yet. Not until it had been made into a lethal weapon. Fairy weddings were known to be the best fun in Shadow. Her own mother had broken several heads right before she jumped the bonfire.

She sat on the floor, took a pinch of fairy dust from her belt and slowly, methodically began to work it into the fabric. The thought of what would happen to Pierus if he so much as laid a finger on her in three days made her giggle madly. It would be the first wedding ever where the groom turned to ash before the vows were through.

CHAPTER THIRTY-SIX

Hippy had some happy dreams about her shiny, shiny, dress. There was an extra sparkle to every inch of it when she hung it on the wall before going to sleep that night. When she woke up, the sight of it made her smile.

The warmth of a hand resting on her thigh quickly tarnished her good mood. She turned her head. Pierus was fast asleep, eyes closed, chest rising and falling evenly. His hand, resting so casually on her leg, felt like a dead weight. She could fairy dust him right now, but she only had a very small amount left and she wanted to save it.

She eased herself away from him and out of bed. The castle was quiet and empty; she wondered if the stranger still slept.

She headed for the kitchen, where Nikifor sat at the wooden bench, his head resting on his arms.

"Nikifor?" she went in and tapped him on the shoulder.

Nikifor jumped, raised his head and looked about wildly. When he saw her he looked so relieved he almost fell out of his chair. "Hippy, thank Shadow you're okay." His hands trembled over the counter. "Let me make you some breakfast."

She studied him. "Of course I'm okay. You're not though."

"Don't worry about me." He went to the pantry and took eggs and bread from the shelves. "But don't ever do that to me again. I thought he warned you about the roses. Please, Hippy, I know you don't like it here, but you must not leave again. You must trust him. He has a plan, he knows what's best."

"What plan?" Hippy took the food out of his hands, pushed him gently into a chair and put a heavy skillet on the hot fireplace. She broke the eggs into it.

"To bring order to Shadow," Nikifor said. "To ensure all the tribes are safe from another invasion from the Darkness."

She tilted her head. "That doesn't sound so bad. Of course I don't believe a word of it. What's his real plan?"

Nikifor stood up so fast his chair clattered backward. "You must not question the king!"

Hippy looked over her shoulder at him. The eggs sizzled. "Sit down, Nikifor. And don't shout at me. You and I are in serious trouble and if we don't work together we'll probably both end up dead."

Nikifor sat down and put his head in his hands.

Hippy flipped the eggs, carved two thick slices of bread and set out the meals on two wooden plates. She set one down in front of Nikifor and sat next to him. "Eat up," she said. "You need fattening up. I can see your bones."

Nikifor looked at the food, then away. "I can't," he said. "I feel sick."

Hippy shrugged and ate her breakfast. "Have you seen Fangs?"

He shook his head.

Disquiet settled. Surely he wouldn't harm Fangs as well. She shouldn't have left her alone. She jumped up as soon as she'd finished. "I'm going to go find her. Will you help me?"

Nikifor sighed. He didn't move from his spot.

Hippy leaned closer. Something red and raw peeked out from the edge of his sleeve. "What's that?" She lifted the sleeve, then frowned. "Nikifor what happened?"

He jerked away from her. This time his chair clattered right across the kitchen. He clutched his arm to his chest, stumbled into the corner and sank to the floor. "No," he said. "No my king. I must not–I must not–"

Hippy went and crouched in front of him. "It's okay." She patted his head like she would have done a frightened animal. "I'm not going to hurt you."

"But you do," he whispered. "Every time the fairy angers him, he will hurt me, because I am weak. I must learn to make the fairy behave. I must keep her in line."

Hippy swallowed her anger and kept her voice gentle. "It's not right," she said. "He's trying to make you like him." She reached slowly for his arm. This time he let her draw the sleeve back and study the angry burn there. It was in the shape of a nine-pointed star, just like the wrought iron on Mr Silver's gates. She frowned. "Why this star?"

"It is to remind me weakness is disloyalty," Nikifor said. "If I cannot control a mere fairy I am of as little use to him as a member of the Invisible Army."

Hippy gently replaced the sleeve. "You have to fight him."

"Nobody can fight the king. He is all powerful. He sees everything."

"Does he?" Hippy stood up. "You need to get that burn in some water, Nikifor. And you need to get away from here before he kills you." She walked away.

"Get away?"

She turned back. The pathetic note of hope in Nikifor's voice made her smile. She made her voice firm. "Yes. Both of us need to get away, the sooner the better. We just need to find out how to get past the roses. You especially, because you have a destiny waiting for you."

"My destiny is to serve my king."

Hippy went back to him and grabbed his face. Her anger bled into her words.

"Your destiny is to kill your king. You and my daughter. Now pull yourself together, because we're only going to get out of here if we work as a team."

There was a horrible sense of déjà vu in searching for her fetch. Hippy started in the garden, because Fangs liked to play outside. She stared at the carvings of fetches on the castle walls, thinking about where a frightened little creature like Fangs might hide. She didn't go anywhere near Fluffy Ducky's new home, but she searched all around the fountain, then stuck her head into the thickest parts of every other bush.

The back of the castle was a cold and shadowed place where old fig trees raised stunted branches towards the distant sunlight. The stones of the castle wall were black with mould. The back of her neck prickled. She turned in a cautious half-circle. Nobody there. She turned again and almost yelled out loud to see Clockwork's upside down face in front of hers. He grinned and quickly covered her mouth to stifle the yell.

Hippy made a furious noise.

"Up here," he whispered and disappeared up the tree he'd been hanging out of.

Hippy scrambled up the big, damp branches until they were both hidden in the centre of the boughs. She rested against a branch and looked at Clockwork with wide eyes. "What are you doing here?"

"I have the best news," he burst out, although he kept his voice very low. "The forest people came to get me yesterday, because people were looking for me, and it was Fitz and Ana! My dad sent them to look for me and check on you and when they found out what he told you to do, they were so angry–at least Fitz was, Ana said one less fairy wasn't going to hurt anyone–but then when I told them everything I knew they said we had to abort the whole thing, get you and get out, so I came back last night and came up here. We can go, Hippy. We can go right now!"

Tears welled. She blinked them back. "Clockwork Silver, why do you have to be such a beautiful, adorable idiot?"

"Idiot?" The smile dropped from his face. "Don't tell me you're not coming with me. You have to come. Don't worry about the Apple, Fitz and Ana said they'd find another way."

Hippy shook her head. "I tried to leave yesterday," she said. "I came to find you, but–but he's planted these roses all around the castle, for miles and miles. They'll let you in, but if you try to get out, they'll poison you!"

"What are you saying?" Clockwork looked graver still. "Those are killer roses?"

Hippy showed him her bandaged foot. "They got me and I lay out there for hours. I couldn't move. If Pierus hadn't found me I would have died. Now we're both trapped here."

"I suppose you're a big fan again, now he's saved your life." Clockwork pouted and glared at the same time, a sight which made Hippy want to giggle, but she didn't. The situation was too serious for that.

"Sure, I'm a massive fan." She punched him on the arm. "The muse king is completely insane and he's driving everyone else around him mad too!"

Clockwork reached out and held her hand. They looked at each other over the single worm-eaten fig hanging from the branch overhead. "I guess we'd better figure out how to get out then," he said.

"Yeah." Hippy squeezed his hand. "Want to go see his laboratory?"

They climbed up the outside walls of the castle and then crept down the stairs that led from the roof. Hippy held her breath until she got to the bottom. The laboratory was empty. For how long it would stay that way she didn't know. "We have to be quick," she said. "He could come up here anytime."

Clockwork looked around with intense curiosity. "What are we looking for exactly?"

"I don't know. Anything. Any clue about the roses. And a way to get at the Apple of Chaos." She hurried over to the curtain and opened it. "See?"

Clockwork reached out toward the shiny light-cage, just as she had, then snatched his hand back. "That's not the whole Apple."

"No. He's hidden bits of it already." Hippy swallowed. She wasn't ready to talk about Fluffy Ducky yet. "But your dad said we only had to get one bit of it."

"Is that electricity?" Clockwork looked closer at the cage.

Hippy shrugged.

"I like electricity. They use it for everything in Dream." Clockwork began to investigate the walls around them. "Just give me a minute."

"Okay." Hippy went to explore the rest of the laboratory. She skirted the skeleton, the cage, ran her hands over the shiny things on the tables. She pushed aside a screen to find out what was shimmering behind it.

She blinked rapidly. Her mouth opened in surprise. "Fangs?" she squeaked.

Fangs, asleep with her head on her claws, opened her eyes and made a piteous whine. Several scales had been hacked off her back. There were tiny iron shackles around her forelegs. Around her were fifteen large green eggs. Their shells were rough and crackled, and they each lay in a wet, sulfurous substance.

"Clockwork," Hippy said.

He hurried over. "I can't find a way to turn the cage off. What's that?"

Hippy took the tiniest, tiniest pinch of fairy dust and wiped it on the shackles. When they crumbled, she lifted Fangs away from the eggs.

A hairline fracture appeared in one of the shells.

"This is Fangs," Hippy said. "I found her in the forest."

"Is she having babies?" Clockwork stroked her scales. Fangs halfheartedly nuzzled his hand.

Hippy shook her head. "I don't think so." She backed away. "I don't like this at all. Let's get out of here."

"But we haven't found a way out!"

"We'll figure something out. Come on."

They hurried through the laboratory, but Clockwork skidded to a halt in front of the wall full of maps. "Wait."

Hippy went to him. "What is it?"

He pointed at a map of Shadow. "Look at this."

She studied it. She recognised Bloody Fairy territory; there was a big red cross over it. There was another cross over the forest people's territory, then arrows radiating out from Shadow City.

"Look," Clockwork said. "Here, he's got a map of Dream."

Hippy studied it. Dream was much, much bigger than Shadow. "Hey he's put a cross on Greece," she said. "Oh, now I understand, Athens is in Greece–what do those words say? Can you read them?"

Clockwork spelled them out silently. He shuddered. "It says "then take back Dream."

They looked at each other.

"He's not happy just being the muse king," Clockwork said.

"He wants to be king of Shadow? And of Dream?"

Clockwork nodded. "He's going to war. On everyone."

CHAPTER THIRTY-SEVEN

She spent the whole day hiding out with Clockwork in the old fig tree, giving Fangs all the attention she could take. They fed her bits of fig, leaves, bugs, anything she would eat. Hippy cleaned down the hacked out scales while Clockwork came up with fifteen different ways to kill the muse king, each one more gruesome than the last.

It was a good day, but when the sun started to go down Hippy knew it had to end. She cast frequent glances at the lengthening shadows. Clockwork fidgeted with a dead leaf.

"You don't have to go in," he burst out.

"Yes I do." Hippy pouted. "But I don't want to."

"Then don't!"

"If I don't, he'll send someone looking and they might find you and Fangs. He brought someone new to the castle last night. I didn't like him at all." Hippy chewed on her lower lip. "You have to stay hidden. Promise me."

"What about you? What if they try something?"

"I'll break teeth. He's not going to hurt me. At least-" Hippy considered. "For another three days."

Clockwork chuckled. He already knew about the fairy dust on the wedding dress. He leaned toward her and kissed her on the lips. "Be careful. I'll see you in the morning."

"Promise me you'll stay hidden. And look after Fangs."

"I promise. It'll be me, Fangs and my shiny axe, right here." Clockwork pointed at the double-headed axe, which was wedged into a branch above his head.

Hippy had deep misgivings, but it was almost dark. She dropped from the tree and walked slowly around the castle, resisting the urge to glance back. The windows felt like eyes.

She tip-toed into the big entrance room. Voices murmured from somewhere in the belly of the castle. Not the dining room or kitchen, they were cold and empty. Her misgivings turned into great cold wedges of dread. She walked softly up to the room where she'd found the empty vibe glasses the other night. The door was ajar.

She stopped just outside, protected by the shadows, and looked in. A single candle burned at the table where Pierus was seated, his long coat flowing out around him. He strained green liquid into two glasses. Nikifor was curled up on the ground opposite him.

"Come now Nikifor." Pierus's voice was smooth and mildly amused, as though he spoke to a recalcitrant child. "You know you want this."

Nikifor shook his head, but otherwise did not move.

"You prefer death?"

Again, he shook his head.

Pierus pushed one glass toward the edge of the table. "I knew from the moment I first saw you amongst your books you were too weak to be the champion. It's no wonder your father couldn't stand the sight of you."

Nikifor flinched.

"I'm only saying it for your own good. I have plans for your future, my dear boy, but you must correct your faults. Overcome your fears. There's only one way to do that."

"My king." Nikifor's voice was muffled. He lifted his head and looked out through strands of dishevelled hair. "I do not doubt your words. Not one of them. But I do not like what the vibe does to me."

"I'm not interested in what you do or do not like." Pierus sipped from his own glass. "You're a coward, boy, and a coward is of no use to me. Now get up off the floor and drink."

"And then?"

"And then what?"

"Then what nightmare will you force on me next?" Nikifor's voice trembled, but with an edge of anger, not fear.

Hippy's eyes widened. Yeah!

Pierus drained the rest of his glass in a single breath. Then he slowly rose to his feet. "If I didn't know better, Nikifor, I would almost swear you just showed disrespect to your king." He paced to the other muse and curled his hand into his hair. "Did you?"

Nikifor stayed perfectly still. "No, my king."

"Are you loyal to me?"

"Completely, my king."

"Then do as you are ordered. Drink." His hand tightened. Hippy couldn't tell if Nikifor rose of his own volition, or if Pierus dragged him by the hair.

"Drink." Pierus's voice softened. "Drink, Nikifor. Then show me what kind of muse you really are."

Nikifor's eyes fixed on the glass. He reached for it, his fingertips trembling.

He wanted it. Even Hippy could see that. He wanted it as badly as he was repulsed by it.

"Everything you want is right there, in this glass." Pierus had let go of his hair. He spoke straight into his ear. "It's so much easier to give in, my boy, you know it is. Be the muse I want you to be."

Nikifor picked up the glass.

"Don't do it," Hippy breathed.

Nikifor raised the glass. Then he flung it against the wall with a motion so violent it shattered into tiny pieces. Green drops stained the stones.

Pierus's laughter rolled around the room. "Oh Nikifor," he said. "You never did know the right time to show courage. But you'll learn." He grabbed the pitcher with one hand and Nikifor's hair with the other. He propelled him to the wall, yanked his head back, pinned him there with one knee and poured the contents of the pitcher over his face. When Nikifor closed his mouth, Pierus pinched his nose until he gasped for air, then tipped more vibe into his mouth. Nikifor choked and spluttered. Pierus shoved him to the ground.

Hippy smothered a squeak of dismay, but too late.

Pierus turned toward her. "What an unexpected pleasure. Do come in, Hippy."

She would rather have run, but she had an idea it wouldn't get her anywhere. She took a hesitant step into the room.

Pierus went to her, put an arm around her shoulder and propelled her all the way in. He rather forcibly assisted her into a chair at the table. "My dear girl, how long were you standing out there?" He didn't give her a chance to reply. "It wouldn't have been all day, by any chance? I was so terribly perplexed when I couldn't find you earlier. I hadn't expected my lovely bride to be to spend all day hiding from me. I'm not that frightening." He bent down and eyeballed her. "Am I?"

Hippy looked away. "I was thinking about this wedding thing," she said. Then, in a burst of inspiration, "If I'm to be married, I want my sister here. Let me send her a message."

"No." Pierus paced around the chair and leaned his hands on the back of it. His breath on her neck made her skin crawl. "I won't have two Bloody Fairies in my castle," he said. "Or really–" he traced a fingernail down the line of her neck "–should that be three?"

Hippy stiffened.

Pierus curled his fingers around her shoulder. "Tell me where you've been, Hippy Ishtar."

"Out." Her fist curled in her lap. Her eyes narrowed.

"I keep asking myself why I had to choose the stupidest Bloody Fairy in Shadow," he said. "Or then again, perhaps it's not so bad. For me, anyway. I enjoy our little altercations. Do you, Hippy? Have you learned yet that the muse king knows all? The muse king sees all?"

Every hair on her spine stood on end. Clockwork. He knew about Clockwork. She snapped her fist backward into Pierus's face and made contact with his eye socket.

Pierus stumbled back, clutching his face. "Nikifor!" he roared. "Get that fairy!"

Hippy bolted for the door, only to find it barred by the tall stranger. The mask was gone, but his face was buried in the shadows of his hood. He made two lazy sidesteps to block her attempts to get past him.

"I seem to recall warning you this would happen, Fairy," he said. "You do make some poor choices, don't you?"

Hippy took rapid backward steps, away from the stranger, away from Pierus. She backed into a corner across the room. Her frozen brain finally decided to work. "Rustam Badora!" Her voice was little more than a squeak.

"I thought I told you to keep the mask on," Pierus said.

The vampire king shrugged. "She knows who I am anyway. I'm rather interested to see what progress you're making on this little fairy problem." He dropped into the chair Hippy had vacated, sniffed the empty glass there and chuckled. "What a hotbed of vice this is."

"As a matter of fact," Pierus said, "It seems my fairy problem is not so little, Badora."

"Oh?" the hand playing with the glass stilled.

"There is an intruder in the grounds. I want you to find him."

Badora rose to his feet. "He's not one of your fairies then?"

Pierus made a dismissive motion. "She's the only fairy I have any use for. But considering it's unlikely any more will stray in here, don't kill him right away. Ration yourself."

Badora disappeared in a blur of motion.

Hippy screamed the baddest word she knew and raced after him.

"Nikifor!" Pierus yelled. "Get after her! Now!"

Nikifor was on her before Hippy had gone ten feet from the room. His hand closed around one wrist with a grip like stone.

Hippy struggled against his hold until she saw the pleading in his eyes. Yes, he was in the grip of the vibe, but something of Nikifor remained this time. He was terrified.

Hippy let out a yell of frustration, stopped struggling and sat down on the flagstones. She glared every kind of hatred she knew at Pierus.

"Nikifor my boy, you're learning." Pierus stooped, grasped her other arm and dragged her to her feet. "Come along my love, I have something to show you."

Hippy allowed them to escort her up the stairs in this undignified way only because she didn't want Pierus to hurt Nikifor again. He'd been through enough tonight. When they continued all the way to the third floor, however, she knew that had been a mistake. She resisted the pull when they approached the door of the laboratory. "No. I don't want to go in there!"

"Really? You didn't seem to have a problem this morning." Pierus yanked her through the door.

Hippy closed her eyes and thought about her green-haired daughter and how she was going to kill Pierus until he was really, really dead.

Then she looked over to where the eggs had been. Now, little grey winged shapes dragged themselves about. Globs of yolk clung to their scales.

"Do you like them?" Pierus closed the laboratory doors. "They grow fast. They'll be adults soon. I used your dreadful little pet's scales and blood to replicate each one of them. Then I improved on them." He gave a thin smile and replaced the screen. "But that's not what we're here for. Nikifor, watch carefully. I'm going to teach you how to control a fairy."

Hippy snapped to attention. She regarded Pierus with every burning inch of hatred she felt. "I'm going to kill everything you create."

"No, you're not." Pierus prodded her toward a table on the far side of the room, near the skeleton and the Apple of Chaos. The curtains were open.

"I'm going to tell the forest people you have one of their skeletons," she said.

"They already know. I told them I wouldn't use the skeleton to create any nasty diseases if they stayed out of my way."

Hippy took a deep, shaky breath. "I'm going to make you sparkle. Just like a vamp. I'm going to play kick with your petrified corpse ash."

"Really?" Pierus grinned and kissed her on the cheek. "I've seen my death, my love, and it's not at your hands. In fact, it's entirely preventable. You wait and see."

One hand went involuntarily to her belly. He didn't miss the move, but he just raised an eyebrow and said nothing. He picked up a little glowing ball from the table and put it in her hand. "Here. This is what I wanted to show you."

Hippy looked at it. Ordinarily she'd have been delighted to play with it for a while. It was very shiny, but right now she just wanted to smash it into Pierus's face. She shrugged and threw it over her shoulder. "What are you showing me that rubbish for?"

"Because you are what humans would call my lab rat." He handed her a crystal. "How about this one?"

The crystal was shinier still. The gleam was enticing, but she still felt none of the usual fascination. An idea slowly dawned in her mind. She kept her eyes down to hide it from Pierus. The child she carried was part muse. She must be shielding her from whatever Pierus was trying to do.

She dropped the crystal. "No, that one's no good either. Next?"

Some of the smugness dropped from his expression. His mouth tightened. He picked up a bowl that glowed with light from some hidden source within.

Hippy peered in. Then she tipped it upside down. Something rolled out and clinked across the floor. The glow disappeared. "What was the point of that one?"

"Here." Pierus handed her a box.

Hippy opened it. Little lights danced around inside. So pretty. She wanted to touch.

She tore herself away and closed the box. "Boring." She pointed at the Apple. "What are those lights? They're shiny."

"These?" Pierus motioned to the cage. "You like electricity?"

"I do." Hippy moved toward it and reached out.

Pierus caught her wrist. "That's dangerous, my love."

She pouted. "Why? What does it do?"

"It fries little fairy fingers."

"How does it work?"

"I know what you're trying to do." Pierus drew her away from the Apple. "Which is why I have one more shiny thing to show you." He threw aside a curtain and thrust her toward a light.

Hippy's eyes widened. She tilted her head. What a pretty, pretty light it was. It was just small, about the size of her hand. Little sparkles floated around it, danced, made rainbow trails. She giggled. It was so pretty it made everything warm and bright and shiny again.

CHAPTER THIRTY-EIGHT

Intense fury seared every brain cell, rolled through her blood like thunder. Hippy slammed her fist into the nearest target.

She yelled in pain and hopped up and down. She'd just punched a stone wall. Tears sprang to her eyes. Where had her shiny thing gone? It was all dark and cold and she'd been in the nicest–loveliest– she dropped her aching hand and said a very bad word.

A flame hissed into life across the room. The glow of a gas lantern lit up the space around Pierus's shadow. The white dress shone like a ghost. The light grew to encompass the whole bedroom.

Pierus took a few steps, stumbled, then fell to his knees in the middle of the floor.

Hippy backed away from him. She wondered if the door was locked. She'd rather chance an encounter with Badora than listen to another one of his depressive episodes. She pressed her back into the wall.

"Pandora," he said

Too late, there he went. She edged along the wall.

"Pandora, I'm afraid." His voice was hoarse.

"You could try smacking your head into the wall. I hear it works." Hippy brushed past the wedding dress. Her insurance. If anything had happened to Clockwork she was going to have trouble deciding whether to use it to smother the vamp king or the muse king.

"Every time I look at her I'm afraid," he said. "From the first moment I saw her, it was you come back to haunt me. I had to have her. Now I have to kill her. Only then will you be dead to me."

Hippy picked up her pace and pushed at the door. It was locked fast. Great. She wondered if Pierus had any idea at all what he was saying, or to whom. She asked the first question to pop into her head. "Well then, why haven't you done it already?"

"And waste an opportunity?" He curled up and clutched his stomach. "Oh Pandora my love, you were always simple."

"Opportunity?" Hippy continued to push at the door. Just in case.

"Oh yes. She was so perfect. I knew I needed a fairy to get the Apple of Chaos, and then to start another war to keep the irritating creatures busy for a few more years. Decimate their numbers still more and turn them against my enemies, all in one stroke."

Hippy felt sick. "What war?" she whispered.

He laughed. The gravelly sound descended into a coughing fit. "Kill her. Blame Fitz and Ana Falls. The fairies go to war on the forest people. And on the Invisible Army. If I play the right cards the Bloody Fairies will declare war on the Freakin Fairies too, and there will be a decade of chaos while they all kill each other off. When I offer law and order the rest of Shadow will fall in behind me."

Hippy tried to control her breathing. And her fists. He was right, she knew he was. If her family was told she'd been murdered by forest people, Invisible Army or not, they'd go to war. It was required. "But why marry her first?" she whispered.

"There are muses who work against me," Pierus said. "There are always rebels and dissidents and traitors. They pretend loyalty and then say behind my back that I'm mad. But if my enemies were to murder my wife, then they could not refuse me. They must fight for their king. Oh Pandora, I promised you one day I would make you a queen. Why did you leave me?" He arched his back and raised himself up on his arms.

So she was safe, at least until the wedding. Hippy flattened herself against the door. He got to his feet and turned in a slow circle. When he finally saw her his eyes were vacant. The Pierus she knew and despised wasn't home.

"Pandora." He reached out a hand. "Come to me."

"I don't think so."

"Pandora." His voice developed an edge. He stalked toward her, curled his hand into her dress and pulled her against him. Then his fingers were in her hair. They squeezed her scalp. He put his mouth on hers.

Hippy pushed against him. This wasn't a kiss. The familiar cold seeped into her toes. She hooked her nails into his arms and dragged them along his skin. When he flinched away she broke free, balled a fist and punched him in the face.

He dropped like a stone.

Hippy scowled, kicked him in the ribs and went to bed. It was going to be a long day tomorrow.

It was hard to wake up the next morning. Her eyes felt like they were glued shut. The bed was warm. Too warm. A weight pressed her down.

Hippy forced her eyes open. Pierus's arm laid across her shoulder and one of his legs was tangled with hers. She didn't know whether to laugh or throw up. He had two black eyes.

She disentangled herself, slid off the bed and brushed herself down. When she tried the door it was open.

She bolted downstairs and didn't even stop to say hello to Nikifor, whom she glimpsed in the kitchen. She ran outside, washed her face in the fountain to wake herself up and then ran around the castle to the old fig tree.

"Clockwork?" She looked up into the branches, but could see nothing.

Silence.

She scrambled up the tree, only to have it confirmed he wasn't there.

It felt like somebody squeezed her lungs with a big, calloused fist. Hippy searched all of the other trees, but there was no sign of Clockwork. Or Fangs. Her mind sent her nasty pictures of what might have happened to them, trapped out here with Rustam Badora on the hunt while she was hypnotised inside by shiny things.

Shiny things. Something gleamed under a tree ahead. Hippy swooped on it and dragged Clockwork's axe out of the long grass. Her knees would no longer hold her up. She collapsed. A big fat tear ran down her nose. She hugged the axe.

A thin, high-pitched whine threaded through the trees.

Hippy snapped to attention. "Fangs?" she scrambled to her feet, followed the sound around the side of the castle and ran back into the garden. Nikifor had been busy at some point, because most of the bushes had resumed their fantastical shapes.

A gleam came from a little clearing between two bushes shaped like rearing winged horses.

"Fangs! Thank Shadow you're okay!" Hippy ran toward her.

Shadows raced over the garden. Before Hippy could get any closer, twelve shiny shapes plummeted from the sky and landed in a circle around Fangs.

Hippy held her breath. She slowed to a creep. Pierus's fake fetches clawed at the grass and hissed. Fangs let out a second piteous whine.

The fake fetches tightened their circle. Then they leaped. Fangs disappeared under a tumble of shiny scales.

Hippy screamed, bolted forward, raised the axe over her head and swung it into their midst.

She hit two fetches hard enough to split their scales. They exploded into clouds of foul-smelling gas. Oh Shadow. Hippy retched, but she swung the axe again. With five swipes, she blew up every single fake fetch.

Then she could hold it back no longer. She dropped to her knees and threw up under a winged horse.

When her body would let her she stopped, took a deep breath and went to Fangs.

But there was no more Fangs. There was nothing left except three shiny scales and a wing tip.

At a time when even a fairy would have been forgiven for crying, Hippy's eyes were dry. She put the last remnants of Fangs in the pouch Fluffy Ducky had once lived in, picked up the axe and looked at the castle. She'd thought it was so beautiful when she arrived an eternity ago. So had Pierus. And he'd been planning to kill her from the day they met.

She walked straight to the castle wall and climbed up it. There must have been a hundred beautifully carved fetches on that wall, under each window, over each door. Somebody had crafted them with the same love and care she and Clockwork had given Fangs after rescuing her yesterday.

She raised the axe over her head and smashed it down on the first carving. Its head flew off, bounced on the wall below and broke. She moved onto the next one.

Flying chunks of rock. Clang and flash of steel. Broken wings and shattered scales. Nothing existed but her world of destruction halfway up a castle wall. Nikifor had at some point come out and begged her to stop, but he'd quickly given up when she ignored him. Then he'd sat on the fountain wall and watched her frenzy like a man under a spell.

It was a methodical frenzy. She walked along the castle wall and smashed every carved fetch she could find into tiny little pieces of rubble.

She was almost done when she heard Pierus calling her from below. He looked terribly small from here, just a gaunt, long-haired figure with a face she wanted to smash. She raised a finger. "Wait. I'm almost done." Then she turned her attention to the last unsmashed carved fetch, raised the axe and smashed it into tiny little pieces. The rubble clattered on the ground below.

"Hippy." Pierus's voice was stern.

She let go of the castle wall with her feet, plummeted to the ground and landed evenly in front of Pierus, axe poised across her body. "What?"

He didn't look angry, which was disappointing. In fact he looked mildly amused. "What are you doing?"

"Smashing your fetches. What does it look like I'm doing?"

"Why?"

"Your fake fetches tore my little Fangs to pieces." Hippy's fury rose and hissed out with the words, but still there were no tears. "So I killed them. Then I smashed up your carvings. I was thinking about your teeth next, to go with your black eyes. Should I warn you, you are now at war with a pregnant Bloody Fairy?" She raised the axe and stepped toward him.

Pierus stood his ground. "I'd be careful, if I were you."

"Why?"

"Because I may be disinclined to prevent Badora from doing further harm to your little friend when he awakes tonight."

Hippy froze. "What? What have you done with Clockwork?"

Pierus closed a hand around the axe and took it from her numb fingers. "Nikifor," he said, without looking around. He held the axe out.

Nikifor walked over and took the axe. Hippy met his eyes over Pierus's shoulder. He gave her a single nod.

"There. Now we're all friends again." Pierus curled his fingers into Hippy's shoulder a little harder than was necessary. "Come along my dear, and I'll show you where your little friend is. Nikifor, get rid of that thing. I don't want her wandering around with any sharp implements."

Hippy walked into the castle with her head down. She didn't want to look at him. Or at the castle. Right now she'd have braved the roses if she had Clockwork with her. She wondered if Pierus remembered any of what he'd told her last night.

The stairs rose up beneath her feet. Of course they went up all three flights and into the laboratory. Where else would he keep a prisoner?

"There now." Pierus settled his arm around her shoulders. "You see? He's quite happy. As were you for some time last night."

Hippy looked up. Clockwork did indeed look quite happy. He stood in the corner near the Apple, just where she remembered being. His eyes were fixed on a glow that was contained inside his cupped hands.

"Clockwork," she said.

He didn't react.

"Clockwork!"

Nothing.

Pierus grinned. "It's all down to you, my love. You gave me the idea when you asked how shiny things could possibly harm anyone. There you see the result. I can take you and all your kind prisoner and you will know nothing. In fact you'll be happier than if you were quite free to run around being destructive like you normally do. Genius, is it not?"

Hippy moved aside the stained collar of Clockwork's shirt. On his neck was a gaping wound, a tear crusted over with dried blood that looked as though it had been made by a set of fangs.

"Oh yes," Pierus said behind her. "This fairy trap is just a prototype. When I build bigger, better ones, entire tribes will cluster around them, ripe for harvest. My love, I'm going to turn all your people into vampire food."

Hippy spun around. "Not if I throw you from the roof of this castle." Her fist curled and she stormed toward him.

"Tut, tut." Pierus shook his finger. "You're going to behave from now until we wed tomorrow morning. If you don't, I will make you watch him die."

CHAPTER THIRTY-NINE

Hippy felt like Pierus had put his hand through her ribs and torn out her heart. Her fists unclenched. She wondered if she'd just fought the shortest-lived war in history. How could she have ever thought she'd win against the muse king? He had three thousand years of experience at tearing people's lives apart. He was going to destroy her, just like he'd destroyed Pandora. Her legs wouldn't hold her anymore. She collapsed to the ground at his feet and buried her face in her hands.

There was silence above her. Then Pierus crouched next to her and she felt, of all things, an awkward pat on her shoulder.

"Come now Fairy," he said, his voice gentler than it had been. "This is your surrender? This is all it takes?"

Hippy turned her face away. A huge tear leaked from one eye, ran down her face and splashed on his coat.

"You're crying?" There was an edge of exasperation to his voice. "Really, you are the most impossible creature. You know I can't stand to see you cry. Come on." He put an arm around her shoulder and drew her to her feet. "Let's go downstairs. You must be hungry."

She wasn't. She was too upset, but Pierus wouldn't even allow a backward glance at Clockwork. His hand obscured her view while they left the room. He didn't let go of her all the way down the stairs. Her numbed brain failed to make sense of his actions altogether. He couldn't stand to see her cry, but he planned to kill her. The man was completely insane.

They went into the kitchen and found Nikifor sitting at the table, head resting on his hands. When he saw Pierus enter he jumped as though a bolt of electricity had hit him. "My king?"

Pierus gave him a smile as pleasant and fake as anything Hippy had ever seen. "Nikifor my boy, don't look so frightened. The fairy has surrendered. Why don't you make her a nice cup of tea? She's rather upset. And me a coffee."

Nikifor gave him a blank look. "What's coffee?"

"You have coffee?" Hippy asked in surprise.

Pierus sat her at the table. "I had a supply smuggled in a long time ago, but I only drink it on special occasions." He disappeared into the pantry.

Hippy could hear him instructing Nikifor on how to make the coffee and why it should never be given to fairies. She opened the pouches at her belt and went through them. Fang's scales glittered. A knot developed in her throat. If she choked on her own grief, she'd just be making Pierus's job all the easier for him.

Choking. Ishtar.

She frowned. She'd long since fit all of Ishtar's gifts into the various pouches she carried. With trembling fingers she went through them. Yes, there it was. Just a tiny little hard ball, to be dropped into any liquid. She hid it inside her hand.

Water bubbled on the fire behind her. Hippy stayed in her chair while Nikifor prepared drinks and Pierus sat beside her.

Nikifor looked pale and frightened at being in the same room as Pierus. When he set hot cups down, their eyes met. Hippy gave him a hard stare, hoping desperately he'd understand. She flicked her eyes to Pierus and back.

Nikifor cleared his throat. "My king-"

Pierus glanced at him. "What is it?"

It was all she needed. Hippy dropped the ball into his coffee and snatched her hand back with one quick motion.

"My king I hope your coffee is to your taste." Nikifor's hair fell across his face. The shadows under his eyes made him look like the skeleton in the laboratory.

"Well surely you can get a simple thing like coffee right."

Hippy hid her face in the steam rising from her cup. The heat warmed her fingers. Her eyes widened. That didn't smell like tea. She took a cautious sip. The coffee slid down her throat like honey. Her brain began to thaw.

Pierus raised his cup to his lips. Hippy watched him over the rim of her coffee. She took continual tiny sips in case he found out and took it away from her.

He made a satisfied noise. "Not bad for a first attempt, Nikifor." He took another mouthful. "There's a flavour here I don't recognise, but it's rather good."

Hippy giggled into her coffee. She took a gulp.

Pierus swallowed another mouthful and turned to Hippy. "What's so amusing?"

She shrugged and tipped the rest of her coffee down her throat. Her blood raced.

Pierus brought the cup to his mouth. Hippy watched with big eyes over the rim of her empty cup. He'd drunk almost the whole thing. Most people only got through half of a drink before it started.

He rubbed his throat.

She giggled again.

Pierus sprayed coffee all over the table. "What have you done?" His breath rasped.

Hippy gave him her sweetest smile. "I gave you choking powder."

Nikifor dropped what he was carrying. Glass smashed on the flagstones.

Pierus rasped again. His hand went to his throat. He made a sound like a sick bullfrog. "Nikifor," he rasped. "Help me. No, stop her!"

Hippy sent her chair flying into the wall. She winked at Nikifor, who was pale and frozen. "Thanks for the coffee," she said. "You won't die, Pierus, if you don't fight it." Then she bolted.

She ran up the stairs twice as fast as normal, burst into the laboratory, tore a piece of the curtain and threw it over Clockwork's hands.

The glow disappeared. Clockwork looked around, his eyes unfocused.

Hippy clicked her fingers in front of his face. "Clockwork. Clockwork! Look at me now. We have to go. Fast. Very fast. I like coffee."

He focused and looked around the laboratory, then back at his hands, still covered by the curtain. His lips drew back and he gave an angry yell. "Where's my shiny thing?"

"It's a trap," Hippy said. "It's not a nice shiny thing." She jumped up and down on the spot. "Come on, come on, we have to go!"

This time Clockwork focussed on her. Then his hand went to his neck. His fingers explored the wound. "What in Shadow happened?"

"Pierus made you look at the shiny thing while Rustam Badora drank your blood please can we go?"

Clockwork dropped the curtain and the fairy trap. Then he jumped up and down on it. Something smashed. He pulled aside the cloth.

They crowded over what was underneath. A thin plume of smoke rose from the smashed glass and copper wires. Clockwork leaned in and picked up something small and metallic. "It's a conduit," he said.

"What's that?"

"It holds electricity." He turned toward the bright electrical cage. "Stand back."

Hippy backed up several paces and kept jumping up and down on the spot. "What are you doing? Can't we just go? I swear I can outrun the roses. Pierus isn't going to choke forever."

Clockwork looked over his shoulder at her. "Are you okay?"

"I had coffee."

His eyes widened. "Really? Well, just wait a minute. We're not going without the Apple of Chaos." He went to the forest person skeleton, considered for a minute, then secured the conduit in the bony fingers. He carried the skeleton to the cage, positioned it, jammed the conduit into the electricity, ran to Hippy and backed away with her fast.

Sparks flew from the cage. Lightning cracked through the air and poured into the conduit. The skeleton trembled. A couple of sparks shot out of the skull. Then the cage exploded in a brilliant flash of light and clap of thunder.

Hippy clapped her hands. "Yay! Can we do it again?"

"No." Clockwork grabbed the curtain and wrapped it around the skeleton. "But if I'm not mistaken, we can find out how those roses feel about electricity."

Hippy searched through the rubble on the floor for the Apple. "Hey," she said, "How come there's only this one little bit left?"

"He must have hidden all the rest already." Clockwork studied the piece, which was the size of her little finger. "Never mind. It'll be enough."

"Enough for what?" Hippy followed when Clockwork picked up the skeleton and ran for the door.

"You'll see."

They raced down the stairs. Hippy grabbed the feet of the skeleton to steady it, since it was a good deal taller than either her or Clockwork. "How come we're taking Bones?"

"I think the forest people might want him back."

They skidded to a halt at the bottom of the stairs. Pierus curled over on himself right in the middle of the floor, retching, choking, gasping for air. He dragged himself toward the fairies and pointed with a bony finger. He tried to articulate a word, but choked before the first syllable.

"Choking powder?" Clockwork said.

"My sister gave it to me. She's the smartest fairy I know."

They edged around him.

Pierus made a furious hissing noise and struck his fist on the ground.

They ran for the door, but were once more forced to a halt when Nikifor barred the way.

Clockwork brandished a fist at him. "Move, Muse!"

Nikifor looked from one to the other.

"We're going now," Hippy said. "Come with us, Nikifor. You don't have to serve the muse king anymore."

"The roses," he said.

"Clockwork has a plan."

"It's not going to work for three of us unless we can get up high," Clockwork said.

"The cart." Nikifor strode into the garden.

"A cart would work." Clockwork ran after him.

Behind them, Pierus was still struggling to articulate. "Bad-" he choked. "Ba-Bad-"

Only after they had run after Nikifor could they hear his roar as he finally got out the whole word, followed by a prolonged choking fit.

"Badora!"

Nikifor went straight to a tumbledown shed at the corner of the garden, where he dragged out the big, clumsy covered cart. He went around the side and unpenned the donkeys.

Clockwork jumped onto the back of the cart. "Too slow," he said. "And heavy. We need to get rid of this roof."

Nikifor drew his sword and sliced it through the sides of the heavy leather walls. Hippy and Clockwork caught the roof and pushed it into the grass.

Nikifor went to herd the donkeys out.

"No!" Clockwork yelled. "Too slow. Hippy help me here."

Hippy helped him lift the skeleton onto the cart. Clockwork secured the skeleton in place, standing up, with the halters not needed for the donkeys.

"What are you planning?" she asked.

"I'll pull the cart," he said, beckoning Nikifor closer. "You two push. When the sparks start flying, get on and stay low." He grinned. "Trust me, this'll work. I thought of it myself. Are you okay, Muse?"

"Fine." Nikifor gripped the side of the cart and bent over slightly. His face had gone white.

Hippy cast him a worried glance. "The vibe's making him sick," she whispered.

Clockwork shook his head. "Stupid muses. Come on." He picked up the shaft and pulled the cart away from the shed.

Hippy and Nikifor leaned on the back and pushed. The cart was heavy. Hippy really had no idea how this was going to work, but the coffee was still making her blood race. She felt really, really good and definitely up for racing toward certain death by baby killer rose.

They picked up speed when they passed the fountain. Then they faced a sea of killer roses grown into knee-high bushes. A low wind made the leaves tremble as far as the eye could see.

"Hippy, the Apple." Clockwork hopped onto the cart.

Hippy joined him and handed over the sliver of Apple.

"Stand back." Clockwork strapped the sliver of glass into the skeleton's wrist bones, right next to the conduit still held in the finger bones. When it was secure, he pushed it until it just touched. A spark flew out. "You two," he said. "Think about speed. Now let's go."

Hippy jumped down the back. "Think about speed," she said to Nikifor.

He took a deep breath. Sweat stood out on his forehead. "Speed," he said.

"Go!" Clockwork yanked the cart forward.

They ploughed into the roses. The cart picked up momentum. Sparks exploded from the skeleton's hand and rained down on roses turning their way.

"On the cart!" Clockwork yelled. He jumped up, ran all the way across and hauled Hippy on. They both grabbed Nikifor's arms and hauled him up too.

Instead of slowing and stopping as Hippy expected, the cart picked up speed. Sparks continued to fly from the skeleton's hand. The sliver of Apple glowed with bright white light.

"It's working!" Clockwork grabbed both Hippy and Nikifor and pulled them down low. "The Apple's not only releasing the electricity in the conduit, it's generating an electric field!"

Hippy didn't understand a word of it, but she whooped with excitement anyway. All around them she could see roses jerking and twisting toward the cart, only to be driven back and burned every time a spark fell on them. They sped under the arch and out into the endless garden. She hugged Clockwork. "You're a genius!"

"Keep thinking about speed. This is really working!"

The cart hurtled through the roses. Sparks flew faster and faster. The forest sped toward them.

Nikifor's eyes rolled back in his head and he fell backward.

"Nikifor!" Hippy grabbed him and dragged him away from the edge. She shook him. "Nikifor wake up!"

"We need him!" Clockwork yelled. "The cart's slowing down!"

Hippy looked at the sea of roses behind them and wished she hadn't. There was a blur of movement through the bushes. A flash of black and a glimpse of silver. Her breath caught. They were so close to the end of the roses. At least two of them could escape if the third provided enough distraction.

She seized Clockwork's face and kissed him hard on the lips. "Don't look back," she said. "No matter what. You have to go get my sister Ishtar and bring her back here. Run as fast as you can, they're not planning to kill me until tomorrow."

"No!" Clockwork tried to hold her back.

"Get my sister here." Hippy jumped off the slowing cart and shoved it as hard as she could.

The cart hurtled to safety.

Hippy turned in the direction of the castle. The roses that had been reaching out for her pulled back.

Rustam Badora, every inch of skin suited and masked, had been going so fast clods of turf went flying up around him when he skidded to a stop. He picked her up by the back of the shirt and dangled her in the air.

"Apparently," he said, "You've been a very bad Bloody Fairy."

CHAPTER FORTY

Badora returned to the castle as swiftly as he'd left it. Hippy, clamped under one of his arms like a rag doll, spent the whole time with her hand pressed to her face to block out the acrid, metallic stink of vamp sweat from his armpits. By the time they reached the castle she was ready to throw up.

The vamp strode inside, straight up the three flights of stairs and threw her to the ground at the muse king's feet. "Your fairy."

Hippy landed on her knees. She looked up at Pierus.

"I thought you were going to behave," he said.

"You never said *how* I should behave." She tilted her head and studied him. "Don't go getting all choked up over it."

His palm cracked across her face.

Hippy raised her hand to her stinging cheek and glared at him. "That *hurt!*"

"Get her off the floor." He walked away.

Badora hauled Hippy to her feet. He gripped her shoulders, bent down and spoke into her ear. "Do you remember my promise, Fairy? I said I'd kill you when you returned to Shadow. I'll be dreaming of that moment tonight. The taste of your blood. The sound of your last scream."

"Shut up one eye, or I'll pour fairy dust down your throat and make you vomit sparkles."

Pierus returned with a knife in his hand.

Hippy flinched. "What are you doing?"

"Something I've been wanting to do for weeks." He grabbed her one dreadlock. The blade flashed, sliced through hair. Pierus tossed the dreadlock over his shoulder. "That should help tomorrow. I want a blushing, beautiful bride, not a little monster with knots coming out of her head."

It took Hippy a minute to realise what he'd done. When it finally registered that he'd killed her only dreadlock, she screamed and leaped at him.

Badora grabbed her in midair and held her, kicking and screaming, inches out of reach of the muse king.

Pierus put his face close to hers. Only then did Hippy see how truly furious he was. His skin was white and his eyes so deadly cold they could have snap-frozen every killer rose in the garden. "Where is Nikifor?"

"Gone!"

He spoke to Badora without ever taking his eyes off her. "Lock her up. I don't want to see her until the wedding."

It was a long, long day. Alone in the bedroom with only the shiny dress for company, Hippy sat on the bed and thought about everything. She thought about Badora prowling the hall outside like a hungry dog, waiting for her to try to escape. She thought about Clockwork's face when she gave the cart that last shove. She thought about Nikifor dying of the vibe. She thought about Ishtar's warnings, about her mum and dad and her banishment from the tribe. Tears prickled her eyes. She thought about Poppy, waiting back in Dream to hear something. She thought about Mr Silver and his insistence that she was the only one who could save Shadow. He'd had faith in her. He'd been the only one who didn't consider her a fumbling child. Right now, for the first time in her life, she wished she could be that child again, that innocent creature whose biggest problem was an overprotective family.

There was nobody left here to protect her now. Not even Fluffy Ducky. At least Clockwork had the last piece of the Apple of Chaos safe and sound.

She watched the light fade outside the window. Listened to the footsteps in the hall and the distant voices. She sat with her hand on her stomach, thinking about the child who would kill Pierus, and how that would never happen if she didn't think of something before morning.

She discovered her belly had developed a very slight curve. She wondered what the green-haired woman would think of her father. If she would turn out like him or be Bloody Fairy through and through.

She fell asleep, exhausted and hungry, sometime after dark.

Hippy woke with a start when the door burst open. Morning light flooded the room and Rustam Badora's mask filled the doorway.

"Wakey, wakey, fairy. The muse king says you're to make yourself beautiful for him. It's your wedding day."

"I'm going to kill you today," Hippy said.

The mask remained smooth and expressionless. Behind it, Badora gave a low, amused chuckle. "Back at you, sweetheart. You're really a very unlucky fairy. Are you sure you were just dropped on your head as a kid and not cursed outright?"

The door closed. Hippy sat on the bed, eyes wide. Cursed? That was it. That was what she had to do. She'd seen it done. She knew she could do it, every fairy could. Pregnant fairies could curse best of all. She just had to get it right.

She went and studied the dress. She stripped and pulled it on over her head. Folds of shiny, shiny cloth settled over her hips and legs, brushed her skin. The fabric sparkled. She tied her belt with its pouches around her waist and combed her hair. This wasn't quite the wedding she'd dreamed of. She'd always thought her mother and sister would be there. At least there'd be Badora. A bit of vamp killing never hurt at a wedding.

The door opened again. Badora looked her up and down. "You look good enough to eat."

"I'm going to make you sparkle brighter than this dress."

The vamp king walked into the room, rather forcibly linked his arm through hers and led her back out. "You can't upset me today," he said. "It's far too special a day. I've been waiting to taste your blood for a long time."

"How disappointing for you." Hippy lifted her skirt so as not to trip while she descended the stairs. She decided not to point out to him the dust holes her dress was burning through his coat.

Pierus waited at the foot of the stairs. He wore a different suit than usual. It was dark blue and white, a tailored long tailcoat over wide-legged pants. His hair was immaculate. He smiled like a groom watching his bride approach, a sight that made her skin crawl. When she neared, he held out his hand. "My dear, you are a vision of loveliness."

Hippy smiled and placed her hand in his. "If Poppy was here, she'd shoot you."

Pierus led her to the centre of the entrance hall, where a circle of five fat candles burning on tall candlesticks gave the room an appearance of formality.

Badora stood in front of them. He picked up a big, heavy book from the small table and cleared his throat.

"Wait a minute," Hippy said. "Where's the bonfire?"

"You don't think I'm going to lower myself to such a crude fairy custom?"

"But I'm a fairy. I can't get married without jumping a bonfire."

"Once you're married to me you'll be a muse. Sort of. You don't need a bonfire."

"Then what's he doing?" She pointed at Badora.

"Officiating." Pierus jerked her closer to his side. "Since there's nobody else here to do it. Count yourself lucky, my dear girl, we're only performing the short version of the ceremony. Normally these things take days."

"Oh." Hippy gave him a big smile. "Okay."

A flicker of suspicion crossed Pierus's face. "Get on with it, Badora."

Hippy waited. She had to have the right moment. Really she could do it anytime, but a marriage ceremony was a serious thing. It required the raising of some kind of power, which would help. At least she hoped it would.

Badora intoned several words Hippy did not recognise, but that sent shudders down her spine. Vampish always had. Cold crept into the circle. Her fingers tingled. There was power.

Pierus sounded testy. "In words we can understand, Badora."

The vamp rolled his eyes. "Alright, alright. In the name of Mnemosyne I pronounce you married."

"What, that's it? Who's Mnemosyne?" Hippy asked.

"The Goddess of the muses. And my mother." Pierus smirked down at her. He laid his fingertips on her face, but spoke to himself. "And now you are my wife, and you look at me just like Pandora did on our wedding day."

The tingling in her fingers spread to her skull. Hippy hoped Mnemosyne hated Pierus as much as she did. She broke away from him and sank to the ground. The skirt pooled around her. She laid her hands on the flagstones, closed her eyes and breathed deeply. Yes, there it was. She could feel every current of power in the circle.

The muse king's magic, the vamp king's deeply suppressed rage, the unformed energy of her unborn child.

"What's she doing?" Badora sounded concerned.

"Hippy. Get up." Pierus reached out for her.

She opened her eyes and connected with his gaze. His sleeve brushed her shoulder, and where the fabric touched, turned to ash.

Pierus uttered an exclamation and snatched his arm away. "She's covered the dress in fairy dust!"

"Pierus, king of the muses." Hippy felt the power flow into her hands from the very castle floor. The candle flames around them flared and grew to three feet tall, casting deep shadows amidst the bright light. "I curse you to live in Pandora's shadow until the day you die at our daughter's hands. I curse your castle to fall into ruin around you. You will walk amongst mould and rubble." She tilted her head, still holding his eyes. He looked like a big trapped snake. "And I curse you to wear the most hideous clothes you can find. Forever."

She stood up. The power streamed from her fingers. She took a deep breath and made the last part echo while she pointed all that power at the muse king. "In the name of every Bloody Fairy in Shadow, I curse you!"

The bolt of power that passed from her to him almost knocked her off her feet. Then that power exploded outwards into the castle. Windows smashed. The stone under their feet cracked. Rocks showered from the roof.

Pierus uttered a yell and fell to the floor when a rock struck him on the head.

Hippy turned to Badora. "Play time."

Badora took the mask off and stared at her with his one eye. "What in Shadow was that?"

"Fairy curse." Hippy balled a fist and punched him in the good eye. The power must have been with her even then, because Badora went flying into the nearest wall.

Hippy fled.

"Stop her!" Pierus roared.

She bolted down the stairs, around the fountain and straight out into the roses. She ran faster than she'd ever run. Her feet barely touched the ground. The Arch passed over her head. She set her vision on the distant end of the garden and ran for all she was worth.

The leaves turned toward her. The first twig to strike tore her dress and turned to dust in her wake. Hippy ran harder. She leaped the tendrils and vines sent her way. She could see the distant forest. The smell of fresh, loamy mud tantalised her.

Another thorny tendril tore her skirt and turned to dust. Then another, and another. The bottom of the skirt tattered into rags and shreds. She leaped and twisted and just barely kept ahead of the roses. A few more heartbeats and she'd be clear. She set her teeth. So close.

There was a tiny sting on the back of her heel. Hippy leaped clear and landed on the other side, out of reach. She scrubbed the back of her heel in the wet grass and took momentary stock. Yes, she felt fine.

She got up, picked up her skirts and ran for the forest. How far could Clockwork have got last night? Could Ishtar be on her way?

Footsteps pounded the ground behind her. Hippy ran harder, but she was starting to flag. She needed to rest. If she could only gain the shelter of the trees and get a minute-

A blow to her back sent her sprawling into the grass.

Hippy rolled, jumped to her feet and faced Rustam Badora. He'd already moved between her and the forest. Mask and costume in place, protected from the sun, he carried Clockwork's axe. "Time to die, fairy," he said. "Pity you used all that energy cursing the muse king for nothing."

Hippy circled him. The short space of time allowed her to catch her breath. Her heart pounded. "Where did you get that axe?"

"I took it off Nikifor yesterday." He chuckled. "Most pathetic muse I ever saw. I must say it's been interesting to observe how the muse king beats the character out of his subjects."

"You think the vamps will escape what he has planned?" Hippy flexed her hands. "He'll destroy everyone in his search for power. You know it. You tried to warn me."

Badora shrugged. "I have joined his cause. My people have everything we wanted. Territory and food. We're simple creatures with simple needs, really." He raised the axe and took a swipe.

Hippy sprang out of the way. The axe embedded in the turf. She ran in under his arm while he retrieved it and drove her fist into his ribs.

"What are you trying to do, tickle me?" Badora brought the axe in a wide arc toward her head.

Hippy ducked under it and leaped onto his back. She closed her hands around his throat and dug her knees into his ribs. "Does this tickle!?"

Badora jerked to try and throw her off. He flung himself backward, but she clung on. He clawed at her arms, but the gloves would allow him no purchase. His clothes turned to dust on his back everywhere the dress came into contact.

"Oh my, where'd your nice coat go!" Hippy yelled in his ear.

"Ow! Do you have to yell?" He flung himself again, then realised what she'd said. He uttered a whole string of nasty words and swung wildly with the axe.

Hippy let go of his neck, grabbed the axe and used her feet to launch herself off his back and snatch the axe away at the same time. She landed on her back.

The vamp twisted to come after her. His exposed back smoked. He regarded her for a moment, then pointed at the sky. "Overcast day," he said. "You can't kill me like that. Stupid Bloody Fairy." He strode toward her.

Hippy rose to her feet. The axe felt good and solid in her right hand. The left dipped into the pouch that held the very last pinch of fairy dust. "You're so right," she said. "But you know what?"

"What?" He ignored the axe and reached out for her throat.

"Today's my wedding day." She flung the fairy dust in his mask.

Badora yelled and clutched his face. The mask crumbled.

Hippy swung the axe in a wide arc. It sliced into his shoulder like butter. Blood spurted in a fountain so big it sprayed the nearest trees, the grass, the path they'd fought their way onto.

The vamp king fell to his knees. He tried to say something, then slumped onto his face.

Hippy put her hands into the blood fountain. She painted two streaks of blood from the corner of her eyes to her mouth. She yanked the axe from his back.

Somewhere in the distance were voices and the sound of running footsteps. Only fairies ran like that, in a convoy, fast. Ishtar. Ishtar was coming.

From the other direction a lone figure strode across the grass. He was pretty fast too. Hippy blinked. Her head spun. Had she fought too hard? Had Badora bit her without her realising it? She put a hand to her head. Dizzier and dizzier. No, she recognised this feeling. But it couldn't be. It was just the merest scratch.

She looked at her heel and found it was bleeding.

Pierus stopped in front of her and looked down at Rustam Badora's body. His voice echoed. "You killed him."

"Not such a child now, am I?" She couldn't move. The sound of the fairies footsteps was like thunder.

Pierus's lips stretched into a thin, cold smile. "No matter. Obviously the roses got you. You won't last a day. With any luck the fairies will bury you alive."

"Hippy!" Ishtar's voice deafened her.

Hippy staggered and turned to face her sister.

Ishtar raced toward her, Clockwork only seconds behind.

"Ishtar." Hippy smiled. The axe fell from her fingers.

"Is that a vamp out in daylight? Did you kill him?"

"Rustam Badora." The words came from numb lips. "I killed Rustam Badora."

Ishtar's voice rose. "Clear off Muse King!" she yelled. "We're taking her home!"

Pierus grasped Badora by the shoulder, turned his back and dragged him away.

Hippy reached out for Clockwork's hand, but before their fingers touched, her knees gave way beneath her. She collapsed on the road at her sister's feet. Her muscles would no longer work. She couldn't even blink.

CHAPTER FORTY-ONE

All the fairies thought she was dead. Hippy could tell from the way they carried her on a hastily constructed stretcher, from the way they were so silent. The sky passed overhead for hours. Sometimes she saw leaves. Once, the stretcher dipped and she saw the forest people lining the road. They said nothing to the fairies.

Clockwork was always at her head, carrying one corner of the stretcher while three of her brothers carried the others. The sight of his stony face made her want to die for real.

All she saw of Ishtar, walking just ahead of the stretcher, was her dreadlocks.

The day wore on and the sky grew dark, but the procession kept going. When the darkness was broken by firelight she knew they were home.

Ruined fortifications loomed over her head. She was carried through the burned walls; all the familiar voices reached her ears like thunder. She wished once more for the silence of the forest.

They laid the stretcher in the centre of the camp. Light from the bonfire flickered and threw shadows across her vision.

Her father bent over her, his face lined and grim. His eyes shone with tears he would never allow himself to shed. "I'm sorry," he whispered. Then he disappeared.

Willow's face appeared. She too was grim and dry-eyed. She glanced over her shoulder. "Hey!" she yelled. "Are you sure she's dead? I could swear she's staring at me!"

Ishtar joined her. They both stared down into her face for a long time.

"No," Ishtar said, at length. "She's dead. Dead a hero of the fairies. She killed Rustam Badora." She reached out and closed Hippy's eyes.

With nothing to look at, Hippy listened harder. She heard Ishtar climb up on something and yell so all the fairies could hear.

"You hear that, Bloody Fairies? My sister killed Rustam Badora!"

The cheering hurt her ears.

Later, the stretcher was moved inside. Low voices murmured in the other room, then Ishtar and her mother came in. They stripped off the ragged dress and cleaned the blood and mud from her skin.

"What's she wearing this raggedy thing for?" Willow said.

"It's white," Ishtar said. "The Freakin Fairy said the muse king was talking about marrying her, remember? This must be the wedding dress."

"No daughter of mine would ever agree to marry a muse." Willow sounded furious.

There was a moment's silence, as though they were considering that.

"No." Ishtar's voice was firm. "Not even Hippy. The Freakin Fairy said she was a prisoner, remember?"

"We'll never know what really happened now. Look at all this blood here. My poor girl."

Water dripped over her heel.

Ishtar's whisper came from close to her head. "I think the Freakin Fairy's in love with her, Mum."

Willow snorted. "Don't be ridiculous. That's worse than her running off with a muse! No daughter of mine would fall in love with a Freakin Fairy."

Her heart hardened like a rock in her chest. Exhausted, Hippy let sleep overtake her.

She had no idea how long she slept. She expected to be dead when she woke up.

Hippy sat up. A sheet slid off her face. It was completely dark. She patted down her face and arms. They were warm and clean. She wore the leather tunic and pants her mother and Ishtar had dressed her in.

Wait, she was moving.

She pinched herself. That hurt, so she must be alive.

She patted down the bed she was lying on and found it was a piece of coarse canvas stretched over stone. She swung her legs over the side. She must have slept a long time, because she was in the mound where all the fairy dead were buried, a cavernous underground chamber filled with different rooms. She was probably in the same room her dead brothers had been buried in.

Hippy put her hands out and walked through the darkness until she encountered a wall. She felt her way along it until she came to a flimsy wooden door set into the stone. A hard push and she was out. She knew the way well; fairies died all the time. She hurried through three stone passages, up a flight of stairs and then out of an entrance sheltered by a curtain of tangled, overgrown vines.

A full moon bathed the nearby forest in silver light. She stared up at the moon for a long time, thinking about what it meant to be alive. Her hand rested on her belly, on the child she had to keep safe now.

The fairy camp slumbered not far away. Ishtar and her mother and father would be asleep in their beds. She imagined their faces when she woke them up and told them she was alive.

But no child of theirs would fall in love with a Freakin Fairy. And if she stayed, if word spread she were alive, Pierus would come back and try to kill her again. He'd never leave her alone.

A long sigh escaped her lips. So there it was. She couldn't go home, not for a very long time. Not until her daughter was old enough to kill the man who had fathered her.

When she looked away from the moon, a shape moved toward her in the night. His walk was hesitant, his voice unsteady. "Are you a ghost?"

Hippy smiled and reached a hand toward Clockwork. "No."

He ran to her, but stopped just short. He touched her face very, very gently. "Are you sure? I watched them bury you today."

"Apparently all you need to do is wash the poison out when a killer rose bites," she said. "My mum did that. She didn't even know."

Clockwork threw his arms around her and squeezed her so hard her ribs almost cracked. "I knew it! I knew you weren't dead, I just felt it, and then I had a dream and I came out and here you are!"

"Shh." She rested her head on his shoulder. "Nobody else can know."

"Why not?"

"Because Pierus will come back." Hippy took his face between her hands. "Clockwork, I'm going to hide in Dream with my daughter until she's old enough to know who she is."

"Good. I'm coming too."

"Really?" She felt a whole lot lighter.

"Try and stop me."

"Do you have the Apple of Chaos piece?"

He nodded. "Fitz and Ana are waiting for me."

"We'd better go find them then," Hippy said.

Hippy and Clockwork walked hand in hand into the forest.

It wasn't easy. Every instinct screamed for her to run home to the fairy camp, meld back into her family and lose herself in day to day life again.

But she couldn't and she wouldn't. There was no going back.

"Do you know where you're going?" she whispered.

"Of course," Clockwork said.

A Thump Owl screeched overhead, exploded out of its nest, swooped them twice and settled back with an angry hoot.

"I think," he added.

Hippy giggled and squeezed his hand. "Don't worry, with this amount of noise they'll probably find us first."

"It's just through here." Clockwork lifted aside a branch hanging over the trail they followed. "They're not as far in as the forest people."

They followed the path around several bends and under some more low-hanging branches before it ended at a clearing where a campfire burned brightly. Fitz and Ana sat over the flames talking.

Clockwork and Hippy walked into the clearing together. Clockwork cleared his throat.

Ana dived for her spear.

"Just us." Clockwork's cheery voice stopped her.

"Us?" Fitz looked up sharply. He stared at Hippy. "Hippy Ishtar! I thought you were dead!"

Ana returned to her seat by the fire and looked the two of them up and down. "Oh good." Her voice was flat. "Another fairy."

Fitz came around to them and seized Hippy in her second bone-cracking hug of the night. "It's good to see you."

Hippy hugged him back. "You too, Fitz."

They all sat around the fire. She reached her hands to the warmth.

"So what happened?" Ana said. "Why aren't you dead?"

Hippy shrugged. "Didn't really feel like dying today."

Clockwork told them the story. Hippy let the words float over and around her; she was too hungry to pay attention.

"So what now?" Fitz finally asked.

Hippy and Clockwork glanced at each other.

"You'd better tell them about the-" Clockwork glanced pointedly at her belly.

"Oh, right." Hippy picked up a stick and poked at the fire. "I'm pregnant."

Silence.

"To the muse king."

"Ew," Ana said.

"Don't remind me. The thing is, the Apple told him the child is destined to kill him. So I'm going to be hiding in Dream for a long time." She glanced around the circle, but there were no arguments. "What happened to Nikifor?"

"Some of our tribe took the muse to Shadow City," Fitz said. "They left him in the care of another muse named Flower. He may or may not survive."

"They were pretty upset about the skeleton," Clockwork said in a low voice. "They didn't know the pretender had it. They would have attacked the castle straight away, but I convinced them about the roses. Then I ran all the way to the Bloody Fairy camp and got your sister. I thought she wouldn't believe me, but the minute I mentioned your name, she and your brothers started moving." His voice trailed off. "I'm sorry."

"Sorry why?" Fitz said.

"Because they all think I'm dead still," Hippy said. "And it has to stay that way."

"Well that's that then," Ana said. "I suggest we go."

"Now?" Hippy sat up straighter. Excitement burgeoned inside. Sure it was mixed with some dread and a lot of regret, but she really liked the idea of going back to Dream for good. "How do we do it?"

Fitz smiled. "Easily, my friend. Anyone who has made the crossing once can make it again."

"Are you serious?" Clockwork sounded outraged. "We could have stepped back anytime? How come nobody told me?"

"You can ask your father that. Come along." Fitz stood up and beckoned them all together. Ana stamped the fire out. Then the four of them gathered into a tight group.

Fitz closed his eyes and raised his hands. The air in front of them distorted. On the other side, as if in a mirror covered with water, could be seen a fire-lit room. He stepped through and disappeared.

Ana followed.

Clockwork and Hippy joined hands. Hippy took one last breath of the mossy forest and the cold night air of home. Then they stepped out of Shadow.

The End

Would you like to know more about Shadow? Then visit The Shadow Project to keep up with all the latest news, and to look out for book two in the Shadow series, *Curses.* http://ninasmithauthor.weebly.com/shadow.html

This is an independently published book, meaning it is produced solely from the author's limited resources. Its success is dependent on you, the reader.

Did you enjoy this, or any other Indie book? You can support an Indie author by mentioning their work on facebook and twitter, leaving a review on Amazon or Goodreads and telling your friends.

ABOUT THE AUTHOR

Nina Smith has been writing stories since she first held a crayon. Now she's grown up, she uses a word processor. She writes thrillers on subjects ranging from political dystopias to small town murders, and fantasies where bloodthirsty fairy folk take nothing seriously against the backdrop of a violent and oppressive dictatorship.

She leads a secret double life as a journalist, theatrical and gothic bellydancer and designer of steampunk and bellydance costumes, all while looking after a family obsessed with all things medieval, a cat obsessed with milk and thirty grouchy chickens.

Facebook: Nina Smith Author
Twitter:@Kilili13